ADRIFT IN
PARADISE

SHIRLEY THOMPSON

BREWIN BOOKS

First published by
Brewin Books Ltd, 56 Alcester Road,
Studley, Warwickshire B80 7LG in 2009
www.brewinbooks.com

© Shirley Thompson 2009

All rights reserved.

ISBN: 978-1-85858-447-8

The moral right of the author has been asserted.

A Cataloguing in Publication Record
for this title is available from the British Library.

Typeset in Baskerville
Printed in Great Britain by
Athenaeum Press.

CONTENTS

About the Author	vi
Acknowledgements	vii
Chapter One	1
Chapter Two	13
Chapter Three	18
Chapter Four	27
Chapter Five	34
Chapter Six	42
Chapter Seven	49
Chapter Eight	57
Chapter Nine	68
Chapter Ten	80
Chapter Eleven	84
Chapter Twelve	90
Chapter Thirteen	99
Chapter Fourteen	105
Chapter Fifteen	111
Chapter Sixteen	121
Chapter Seventeen	129
Chapter Eighteen	138
Chapter Nineteen	146
Chapter Twenty	154
Chapter Twenty-One	157
Chapter Twenty-Two	161
Chapter Twenty-Three	170
Chapter Twenty-Four	178
Chapter Twenty-Five	180
Chapter Twenty-Six	187
Chapter Twenty-Seven	191
Chapter Twenty-Eight	196
Chapter Twenty-Nine	200
Chapter Thirty	207

ABOUT THE AUTHOR

Shirley Thompson was born in 1949 and educated at Malvern Hall Grammar School, in Solihull. In 1973 she qualified as a primary school teacher, teaching for almost 25 years in Solihull and Birmingham schools. She also obtained a B.Ed. Honours degree, specialising in research techniques, English and Creative Writing in particular.

She is a 'chameleon' writer, because although primarily a biographer, she writes is a variety of genres, encompassing an eclectic range of fiction, magazine articles, songwriting and poetry; her poems have been published in a range of anthologies.

Shirley has maintained a special interest in the performing arts, since her first solo at the age of six and has participated in and directed a variety of pantomimes, musicals and plays. She has been a member of several choirs, a folk group and an amateur dramatics company and enjoys singing regularly in concerts, as one of the *Fellowship Singers of Shirley*.

Thirteen years ago she took early retirement from teaching. Her seven books to date include *There's More Out Than In*, *If – The Pat Roach Story*, *The Original Alton Douglas*, *Pat Roach's Birmingham*, *Auf Wiedersehen Pat*, *Finally Meeting Princess Maud* and *King Of Clubs – The Eddie Fewtrell Story*.

Other interests include photography, foreign travel, parapsychology, computers, reading and gardening. The author gives talks to societies at home and abroad, about writing in general, and novels and biographies in particular.

For further information visit her website: www.shirleythompson.me.uk.

ACKNOWLEDGEMENTS

The author is indebted to the following people, companies and organisations for their valuable contributions, various favours and support, which have been of great assistance in the publication of this book:

The *Society of Authors*, as Literary Representative of the Estate of John Masefield, for granting permission to publish the extracts from John Masefield's *Sea Fever*, as a 'scene-setter' for this novel.

Lyricist C. Mordaunt Spencer (d.1888) and musician-composer Charles W. Glover (1806–1863), for the eight-line extract in Chapter 17, from their evocative song, *The Rose of Tralee*, which is central to the story.

For invaluable help with promoting the Irish aspects of the story: Maria Cleary, co-organiser of the Birmingham branch of the annual *Rose of Tralee* event; Pat Wright of the Birmingham Irish Community Forum Ltd and their Information Officer, Claire Rooney.

Thanks are due to Anne and Peter O'Brien, proprietors of *O'Connor's Seafood Restaurant & Bar* and to my husband Dr. David Thompson – not only for his patience in general, whilst I'm writing, but also for helping me with some of the Irish research.

My particular thanks to the descendants of the Earls of Bantry, Egerton and Brigitte Shelswell-White and their family, for advice regarding their ancestral home, Bantry House, featured in the closing chapters; permission to use a photograph of their magnificent home, on the back cover of this novel – and also for their generous hospitality. Rear cover photograph of Bantry House by Dennis Connolly.

Newspapers: The Solihull Times (Editor Enda Mullen).

Poppy Brady, freelance journalist.

Gordon Creese, Fundraising Manager, *Birmingham Mail Charity Trust*.

Publishers: Alan and Alistair Brewin.

I must go down to the seas again, to the lonely sea and the sky,
And all I ask is a tall ship and a star to steer her by,
And the wheel's kick and the wind songs and the white sail's shaking,
And a grey mist on the sea's face and a grey dawn breaking.

And all I ask is a merry yarn from a laughing fellow-rover
And quiet sleep and a sweet dream when the long trick's over.

Extracts from *Sea Fever,* **by John Masefield –** *Salt Water Ballads, 1902.*

(English Poet Laureate, 1930 – 1967)

CHAPTER ONE

It's a sobering thought, that a single twist of fate, on one particular day, can trigger an irreversible chain of events... leading someone down a totally different path in life.

Standing by the jetty, she scanned the horizon for Patrick's boat, which was due back within the hour. As there was no boat in sight, she seated herself on a bench, a few yards away: one of a set of eight identical seats, situated at intervals, around the perimeter of the huge lake. While she waited she watched the water birds preparing for twilight and listened to the sounds of small creatures, scuffling about in the undergrowth.

Gazing across the water, her mind began to wander back to that eventful day, her eyelids growing heavier by the minute. There was no way that she could have predicted where it would all lead. Although just ten short years ago, the events of that hot summer had completely transformed her life. She shuddered to think how different life would be for her now, had she stayed in her apartment that day, taken the bus into town, or visited one of the neighbouring islands.

In her 'mind's eye', she saw a young woman, walking pensively along an almost deserted Skiathos beach. The sea air was bracing, with the faintest hint of seaweed. A lone seagull screamed and swooped overhead in the bright morning sky, while a short distance away, his companions shrieked and called, born up by thermal air currents; twisting first to the left and then to the right – like demented hang-gliders!

Her shoulder length dark-auburn hair caught the sunlight, revealing a lighter auburn element. Frothy waves ebbed and flowed onto the shingle. Although it was the middle of May, she practically had the beach to herself, except for a young couple, walking some distance away, in lively conversation. They were holding hands – stopping every few seconds to kiss. Fiona sighed – as she remembered.

In her right hand she'd been clutching a light-coloured straw hat: wide-brimmed with a pale pink band of ribbon and two pink tails trailing down at the back – bought six years previously – from a Portuguese market in Portimao. She could still picture that early morning stroll so vividly... like a film scenario. With her left hand she'd picked up a smooth dark pebble, hurling it viciously out to sea – as if to jettison the memories that tormented her. If only it were that simple!

Lost in thought, she ambled further along the beach for a few more minutes. Then, as the sun's heat intensified, she rested on a smooth rock, in the shade of a larger overhanging one. Taking a notebook from her straw shoulder bag, she began to write. At first her thoughts came slowly, but then they gathered momentum and she wrote as if her life depended on it.

She was vaguely aware of the shouts of holiday-makers in the distance, coming from the chalets, in the holiday village known as *Club Skiathos,* set back a short distance behind the beach. Somewhere… a child was crying. The brochure described the club as *luxurious and secluded.* The cost of the holiday certainly matched its description. Skiathos seemed an idyllically beautiful island.

She desperately needed a means of escape from the solicitous, although well-meaning advice of friends and relations; a place where she could unwind and begin to free herself from the mind-numbing grief which held her in its grip. Away from the cold empty house that had once been a haven for Ian and herself.

These feelings had overwhelmed and depressed her for two long years. Her eyes filled with tears as she remembered the dreadful telephone call. She had been working in a local bookshop in the centre of Solihull, the small town where she lived.

The manager, Paul, handed her the phone, apprehensively: "It's your neighbour, Simon." "Get back quickly Fi!" Simon practically shouted down the phone at her. "I've just had an urgent phone call from Ian. He needs you. Please hurry!"

Although it was only a five-minute drive from the town centre, it had seemed an eternity. On arrival, Simon's wife, Carol, was waiting for her at her own front door, which was already open; their neighbours always kept a spare key for them. Carol was in tears. She followed Fiona, as she rushed upstairs – but it was too late. Ian was lying on their double bed; two dark blue pillows propped under his head. He was as white as a sheet; with eyes staring straight ahead – and ashen lips.

She reached for his hand, but it was cold as ice. Staring at his face, she knew in a moment that this stranger in the bed was simply an empty shell. What had been Ian… his soul, has disappeared – had fled. Simon was seated close by, on one of their bedroom chairs, his head in his hands. Fiona couldn't take it all in. They'd had breakfast together that morning, as usual. Everything had been fine when she left for work.

CHAPTER ONE

She opened her mouth to make a sound... But nothing came. Then as if from a great distance, she heard violent, uncontrollable sobbing. For what seemed like hours she was unable to stop. Carol helped her to undress and put her to bed. As it was a sudden death, Simon telephoned their local surgery and the police.

The months that followed were like a nightmare – played in slow motion. She wanted to die herself: she longed for it, over and over again. Her soul and heart ached so much. It would have been such a relief to sink into nothingness. Two years later, she was still trying to pick up the pieces.

There was just time to complete her walk. Putting her notebook away, she continued along the beach. Her beach shoes scrunched over the pebbles to a regular marching rhythm.

She noticed a figure in the distance. Drawing closer, she realised that he was painting at an easel; a palette in one hand and a brush in the other. He wore a straw trilby hat and sunglasses and seemed totally absorbed in his task. His dark blue shirt was streaked with flecks of paint.

Fiona maintained a respectable distance; not wishing to disturb him but nevertheless fascinated. She envied him his skill. He was painting a seascape. There was a small white yacht in full sail in the foreground. The edges of the clouds were tinged with sunlight. Slowly, she walked behind the artist to the other side, trying to be as unobtrusive as possible.

"Come take a closer look." His voice had a deep, resonant quality. The accent was unmistakably American, with a slight lilt to it. Fiona hesitated, reluctant to move any closer. The man half turned and looked over his shoulder. Still no response.

Turning right round, the stranger removed his sunglasses, studying her intently, with intelligent brown eyes. He had fair hair, slightly greying at the temples; a beard and moustache gave him a quite noble appearance. "Come take a look. It's almost complete." A lock of wavy hair lay carelessly across his forehead. Most of his hair was still blond and quite long. It came well down over the collar, at the back of his shirt. Responding to his warm smile, she stepped forward.

"I was just admiring your work," she explained. "It's so accurate... almost like a photograph. You've captured the atmosphere and the effect of the sunlight perfectly." He thanked her and seemed pleased. The lilt in his voice suggested that there might be a touch of the Irish in him.

"I should introduce myself," he ventured, offering his hand. He had a firm, forthright handshake. "The name's Patrick – Patrick Maitland."

"Fiona Eastley," she said, returning the handshake and the smile.

"Are you staying at the club, or just passing through?" asked Patrick.

"I've rented one of the apartments."

"Then I'll walk you back if I may. I'm about done here." The suggestion took her by surprise. He began to gather up his painting equipment.

"Can I give you a hand?" she found herself asking.

"Fine." He passed her a large canvas bag, containing some of the equipment. As they strolled back along the beach Fiona studied the ground intently. Sensing her mood, Patrick said suddenly, "Hell, I don't usually make a habit of chatting up women while I'm painting!" Fiona quickly responded: "That's okay. I'm not very good company, I'm afraid." "Doesn't bother me none," he reassured her. "I'm like that myself – when I'm working – that is."

After ten minutes or so, they reached their chalet-style apartments. Each building was white and more or less identical to its neighbour. Fragrant clusters of cherry-pink bougainvillaea adorned either side of each entrance. Behind every chalet was a private patio area with wrought iron furniture, striking sunshade and matching cushions. The chalets were well spaced out; each group of six had a private swimming pool.

"May I offer you a drink?" Patrick suggested. Again, Fiona hesitated. But something about his warm, friendly eyes and his good-natured smile reassured her. "Well – maybe just a small one, before lunch." They strolled on, towards the next group of buildings. "Here we are. Number thirty-seven," he announced. The cool marble floors and the shade of his apartment were a welcome relief after the sun-drenched beach.

"Let's sit in the shade," suggested Patrick, as they moved out onto the patio area. "What's your poison? I've only martini or scotch. Haven't gotten much in yet – no time... too preoccupied I guess." "Martini would be fine – got any lemonade?" She could feel herself beginning to unwind.

"Cheers!" he said, holding up his glass of scotch. Seated opposite each other, they leant forward to clink glasses and she smiled a warm, sunny smile; something she hadn't done in a long time. "You should do that more often," he observed. "It suits you!" As he studied her, with a warm but penetrating gaze, she felt suddenly uncomfortable – like a specimen under a microscope. There was a long silence.

"So," he drawled, "what brings you to this part of the globe?"

"Probably the same as you. Trying to find some solitude to work in... some peace and quiet."

"And what kind of work would that be?"

She hesitated, then took her notebook out of her straw shoulder bag. The bag was decorated with coloured raffia flowers within its circular centre. "This kind!" she said, waving the book at him.

CHAPTER ONE

"Don't tell me you're a writer!" He grinned broadly.

"*Trying* to be," she replied. He had such an infectious sense of humour. She felt herself warming to him, more and more.

"Well – two creative geniuses in one resort!" he laughed. "This is too much!" He was studying her even more intently now... still smiling, but scrutinising her, as though searching for something that he couldn't quite fathom.

"Tell me about yourself," she found herself saying.

"What's to tell?" Patrick replied. Time passed quickly, as they talked about their past histories, becoming progressively more relaxed in each other's company.

She began to tell him things, which had lain deep and buried within her, since Ian's death; things she had never told a living soul... let alone a stranger.

Fiona explained that for several years she had been a primary school teacher, until about a year before Ian's death. At that point, needing a career change, she'd worked in a bookshop, on a part-time basis. Patrick listened intently and patiently for some time, until she realised that she'd been monopolising the conversation.

"So why did you become an artist?" she asked.

"I kinda drifted into it, I guess. A close relative – my Uncle Dan; a bit of a maverick, I suppose, but a great guy and an extremely talented artist, got me started... as a kid. I tried my hand in the family finance business for a spell, but soon realised I wasn't suited. The cut-and-thrust and wheeler dealing went right against my natural temperament. Too stressful – so I quit."

He refilled their glasses, as they continued their conversation. The sun grew higher in the sky, the brightly coloured sunshade providing a welcome canopy from the intensifying heat. "Oh no – is that the time?!" Glancing at her watch, Fiona suddenly remembered a pre-arranged appointment with a holiday courier, to finalise some details about local trips. "I'll have to go. I'm already late." She stood up and slowly extended her hand. He paused for a moment.

"Must you?"

"'Fraid so, but maybe we could meet some other time? I've really enjoyed your company." He showed her to the door of the apartment, then asked,

"What's your apartment number? I'll call you."

As they parted she felt a sudden sense of loss: as though she'd left some treasured possession behind. The feeling remained with her... all afternoon.

* * * *

The warm blue waters of the Aegean lapped gently onto the beach, some distance below. Hot afternoon sunshine and warm gentle breezes caressed the terracotta tiles on the roofs of the fishermen's houses. Olive-skinned, half-naked inhabitants were going about their business. Yachts and fishing boats twinkled in the sun's reflection: rocking with the gentle motion of the waves, in the azure harbour. A few cars, trucks and carts moved about, like so many dinky toys.

They were high above, on a promontory, jutting out from a jagged cliff edge. Fiona felt pleasantly cool up there, on such a vantage point... in this place of a thousand islands. Gazing far out to sea, she shaded her eyes with her right hand, to gain a better view. A warm wind played against the back of her legs. She felt a slight burning sensation there already; being fair-skinned, she always burnt, before achieving any semblance of a tan.

Although Skiathos lay out in the Aegean Sea, it was situated only a few miles from the Greek mainland. Many of the other islands, such as Mykonos, Crete, Limnos and Rhodes, lay much further out.

"Ladies and gentlemen – your attention please!" The cultured tones of their guide interrupted Fiona's daydreaming. She turned sharply around, then re-joined the group of six other tourists. They were a cosmopolitan crowd: a young Italian couple, two thirty-something sisters from Perth in Scotland, an elderly American woman and a French student.

"As you're new arrivals, allow me to introduce you to our beautiful island of Skiathos, set in the middle of the Aegean Sea. The name *Skiathos* means, 'Shadow of Athos', *Athos* having been a holy mountain, one hundred and fifty kilometres away by open sea. In our clear waters its shadow is frequently visible, from some of our main vantage points. As you will doubtless discover, the island is renowned for its golden beaches: there are over sixty of them."

'It's a pity', mused Fiona, 'that the beach below *Club Skiathos* is only shingle. But, who knows? Maybe there were more important reasons for locating the club in that particular spot?'

"At our next stop," continued the guide, "you will see one of the most extensive of these sandy beaches. Hopefully, as it's a clear day, the view will be superb!"

They returned to the minibus, their transport for the day. A second minibus followed, about ten minutes behind. This particular excursion, to the fishing villages and along the south coast, was a popular one.

Their guide, Robert Osborne, was also the driver. He was tall, lean and tanned, with dark hair and intelligent blue eyes. His body was athletic and muscular. Fiona found herself wondering about him, as the bus continued

CHAPTER ONE

on its way. The combination of physical attraction and cultured accent was very appealing.

The young Italian couple seemed to speak only their native language, so conversation with them seemed unlikely. Besides, they were totally engrossed in one other. The two sisters from Perth were a different case altogether. Sally and Josie were a pair of articulate, seasoned travellers, who had taken a whole series of continental holidays together.

"What about your husbands?" Fiona enquired, on hearing that they were married. "Och! They cannae stand the sun!" Josie replied. "The two of them go fishing every year – in the River Tweed," explained Sally. "It's the only bit o' freedom we get from each other, all year. It does nae harm!" They entertained her with details of previous continental holidays. As two unaccompanied, but attractive women, they had some rather lurid tales to tell!

The French student, Jean Pierre Lefevre, was young, olive-skinned and charming. Fiona's French was reasonably good, although not up to the same standard as Ian's had been; nevertheless, she was able to hold a conversation with him. She told him about her French friends in Montpellier – Serge and Catherine. Also, about another French family, whom she and Ian had known for years: the Bouviers, who lived in the Seine-et-Marne region, not far from Paris.

Jean Pierre reacted with some surprise when she mentioned the area. Coincidentally, his family home was in that same region – in Brie Comte Robert. His father, Claude, was a wealthy financier based in Paris, with offices adjacent to The Bourse. Jean Pierre declared proudly, to anyone who cared to listen, that he planned to work for his father, once he'd gained his Economics Degree, from the Sorbonne.

They arrived at a taverna for lunch. A large table was set out under the trees in readiness for them. Fiona found herself seated between Robert Osborne and Jean Pierre, who was to her left. She needn't have worried about her standard of French; it emerged that Jean Pierre was an accomplished linguist. He surprised her by speaking quite rapidly, in fluent Italian, to the young couple. Later, he explained that they were on honeymoon or their 'lune de miel' as he put it.

"So, what do you make of our club so far?" Robert asked, when they were all seated, waiting to be served. Addressing the waiter in fluent Greek, he had ordered wine for the whole party, as the majority weren't sure which one to choose. He selected several bottles of the local *retsina* wine, explaining that it was a more-than-adequate accompaniment for most Greek dishes.

He had a habit of looking in someone else's direction, when asking a question. Fiona found this somewhat disconcerting. Robert repeated the question, this time looking more directly at her. She smiled, then replied,

"Well so far, it seems to be exactly what I'm looking for."

"Which is?" he queried, looking across her, towards Jean Pierre and nodding to him with a friendly gesture. "Somewhere to relax and forget about the cares of the world. To unwind and give free rein to my imagination."

"Imagination can be a *wonderful* thing!" This time, he looked directly at her. His eyes, which suddenly seemed to be of a more piercing blue, met hers. He smiled at her. She felt slightly uneasy. He poured a glass of red wine and passed it across to Sally. Further bottles of retsina were brought in and placed at intervals, along the middle of the table.

Robert began to discuss *Club Skiathos* in great detail, especially the amenities, asking if she was satisfied with them. "Well, yes," she answered, with some surprise. Then added: "You seem quite proprietorial."

"You *could* say that. Miklos Atronoides and I are the co-owners."

Fiona reacted again with surprise. Robert laughed: "So you thought I was just an Englishman, on a working holiday, with a smattering of Greek and a brief knowledge of history!" "I hadn't really thought about it," she replied, although, in fact, she felt quite embarrassed. "Anyway – no matter," he replied. "Let's enjoy the meal."

As they approached *Club Skiathos*, much later that evening, it was bathed in the glow of a golden-orange sunset. Fiona immediately found herself thinking what a beautiful subject it would make... for one of Patrick Maitland's paintings.

By the time they reached reception, she'd begun to feel more at peace with herself – although rather sleepy. Taking her leave of everyone, she went straight back to her apartment.

* * * *

The radio inside the apartment was playing a classical violin concerto. The French windows, leading on to the patio were wide open to the world.

Fiona had been reading a romantic novel, the kind of easy-read that she enjoyed on holiday. The book lay, half-open, on the patio table; a slight breeze played with the pages. She was just drifting off to sleep in the warm morning sunshine. Suddenly, a voice broke through her dream. Someone was calling her. She woke with a start. Robert was standing, hands on hips, at some distance from her.

CHAPTER ONE

"Are you not coming on the trip today?" he shouted. "It's to Olympia Bay – an old haunt of brigands and pirates; lots of caves and sandy beaches – very dramatic! You've got ten minutes – if you're interested."

She glanced at her watch – there might just be time to throw some things into a bag. Minutes later she jumped into the minibus outside reception, taking the passenger seat beside Robert.

It took her a while to recover her breath, by which time the 'bus was wending its way down the narrow twisting lanes, leading from the resort. Fiona glanced behind to greet her fellow passengers, but realised, with a shock, that the only other travellers beside her and Robert, were the Italian couple. She felt herself blushing... closely followed by a feeling of panic.

"Where are all the others?" she asked. Robert placed his left hand on her bare sun-tanned arm, whilst continuing to drive with the other. "That's not a problem. We've got it mostly to ourselves." Despite initial misgivings, she felt a tingle of excitement. The sensation of strong fingers on her exposed flesh remained, long after his hand had returned to the steering wheel.

After what must have only been half an hour or so, but seemed like an age, the minibus arrived at the bustling market place. The four travellers alighted from the bus, and began to explore the richly coloured and often heavily scented goods, displayed by the stallholders.

The atmosphere was noisy, hot and sticky, although at the same time vibrant and welcoming. Fiona became completely engrossed in a leather goods stall. After a rather tricky bartering session with the stallholder, over a leather wallet, she realised that she was alone. There was no sign of Robert, or the Italian couple.

She began to panic, her eyes searching feverishly around for them. Suddenly, she felt a light touch on the back of her arm. Turning quickly around, she found herself face to face, and at *very* close quarters, with Robert Osborne. They were being jostled by the now tightly packed crowd of holiday-makers and locals... practically pushed into one another.

His attractive blue eyes were sympathetic, as he steadied her and prevented her from falling. "Come with me!" he shouted, quickly leading her towards a quieter section of the square, where they could at least hear one another speak.

The din from the market was by now quite deafening. It was a relief to find a quiet corner, several yards away from all the action. "Is it always like this?" she asked, laughing nervously, trying to contain the panic which she had felt, just seconds earlier. "On Saturdays – yes," replied Robert. "But that's when they sell a wider range of goods. A *Catch 22* situation," he joked.

Marco and Gabriella, the Italian couple, joined them in their quiet corner, over by the fountain. Unlike Fiona, they were in their element and wanted to stay longer. "We enjoy de market zo match!" Marco informed them. "It eez jus lak are own 'ome tarn, near Portofino. Everywhere, zee naws, zee bassel! Zo full av life!" His grasp of the English language was better than she'd imagined.

Somewhat reluctantly, Fiona returned to the minibus with Robert, but hesitated before getting in: "If you'd rather return to the hotel, that's fine with me, especially as there are now only two of us. You must have lots of other things to do."

"But why waste a beautiful day?" he replied nonchalantly. "Besides, the Italians want to meet us later, down by the bay." Climbing in beside her, he added with a sudden smile and a sideways glance, "I promise not to ravish you!"

The minibus descended from the market, along a narrow winding mountain road, which became increasingly treacherous. Robert had to sound a warning blast of the horn, on every bend. Despite her seat belt, Fiona held grimly onto the dashboard, as they turned each corner. Each bend in the road threw her closer to Robert. Despite the air-conditioning, the air inside the minibus grew hotter and more stifling, as the outside temperature increased ... or was that just her imagination?

Luckily Fiona had a white lace fan handy – bought in a souvenir shop in Pisa, whilst holidaying with Ian, eight years ago – yet another reminder of happier days.

The shop had been just a stone's throw from the *Leaning Tower* itself. She fanned herself rapidly, and in truth, a little desperately.

"The bay's not far away now," Robert reassured her, "then we'll find some shade."

As he drove, he explained that, from the close of the so-called *Classical Era* onwards, piracy had been the scourge of many an Aegean island. The inhabitants of Skiathos were renowned for the settlements they had built to repel the invaders. 'Great – we can all rest easy in our beds!' thought Fiona.

Five minutes later, they reached the golden sands of Olympia Bay – as dramatic a setting as Robert had promised. Fiona could just discern a few sheltered caves, in the distance, set back from the shimmering beach.

Robert lifted a picnic box out of the 'bus. They carried it across the golden beach, towards a more shaded area, close to one of the caves. The box was surprisingly heavy! White frothy waves ebbed and flowed their greeting, making a swishing noise. Fiona enjoyed the pleasure of fine, hot sand, trickling through her open-toed sandals, as they headed for a suitable spot.

CHAPTER ONE

They ate a fine picnic lunch, washed down by a fairly heavy retsina wine. She began to feel drowsy. As she lay in the shade, she felt deliciously relaxed... for the first time in many months. A glow of happiness spread over her, as she listened to the distant waves lapping on the beach. Remembering to apply suntan lotion she lay back once more – totally relaxed.

Suddenly, she started with surprise, feeling felt hot sand, on her navel. Opening her eyes in alarm, she found Robert lying beside her, his muscular torso and hairy chest clearly visible between the folds of his open shirt.

He grinned, as he continued to sprinkle the sand. Fiona wore a pair of faded blue denim shorts, frayed at the edges, and a pink halter-neck top. There hadn't been time to sort out a swimming costume. Despite the apparent shade, her shoulders had begun to burn. She looked up into Robert's handsome, tanned face. "Is this what you'd call the gold-star treatment?" she asked – as casually as she could.

"It's what the management reserve for all their best customers," he quipped. At the same time he began to gently trace circles with his forefinger, along the base of her throat; the expression in his eyes slowly changing, from a warm smile, to something more sensual and hungry.

She tried to extricate herself, but he moved closer, pinning her down, with the weight of his body. For an instant he rolled back over. Seizing the opportunity, she jumped up and ran towards the nearest cave. It led some distance back into the jagged rocks, like a subterranean tunnel. Robert quickly pursued her, calling out for her to stop. She could hear his heavy breathing, close behind her.

She realised her mistake too late. He soon caught up with her and pinned her against the jagged, damp wall of the cave. His breath was hot and searing. Robert's kisses were frenzied and demanding. She felt herself weakening under their force. His hands reached up under the silkiness of her halter-neck; he began to fondle her.

All of a sudden they heard voices – excited shouts. It was like receiving thousands of volts from an electric shock! Fiona began to hastily adjust her clothing. Her face was hot and flushed. Robert quickly turned away from her and after a few seconds, began to walk slowly back toward the mouth of the cave. She tried to collect her thoughts, and resume as normal a demeanour as possible – but her heart was pounding.

Robert was back on the beach. She could hear him, from a distance, speaking to someone, in Italian. Dazzling sunlight hit her, as she emerged from the mouth of the cave. She could see the remains of their picnic, spread across the red and white checked cloth. An empty green wine bottle, tipped over onto its side, was coated with sand.

Fiona heard Robert giving a light-hearted explanation, having now switched back to English, to Marco and Gabriella; going into lengthy detail about how they'd been exploring the cave, in the hope of finding treasure trove left by the pirates, centuries before. He further joked that, so far, they'd had no success! Judging by their laughter, the Italians definitely had a greater understanding of the English language than she'd thought... or maybe of human nature?

She remembered their earlier arrangement, to meet the couple in the area around the bay. The picnic hamper, which was labelled *Club Skiathos*, had helped the couple to locate them. Fiona realised, with relief, that as the pair were still so besotted with one another, they were totally unconcerned about the feasibility, or otherwise, of Robert's explanation. They were simply pleased to have found them. Marco and Gabriella discussed and examined their purchases from the market – blissfully unaware of the painful silence between Robert and herself – lasting the entire length of the return journey.

Neither of them gave the slightest glance toward the other. Fiona felt a sinking feeling in the pit of her stomach ... as though she had betrayed some sacred, innermost part of herself. 'Trust me to get stuck with the biggest lech' this side of Christendom!' she thought wryly. Robert gazed fixedly at the road ahead: his jaw set rigidly and his lips clenched tightly together. His knuckles showed white as they gripped the steering wheel.

Once back at the resort, Fiona said hurried goodbyes and ran immediately back to her apartment. The door locked automatically behind her. She heaved a huge sigh of relief. Robert, meanwhile, drove the white minibus back to the car park at the rear of the main hotel building. He was *furious* with himself. Striding purposefully, he took the lift up to his spacious apartment suite on the fifth floor. Snatching a can of lager from the enormous, American-style fridge in his designer kitchen, he slammed the door shut. Accustomed to thinking of himself as a 'man of the world', he felt uncharacteristically deflated: "Damned idiot! What the hell was that all about?!"

CHAPTER TWO

Fiona decided to avoid the hotel restaurant that evening. She threw herself onto the large double bed in her apartment and slept soundly, until just after nine o'clock, the following morning. She remembered, with chagrin the events of the previous day and fell into a very depressed mood. Since Ian's untimely death, she had organised her life into neat little compartments, despatching her emotions to such subterranean depths that nothing could reach them.

To all outward appearances, she had been content to lead a well-ordered, sensible and self-protective existence. But yesterday's encounter with Robert had shaken her, badly. Over the course of the last few days, she'd begun to develop a sneaking admiration and affection for him, but yesterday had left her feeling cheap and somehow tainted. Particularly hard to accept was the willingness with which she'd been ready to surrender herself to him. But, in the cold light of day, she realised that he was practically a stranger to her.

Fiona took her time, making a light breakfast of cereal and fruit juice, then settled down at the breakfast bar to eat it. The slow, almost ritualistic nature of the process was therapeutic. Lost in thought, she considered the difficulty of facing Robert; it was inevitable that they would meet again, possibly several times, during the remaining week-and-a-half of her holiday.

The sudden, sharp ringing of the telephone startled her. She almost fell off her stool. A deep, velvet-brown languorous voice on the other end of the line brought her back to her senses.

"Hi stranger," drawled Patrick. "What does a fella have to do to get a date around here? I'm beginning to think you're avoidin' me!"

A wave of relief washed over her; the sound of his voice alone was enough to raise her spirits. Patrick explained that he had been for a walk the previous day, along the beach, hoping to find her there. He had planned to paint, but her absence had unsettled him. Unable to concentrate on his work, he had simply read for a while. In the afternoon he'd taken a taxi into the town of Skiathos – a haunt of the rich and famous; known to the locals by its more familiar name of *Chora*.

Taking a leisurely stroll, he wandered through crowds and around the waterside cafes and shops, with their bright awnings. The smart restaurants, bars and boutiques oozed sophistication and style. He'd explored the small, whitewashed, red-tiled houses, which were clustered around two hills, then shopped for presents for his sisters, back home in Canada. The narrow winding maze of back streets proved a fascinating place to explore, he explained; many of them were still cobbled. He had spent time browsing through several antique shops, then headed back, towards the harbour. Chora was also a port, for ships arriving from Volos, Ayios, Constantinos and Kimi. Patrick rested, for a while, on one of the lower harbour walls, watching the passers-by and admiring the graceful yachts.

Fiona was more than happy to accept the invitation to lunch, at his apartment. The hotel's *Sandpiper* restaurant was usually packed at lunch times and Robert was sure to be somewhere in the vicinity.

Replacing the receiver, she felt in an altogether more optimistic mood. How did he *do* that, she wondered? It wasn't simply the invitation to lunch. Maybe he was one of those life-enhancing people, who could make you feel good, just by being in their company.

She changed into a peach-coloured dress, which accentuated her figure in all the right places. The addition of gold jewellery and French perfume completed the effect. Patrick was in the process of opening wine, when she walked through the already open doorway of his apartment. His hand stopped in mid-action, as he gave a low whistle.

They ate inside the apartment this time. Patrick had set the table with artistic panache. An elaborate arrangement of fresh flowers, their citrus colours exquisitely blended together, adorned the centre of the table, with lighted candles on either side. The pale-green, velvet curtains were drawn halfway.

The meal began in total silence. After a couple of glasses of red wine however, they began to unwind. "You know, there's a *great* place I'd like to show you, close to the town," enthused Patrick. "I found it last year. Makes a helluva walk. It's called *Bourtzi* – a kind of promontory that juts *right* out over the water." He emphasised the point with his hands. Fiona studiously avoided the events of her previous day; thankfully, Patrick didn't ask.

After lunch they moved across to the soft white leather sofa, and sank gratefully into it, feeling pleasantly drowsy, after the wine. Patrick put his arm around her, pulling her closer to him. Fiona rested her dark auburn curls, on his shoulder; her eyes a subtle mixture of green and blue, as she gazed at him seductively, from beneath long auburn lashes.

CHAPTER TWO

He began to run his fingers softly and delicately through her perfumed hair. She sighed and their eyes met... in a gaze full of passion and longing. At first, their kisses were gentle and exploratory, but they quickly became more urgent. He put his tongue inside her mouth. As he probed deeper, and more passionately, she felt a flood of excitement, from deep within her. She began to loose control.

"Come on darling." Patrick's voice was husky, as he led her towards the bedroom. She fumbled, as she undid his shirt, then ran her hands across his bronzed, muscular chest. One of her fingernails snagged the still blond, but slightly greying hairs. His mouth became ever more demanding. Quickly removing one another's clothes, they flung them across the bed, then made love with tremendous passion, completely consumed, releasing a deeply-rooted hunger in both of them.

* * * *

When Fiona awoke, she glanced at the white digital clock, on the bedside table. Patrick was still sleeping, his tousled, wavy hair framing his handsome, bearded face. Not wishing to disturb him, she dressed hurriedly then tiptoed out to her apartment, closing the door quietly.

They had agreed over lunch to attend a meal with cabaret, being held in the cocktail bar of the hotel, that evening. Having booked a table for eight o'clock, Patrick arrived at her apartment ten minutes before, to escort her.

As it was quite a formal occasion, he was wearing a smart evening suit. He looked very suave and sophisticated. Fiona's heart leapt when she saw him. She wore a long, slinky-black evening dress with a diamante, diamond-shaped panel, in the centre of the bodice. The back of her dress was rather revealing: thin straps edged with tiny zircons. Diamond pendant earrings completed her ensemble.

Patrick gave her one of his warm, heart-stopping smiles. His deep brown eyes were full of admiration and ... something quite intangible... which had not been there before. As they enjoyed the cabaret, Fiona began to feel uneasy. She had heard that Robert usually compèred these shows. Her heart sank, at the thought of being anywhere near him again. The female singer sang in a similar, dramatic style to Shirley Bassey and wore a dress of shimmering gold. Ironically, the songs she had chosen that evening seemed to mirror Fiona's emotions.

Robert *was* compèring the show, although he didn't appear until after the first two acts. He was making a very creditable job of it. The initial shock of seeing him again, soon gave way to a stalwart resolution, to pretend that nothing had happened between them. Two-thirds of the way through the cabaret, while Fiona was laughing and joking with Patrick, the waitress came over to their table for two. She was carrying a silver tray, two goblets, and a complimentary bottle of *Zitsa*, the Greek equivalent of champagne – courtesy of the management.

Fiona blushed bright red, but hoped frantically that Patrick hadn't noticed. Robert was standing over by the piano, watching them closely. His tall, rugged good looks were accentuated by the formality of his attire. He caught their respective eyes and raised a glass to them. To Fiona's chagrin, Patrick reciprocated, raising his glass to Robert.

She reminded herself that this was a perfectly natural reaction. After all, the two men apparently knew each other quite well. Patrick had already explained that he had holidayed at *Club Skiathos* for the past four years. The scenic nature of the island provided him with an inexhaustible selection of subjects for his landscape paintings.

Just at that point, the music began again. The female vocalist began to sing another, much more plaintive song.

>   *Thinking of two lovers*
>   *Loving them the same*
>   *Loving's for eternity – it isn't just a game.*

She continued with the song, but the effect upon Fiona was devastating. She tried to keep her composure, but found herself gradually dissolving into tears. The strain, despite her best efforts, was too much. She murmured something to Patrick about needing the Ladies Room, then disappeared, as quickly as possible.

Once there, she hastily found a cubicle, pulled down the seat cover and sat there shaking, trying to control herself. Thankfully, the place was deserted. Although upset, she was, at the same time, very angry with herself. What on *earth* was the matter with her? She was behaving like an immature schoolgirl!

She could still hear the strains of the song, filtering through from the lounge. The singer's voice was so soulful and melodic. It seemed to reach into Fiona's very soul. She began to fumble in her black, sequinned evening bag, for a handkerchief. The bag was so delicate that as she rummaged around, she feared that she might pull it apart. She dabbed the area around her eyes with a lace handkerchief, trying to recover her composure. Then she began to worry. What would Patrick be thinking of her? She must try to redeem the situation, as quickly as possible.

CHAPTER TWO

Fortunately, there was still no one around as she used the illuminated mirror, which covered an entire wall, to repair her make-up. She quickly applied fresh plum-coloured lipstick, dabbing the area under her eyes once more, with a little cold water.

Just then two elderly women guests burst into the room, laughing together over some private joke. They glanced at Fiona, but she must have looked reasonably normal, as they paid no further attention to her.

Feeling more like her normal self, she slipped back into the dimly-lit cocktail lounge. A comedian was performing. The riotous laughter from the audience lifted her spirits further. When she finally reached the table, all trace of her former mood had, ostensibly, vanished. She smiled reassuringly at Patrick, who was looking rather concerned. She quickly put his mind at rest, explaining that the champagne must have been more potent than she had realised. As he squeezed her hand tightly, she felt once again safe – in his company.

The evening was drawing to a close – although there was no sign of Robert. His partner Miklos, at least ten years his senior, thanked everyone for attending – adding that he hoped that they had enjoyed themselves. Most of the guests took the polished oak floor for the final waltz; the multi-coloured lights of the strobe covered the dancers and the floor beneath, with a magical, sequinned quality.

Such a marked contrast: the vibrant, artificially-created atmosphere of the cocktail lounge – and the fragrant stillness of the Mediterranean night that awaited them. Couples wandered back, hand-in-hand, within their own, unique worlds; sharing the same Greek setting, for just one moment in time – like so many oases, within the unpredictable desert of the world.

The timeless wine-dark sea ebbed and flowed all around them. Fiona imagined the myriad of worlds, co-existing alongside theirs; within this same moment in time that she and Patrick happened to be sharing. Arm-in-arm, they followed the resort pathways, accompanied by the relentless noise of the cicadas, rubbing their back legs together – or maybe it was their wings? Fiona could never remember precisely which part of their anatomy produced that distinctive sound!

As they kissed goodnight, outside Fiona's villa, Patrick suddenly suggested: "How would you feel about moving into my apartment, for the rest of the vacation? After all, there's plenty of room... for both of us."

CHAPTER THREE

Friday morning dawned, bright and early. Bookings at the resort ran from Sunday to Sunday. The end of her first week in Greece was fast approaching, with only one week remaining. Despite Patrick's suggestion about moving in together, she decided against broaching the subject again, unless he did.

Time was passing so quickly – if only she'd booked a month! The idyllic atmosphere of this beautiful Greek island was beginning to cast a spell; the *Sirens* of the mythological tales, were singing their captivating but fatal songs – drawing her ever closer to the rocks. She was in a rather whimsical, but fatalistic mood that morning, as though something was about to happen, over which she had no control.

During the last few days, Patrick had been hinting that he would have to spend more time painting, to meet the deadline for his forthcoming exhibition, in Victoria. He had an additional week to complete his work, following her departure.

However, he had originally planned to complete six paintings, by the end of his three-week stay. Fiona began to feel guilty about keeping him from his schedule, so she telephoned him to suggest that she should take a trip to a much larger supermarket, a fair distance away, almost on the outskirts of Skiathos town. One of the receptionists had recommended it. This would serve the dual purpose of providing items unobtainable in the on-site grocery store, whilst giving Patrick additional time to focus on his painting. She could then conjure up a more ambitious meal for them that evening. To her relief, he readily agreed.

Patrick decided to make an immediate start on his next project. This was to be a particularly dramatic landscape painting of the wooded promontory at *Bourtzi*, which he had described to her the previous day; a place where fishermen frequently took siestas, or gathered in conversation in the trees' shade. He planned to make some detailed sketches initially, selecting the precise subject of the painting later.

Half an hour later, Fiona took the winding lane that led to the front entrance of the club. Passing under the white stone archway, she turned right onto a pathway, alongside the main highway. There was just one main

CHAPTER THREE

road on this small island. It stretched from Skiathos town, all the way down to the south coast.

She caught the local bus, which ran every thirty minutes, armed with a copy of the timetable from reception. When the bus arrived it was almost empty. Having paid her drachmas, she was soon speeding on her way, in the direction of the main town. The bus followed a breathtakingly scenic route. Every corner seemed to provide a glimpse of yet another sunny cove, washed by vivid blue seas.

The supermarket was much larger than she had expected – almost like shopping at Tescos – although the range of fresh goods, such as meat, fruit, fish and vegetables, was more varied and exotic. There were however, a few familiar brand names, like Kellogg's, Cadbury's and John West, common to many international supermarkets.

She emerged from the cool air conditioning, with two large brown paper sacks of provisions. Fiona realised, to her dismay, that she had missed the return bus, by seconds; she could see it disappearing into the distance. As she was exactly on time, being a rather well organised person, the bus must have left a couple of minutes early.

It was still only ten o'clock in the morning, so luckily the May sun was nowhere near its zenith. She began to trudge along the main route, back towards the resort, thankful that she was wearing casual shoes. On the outward journey she had noticed a taxi rank, about a mile or so down the road from her present position. Although the sacks were heavy, she could probably make it that distance.

However, the sacks proved heavier than she had realised and one of them was slightly torn. Her arms began to ache. She walked on a few more yards, then put her load down at the side of the road, to rest her weary arms. Picking both sacks up again, she prepared to continue her laboured progress towards the taxis. Suddenly, she was startled by the sound of a car horn behind her.

As she had been walking carefully along the side of the road and was clearly in no danger from traffic, she turned around quickly to protest. But it wasn't a car at all. It was a minibus. The driver had parked some distance behind her. He got out and strode casually over to her. Fiona noticed that he was dressed in white shorts and T-shirt. His limbs were muscular and tanned. It was difficult at first to see his face, because as she turned, she found herself looking directly into the sun. As the driver drew closer she realised that it was Robert Osborne. He greeted her in friendly way: "Hello there. I was on my way back to the hotel, but those bags look heavy. Would you like a lift?"

19

ADRIFT IN PARADISE

Fiona had no desire to see him at all. She knew that it was probably a totally unreasonable response to his offer of help... but her instincts were ringing alarm bells, loud and clear. She began to make a feeble excuse about heading for the taxis. Robert laughed good-naturedly.

"You'll never make it," he said, in a light-hearted fashion, but the expression on his face was one of genuine concern. Reluctantly, Fiona saw the sense in his offer.

"Hop in," he insisted. "I'll take you back. It will save you time." Climbing into the minibus, they began to head back, toward the resort. He whistled as he drove and seemed in good spirits. He explained that he had been down to the harbour, below the town, to discuss business with one of the wholesalers, who supplied fish for the club restaurant. "You should take a closer look at the harbour sometime," he advised her. "It's built on the site of an ancient city. The Persian king Xerxes used it centuries ago, as a ship-repairing base.

"Niklos, my supplier, drives a very hard bargain," he continued. "He knows that his merchandise is in great demand, so he's trying to increase the price. We managed to settle the matter over a glass of ouzo."

Fiona replied that, despite being in Greece for a week she hadn't yet tried the national drink. "But you must!" retorted Robert. "Is this your first time in Greece?"

"Yes, I've not even visited the mainland before. But I *have* travelled the world a great deal," she added. She didn't want him to think of her as a provincial ignoramus.

He drove a few yards further along the road. They were approaching a rather attractive looking taverna. Its whitewashed walls were covered in vines. "I've just had a *great* idea!" he said, pulling swiftly over, onto the car park. "Come on." He extended his hand to her. She glanced nervously at the parcels. "Oh, drop those down behind the seats," he advised. "They'll be much cooler there." She took his hand, as he helped her out of the vehicle, feeling a tingle of excitement, as his skin touched hers.

Once in the taverna, she selected a secluded corner right at the back, overlooking small but attractive gardens. Fiona was fascinated by plants of all kinds, especially those from foreign climes. At home, she was a keen gardener. Four years previously, she had bought some African Lily bulbs back from Madeira, which she'd managed to grow successfully in her conservatory. 'Those were happier times', she thought sadly... 'before I lost Ian'.

Fiona loved nurturing plants. She was of a kind, considerate nature with birds, animals... and the more human variety. Each morning, on her three-tiered brown bird table she would place morsels of food,

CHAPTER THREE

especially during the winter months. As she waited for Robert, she thought about her lovely garden, back home – suddenly feeling tearful and homesick.

He came over from the bar, with two very small glasses of an almost clear liquid. "Here you are, try this," he suggested. She took a fairly small sip, but nearly choked. He laughed and patted her gently on the back, explaining that it was ouzo that she was drinking. After cautiously taking a few more sips, she realised that she quite liked it.

"I noticed you admiring the plants," Robert commented, shortly afterwards. 'He doesn't miss a trick', thought Fiona. She explained about her gardening hobby and her love of plants... and nature in general. The two of them began to talk in a more relaxed and friendly manner than before.

"I've been wondering what brought you to the island in the first place. You seem so at home here, in this type of setting," she observed. Robert explained that as a young man, he had graduated from Oxford University, with an Honours Degree in History. He had subsequently visited the Greek Islands for the first time as a research student: studying for a Masters Degree in Classical History.

Greek History had fascinated him, since his schooldays, but his visit to the islands and to Skiathos in particular, transformed what had originally been academic curiosity into something closely akin to an obsession. The more time he spent in Greek company, the more convinced he became, that his own, more direct and passionate nature, was far closer to the Greek temperament, than that of his fellow Englishmen. It was a major breakthrough for him – he'd discovered his natural home.

He had met his wife Barbara when they were studying together for their Bachelor of Arts Degrees. They had both attended the same college, lectures, social venues, and had fallen in love. They were married shortly after completing their first degrees.

At this point in the conversation Robert offered to buy her another drink. But this time Fiona insisted on buying them, returning with two glasses of white wine; a second glass of ouzo at that hour of the day might be a bridge too far!

While they were on their second drinks Robert asked about her husband. She explained that he had been a kind, considerate man. Like himself, he was highly educated, but in Ian's case at London and Cambridge Universities. His specialist subject was French – particularly, the French Classics. Like herself, he'd been a school teacher, albeit at secondary level.

"What happened to Barbara?" Fiona asked the question on impulse, then immediately regretted it. He seemed to react negatively; his previously amiable expression became brooding and morose. "I'm sorry," she said. "I didn't mean to pry." "No problem," he replied, after a pause. "It *was* a long time ago."

"Had we better be getting back? I've no wish to delay you," she said, trying to change the subject. "You're *not* delaying me, Fiona." His reply was measured and incisive. The tone of his voice caused her to look directly, into his blue eyes. They held each other's gaze for several seconds – unable to extricate themselves.

Finally, Robert broke the spell. "Come on young lady!" he said, jumping to his feet.

Once back in the minibus they drove on for a few kilometres. He seemed rather preoccupied. They reached a fork in the road. The lower coastal route on their left took them back towards *Club Skiathos*. The higher, grey serpentine road insinuated its way, up into the ancient, olive-clad hills. Robert stopped at the fork, hesitating for a few seconds. He gave her a quick glance, as though changing his mind about something. Just as suddenly, he changed gear, then checking in the rear view mirror, deftly swung the bus over to the right, taking the higher mountain road.

It was a few seconds before the full implication of what he was doing registered with Fiona. He had taken her completely by surprise. "Wh – what are you doing?" she asked nervously. His expression seemed quite steely and his jaw was set, in a similar manner to the one he'd adopted, on the return journey from Olympia Bay, a few days earlier. "There's something I must show you," he replied tersely. Fiona felt helpless, as though in a dream. At the same time, she felt sure that Robert meant her no harm. She was gradually regaining her trust in him. He must have a very important reason for changing their route, she reassured herself.

Robert was driving very quickly now, along this high mountain road. He explained that the route eventually led to Kastro, a pirate stronghold centuries before. Fiona had heard that it was only possible to drive along this route, up to a certain point. The remaining part of the journey to Kastro was part of a popular walking itinerary for tourists.

According to the *Blue Book*, which she had bought in one of the local shops, the monasteries of Taviarkhis, Evangelistra and Karalambous lay somewhere along this trans-island part of the route. She imagined them, shrouded picturesquely by forests. Patrick had previously explained that it was much easier to reach Kastro by boat, than by any other means. Apart from themselves and the occasional peasant or cart, the road was almost deserted – just as well, in view of his speed! He seemed to know every twist and turn of the road.

CHAPTER THREE

Within ten minutes they had reached a very high point, right up in the hills, miles from anywhere. Vivid green pines shaded the many tracks and lanes leading off the main road. He suddenly turned off along one of these smaller dirt tracks, following it as it sloped gently upwards, for about a minute. Then he swung completely off to the left and came to rest behind an old, whitewashed stone building.

The roof was rather worn in places; some of the terracotta tiles were particularly weathered. The whole building was surrounded by grove upon grove of olive trees. Robert motioned for her to get out of the vehicle. Having done so, she glanced behind. The land to the rear was on an even steeper incline. The whole landscape, as far as the eye could see, was studded with varied textures of green.

The air was heavily perfumed with the aromatic scent of olive leaves. She could also smell the fragrance of orange trees. Everywhere was unbearably quiet. Nothing moved. There wasn't a sound. She looked towards Robert, but he wasn't looking in her direction. He still seemed completely preoccupied. "Come and take a look for yourself," was his brief comment.

The interior of the building, as she stepped into it, was a complete surprise. She had expected it to be derelict, crammed with old furniture, cobwebs and insects; her imagination working overtime, as usual. Instead, it was neat, tidy and well ordered. It seemed to be a cross between a studio-cum-workshop... and someone's home. The interior was much larger than was apparent from the outside. It looked, for the entire world, like a very large but comfortable, studio apartment!

The floor was carpeted with almost new rush matting. Over by the wall, on the right-hand side, was an ample bed, with pillows and a covered duvet. At the back of the room, a small kitchenette area contained a compact white oven and hob. Across from the bed, on the opposite wall, were long, extensive shelves of neatly ordered books. The topmost shelf housed foreign language books, encompassing most of the European languages. Alongside these, she was slightly unnerved to discover, were several books about alternative religions, the occult, shamans, and parapsychology.

The two shelves, immediately below the language books, contained copious volumes of Classical English Literature and Poetry. Dickens, Thackeray, Hardy and Shakespeare lay alongside tomes devoted to several well-known poets of different nationalities. She was amazed to discover a copy of her favourite book of poetry. Selecting the *Poetical Works of Rupert Brooke*, from the second shelf, she scanned the contents page. On page one hundred and forty-two, she found her favourite poem, *Day That I Have Loved*: "I can't believe you actually have this. I've an identical copy at home!" Warmed by her enthusiasm he said, "My favourite lines are in verse two. Now, how does it go?" He began to quote,

'Where lies your waiting boat, by wreaths of the sea's making...'.

He recited the remaining eight lines of the stanza, word perfectly. The accuracy of his recitation and his sensitive delivery of the lines aroused her.

"That's wonderful Robert," she said breathlessly, when he had finished. "But how could you possibly have known about that particular poem?"

"Well, it does help to have a father who read English at Cambridge. Besides, there's a great deal you don't know about me young lady – nor I about you. It's a situation I intend to remedy with all possible haste." Taken aback by his comment, she returned to the previous subject: "Poetry shouldn't be purely educational. It should be about real life too, don't you think?"

There were two comfortable sofa chairs upholstered in blue, in the centre of the room. Robert suggested that she take a seat while he made two mugs of tea, in the kitchenette. Luckily he had a supply of powdered milk. He kept an ample stock of basic provisions, in a white cupboard below the sink.

Fiona noticed that the lower of the two bookshelves contained several Ancient History books and a few about epic voyages and sea exploration. Robert pointed out that he also had some popular novels by Alexander Papadiamantis, a native of the island. Alexander was the son of a local priest. His stories were concerned with the lives of local seamen and farmers.

He handed her a mug of tea and sat down beside her on one of the sofas, cupping his mug in his hands and sipping the hot, sweet liquid. "If you visit the *Bourdzi* area," he explained, "you'll see a statue of Papadiamantis – right at the entrance." Ironically, this was the same area which Patrick was visiting that very day – the subject of his next painting.

For a short while, they fell silent. Fiona sank back into her half of the blue sofa, feeling cosy and comfortable. She stretched her legs out in front of her – suddenly feeling very much at home. It was a strange, almost eerie feeling, as though she had been there before; but of course, that was completely impossible.

"Tell me more about Barbara," she found herself saying, before she'd even realised that she'd said it. He eyed her quizzically and for a moment, seemed somewhat surprised. "It's not a subject I normally discuss in any detail," he replied, evasively. "In fact I haven't discussed her with anyone since we parted."

CHAPTER THREE

"I'm sorry," she apologised. "It's just that you mentioned her earlier and I thought..." "So I did," he interrupted. "Well, what does it matter anyway? We've been divorced for at *least* seven years." There was a long pause. Somewhat embarrassed, and anxious to change the subject, Fiona left the sofa and wandered over, to look out of the large glass window at the rear of the workshop, immediately behind his writing desk.

"What a fantastic view!" she observed. The olive groves rose up, to the green hills beyond. In the far distance was a row of cypress trees. To her right, far below, nestled a tiny valley. It hadn't been visible when they'd arrived in the minibus. It was a grassy area, with a small stream flowing through it. She could hear the faint trickle of water from the stream, through the glass window, intermingled with the delicate tinkling of bells, around the necks of three small white goats, which were grazing in the area. A fourth goat was drinking from the stream.

"It must have been very tranquil, yet *so* inspirational for you, whilst you were writing." "It was," he remembered, wistfully. Then added, in a more jocular vein: "I call this place my 'Den'." Joining her at the window, he placed his right arm casually, around her shoulder. "*Very* inspirational," he echoed. With his left hand, he turned her around to face him. There was a moment's pause. Then he cupped her chin in his right hand, drawing her gently towards him. When his mouth came down on hers, however, there was nothing gentle about it. His kisses were at once fierce and demanding. He pulled her ever more tightly towards him.

She felt as though she were being crushed. Steadying herself with one hand, on the desk behind her, she tried to break free. She opened her mouth to protest. Robert quickly slid his tongue inside and began probing. Fiona found her resolve ebbing away. She tried to control her reactions, but she was totally overwhelmed by sensations, which were welling up... from somewhere deep inside.

He continued to kiss her hungrily, as he moved her towards the ample bed. She sank down onto the pillows, Robert's body heaving with passion above her. She could feel his heart beating rapidly. "Please, don't," she whimpered, at the same time thinking: 'I can't – I've got to get back to Patrick'.

He only groaned in reply, as his fingers began to deftly undo the buttons of her dress. She realized, with horror, that he would be able to open the dress quite easily. It was a floral print Laura Ashley, which unbuttoned straight down the front. Oh *why* had she chosen to wear it that day? But how could she have known that she would meet Robert Osborne – by pure chance?

"No, *please* Robert. Don't touch me. Leave me alone!" she pleaded, as she struggled desperately, to free herself from the weight of his body. He moved to one side. The strength of his right arm was pinning her down to the bed. "You don't really mean that," he whispered huskily. "I know that you don't. For Christ's sake, stop *fighting* me Fiona!"

Unfastening the last two buttons on her dress, he pushed it away from her. Her silky, shell-pink slip was revealed underneath. His mouth came down hard upon hers. Then he lifted the slip over her head. Only her pink silk French knickers and her camisole top remained. She felt all resolve draining away, as he kissed the base of her neck, then travelled slowly down the full length of her body, continuing to kiss her… arousing long-forgotten sensations.

"Please Rob, no," she moaned. "Please don't!" "It's far too late for that my darling," he whispered – almost inaudibly. Nothing mattered now – except the sensations she was feeling. All reason had completely deserted her.

"Fi," he moaned. "My darling Fi!"

As she arched her back in complete abandonment, she realised, half-consciously, that the only man who'd used that abbreviated form of her name before, had been Ian. Their two bodies moved rhythmically together, in perfect time. Locked into one another's pleasure, their hands intertwined.

CHAPTER FOUR

The rays of hot afternoon sun enhanced her long auburn locks, spread out like a beautiful trail behind her. For a moment, Fiona couldn't remember where she was. Then she turned towards the warm, tanned, body beside her. There was just room for the two of them, side by side, on the bed. Robert was sleeping peacefully. The duvet had been tossed to one side, because of the heat, enabling her to admire his muscular, sensual body, as he lay there, oblivious to her presence.

He was very tall, at least six foot two inches compared to Fiona's five-foot seven-inch frame. Although he had a relatively slim waist, his chest and hips were broader and more muscular than she had previously realised. His body was tanned, from years of exposure to the hot Mediterranean sun, but he remained very hirsute: a large proportion of his body was covered in a mass of thick-matted dark hair.

As she admired him he turned over and woke. He gave her a long, lingering smile. A sudden thought occurred to her. She glanced quickly at her watch. "What time is it?" she inquired anxiously, her watch being the only item that he hadn't removed. "Who cares?" Rolling towards her, his hands began once more, to work skilfully along the length of her body. "That was only the entrée, my darling. *This* is the main course!"

Fiona had ceased to believe that she could experience such ecstasy again. A year or so before Ian's untimely death, he had become incapable of lovemaking, except to a very limited degree. As she lay resting, after this second session with Robert, she began to feel guilty, as though she should have realised that Ian's health was seriously impaired. But no one realised the extent of the problem – not even their own doctor.

Casting gloomy thoughts aside, she smiled serenely at Robert. He returned her loving gaze, intertwining the fingers of his right hand with hers. She was lying on the inner side of the bed closest to the wall, feeling protected and content. They rested for a little while longer – but this time Fiona's conscience began to work overtime. "I'll *have* to get back," she protested, but this time more firmly.

They dressed slowly. During the last two hours, Robert's den had become strangely familiar. Having collected their possessions, Robert carefully locked the door behind them, pocketing the key. As they exited the building, Fiona was once more aware of the warm, pungent scents around them.

For the first few kilometres they hardly spoke, being simply content in each other's company. She caught him glancing at her long legs, as they progressed further through the wooded hillsides. They were heading back towards the resort, but still quite a distance from their destination. In her distraction, she had forgotten to button her dress; several of the lower buttons had popped open, revealing a large expanse of thigh. It amused her to realise how alarming such a situation would have been, at the start of their earlier journey into the hills. Now, in view of what had happened between them, she felt no embarrassment at all.

She laughed playfully as his hand moved around the gear lever, then slid down to caress her exposed thigh. Then it began to move teasingly, and by stages, higher and higher, underneath her dress. With the other hand, he continued to drive, albeit more slowly, around each of the treacherous bends.

"Don't," she laughed. "We'll have an accident!" "Will we?" he asked teasingly, feigning a total lack of concern. Meanwhile, his hand strayed in the opposite direction, towards the soft, erotic region of her inner thigh. Gently, he began to arouse her again.

"Look out!" she shouted. He swerved, to avoid one of the shaggy white mountain goats, indigenous to the area. Having strayed into the middle of the road, its bell tinkled wildly, as it jumped quickly to one side, then on to a spot of fresh grazing land. Robert was laughing, as he steered the minibus back onto what was thankfully, a straight section of road.

After a quarter of an hour or so, they arrived back at *Club Skiathos*. It was about three o'clock in the afternoon. The events of the day had relaxed them both. Robert parked at reception, then helped Fiona to carry the two sacks of food, thankfully not of the perishable variety, back to her chalet. He held both bags, as she fumbled for the keys. Her hands were shaking, as she thought of what lay ahead.

Stepping into the entrance hall Robert paused momentarily then carried both bags into the breakfast-cum-dining room area, placing them on the marble-effect breakfast bar. "I'd better leave you to it," he said reluctantly. With equal reluctance, she agreed. "Otherwise Patrick might suspect something," she reminded him.

"You'll have to tell him," he advised solemnly, taking her right hand between both of his, and squeezing it tightly. "I will," agreed Fiona, "but I'll need to choose the moment carefully. I don't want to hurt him any more

CHAPTER FOUR

than I have to." Robert nodded, giving her a perfunctory kiss. Then he left quickly, closing the door gently behind him.

Fiona realised that he was only too aware of the complicated situation now facing her. He had taken his leave in a relatively platonic way – as though making it clear, albeit indirectly, that the final decision, about which lover she should choose, must be purely her own; unaffected by any additional pressure on his part.

* * * *

As luck would have it, Patrick spent most of the day painting. He had returned, tousle-haired, with paint-splattered clothes, collapsing onto his bed at about half past three that afternoon. Seven hours of solid concentration upon his craft had left him exhausted and he slept like a baby, until about six.

He telephoned her to check that their arrangement still stood, arriving on the doorstep at about half past seven, casually but smartly dressed in blue cord trousers and a blue velvet-type top, with a draw cord at the waist. Fiona was genuinely pleased to see him. He handed her a bottle of retsina as he entered. Luckily she had grabbed a couple of hours' sleep, before setting the table, as elegantly as possible; when you're dining with an artist you have to make an effort!

Following the melon boat starter she served a simple meal of lamb kebabs on a bed of rice. She had prepared a Greek Salad, using cucumber, tomatoes, green peppers and twelve black olives. As she added this last ingredient, she was reminded of the dense olive groves surrounding her in Robert's den, just a few hours earlier. She topped the dish with small cubes of Feta cheese, garnished with a special homemade salad dressing.

The meal concluded with a Black Forest gateau, followed by coffee and liqueurs. Thank goodness that the lamb, cheese and gateau had already been purchased and refrigerated beforehand. She imagined the sorry state they would have been in, after a few hours in the minibus!

They relaxed together on the sofa, following the meal. The apartment was equipped with a sophisticated sound system, enabling her to play a selection of classical music CDs that she'd brought with her. Patrick described in his lilting, Canadian-Irish brogue, the progress he had made with his painting.

"Would you care for a few lessons… in the art of landscape painting?" he offered. "They'd be strictly on the house of course," he added, with a twinkle in his eye. Fiona stroked his slightly greying fair hair gently, with her fingers. Despite the soothing effect of the wine and liqueurs, she was experiencing strong pangs of conscience. She hoped that Pat wouldn't detect the edginess in her voice. Since their last meeting he had gently insisted that she call him Pat: "All of my close acquaintances do. Patrick is *way* too formal."

Fiona explained that during her final years of primary school teaching, prior to Ian's death, she had taken a party of schoolchildren to the Birmingham Museum and Art Gallery, adjacent to the Town Hall. It was a day's course on landscape painting. In addition to a tour of the Art Gallery, to view paintings from different centuries, a further component had been basic landscape painting techniques, using watercolours. The woman conducting the tour was an expert. She demonstrated the art of building up a landscape in stages, from a blank canvas.

They had learned about foregrounds, middle-grounds and backgrounds; techniques in the use of paint, light and shade, perspective and so on. On returning to school they experimented with these ideas, as part of a series of Art lessons.

"That's all well and good by way of an introduction," remarked Patrick. Then he lapsed into a broad Irish brogue: "But you'll be wanting a few lessons from a true master of the art!" Fiona laughed. She could always rely upon Pat to make her feel better. After what seemed a lifetime ago, but was in reality just a handful of days, she'd felt herself drawing closer to him, with every meeting. 'But apparently not close enough to stop me falling for Robert!' she thought ruefully. Mercifully, the wine was making them sleepy so they decided to sleep in their own beds, that night, which was fortunate, to say the least! After Robert's ministrations that day, Fiona felt that her sensuality was, at least for the time being, all played out. It would enable them, so Patrick reasoned, to rise bright and early for the artistic work of the following day. He thanked her for the delicious meal and gave her a parting kiss. But as Fiona finally closed the door, she felt overwhelmed with guilt.

* * * *

The following day was a Saturday. Fiona could feel her holiday time ticking away, like a relentless giant stopwatch. She had been woken earlier than usual that morning by the sound of bird song, emanating from the luxuriant foliage, outside her bedroom window.

Tremendously enervated, she jumped quickly out of bed, showered, and changed into inexpensive clothing: a pair of faded, blue denim jeans, white T-shirt and a checked over-shirt, in two shades of blue. She was

CHAPTER FOUR

more than likely to end up with paint-splattered clothing, after a lesson with Patrick!

She wasn't meeting him until nine o'clock. By the time she'd completed a quick breakfast it was only half past eight – still time for an early morning stroll on the beach. The fresh air would be bracing. She could push thoughts about Robert to the back of her mind. She planned to walk along the same area of shingle, just below the Club, where she had first met Patrick.

Passing the plush main hotel building, Fiona peered through, into the ground floor restaurant. Its elegant porthole windows faced out to sea. She loved to sit at a table adjacent to these windows, to watch the breakers, when she ate inside. On warmer days, it was even more pleasant to sit outside, on Japanese-style decking – the wind playing in her hair – and an even better view.

Passing the hotel, she took the left-hand path, which curved around quite sharply, then led gradually down to the beach, via a series of stone steps. The steps were edged with long strips of wood, for reinforcement. Just before the last flight of steps there was a long hedge, stretching for some distance. It served the dual purpose of windbreak and private screen, between the resort itself and the beach below. Fiona was just about to descend this final flight of steps, when something stopped her in her tracks.

She could see something, or rather, *someone,* in the distance… on the beach.

Unable to believe her eyes, she stepped quickly back and out of view, behind the hedge. Then surreptitiously, she peeped around the corner of the hedge again, to take a second look – hoping against hope that her original impression had been mistaken.

Two figures, one male, one female, were standing at some distance from her, right on the edge: where the shingle met the sea. The man was tall, dark and muscular. His woman companion was about an inch or so shorter than herself. She had a voluptuous figure and was wearing a light-green one-piece bathing suit. Her breasts were fulsome, her skin, a light-olive colour. A mass of beautiful, rich ebony hair cascaded down her back.

The man wore white slacks and a white aertex shirt. He seemed to be remonstrating with her. Beyond the two figures a motorboat could be seen, heading out to sea. It was white, with a light-blue stripe across its side; also, a motif, of what looked like a leaping blue dolphin – at least from a distance.

The boat was heading at rapid speed for a much larger vessel, which was anchored out at sea, some distance away. When Fiona and Ian had holidayed in Madeira a few years previously, they had taken photographs of the luxury ocean liner, the *Oriana,* as it sailed into Funchal harbour. She had been on the first stage of her maiden voyage.

The photographs had been taken initially, from a high vantage point at Monte, just below the chapel. The two of them descended later, by car, towards Funchal Harbour, where they had taken close-up photographs of the liner.

The ship towards which the smaller vessel was now speeding, seemed to be of a similar type to the *Oriana*. Perhaps it was transporting a few extra passengers, to join the cruise liner? These details registered in Fiona's mind, in seconds. Then, in a flash, her attention re-focused on the scene immediately below her.

The young girl, she now noticed, was dripping with water, as though she had just emerged from the sea. The man seemed to be considerably older than the woman. He seized her shoulders roughly, with both hands. They were definitely having some kind of argument. As he raised his voice, her worst fears were realised – the man, she was now *certain*, was Robert Osborne. She was also reasonably sure that the girl was the niece of his partner, Miklos Atronoides. Fiona had spoken to her on several occasions. She seemed to divide her time between reception duties and supervision of the restaurant staff.

But why were they arguing? Why was she dressed like that? He's old enough to be her father! Pangs of jealousy began to stab viciously into her heart. 'She can't be much above twenty', she thought, clenching her fists. Her nails dug deeply and painfully into the palms of her hands.

Darting back quickly once more, behind the hedge, she felt ashamed of herself – she was little better than a Peeping Tom! She could stand no more. Hurriedly, she ran back to her apartment, unlocked it and flung herself in fury onto the bed. Was this the man who had made love to her so passionately, just a few hours before? Was he after all, a mere lecher – a seducer of women?

She felt thoroughly miserable and began to sob. After two or three minutes, her sense of reason began to return. It was almost inconceivable that a man of Robert's character and sensitivity could be such a bastard. Her judgement couldn't be that wrong! There *had* to be an alternative explanation. Drying her tears, she composed herself. Looking in the mirror she began to repair her make-up.

Just at that moment the doorbell rang – *Patrick*! She had completely forgotten about him! Having recovered her composure, she swiftly answered the door.

She was about to apologise for being a few minutes late, when he pre-empted her, by explaining that he had overslept. 'That's twice I've been saved from discovery, by Patrick sleeping over. Thank God!' she thought, with relief.

CHAPTER FOUR

He had painting materials with him. Between them they carried an easel, large sheets of white card, paints and so on, down to the beach. Luckily the two figures who'd been there earlier had vanished – as if into thin air.

They walked some distance along the beach. After selecting their spot, they arranged the equipment accordingly. Patrick thought it best to begin with a relatively simple composition, so they began work on what was primarily a seascape. A jagged outcrop of rocks, to the left-hand side, provided an element of landscape.

Starting a painting, he explained, was always a fascinating experience for him, although, at the same time, it could be quite daunting. Fiona replied that they held that experience in common. She felt exactly the same when she began work on a new novel – or even a short story.

Patiently, he worked with her for several hours – expertly instructing her in the art of creating a passably competent painting – at least for a beginner. They used a large blank sheet of white card, sketching pencils and paint. Every hour or so they rested and had a drink. Later they ate a small picnic lunch, which Patrick had thoughtfully prepared.

By now the painting was half complete. The basic features were all present, but he suggested that they should work on perspective, the following day. Fiona was quite weary, due to the intense concentration required. At the same time she felt a tremendous sense of satisfaction with her efforts, as though she had truly accomplished something worthwhile.
Her earlier injured feelings were totally forgotten. Patrick had been so loving, attentive and patient. They both laughed, as they realised that they were splattered all over with flecks of different coloured paints. Some had even found its way into Fiona's fringe. Patrick reached down and tried to brush it away with his hand. He was over six feet tall. As his hand brushed her forehead he seemed so masterful – so at ease with himself. Fiona's heart warmed to him.

CHAPTER FIVE

Patrick had bought tickets the previous day, for a traditional Greek Folk Evening, to be held that night, at a taverna high up in the hills; a suitable reward, he suggested, as the two of them had worked so hard that day. Whilst buying the tickets in reception he had learned that this particular event was one of the most popular on the island. On previous holidays he'd been far too preoccupied with his seascapes to participate.

It was a fortnightly excursion, drawing together a cosmopolitan range of guests from several neighbouring resorts. Fiona laughed when she heard Patrick's description. It sounded like something straight out of a tourist brochure!

She decided to make herself as glamorous and alluring as possible, selecting a white full-length, Grecian-style evening dress, with matching gold jewellery. To heighten the effect, she swept her long auburn curls up at the back, with ringlets of curls falling on either side. A fringe of tiny, delicate curls completed the effect. Having applied her make-up she was well satisfied – *definitely* the Aphrodite look. She slipped on a pair of elegant gold evening sandals. Patrick looked very sophisticated in white evening jacket, bow tie and dark trousers, with a white silk shirt.

Two minibuses were waiting outside the reception area. As the first one was already full she and Patrick climbed aboard the second. Fiona had pushed the early morning incident to the back of her mind. Nevertheless, she still hoped that Robert wouldn't be driving them to the taverna. Luckily, it was his partner Miklos, instead. Whilst en route to their destination, he provided them with information, over the address system. It seemed to Fiona that Miklos embodied some of the finer characteristics of his classical forebears. He seemed a generous, but proud man, with a strong sense of curiosity and a love of hospitality.

Taverna Persephone, he explained, was the brainchild and personal creation of his good friend Iona Thessaloukis, a wealthy Greek landowner and entrepreneur, now in her late sixties. She had created several successful tourist attractions, across the island. For those less familiar with Greek Mythology, he gave a summarised account of the ancient story about the evil god Pluto – the source of Iona's inspiration for the taverna. As God

CHAPTER FIVE

of the Underworld, Pluto had lured beautiful Persephone, Ceres' daughter, into his kingdom of Hades. After eating six pomegranate seeds she was condemned to spend six months of every year, underground with Pluto.

As Miklos continued his explanation, Patrick whispered in Fiona's ear, "I guess Iona chose the right name. *Taverna Hades* might put people off – don't you think?!" On entering the venue, Fiona soon understood why Miklos had been so lavish in praise of his friend. Her imaginative skills, combined with those of the artist she'd commissioned, had produced a tremendously impressive place.

Huge frescoes lined the walls, Da Vinci style. The rather dramatic entrance represented Persephone's descent into Hades: in this case, via an illuminated staircase! Paintings of satyrs and creatures of every weird persuasion stared back at them, from either side of the walls. Small spot lamps were strategically placed, to accentuate particularly ghoulish features.

The enormous restaurant area was tastefully partitioned into different sections, each representing a part of the Underworld story. The section by the dance floor illustrated one of the more light-hearted episodes. There was a huge fresco of Persephone in diaphanous robes, dancing in a field of beautiful spring flowers.

The restaurant held over one hundred large circular dining tables, with eight chairs placed around each one. Every table was tastefully laid out, with an elegant flower arrangement in the centre, flagons of wine and jugs of iced water. The waiters and waitresses were dressed in costume, representing various underworld inhabitants and specific characters from the story.

There was a large raised stage area at the back of an equally spacious dance floor. A group of nine Greek musicians was seated on stage, dressed in traditional costume. Each played a particular Greek instrument: a lute, mandolin, tambour, and something, which looked surprisingly like small hand-held bag pipes. Also, pan pipes, a zither, two individual pipes or flutes and a lyre.

Patrick and Fiona were seated at a table with Miklos and their fellow minibus travellers. Those who had travelled on the first of the two vehicles were already seated two tables behind them. Fiona's heart skipped a beat – Robert was with them. To his immediate left was Miklos' niece, Lydia. Her sultry dark-haired looks were accentuated by a clinging red dress, which she wore at calf length and slightly off the shoulder, split half way up on one side.

Lydia caught Fiona's eye as she stared across, in dismay. Lydia gave her a friendly wave, accompanied by a smile of recognition. Fiona felt obliged to return the greeting, but her *true* feelings were simmering, just below the surface, although she fought valiantly to suppress them. She'd always regarded jealousy as such a pointless emotion – so why succumb?

When the Greek musicians were two-thirds of the way through their repertoire, the myriad company of staff, as if to a signal, began to serve the meal. This consisted of a variety of barbecued meat and *souvlakis*, which were pork kebabs. Also, ratatouille, sauté potatoes and a salad selection. Dessert was a mixture of yoghurt, fresh fruit and cream.

During the course of the meal, as an integral part of the entertainment, special waiters dressed in traditional costume, brought round leather goatskin sacks of wine. Each of the guests was required to drink a stream of the ruby red liquid, aimed at their mouths from a great height! Luckily each victim was provided with a large serviette to prevent clothing from becoming crimson-streaked.

A quintet of modern musicians began to play during the latter half of the meal. Traditional Greek dancing followed, during which some of the audience were invited to participate. The male dancers were dressed in the *fustanella* style. This consisted of white, short-skirted tunics and shirts with billowing triangular-shaped sleeves, criss-crossed at the top with sashes.

A particularly handsome Greek dancer rushed over to their table, grabbed Fiona by the hand, led her over to the dance floor and encouraged her, along with forty or so of the other guests, to join in with a *Zorba the Greek* style dance.

Patrick, Lydia and Robert were also amongst the dancers. Patrick was making a particularly elegant and rhythmical effort. Some of his Irish ancestors must surely have been experts in the art, Fiona thought with amusement. Come to think of it, apart from the variations in tempo, this style of Greek dancing, with its tapping, heel-clicking, and flowing arm movements, wasn't that dissimilar to River Dancing!

Robert, dressed in a dark evening suit, was particularly sensual in his movements, despite his large frame: like a sleek black panther. She noticed with dismay, the adoring expression on Lydia's face as she danced with him, arms-across-shoulders, in a circle.

Fiona's reaction continued to dismay her. Why should she feel like this? She had the gorgeous Patrick after all. Patrick was still totally absorbed in his dancing: a sultry traditionally-dressed, doe-eyed beauty on either side of him. He was seducing them with his charm – the devil! This part of the evening was a particular success. The dancing guests returned to their seats to tumultuous applause, from the less active members of the audience.

CHAPTER FIVE

The mood then changed as the modern quintet, including a keyboard player, pianist, drummer, guitarist and a flautist, resumed their places on stage. Initially their repertoire consisted of mainly disco music, but towards the later part of the evening they switched to ballroom dancing, including quicksteps and several slow, romantic waltzes.

By the time the quintet began to play for the second time, the atmosphere of the place was buzzing and much more frenetic: a mixture of bonhomie and abandonment, as most of the guests had consumed several glasses of wine and ouzo. In true Greek tradition, they were encouraged to participate in plate-smashing sessions – using only the cheapest plates, of course! The only poor souls not allowed any alcohol were the drivers. Fiona felt quite sorry for them, although a quick glance at Robert reminded her that he had no need of such artificial stimulation!

Many of the guests had made several inebriated and by now swaying trips onto the dance floor – swapping partners each time. They were certainly an international clientele. Fiona had danced with two Greek men from a neighbouring resort, and with Jean Pierre, the French student, whom she had met briefly, at the beginning of the holiday. They were able to chat in French as they danced, and even share a joke or two. She discovered that he had a great sense of humour. However, it was becoming more impossible to hold an intelligible conversation, especially in another language, inside the noisy atmosphere of the taverna.

Collecting their drinks they retreated to a spot, just in front of the exit doors. This was a much cooler area, right at the back of the taverna. Jean Pierre spoke in reasonably fluent English, about his future plans. Fiona recalled their previous conversation about his father Claude, the entrepreneurial businessman. Jean Pierre had described his father as having "A finger in several pies."

The effect of the alcohol was abundantly clear. Despite being a few years younger than her, he began to flirt outrageously with her. Taking her by the right hand he kissed the back of it with a flourish, in true Latin style. "Ma chère madam," he declared. "If you are ever in Paris, you come and look me up – non? I will soon qualify and then you will no doubt find me at my father's bureau. As I have already described to you, it is adjacent to the Bourse. You know, the Paris Stock Exchange – close to the River Seine."

"What *exactly* does your father do?" queried Fiona. "Oh, 'ow d'you say? A little bit of this, a little bit of that," replied Jean Pierre, somewhat evasively.

On returning to the main restaurant, Fiona danced with Patrick several times; he had begun to wonder where she was. She was really enjoying the evening. If only Ian had enjoyed dancing as much as she did. They could have appreciated evenings like this so much more. Ah well! That was water under the bridge now.

The evening was drawing to a close. Only a few dances remained. Jean Pierre, meanwhile, seemed to be getting on famously with Lydia; he had danced with her several times. Fiona was relaxing at her table; enjoying her own company for a minute or two. Patrick then invited Lydia to dance, to a slow waltz. That young lady was certainly popular. It wasn't difficult to see why! It was she who had sold the tickets to Patrick, for the event.

Suddenly, she felt a hand on her shoulder: "May I have the pleasure of this dance madam?" A tall dark, handsome gentleman, who bowed as he spoke, delivered the question in mock-theatrical style. Turning slowly around, looking every inch like the bewitching Persephone in her Greek couture, Fiona's heart began to beat wildly. As she rose to dance with Robert, he held her gaze; she felt totally mesmerized. As if in a dream, he escorted her elegantly, towards the dance floor.

Pulling her gently but firmly, towards to his body, they danced slowly and sensuously, around the floor. The touch of his skin on hers, as their hands once more intertwined and his cheek touched hers, was almost too much to bear. Her cheeks were flushed – surely he would be aware of that? Her heart was beating wildly and her hands were clammy. All the telltale signs, she realised, desperately hoping that Robert wouldn't notice. But, if he did, he made no comment.

They simply continued around the dance floor, as though their bodies were meant to interlock together: like two parts of the same soul. Fiona felt, almost through a sixth sense, that they must have been torn apart in some cataclysmic incident, centuries before. Having scoured the universe for several lifetimes, they had finally been reunited. She was seized by an overwhelming, though seemingly irrational conviction... that they must never again be parted. As if by telepathy, Robert squeezed her ever more tightly to him.

The quintet was playing a series of slow waltzes. As each waltz followed the next, the two lovers continued to dance; so mesmerised that they seemed oblivious of any changes between the dances. The spell was finally broken, as Patrick's Irish brogue broke into the dream.

"Mr. Osborne – Sir," he asked, sardonically. "Would you mind very much if Fiona and I had the last waltz?" Robert stared at him, for a trance-like moment, then snapped out of it. "Of course," he replied, with a charming smile, at the same time passing her elegantly across to him: "She's all yours – Mr. Maitland."

CHAPTER FIVE

Miklos approached Patrick and herself, at the close of the evening. Hurriedly he explained that a young American couple, the Andersons, who had travelled out with them on the minibus, had befriended an English couple of similar age, who were also staying at the resort. As the four of them would like to be dropped off at an All Night Disco, on the return journey, they were wondering if the seating arrangements could be changed.

Patrick and Fiona therefore agreed to change vehicles. She managed to convince herself that although this now meant that Robert would be their driver, it would make no difference to her, one way or the other. The five other passengers climbed into the minibus. Patrick was the last of the five and squeezed on to the back seat, waiting for Fiona to follow.

Fiona waited for Robert to help her into the 'bus. He took her hand, but instead of helping her on immediately, hurriedly pulled her back into the darkness, behind the shelter of the second minibus. Its passengers were just emerging from the taverna and were some distance away.

"Hide this note in your bag, *quickly*," he whispered hoarsely. "I've been trying to 'phone you all day!" Then he ushered her into the first minibus, sliding the door shut behind them. She joined Patrick on the back seat, apologising to two of the other passengers, who had to move to one side to give her access. "What kept you?" Patrick whispered, as Robert started the engine and pulled out, to begin the return journey.

"I could have sworn that I'd dropped my evening bag, in the darkness," she lied, trying to think quickly. "But I hadn't after all. It was under my evening shawl. I must be drunk!" The two passengers in front of them laughed at this last remark, but Fiona felt uncomfortable. She wasn't accustomed to lying to Patrick and felt very uneasy.

She squeezed the gold evening bag between her fingers. It was made of silky material; shaped like a rather large purse, with a clasp at the top, which clicked sharply when she closed it. Fiona could feel the note, through the soft golden fabric, where she had pushed it – for safekeeping.

When they finally approached the entrance to *Club Skiathos*, a silver moon was hanging in splendour, like a giant orb, high up in the sky, above the wooded hillside. Rows of cypress trees were silhouetted against its eerie light.

Robert had switched on the radio and, for the last few kilometres of the journey his passengers were entertained by Greek orchestral music. By the time they drove through the broad white stone archway at the entrance to the complex, one of Nana Mouskouri's records from the eighties, was being broadcast. It was the theme song from the film *Mistral's Daughter*.

Being a music lover, Fiona recognised it immediately. It was a sad and poignant song. As the minibus wended its way down the twisting tarmac drive, towards reception, the chorus of the song, about only love being able to make memories, was repeated.

At that precise point Robert turned off the engine, so the radio automatically switched off. The music ceased abruptly, interrupting Fiona's private thoughts. Patrick, noticing her preoccupation, touched her shoulder to signal that it was time to leave the bus.

Robert extended his hand to assist each of the passengers, as they stepped out. He helped all of the women, plus two elderly male passengers. Patrick was the only guest who needed no assistance. Just as Fiona had been the last to board, now she was the last to leave. Patrick walked on a little way ahead towards the reception area, to collect both sets of keys.

Robert extended his hand slowly to her. She wondered if the words of that last song had meant anything to him. He gave her a lingering gaze, as he helped her out. His eyes focused on hers. He seemed distracted.

"Goodnight," was all he said. But as she stepped down, he held on to her hand and then, quite unexpectedly, kissed it gently. Fiona didn't trust herself to remain in that situation any longer. She quickly ran through the main entrance to join Patrick, without daring to glance behind her. She felt like Lot's wife, in the Old Testament story.

Patrick threw her a slightly exasperated look as she joined him. He was ostensibly discussing the night's events with a group of fellow guests. However, as soon as she arrived, he quickly bid the others goodnight.

Before she had a chance to speak he ushered her away, placing her arm through his. They walked smartly out of the main building, following the gravel path and turning in the direction of his apartment, as there was a shortcut to it.

Continuing at a fast pace, past the floodlit flowerbeds, and a large kidney-shaped pool, they turned sharp left, and after a few steps arrived in front of his apartment – number thirty-seven.

"I think that maybe I should go. It's past midnight and I..."

She was unable to complete the sentence. With one swift movement, she was in his arms and he was kissing her hungrily. His moustache tickled her lips and his beard rubbed against her chin. It was a long, lingering kiss. She was quite breathless when he finally released her. "You wont be going *anywhere* tonight Fiona," he breathed huskily. "God, you look absolutely ravishing!" Gripping her left hand, he began to open the door of his apartment using his free hand.

CHAPTER FIVE

For one terrifying second, Fiona was afraid that he had seen Robert, slipping the note to her. Totally misinterpreting the expression on her face, he said, in laughing disbelief, "For God's *sake* Fiona, I'm not going to eat you... you're quite safe with me!" She passed it off as a joke too, then followed him into the sumptuous atmosphere of his abode.

"Just relax," he said softly, indicating the sofa, "Kick off your shoes honey. I'll fix coffee." Fiona did just that. She placed her feet on the footrest, at one end of the white sofa, while Patrick went into the kitchen, beyond the breakfast bar, switching on the light below the canopy.

Half an hour later, she was lying beside him, in the large double bed, her body turned sideways towards him, as she propped herself up on one elbow. She didn't need any further encouragement; the events of the evening had seen to that! They made extremely passionate love, three times over, into the early hours of the morning, then eventually rested, totally exhausted. As Patrick gazed at her, he reached for one hand and squeezed it tightly. His eyes were brimming with tears. Fearing that she had somehow displeased him, she asked if anything was wrong.

He answered directly and very softly – almost inaudibly, "Christ, Fiona... I think I'm falling in love with you..."

CHAPTER SIX

She awoke the following morning, to the sound of breakfast being laid out, in the next room. Rescuing her under-slip, from the green carpet at the side of the bed, Fiona half stumbled out of the bedroom into the kitchen, shielding her eyes from the daylight which streamed through the kitchen window.

"Ugh! Close the blinds," she grimaced. Grinning at her, in an almost paternalistic way, Patrick obligingly pulled down the peach-coloured blind, blocking the light. "What time is it?" she asked sleepily, glancing at the digital clock on the electric cooker. She noted with a degree of surprise, that it was already ten o'clock. So much for their plans to spend the next few days painting!

Patrick had carefully draped the remainder of her clothes, so quickly discarded the previous evening, over the back of one of the single white leather armchairs. Her evening bag and jewellery were, hopefully, somewhere amongst them. "About the painting," she began. "Oh, to hell with that!" remonstrated Patrick. "Come and have your breakfast." As she approached the table he grabbed her around the waist and kissed her.

Once breakfast was completed, she helped him to fill the dishwasher. Smiling conspiratorially at her, he took the *Do Not Disturb* sign from the coffee table, placing it on the outer door handle of the apartment.

He returned to the lounge, closing the inner door behind him. "Guess we'd better find you something more comfortable," he offered. He emerged from the bedroom, just seconds later, holding a pale-blue and white striped shirt. "Slip that on," he said, passing it to her. Fiona thoughtfully bit her lower lip – a habit she had acquired, when deliberating over something. Then, smiling seductively, she lifted her silken slip over her head, revealing her naked body. He took a step towards her.

"Ah-ah," she cautioned, wagging a finger at him. She slipped his shirt over her head immediately, doing up all but the top button. It was probably expensive – judging by the silky sensation, against her bare skin; reaching half way down her thighs, it covered most of her erogenous zones.

CHAPTER SIX

"You know," continued Patrick. "We've no need to continue the landscape painting part of the course; that's the intermediate part of the program anyways."

"How do you mean exactly?" she asked, draping her arms around his neck – seductively close to his body. He could feel her warmth, through the half-open blue silk of his bath robe, which had a white, abstract motif on the right lapel – like a tiny bird in flight.

"Well," he drawled, "it's like this. Ya see, the management of this resort like to offer a comprehensive and well-structured itinerary, during your stay."

"You don't say!" said Fiona mockingly, placing her hands defiantly on her hips.

"Oh *certainly* ma'am," he continued, slowly undoing the second button. "Ya see, you haven't completed the foundation part of the programme yet."

"Okay Mr. Maitland. And what is that – exactly?"

He'd been slowly working his way down, undoing all of the buttons in sequence. She watched his face, focusing on his beard. It made him look so bohemian and yet at the same time, rather sophisticated. Her eyes travelled up from his beard, to the seductive moustached area above his generous lips, and finally, his smouldering brown eyes.

Patrick pulled her closer and gave her a long, passionate kiss. She opened her mouth invitingly, sighing as his tongue entered hungrily into it. After a further exploratory half minute he drew his mouth away, breathing heavily. "You haven't yet completed the twenty-four hour, intensive part of the course; are you familiar with its components?" He pushed his shirt from her shoulders; it fell to the floor.

Their lovemaking continued throughout most of the day, in a variety of places: on the sofa, in the bedroom, even on the kitchen table, which luckily, was very sturdy! They paused only for occasional food, drink, and the obvious calls of nature.

Although Patrick seemed reluctant to reveal much about his past, it became apparent that he had certainly 'known' a variety of women – in the biblical sense! Such was his sexual expertise, and range of techniques, some of which had never occurred to her, that she felt certain that he'd had a colourful past.

Patrick was the first to wake a couple of hours later. Carrying a circular tray of two martini cocktails with cherries, he placed them on the bedside table. Then he lay forward on his stomach, gazing into her sleepy, but gorgeous eyes. They were like two limpet pools, under long auburn eyelashes.

They held each other's gaze for several seconds. Then he rolled over, passed the drinks and they sat together on the edge of the bed. They sipped the drinks silently.

Patrick began to stroke the forefinger of his left hand lightly down the middle of her spine. She turned lovingly towards him. As he continued to trace her spine, he asked casually: "Are you ready to tell me yet?" "Tell you what?" she asked automatically, without giving it a great deal of thought.

"If I have to spell it out for you," he replied, a note of exasperation in his voice, "then you certainly aren't!" There was a stunned silence.

"It's very difficult for me Pat," she explained, hesitantly. "I've had this barrier – a kind of defence mechanism – since Ian died. I don't even know if I know *how* to any more." Tears welled up in her eyes as she spoke.

He led her back to the lounge, where they both dressed, he in his dressing gown, she, slipping the blue shirt back over her nubile body. As they sat together on the white sofa Patrick put a comforting arm around her. At length he said, "I know you've had a rough deal lately. I truly don't want to pressurise you. It's just that I feel closer to you than any woman I've known, since my wife died. Being like this, the way we are… seems so right… so real somehow. Do you understand what I'm saying?"

Fiona felt such a surge of passion, such a need for him that she knelt upon either side of his thighs. Then she kissed him with such prolonged, fiery passion, that he had to struggle to recover his breath. He quickly rolled her onto her back, on the sofa, and kissed her equally passionately, until they both surfaced for air. Slowly they sat up again, with tears in their eyes – locked into each other's gaze.

Patrick took one delicate white hand. Slowly and silently, he placed it between his own, much larger muscular hands, fondling and caressing it with infinite care. They looked at each other again. He was unable to speak.

"I love you Pat," she said.

* * * *

Fiona rested her head against the arm of the sofa, allowing the strains of Pucinni's *Madam Butterfly* to wash over her – like waves on a sea-shore. She was stretched full length, with her eyes closed. Patrick was in a similar position, on the seat opposite. "I thought you didn't particularly like opera," he commented, opening his eyes. "Did I say that?" she queried. "I thought that I'd said I didn't know much about it. Light opera's about my limit, you know," she explained, sitting upright. "I do find it very sad

CHAPTER SIX

though, that her American lover has left her and although she doesn't realise it, she's never going to see him again."

Patrick moved over, to sit beside her: "That's *one* problem honey that you'll never have to wrestle with." There was a long, uncomfortable pause – she wasn't sure what to say. "Light opera's all I've really experienced, in that field," she continued – "Gilbert and Sullivan, and so on. On the other hand, classical music is definitely my scene. Tchaikovsky, Debussy and Elgar are my favourite composers. Oh, and I love *Rodrigos Guitar Concerto*. It reminds me *so* much of making love – especially the crescendos and climaxes!"

Patrick looked genuinely taken aback.

"You gotta be kidding me!" He exclaimed. "Have you been looking through my CD collection? Those are four of my favourite composers too!"

"They can't be... you're winding me up!" she protested. "You wanna bet?!" He leapt to his feet. Taking four CDs from his collection, he placed them on the coffee table, in front of her. They were actually the self-same composers.

"I'm sorry I doubted you," she mumbled, "but you've got to admit, the odds are loaded against it!" They discovered that some of the actual compositions by three of the composers were also mutual favourites: Elgar's *Nimrod*, from the *Enigma Variations*, Tchaikovsky's *Romeo and Juliet* and Debussy's haunting *Claire de Lune*. Patrick had those on CD too. They spent the next few minutes listening to extracts from all three... rediscovering them.

As the beautiful, haunting notes of the piano played *Claire de Lune*, Fiona explained that as a young girl she had played the piece over and over again, on her mother's old 78 r.p.m. record player. "It always made me cry," she confessed.

"The last time I heard this," recalled Patrick, tearfully, "was when Julia and I played it, back home in British Columbia. It was summertime. We were having tea on our patio, enjoying the music – looking forward to the birth of our first child. In reality, she only had a few weeks to live. The tragedy was that we were living in a 'fool's paradise': there was no way on earth that we could have known – that her pregnancy would go so disastrously wrong!"

Fiona's eyes filled with tears. No wonder he'd been reluctant to speak about his past. It seemed that, despite their relative youth, both of them had *already* experienced more than their fair share of unhappiness. They played music for a little while longer. Then, as it was nearly eight o'clock, they decided to have an early night, making a prompt start on their painting the following morning.

Patrick gathered her clothing and belongings and placed them in a bag. Then he changed into trousers and a shirt, covering her with his silk dressing gown, which reached somewhere below her ankles. She had to hold it up at the waist to avoid tripping over. It did however enable her to return to her apartment, with a modicum of decorum.

"Take your time over breakfast tomorrow honey," he advised. "I'll need to make an early start myself – about 6am. Meet me on the beach, whenever you're ready. I promise not to oversleep this time. It's weird – guess that only happens to me on vacation." He escorted her back. Once in her hallway, she quickly passed his dressing gown back to him – depriving any passing guests of a semi-nude shirt-clad view of her!

Patrick turned on his heels and returned to his apartment. She closed the door behind her. Three or four minutes later, just as she was about to step into the shower, the doorbell rang. Clad only in her own skimpy dressing gown, she opened the door cautiously. To her surprise, Patrick was there again, holding something in his hand. "Pardon me madam, you've left this behind – see you in the morning!" He passed the item to her, through the half-open doorway, then disappeared as quickly as he had arrived.

Fiona stared down at the object in her hand. It was her golden evening bag... she had forgotten all about it! Then she suddenly remembered Robert's letter. Closing the door quickly, she stood with her back against it, frozen with terror. What if Patrick had already examined its contents – and discovered Robert's letter? Their vows of love would count for nothing! Fiona was convinced that, certainly up to that moment, Patrick had no idea that any relationship existed, between herself and Robert.

She couldn't bear the thought of losing Patrick – not now. Now that she had exposed her feelings – her love for him – in such an open way. The prospect of losing his love, and his trust, was unthinkable.

Quickly, she ran to the kitchen. In panic she shook the entire contents of her evening bag out, onto the pine table. Make-up, compact, lipstick, perfume spray, comb and handkerchief – they all tumbled out. She lifted up the embroidered handkerchief. Lying beneath it was a crumpled piece of paper. Thank God, it was still there, and apparently, undiscovered.

She opened the cutlery draw, and holding it as though it were a lump of hot coal, or a rattlesnake, dropped the offending paper into its depths, closing the draw again quickly. Fiona wasn't sure whether she even wanted to read the note. Anything that might cause a rift, between herself and Patrick, was anathema to her.

During the teenage years and certainly throughout the passionate years of her twenties, she had possessed a great capacity for love. As she

CHAPTER SIX

had turned the corner into her early thirties however, and with Ian's ever decreasing ability to make love, she had been forced to suppress this vital part of her nature: to sublimate it. Since his death her love had been like a tiny seed, trapped and suffocating beneath the frozen earth. Patrick's tenderness and care, were like the warm rays of the sun, gradually thawing out her reserve; allowing her love and passion to once more burst into bloom: like a beautiful but tender, exotic flower. She couldn't bear to return to that cold dark place. She needed to live… to feel warmth and happiness again.

As she stepped out of the shower, she felt instinctively that Robert's letter might be the catalyst that could kill such a love; destroying all hopes of future happiness.

If Robert proved to be a womaniser, responding to his letter might be her downfall. At that precise moment, she was seized by an irresistible urge, to burn it. For the time being, however, she left it where it was, undisturbed in the drawer, and staggered wearily to bed.

But there was to be no peace that night. She tossed and turned for hours over the advisability of reading it; tormented by the thought that if she didn't, she would forever wonder about its contents. Realising that she'd get no rest until she resolved the matter, she turned on the bedside lamp, checking the digital clock. It was only three o'clock in the morning! She must be *completely* mad!

Disregarding her conscience, she pushed her feet into warm pink slippers and walked slowly out of the bedroom, into the kitchen. Opening the draw cautiously, she took out the crumpled paper. Turning on the green pendant light which overhung the table, she flattened the paper out, as best she could, so that she could read it more clearly.

The note was written in beautifully scripted handwriting. It seemed to be an intrinsic part of Robert's nature, she reflected, to be meticulous in everything. He had obviously taken some time and care over its composition. She read it carefully.

My Dearest Fiona,
I received a telephone call from my publisher, yesterday evening. I have been trying to telephone you, ever since.
Several months ago, I made arrangements to meet with one of their representatives, at their Athens office, on the mainland. The pre-arranged date was May 27th. I am required to remain in Athens, for a period of at least three days, as my forthcoming publication is to be my most ambitious yet. It requires discussion and planning of a highly complicated nature.

Had I known in advance that we were destined to meet, I would have put the arrangement on indefinite hold. As it is, I am now obliged to accommodate them.

Please believe me when I say that I would far rather be spending the time with you. I will certainly take steps to ensure that I have returned before your departure date, of June 1st.

It was signed, simply – 'Robert'.

She sat at the table reading it, several times over, despite the fact that her eyes were extremely sore, through trying to read at such an early hour.

She had mixed feelings about its contents. There was no denying that having a note, actually if front of her, in his handwriting, made her heart beat faster. Conversely, her feelings for Patrick had developed in such a dramatic way, that she began to wonder whether Robert's actions could be of any consequence. Perhaps she no longer cared for him?

She found herself returning back to her grammar school days. In particular, to the words of the New Testament: *No man can serve two masters,* and the text that followed it.

Not that she regarded herself as the servant of any man. Being a modern woman, like many of her contemporaries, she had always tried to keep a reasonable degree of control over her own destiny. Since the start of this holiday however, that was becoming increasingly difficult.

It felt as if something in the charmed atmosphere of this idyllic island was lulling her into a trance… hypnotising her. An image of the sweet-voiced, mythological Sirens came once more to mind. She had a powerful premonition – that some unseen force was attempting to control her destiny – to destroy her own free will.

She must break free… before it was too late. But how? And from whom?

CHAPTER SEVEN

She rose quite early, to take full advantage of the day. It was Friday: the penultimate day of the holiday. Time was rapidly running out. When she booked the holiday, two weeks had seemed ample time for a lone holiday-maker, in a depressive state. But now, she wanted to remain forever on this beautiful island, with Patrick, her handsome and oh-so-ardent lover. The saying, 'time and tide wait for no man', had taken on a whole new significance.

The waves out to sea were galloping in at tremendous speed, like a herd of untamed horses. Reaching her vantage point, they crashed wildly through her thoughts, smashing against the jagged grey rocks to her right. The rock formations, on either side, to the extreme right of the main hotel building, were rather dramatic; one in particular resembled the craggy ruins of an ancient castle. From this semi-enclosed sixth floor balcony the sea air was particularly bracing.

During a conversation at *Taverna Persephone*, Miklos had recommended taking a lift up to the balcony, to see for herself. She'd explained that Patrick was encouraging her to paint seascapes; such a spectacular view, suggested Miklos, would make an excellent picture.

Descending by the lift, a few minutes later, she treated herself to breakfast in the hotel's *Sandpiper* restaurant. It was quite expensive, but she decided to indulge herself. She still had several thousand drachmas left, with only two days to go. She didn't consider Sunday, the day of her departure, as part of her holiday; it was more of a chore day really, with all the packing, travelling and deadlines to meet.

The temperature had increased by several degrees since her arrival, so she adapted accordingly: a pair of stone-coloured Bermuda shorts threaded with a narrow brown belt, short-sleeved green ribbed top, and a loose-fitting green over shirt, which would protect her arms from sunburn whilst painting. Her indispensable straw sunhat and shoulder bag were permanent features.

After breakfast, she left the main hotel building, taking the by-now-familiar route: down the steps, past the screen of hedges, sharply round to the left, then onto the shingle. She walked for three minutes or so, along the less rugged beach, until she spotted Patrick in the distance – right at the far end.

She ran to meet him. He had set out painting materials for both of them. As promised, he really *had* made an early start. As soon as he spotted her he ran to meet her too. They embraced passionately. He was so overjoyed to see her that he swept her off her feet, turning a complete circle. She reminded him that he'd asked her to take her time. "I guess I did," he replied. "But even an iota of time can seem like an eternity – when you're in love." "That's rather poetic darling; perhaps you're in the wrong artistic field!" she replied, laughingly.

Patrick had placed her half-completed seascape-cum-landscape painting, on one of the two easels. She scrutinised the work that she'd already done. Then he helped her to add a couple of sailing ships: one fairly close to shore, another in the distance; also, trees, and other flora and fauna, adding perspective to the picture. The additional technique of adding light and shade to the composition was a painstaking process, but she particularly enjoyed the fluidity of movement which watercolours afforded her.

He had begun a careful study of an outcrop of rocks, combined with a cliff edge nearby. It required many intricate, detailed lines; she was lost in admiration for his talent, and for the years of practise that he must have put in, to reach that degree of expertise, combining precision with speed.

As they worked, they revealed further intimate details, about their past and present lives. Yesterday, they realised, had been a significant watershed: breaking down barriers, both sexual and emotional, which they had both erected for self-protection; impregnable to everyone else around them.

Now, by some miraculous stroke of fate, by daily degrees, they were drawing significantly closer to one another. They returned to Patrick's apartment, just after one o'clock in the afternoon, depositing the painting equipment in the kitchen. Then they adjourned to Fiona's patio for a light lunch of salad and quiche, served with chilled German Riesling.

Over lunch, Fiona described the dramatic seascape which she had seen earlier that morning. As a frequent visitor to the resort, Patrick was already familiar with the area she was describing. He readily agreed that they should head for the spot after lunch, adding that it was also ideal for sketching.

They took a large sketchpad and several sticks of charcoal. Although Fiona had some experience of instructing primary school pupils in the art of charcoal sketching, Patrick's level of expertise enabled her to produce work of a far more professional calibre; she was rather pleased with the end

CHAPTER SEVEN

result. Patrick placed all of the work carefully in a folder, collected the charcoal from her, then returned it to its box. She had a smudge of charcoal across her right cheek; he grinned, as he wiped it off with his shirtsleeve.

Many of the rocks at this end of the beach were huge – providing shelter from prying eyes. They were several hundred yards away from the club; the beach stretched for several miles. They could just see the edge of the hotel building in the distance. The entire area was deserted. Just a little way out to sea was a motorboat, with a water skier trailing behind.

With work completed, they lay down on two large beach towels for a well-deserved rest. Patrick drew Fiona to him and held her closely for a while. She rested her head contentedly, in the cusp of his broad shoulders. They continued to discuss their past lives. Patrick confided more about his wife, Julia. He opened up his heart to her, speaking rapidly and with great passion; the pain and anguish, locked away, deep inside of him, came flooding out.

He described how they had enjoyed an almost idyllic marriage. Fiona realised as Patrick's account unfolded, that there were similarities between herself and Julia – especially their creativity and love of nature. They also had music in common; the difference being that Julia had been an accomplished pianist, whereas Fiona sang and played the guitar.

Her eyes filled with tears, as Patrick described how his young wife, just twenty-six years of age, had died in childbirth – along with their stillborn son. They talked well into the afternoon, sharing their most intimate secrets; speaking of things that had delighted or tormented them... and had a profound effect on their respective lives.

At one point, Patrick took her by the hand, leading her to a sheltered area of rocks, far from anyone's view. There they disrobed and made wild and passionate love, totally oblivious to anything else around them. The waves rose and crashed on the rocks as they reached climax after climax.

As the day ended, and the sun disappeared behind clouds, they strolled back hand in hand along the beach. Patrick clasped her hand tightly as they walked. They looked neither to right nor left. Neither of them spoke. There was no need for words. They had each other.

That same evening Fiona and Patrick took the small bus up to a local taverna, situated on a promontory. It overlooked both *Club Skiathos* and the area of the town known as Tzanaria. The *Club Skiathos* complex lay far below them, on the right. To the left, but at a much greater distance, the lights of a Timeshare Village were a prominent feature. Below the village was a small marina. Several small boats were anchored there. Multi-coloured triangles of tiny lights marked the outline of their sails.

They were seated at a table right next to a huge window, which provided a superbly panoramic view of the whole coastal area, for miles around. This particular taverna had been carefully selected as the venue for their final evening together; not only for the magnificent views, but also because they had heard that most of the tourists and local population would be heading into the main, central area of Skiathos, on a Friday night. That was where all the action was – the up-market discotheques and tavernas. But the two lovers simply wanted a quiet evening, in each other's company; they had no need of outside stimulation. This was *their* time together, in their own private world.

Although a three-course meal had been ordered, neither of them was particularly hungry; they just played with their food, for the most part. Their starter was *Fasalotha;* a soup made with onions, tomatoes, carrots and parsley.

As the local bus only ran until ten thirty they planned to take a taxi back to the resort. Their conversation was conducted in hushed undertones… anything louder might break the spell. Below them, far down to the right, the lights of *Club Skiathos* twinkled knowingly; reminding them that this had been their hideaway; the centre of their universe, for the last two weeks. From such a distance the resort seemed tiny, almost insignificant – but they both knew that it had been anything but that.

The second course was a specially prepared Mousaka, followed by Baclava for dessert: a sweet cake, consisting of flaky pastry covered with nuts and honey. Having pushed the cake around for about the fifth time, Fiona allowed her fork to drop. It fell with a clatter onto her plate, causing Patrick, who was equally distracted, to look up at her.

She reached across the table for his hand and squeezed it tightly. The sadness in her eyes was like an icy knife through his heart. He cradled her delicate hand, with infinite care, between his two strong masculine ones. "I'm so afraid of losing you," she said softly, her eyes moist with tears: "I've heard such dreadful things about holiday romances. What happens if once we're back in the familiar territory of our own countries, we forget about each other… if the memory gradually fades? I couldn't bear that."

"You can't imagine that's really going to happen!" he replied. "How could you possibly think that I'm ever going to forget you? I *love* you Godammit. Forgetting you honey would be like forgetting how to breathe. I'll never let you go… *never!*" The last word was spoken with such ferocity, that Fiona was completely taken aback, and slightly afraid. At the same time she was strangely aroused by the passion in his voice and in his gaze. He deliberated for a moment. Then, squeezing her hand even more tightly, he

CHAPTER SEVEN

spoke in a hoarse whisper: "I want you in Canada with me: in my home and in my life and in my bed."

The taped music in the taverna, throughout most of the evening, had been international, rather than purely Grecian. Patrick ordered brandy, to complete what had been an unforgettable evening. As they chinked their glasses together, the lyrics of the music in the background seemed particularly apposite. In a strangely haunting fashion, the female singer sang,
We're the only two people in the world.
At that precise moment in time, gazing at the lights far below them, she could almost imagine that it was true…

* * * *

Saturday was the last full day of the holiday. Having risen bright and early, Fiona was eager to see Patrick as soon as possible. Only two short weeks ago she had imagined the remainder of her life being spent alone, trapped in her own private world. But, after such a transformation, within such a short space of time, life without him was unimaginable.

She'd made an early start with her packing, so that it would be completely out of the way; she and Patrick could then make optimum use of the remaining time. Her smart green-and-tan suitcase lay open, ready and waiting, on the bed. Whilst packing her underwear, in the special section of case which she always reserved for that purpose, she found a pack of three silk and lace, thong-style panties: a present, the previous Christmas from Claire, one of her more provocative female friends. When Fiona had protested, half-vexed, but also rather intrigued, Claire replied, with a wicked grin, that she should 'learn to live a little'.

In her present mood, she felt like hugging her, making a mental note to give Claire something extra special, next Christmas. Removing a pair of white lace thongs from the packet, she slipped the remaining two into her hand luggage. Having completed most of her packing except for the hand luggage, she returned to the bedroom, selecting a pair of crisp white slacks and an orange short-sleeved top.

As she turned around to view her buttocks in the mirror, the effect was still more electrifying. "Oh my God!" she whispered. Before she could change her mind, she hastily threw on her white slacks and the orange top. Her make-up complete, she added gold earrings and a bracelet. Patrick would be expecting her. They had planned a 'farewell' two-hour boat trip around the island that morning. There'd been no previous opportunity to view the island from the sea, so she was really looking forward to it.

On arriving at his apartment Fiona found Patrick ready and waiting. He was gathering up some loose change, to put in his pocket and checking the notes in his wallet. He offered her a cool drink before they left. Like her, he was dressed in white slacks, but he was also wearing a blue and white striped T-shirt with an anchor on it – *very* nautical!

The prospect of a boat trip reminded him of his maritime home in Victoria, British Columbia, which he began to describe, albeit briefly, as he put his arms around her. The intensity of his caresses increased, as he continued to describe his home. She told him about her large detached house in the countryside, immediately adjacent to a park. They became so interested in describing their respective homes that the minutes began to slip by.

Fiona's hand slid, almost unconsciously, to the inside of Patrick's muscular thigh. His pleasure was increased one hundred fold, by the knowledge that Fiona was not simply arousing him through lust, but because of much deeper feelings for him.

"Ah – to hell with the boat trip!" He stripped off, while Fiona feverishly pulled off her orange top and bra. She stood up, slowly and deliberately removing her white slacks. He gasped, as the white lace front of her garment was revealed. Even more slowly, and with deliberate steps, she stepped backwards towards the bedroom door, as if she might leave, then turned around.

Moving quickly towards her he dragged her back on to the bed. The softness and tickling sensation of his full beard and the impact of his hot, greedy lips were heightened, as his tongue eagerly sought hers.

Minutes later, the two of them lay side by side, hardly moving. Despite the aborted boat trip, the two of them went on a voyage that day, into uncharted waters that neither had experienced before. The scenery, en route, was fascinating, and of a totally unique variety.

They stopped briefly, during the mid-afternoon. Patrick phoned reception to order a bar snack and drinks. Clad only in his half-open dressing gown, he answered the door to one of the young female staff – the startled expression on her face amused him. As he re-entered the lounge with the tray he was chuckling to himself. "I wonder if they'll put *that* in the brochure next year?" he quipped. "Guess they could attract a whole new clientele!"

They ate the meal, sitting on the lounge carpet; the formality of sitting at the kitchen table had long since passed. As they ate, Patrick explained that he had spent the last two nights tossing and turning, while he devised a game plan for them. He had figured out all of the details. On his return to B.C., as he liked to call it, via Vancouver, he would book a set of return

CHAPTER SEVEN

tickets, between England and Vancouver, in Fiona's name. He would arrange the final stage of the journey for her, from Vancouver to Victoria, at a later date.

Following a further week of intensive painting, he planned to depart for British Columbia on the evening of June 8th. From then onwards a further month would be spent, preparing and exhibiting a whole year's collection of his paintings, at the prestigious Halcyon Art Gallery, in the centre of Victoria. During this period, he cautioned her, she should avoid him at all costs, remaining at home in England. This would not only give her time to re-organise her own affairs, but would also avoid any friction between them. He explained that whilst engaged in exhibiting his work, he inevitably became neurotic and uptight – like his country's national symbol: the proverbial 'grizzly with the sore head'!

"I should imagine that it's similar to when you're caught up in writing a novel. You have to draw upon you own resources to such a pitch that you're left feeling emotionally drained and morose. When I'm exhibiting, I'm forever searching for ways of boosting my ego – to keep me on track. But I'm an absolute 'pain' to live with!"

Having cleared away the remains of their meal, they converted the sofa into a sofa bed, which was surprisingly spacious. Being both fairly exhausted by now, Patrick advised Fiona to lie back and completely relax. He selected one of his cassette tapes. It was a collection of film theme music: recorded by the Boston Symphony Orchestra. It included one of his most favourite pieces of music of all time – a violin concerto composition, by John Williams: the theme music from *Schindler's List*.

So beautiful, and yet so sad was the piece, that as she lay listening to it on the sofa bed, she began to weep, almost involuntarily. Patrick removed all of their clothes, slowly, by degrees. Then lying down, gently covering her with his entire body, he made love to her in such a magnificently sensual, yet at the same time, a more tender and caring way, than she could possibly have imagined. His lovemaking was synchronised so closely and sensitively with the slow haunting strains of the music, that she felt as if she were having a totally metaphysical out of body experience.

When they were both finally and completely satisfied Patrick staggered over to switch off the music, returning to rest alongside her. At length he sat up, running his fingers through her beautiful long auburn tresses, saying,

"From the moment you arrive in Victoria, I want you to quit taking the pill." She sat up, with a look of surprise – tinged with caution. When they had discussed the matter, only a few days previously, they had decided that the wisest strategy would be for her to continue taking a contraceptive.

Neither of them felt ready, at that point, to make a firm commitment to the other.

Since then, with their relationship on 'Fast-forward', Patrick had been giving the matter considerably more thought He was now forty-two years of age, whilst Fiona was still a young thirty-three. If they wanted children, he argued, they couldn't afford to delay much longer.

"I guess you'll have to exercise particular care though."

"How d'you mean?" she asked.

"We – ell," he drawled, in his deep Canadian tones, "if you quit taking the pill, you'll have to make damn sure that you're not having sex with any other guy!"

"As if I would!" protested Fiona, quite outraged, hurling one of the soft cushions at him. "All the same," he warned... deflecting the cushion. "You never can tell."

CHAPTER EIGHT

Fiona's two green-and-tan leather suitcases stood in readiness by the low brick wall, at the entrance to reception, together with a dozen or so others.

Miklos planned to transport herself and five other guests to Skiathos Airport, within the next hour or so. Still no sign of Robert, she realised, with a kind of satisfaction. So much for his letter! It lent further weight to her theory that he was nothing more than an unreliable philanderer. She hadn't seen him anywhere around the resort, during the last two days, but then, she acknowledged wryly, she hadn't been out of doors much either!

She was just about to return to her apartment, to check that she hadn't left anything behind, when a sudden thought occurred to her. Robert had mentioned, at one stage, during the course of their trip to his den – an event which she preferred to forget, that he had his own private Range Rover. With her transport to the airport already arranged, she decided to take a minute or two, to check the other car park behind the hotel, on the off-chance that Robert had returned. He had a suite of rooms on the fifth floor, which he had taken great pride in describing to her. There was just time to run over, before meeting her darling Patrick back at his apartment, as arranged.

There were no vehicles of that type in the rear car park, but as she turned on her heels a smart green Range Rover shot into view, from the direction of reception – heading straight towards her. She had never moved so fast! Fiona raced back to her apartment, slammed the door behind her and with flushed cheeks began to make a hurried check. Then she tossed the apartment keys into her navy shoulder bag, slammed the door again and headed quickly for Patrick's apartment.

The reason for her haste, she persuaded herself, was that she wanted to spend those last precious minutes with Patrick – she wouldn't be seeing him again for almost two months. Fiona fairly hammered on his door. As he opened it, she practically fell into his arms.

Patrick didn't consider her behaviour at all unusual; in fact, he was gratified by it. Time was at a premium. Their seven weeks of separation would feel like an eternity; it would be sheer torture for them to be parted.

Patrick reassured her that she would be constantly in his thoughts. She felt exactly the same. They kissed, quite desperately. Just at that moment they were interrupted by the telephone. It was Miklos, asking to speak to Fiona. He sounded quite agitated. "It seems that we have two late bookings for transport to the airport. Would you mind very much if my partner drives yourself and one other passenger to the airport, instead of myself?"

After leaving Patrick's apartment, for the last time, Fiona handed in her keys at reception and settled her account, using some of the remaining drachmas. She had originally planned visits to the Greek mainland. It had been a particular ambition of hers, since teaching Greek history at school, to visit the Parthenon: that temple of 'spare and uncluttered lines', standing on its famous hill, the Acropolis. Ah well, it would have to wait – another time perhaps? She certainly hadn't anticipated having so much cash left over... due to a surfeit of indoor activity!

Patrick promised to check that her luggage was safely loaded into the back of the Range Rover. Having completed her business at reception, Fiona walked purposefully towards the parking area, a few yards away.

Suddenly, she froze in her tracks. To one side of the car park, she noticed Patrick, in conversation with the other driver. The man in question was dark, rugged and an inch or so taller than Patrick. The tone of their conversation suggested that they were on very friendly terms. Patrick turned with a smile as she approached. Placing his arms around her shoulders he said lovingly: "Take care honey. Have a safe journey home."

Then he looked into her eyes, with great seriousness, pulled her to him and gave her a long, lingering kiss. "Remember our arrangement. I'll be thinking of you baby, the whole time." Fiona had eyes only for Patrick. She willed herself not to glance in the driver's direction, having no wish to make eye contact with him. Giving her lover one last frantic hug, she climbed up into the back seat of the jeep. The elderly Spanish gentleman, who was to be her fellow passenger, sat in the passenger seat alongside Robert.

As the vehicle drove off, she waved in sad desperation to Patrick. She could see him clearly through a side window. He looked equally dejected, as he blew a parting kiss. The Range Rover made a quick exit, through the archwayed entrance to *Club Skiathos*, following Miklos' minibus, which led the way. The second minibus was out on a day trip.

Fiona felt as though her heart was breaking. She felt physically ill. A dull ache spread across her chest; she found it very difficult to breathe. The driver was playing a CD of Greek folk music. Luckily, within two or three minutes of leaving the club, the music began to soothe her.

The Range Rover sped further along the route to Skiathos Airport, putting a rapidly increasing number of kilometres between themselves and the resort. Fiona decided to focus on Patrick's plans for that afternoon. He

CHAPTER EIGHT

had told her that he intended to resume painting, immediately after lunch. It made her feel somehow more secure to imagine his itinerary. She found herself begrudging him his extra week, in case he met someone else. Fiona suddenly felt insanely jealous. But hadn't he said that he loved her to distraction? He could surely never betray her. With any luck the next few hours would pass quickly; she would put such foolish thoughts right out of her head!

On arrival at the airport, Robert helped most of the guests to check in their baggage. Miklos made a point of helping Fiona to do likewise. He had been very solicitous throughout the holiday. As he shook her warmly by the hand, she thanked him profusely. He kissed her respectfully on the cheek.

Fiona said that she had been most impressed with the quality of the holiday and would certainly be recommending the resort to her friends and acquaintances. She also thanked him for the very personal nature of the service. There weren't many holidays, she added, which offered such a comprehensive service. Miklos seemed rather gratified by her comments. As he turned to leave however, he hesitated for a moment: "Forgive me Fiona, but may an ageing man offer a little advice?" Taken by surprise, she was uncertain how to reply. Undaunted, he continued, "Love may be found in the most unexpected of places you know… and sometimes, with the *most* unlikely people." "Yes, I suppose that's true," she conceded, although still puzzled by the cryptic nature of his comment, which was quite out of character.

He tried again: "Don't be too quick to judge," he suggested.

"Right…." She was about to ask him to be more explicit, but at that moment he began to leave, turning once to give her a friendly wave. She did the same, although a little uncertainly. What did he mean?

Miklos was normally so straightforward and direct – a facet of the Greek character that, she suspected, had changed very little since ancient times. Recalling the opening pages of Homer's *Odyssey*, from her grammar school days, she remembered being struck by the direct style of Grecian interrogation within its pages; for example, when Telemachus, Odysseus' son was questioning Athena. Fiona could only conclude that Miklos must have a compelling reason for being so uncharacteristically obtuse.

There was lots of time to spare; her four-hour return flight to Gatwick didn't depart until five that evening. Fiona had only one piece of hand luggage, in addition to her navy blue shoulder bag. As she hadn't had much opportunity to take photographs of Skiathos, she hunted in one of the airport boutiques for a book or brochure about the islands, Skiathos in particular, to take home as a souvenir. Having selected a suitable keepsake, she made for the escalator, which would take her up to the first floor restaurant.

Standing on the ascending escalator, she noted a somewhat familiar figure, heading in the opposite direction – on the down escalator. He was wearing sunglasses and was obviously determinedly en-route for somewhere. Her heart suddenly skipped a beat, but she immediately chided herself for having an over-active imagination! She chose a restaurant table designed for four people: not only to give her plenty of space, but also because she had begun to feel slightly uneasy and had a sudden urge for privacy.

She'd just settled back into reading her new brochure when a long shadow fell across the table. She found herself looking up, directly into the piercingly blue eyes of Robert Osborne. Completely taken aback and speechless, she stared back at the prepossessing figure, towering above her.

Responding to her reaction, he silently cleared a place for himself, placing a sandwich and a cup of coffee in front of him. After at least half a minute she muttered, half to herself, "I imagined you'd be half way back to the resort, by now."

"So did I," he replied. He carefully unwrapped his sandwiches and took a sip of coffee. They both ate in complete silence, for what seemed like ages. Fiona felt as if her salad was choking her. How was she supposed to eat, with him sitting directly opposite her? She found it difficult to swallow.

"What time's your flight?" he eventually asked, breaking the silence. "Five o'clock," she replied nervously. 'As if he didn't know', she thought cynically. It was standard procedure for him to check the flight times of all of his guests, at least a day in advance.

They returned to eating in silence; uneasy in each other's company. 'Dammit', he thought. 'I didn't *have* to come back!' He didn't speak again, until they had finished eating. Fiona pushed her plate to one side and was looking distractedly to her left; ostensibly, watching the antics of two small children playing by the fountain, adjacent to their parents' table. What was she really thinking? He needed so *desperately* to know.

"Look," he ventured, "I have a suggestion. It's not quite one o'clock. Rather than wait around a noisy, crowded airport, we could relax more easily on my boat. It's only a ten-minute drive away – moored in Skiathos harbour. We could return here later, with at least an hour to spare. What do you say?"

She looked at him in disbelief – still half in shock. This was crazy! Robert pulled his chair closer around the table to her. It scraped along the hard tiled floor. "You wouldn't miss your flight," he explained, in what he hoped was a reassuring manner. Still, she said nothing. "Look," he said. He was

CHAPTER EIGHT

becoming increasingly desperate, but trying not to show it. "Spend a couple of hours with me Fiona – if only for friendship's sake."

The last remark was a persuasive one, so she finally agreed to his plan. After all, she acknowledged privately, there was no way that she actually relished spending a full three hours in a stuffy airport, surrounded by the ever-increasing hordes around them.

They left the main airport building soon afterwards. Robert held her arm protectively, as they emerged once more into the bright sunshine. She hadn't realised what a glorious day it was, outside. The whole area was alive with noise and activity. Fiona's spirits began to revive. Spending a couple of hours with a friend was surely not a problem? They collected Robert's Range Rover from the airport car park. He manoeuvred skilfully through the complicated Skiathos road system, keeping to the outskirts as much as possible; avoiding the centre altogether. "We could be boxed in by heavy traffic, for at least an hour, if we took that route," he explained, indicating one road in particular.

They followed the right-hand side of the coastal route for a while, then entered a parking area, designated for boat owners. Fiona noticed a special parking disc, decorated with a nautical symbol, displayed on Robert's front windscreen. Locking her hand luggage in the boot, he hurried her down two short flights of stone steps and onto the quayside. They headed swiftly towards one of the smart white motor boats that were moored there; a silver arrow was painted on one side and a smart blue and white sign declared the name of the boat – *Silver's Arrow*. He helped her into it, unfastened the rope and started the engine.

Deftly, he steered the vessel through a maze of bobbing boats in the marina. Soon they were on their way, following the coastline. Fiona's mane of long auburn hair blew out behind her in the breeze. As the boat bounced over the waves, the sea breeze and sea-spray on her face was so invigorating! She began to feel alive again.

Looking across at Robert, at the helm, so masterfully steering the vessel, a ripple of pleasure ran through her body. He returned her glance, with a heart-stopping smile. Ten minutes later, after covering some distance, they anchored the boat in Archelides Bay, a favourite location of his, several kilometres from the airport complex.

In the distance they could just make out a few holiday-makers, moving around like ants on the small area of golden beach. Luckily, the water was reasonably calm, the boat moving slightly with the swell. The motion of the boat had a soothing, rocking quality. Robert assembled two pink and green-striped deck chairs. Fiona seated herself in one, whilst he returned with two hastily prepared Bacardi and Cokes, served in highball glasses with lemon and ice.

"This looks quite professional!" she joked with him. After the earlier tensions of the day she was beginning to relax. "It should do. I worked in one of the local bars, in my student days – when I first arrived on the island."

Fiona held the two glasses whilst he positioned a small round table in front of them. She placed both drinks on it. Robert disappeared below deck for a short interval, then re-emerged, having changed into a pair of navy Bermuda shorts and a white T-shirt. She couldn't help noticing his muscular, hairy legs.

They sipped their long, cool drinks in a very laid-back manner, enjoying the sultry glow of the warm Greek sun. "This is the life," sighed Fiona, her shapely legs stretched out lazily in front of her. A gentle sea breeze played with the delicate curls, across her beautiful forehead.

"Yep! Never let it be said that *Club Skiathos* doesn't provide a comprehensive service – right to the very end!" joked Robert. "You can say that again!" Fiona replied, then added, somewhat meekly, "Thank you for rescuing me."

He was regarding her very intently now, although she couldn't see the expression in his eyes, as they were both wearing sunglasses. "We aim to please," he replied, but in a quieter, more subdued manner.

Fiona was wearing the white slacks and ribbed orange top that she had worn the previous day. Underneath, as a kind of secret memento, she had early that morning, taken a second pair of thong panties from the original packet. Unlike her previous pair they weren't lily-white, but a blood-red colour, trimmed with black lace. The idea had been that once back home in England, they would be the first item that she saw when she stripped off – serving as a perfect reminder of that last lascivious Saturday, spent with Patrick!

Something that Robert was saying pulled her reluctantly out of her reverie. "It was rather disappointing not to find you at the Poolside Barbecue on Saturday evening. I couldn't get back until about six o'clock that evening. As most of our guests always attend the barbecue, I automatically assumed that you'd be there. Where were you?"

He made the last comment in a casual, almost indifferent fashion; but there was a slight 'edge' to his voice. He turned away from her as he asked the question – staring out to sea. Fiona was at a loss for words. What could she say? That she and Patrick had been so exhausted after hours of lovemaking, that they could hardly walk – much less *dance* the night away!

CHAPTER EIGHT

Feeling very much on the defensive she muttered something about needing a good night's rest, before the homeward journey, which hardly sounded convincing. She glanced at her watch, hoping to change the conversation. "It's perfectly all right," said Robert – as usual – one step ahead of her. "We have a full hour-and-a-half at our disposal, so I propose that we make the most of it."

"That's a very cryptic remark!" she retorted sharply. "Wasn't it though," replied Robert. "Come on!" he said, springing to his feet. "There's something I'd like to show you." "Not your etchings I hope!" she snapped back at him, immediately on the defensive. "Not quite."

Slipping his sunglasses into his top pocket, he led her down the polished wooden steps into the cabin area below. There, stretched out on tables, on an old padded sea chest – even spread out around the floor, so that she had to step carefully over them, were a wide range of books. Also, a series of maps, charts and quite complicated documents, all laid out in methodical order.

"Wow!" she exclaimed. "Someone's been busy! You look as though you have the entire reference section of the Bodleian Library laid out here, Mr. Osborne," she added teasingly, referring to his Oxford days. "Several libraries, I should think," he retorted, "although I'm somewhat short of the Bodleian's eleven million books and documents!" He led her around the cabin, explaining, briefly, the significance of a few of the books and documents. "This is how I've been spending my time over the last few days, researching my latest book. It's to be entitled, quite simply, *The Treasures of Greece*. It deals with treasure trove, plus Spanish and French galleons and the like."

"It sounds like a very viable commercial proposition," suggested Fiona.

"My publishers would certainly agree with you," replied Robert, although he seemed to be rapidly losing interest in the subject – rather surprising, considering the time he had already invested in it, and was going to have to invest, in the months to come.

She walked over to the enormous padded sea chest, which she had immediately noticed, on entering the cabin. "May I take a closer look?" she asked, bending down on one knee, for closer scrutiny. "Oh, I'm sorry," she said, realising that he would first need to move several important documents from its top surface. "No problem," he insisted, nevertheless moving them to one side, with great care; one of the documents looked particularly fragile.

The huge chest, he explained, was a family heirloom that had once belonged to his paternal grandfather. It had been crafted out of what appeared to be ancient oak timbers. Although highly polished, it was scratched in several places.

There were wood carvings, around the sides of the chest, depicting various sea creatures. These included a figure with long flowing locks, resembling the sea god Poseidon. The top was inset with a sizeable padded section of red leather, still in fairly good condition, trimmed with gold around its perimeter. Fiona remarked that Poseidon looked as though he was smiling – or maybe it was more like a grimace?

"It's a smile that could hold a multitude of secrets," replied Robert, cryptically.

"It's an incredibly beautiful chest," she gasped, pocketing her sunglasses too. She ran her hands gently across the top of it, feeling the softness of the leather.

"Yes. Isn't it?" he said, in a rather distant voice, kneeling down beside her. She looked up. He was no longer looking at the sea chest; he was scrutinising her face. Cautiously, he reached towards her, running his fingers through her long auburn tresses. Fiona looked at him in alarm. He held her gaze, mesmerising her with his hypnotic blue eyes. She stood up quickly.

"I don't think I should be…," she began, but she got no further. Robert had also stood up beside her, towering several inches above her. Before she could complete her protest, he grabbed both of her arms tightly, pulling her reluctant body towards him, silencing her protests with a long, hard kiss.

Any further protest was useless. Before she knew what was happening, he was kissing her passionately, all over the upper half of her body – her lips, her eyes, her neck, the base of her throat. He placed a hot tongue inside the orifice of her right ear, moving it still further in, then sucking her ear lobe.

She began to whimper and moan, at the same time struggling to break free. Her reaction only served to increase his ardour. As with that day in the Skiathos hills, his hot kisses began to release something wildly sensual within her.

Hardly knowing what she was doing, she began to undo the top two buttons of his white T-shirt. Without ceremony, she drew the shirt quickly over his by now tousled dark locks. She felt her senses swimming at the sight of his broad, hairy, muscular chest. Slowly, he lowered her down, onto the top of the sea chest. "Rob, Oh *God*. Please, *no!*" she called out to him. "*Please* stop – we can't do this!"

But he didn't want this to end. He wanted to make these moments last forever. Robert felt a deep, emotional reaction, as he was making love to her. It wasn't simply a physical act, like so many that he had experienced before.

CHAPTER EIGHT

He realised something that he had been trying to keep from himself; something which he'd been wrestling with for several days and sleepless nights. He knew now beyond any shadow of a doubt, that he loved her, and that he would always love her.

'*Dear God*', he thought, 'if nothing else, I must keep the memory of this moment with her... always'.

They lay still for a few seconds. Then slowly, she rose and began to dress. Robert did the same. Neither of them spoke. Pulling her to him once again, they kissed each other with great tenderness.

"Darling," he said huskily, "we have to sort something out. We can't just leave things as they are." He lifted her delicate chin up, towards his face. Her eyes were brimming with tears. Resting her head against him, she began to sob very quietly, almost like a child: "I'm afraid Rob," she sobbed. "Of what?" he asked. "I'm here... nothing can harm you."

"I'm afraid that I'm falling in love with you." "Is that all?" he said, smiling down at her. "That's nothing to worry about... I have an identical problem with you."

"But what about Patrick?" "Come on," he said, leading her back up on deck. They both resumed their seats there, but this time they sat much closer. Robert put a protective arm around her, pulling her closely to him. There was a long pause; they remained there, as the water lapped around them. Being in each other's company was more than sufficient now. Eventually Fiona said,

"I'm not a promiscuous person by nature, Rob. Before this holiday, I played everything very much by the book. I'm very virtuous, at heart."

"I know my darling," he replied lovingly. "If I'd thought otherwise I wouldn't have come within ten million miles of you!"

"But I feel that I've betrayed Patrick. It's a terrible feeling. I'm not a fickle person. If he knew what we'd done, he'd kill me!"

"He'd probably kill us both," said Robert wryly. "Besides," he continued, "you're not the only one with a conscience. He and I have been good friends for a number of years. We've spent a considerable amount of time in each other's company – I like and respect him. There are so many similarities between us. Even our ages are almost identical: he's just six months my junior."

Fiona took Robert's hand in hers and clasped it tightly. "It's a hopeless situation," she murmured. He paused for a moment; there were tears in his eyes too. When he spoke, his voice trembled with emotion. "The reason I tried to leave the airport was precisely to avoid hurting Patrick. I was almost out of the main concourse building, with the exit doors in sight. I felt like a character out of Dickens' *A Tale of Two Cities* – you know, like Sydney Carton: 'It is a far, far better thing I do now', and so forth. But I finally stopped short of the exit. Do you know why?" She shook her head.

"Because I knew that if I *didn't* return to you, I would never know if you loved me as deeply, as passionately, as I love you. That, my darling, was even more unbearable than betraying Patrick." Holding her closely to him, he kissed her as he had never kissed a woman before.

* * * *

They returned to the main airport building a short while later. Robert bought a copy of the local newspaper; Fiona, an English edition of *Cosmopolitan*, as reading material for the return flight. Clutching her hand luggage in one hand, in as private a corner as they could find, they kissed passionately; with the desperation that comes from knowing that your next kiss could be several weeks, or even months, away.

"Make sure you keep in touch. I shall expect a daily letter," he said huskily.

"At the very least!" she replied, with what was a cross between a laugh and a sob. Both of them had eyes brimming with tears.

"Do you have your passport handy?" Robert asked solicitously, tenderly brushing curls away from her cheek. "Here," she said, producing the document from the confines of her navy shoulder bag. "But I don't want to leave you!" She began to sob again. "Go on. You'd better go now," he said reluctantly, "before I start crying too." He tried to make a joke of it… but he could hardly hold back the tears.

* * * *

Trying to concentrate on reading her magazine, whilst waiting in the Departure Lounge, proved well nigh impossible; the thought of Rob's close proximity, within the same building, as he waited for the departure of her flight, was too disturbing. It took superhuman effort to prevent her from running straight back – into his arms. So near and yet so far, she realised tearfully. Why couldn't she just remain there with him? Why was life so unfair?

Half an hour later he stood in the gallery section of the airport, staring out of the enormous glass window which overlooked that particular area of tarmac. Down below, Fiona's plane waited, with the smartly dressed cabin crew in attendance. The passengers were now boarding. She turned to wave to him, trying to assume a cheerful expression – for his sake. Inside,

CHAPTER EIGHT

she felt *totally* dejected. Fiona turned, at frequent intervals, to wave to him, trying desperately to keep the image of his sad but handsome face, fixed firmly in her memory. Like a precious, never-to-be-forgotten photograph.

As she finally boarded the plane and disappeared into its interior, Robert felt as though his heart was breaking. It was as if some omnipotent being had decided to cut off his right arm, without any prior consultation, then transport it thousands of miles across an ocean.

Choking back the tears, he rushed blindly down several flights of stairs, ignoring the escalators – then straight across the main terminal building and out into a far corner of the nearby car park, where he had parked his green Range Rover. The keys shook in his trembling hands, as he struggled to open the door. He collapsed onto the front seat; his head slumped forward on the steering wheel.

He cried as he had never cried before. This normally stalwart and intrepid explorer was both startled and overwhelmed by the sheer power and intensity of the grief that was pouring out of him – at the prospect of being parted from Fiona. Several times he smote the steering wheel – in an effort to stem the tide of such an emotional outburst. But to no avail. After a while... the tension within him slowly dissipated.

As he gradually recovered, he wiped a few remaining tears away, with the back of his hand. With growing awareness, he realised that the only time he had ever experienced anything approaching such intense despair, was the day that Barbara left him...

CHAPTER NINE

A tiny, powder-blue-breasted bird, alighted on the three-tiered bird table below. Turning its head quizzically towards the ground, listening for something, it chirruped cheerfully. Another of its species joined it, seconds later, imitating the same ritual. They chirruped, almost in unison, each scrutinising the other, with a black beady eye. Then they began to gorge themselves, pecking voraciously away at the tiny white handfuls of bread and bacon rind, which had been placed there.

Behind them and slightly to the left stood an octagonal, honey-coloured summerhouse, with its mottled-green tiled roof and black weather-vane. The cockerel on its pinnacle mounted guard, like a flat and dark, ever-watchful sentinel. A gentle breeze caused an almost imperceptible change in its direction, a slight creaking noise being the only indication that it had moved.

Fiona looked up from the patch of ground just to the right of the rockery, where she'd been doing a little light weeding. It was a beautiful Sunday morning in June. The change in her own life, within just a few short weeks, she reflected, had been *far* more dramatic. Pausing for a short rest she reached into the pocket of her gardening apron, producing a sealed letter. She examined the handwriting on the front of the envelope for a few seconds. Moving across, to a green-cushioned, white wrought iron garden seat, she carefully opened the letter… deep in thought.

The writing was immediately recognisable. She had already received three others from the same correspondent, who wrote in a style with which she was rapidly becoming familiar: a combination of cultured Canadian, mixed with conversational Celtic wit. The letter was full of expressions of his love for her, his impatience to see her again – and his sleepless nights.

The trials and tribulations of the forthcoming Art Exhibition were described in great detail. In addition there were anecdotes about various family members, whose foibles he described in such graphic detail, that she could almost visualise them, although she had yet to meet them. At the very end, he added a postscript.

CHAPTER NINE

PS. I almost forgot. The strangest thing happened, before my departure from the island. My good friend, Robert Osborne, asked me if he could purchase one of my paintings. It was of a sunset; if you recall, you supplied the idea, originally. It's the sunset that can be seen as one descends towards Club Skiathos, from the direction of Olympia Bay. I'd just had time to complete it before I returned home. In fact, it's probably one of my finest paintings to date. Said he wanted it for one of the rooms in his apartment.

P.P.S. I sold it to him.

All my love
Patrick.

The memory of Patrick was so vivid; she could almost imagine him, seated at the garden table alongside her; chatting with the quiet sophisticated charm and good looks which had swept her off her feet.

Darling Patrick. Why, only the day after her return, back home in Solihull, she had answered the doorbell, to be greeted with a beautiful bouquet of red roses, tied with a luxurious red silk ribbon. The card had read simply,

With love from Patrick. My thoughts are with you, always. A bientôt...

Fiona surveyed the garden. The sight of it filled her with joy. It was a riot of colour. A few years of toil, creative planning and patience had been required, plus some help from a local landscape gardener. Now it was finally paying off.

Gardening, she reflected, was rather like painting – only with plants. Each border resembled a unique gallery, a harmony of tints. She felt that in her own small way, she had created a work of art – as surely as any Monet or Renoir... except that this was a living, vibrant creation, as opposed to something static.

Her favourite part was her own *Secret Garden*: a woodland area behind the summerhouse; partly contrived, partly wild. Nature, left to its own devices, seemed to plant in a random, impressionistic fashion. It was a strange irony indeed, that just at a time when she felt most at home in her garden, there was a strong possibility that she would have to desert it, at least for a month or so; to uproot herself to a different country.

She re-entered the house through the utility room. This in turn, led into a large designer kitchen, with ultra-smart shiny white cupboards and fittings. A pristine white, Spanish Octagonal floor, interspersed with smaller diamond-shaped, blue-grey tiles, completed the stylish effect.

Moving towards the spacious study, she seated herself in a turquoise-green, revolving leather armchair, to examine her notes for the following day's tuition. Although she had officially quit school teaching before Ian's death, she still gave private tuition to several local primary school children. There was a great demand for her services in this affluent area, particularly in English and Mathematics.

Normally, Fiona worked in the bookshop on Monday and Tuesday of each week. That Tuesday morning, she drove her white Volvo to a garage in the centre of Solihull, for its annual service. From there it was just a short walk through the main shopping area of Mell Square. Then right, into the cobbled High Street, with its deep blue Victorian style lampposts, and up to the bookshop, on the right-hand side of the street. Mell Square and the High Street were almost entirely pedestrianised, to encourage a quieter, more refined kind of atmosphere, in keeping with Solihull's village ambiance, a century before.

Her presence in the shop enabled Paul, the proprietor, to attend to other business: perusing catalogues, ordering new stock or visiting business colleagues. Over the space of almost three years, what had begun initially as a companionable working relationship had blossomed into friendship.

Today, she would have to explain that she needed a further month's holiday, in July. She was reluctant to ask him, in case he thought that she was taking advantage of their friendship. It might be an idea, she reasoned, to find a reliable replacement herself, from amongst her friends and acquaintances. She considered the matter during the day, finally selecting a suitable candidate of whom Paul was likely to approve.

At the close of the day's business Paul gave her a lift home in his elegant black sports car. He pulled up, just short of the sweeping block-paved drive. She frowned slightly at the sight of a red Nissan, already parked on her drive. She wasn't expecting visitors.

Opening the car door, she swung her shapely legs out first, then eased the rest of her body out of the low-slung passenger seat. She looked very sophisticated in her black and white striped business suit. In her right hand she carried a dark leather briefcase, containing a backlog of administrative paperwork from the bookshop.

She had offered to help Paul clear the administrative backlog, built up over the course of the last few weeks. It would at least be some form of recompense; he had just agreed, albeit reluctantly, to her taking a month's leave of absence, from July 16th onwards; she was due to fly out on the 17th.

CHAPTER NINE

Paul swung the car back round, gave her a friendly wave, then 'roared' off out of sight. The heels of Fiona's black patent shoes clicked on the bracken-coloured driveway, as she approached the front porch of the house.

Stopping half way, to find her keys, she happened to glance towards the large area of parkland, to her left. In doing so, she noticed a tall dark figure walking towards her along the winding pathway, which led towards the house. At that moment, he was passing an island of trees. As soon as he saw her he began to run. In a few seconds more he was close enough to see her clearly.

She couldn't believe it and dropped her case in astonishment. He was almost upon her now – jumping the low stile fence, which bordered the edge of her front garden. He grabbed hold of her, taking her in his arms. Then he twirled her around, with great exuberance, laughing as he did so. "For God's sake Robert put me down!" she protested. She was laughing too, but in her case, in disbelief.

As she fumbled for the keys, having rescued her case, he grabbed her playfully around the waist. "I hope you realise that property prices have just plummeted around here!" she joked.

Once inside the porch, she had a second door to open, into the spacious hall. As they both entered Robert practically slammed the door behind them. He seized hold of her, smothering her with kisses. "Stop!" she protested. "Let me get my breath back – you big ape!"

As he gradually calmed down, she showed him into the lounge. Fiona removed her jacket, in the certainty that it would otherwise be creased; there was a white silk blouse underneath. Robert noticed the outline of her lacy white bra beneath it.

For what seemed like minutes, they just held hands and gazed into each other's eyes. Then she sank back into him – resting her head on his shoulder. His body felt very hot... probably with the exertion of driving, she concluded.

She could hardly breathe for excitement; unable to comprehend fully, that he was actually there. It felt like a dream. "I'm sure I'm going to wake up any minute," she murmured, resting against the warm comfort of his body.

A little while later, Robert explained that he had taken an early Saturday morning flight from Athens to Heathrow, to meet a business associate, who was also a friend of long-standing – from his Oxford days. Rob had mentioned him before, when they were on his boat. Professor Graham Pilkington, he reminded her, was an expert in European Maritime History and a Senior Lecturer at a naval college in Greenwich.

Robert had run into problems with his research into the location of one of the Spanish wrecks: a galleon, which had sunk in 1562, somewhere off the coast of Crete. The implications of Graham's latest research were that the vessel was located several miles further to the north-west of the island, than was previously supposed.

"Whilst in London, I suddenly thought, what the heck! I'm only two hours down the motorway from Fiona. So I hired a car – and here I am."

"Just like that?" queried Fiona.

"Absolutely! Why?" he asked, frowning. "Aren't you pleased to see me?"

Fiona, muttering something about the understatement of the year, offered him a drink. "You could have a double whiskey, that is, unless you're planning to drive." "Well... that rather depends upon you now, doesn't it?"

His rugged good looks were so appealing – totally impossible to resist. Feigning indifference to the effect he was having on her, she merely shrugged her shoulders, offering to prepare dinner, as it was almost six o'clock in the evening. Inside, however, her heart was pounding.

She cooked a light evening meal of mushroom omelette, with salad and baked potatoes. Robert had brought a bottle of white wine, which they chilled, then drank with the meal. They had ice cream for dessert. Fiona apologised for the simplicity of the meal. "If I'd known you were coming, and all that," she said.

When they were towards the end of the meal, becoming quite pleasantly drunk, she said, "I suppose you'd like to stay?"

"I suppose I would."

"Okay... but only for a day or two," she added.

"Well now, let me see. I've been doing some calculations. I reckon that you spent the majority of your fortnight's holiday in Patrick's company, according to his account anyway. Out of that I had only... maybe a maximum of three days in total – if that. So, to even the balance, I calculate that you owe me approximately one-and-a-half further weeks of your time."

"Are you *serious?*" she asked – in mock disbelief.

"Absolutely!" he replied. "At least that would redress the balance a little."

After dinner, Fiona suggested that a shower might be a good idea.

"You must be hot and sticky after your motorway journey," she suggested.

"That's a *very* accurate description," he replied, giving her a knowing wink.

Being a spacious detached house, there were two separate en-suite shower rooms which they used simultaneously. She hesitated, before handing him a large white dressing gown, which had belonged to Ian, then realised that it would be one further step towards putting the past behind her.

CHAPTER NINE

Far better to put it to some use, she reasoned. Nevertheless, she studied Robert's reaction, as she passed the robe to him. Her own pink silk housecoat had a sash belt, which she tied loosely.

By the time Robert emerged from the shower, Fiona had wrapped a pink towel around her head, like a turban. He began to lead her towards the master bedroom. "No, not that one," she insisted nervously. Her emotional recovery hadn't progressed to that extent. "It would feel as if Ian were watching us," she explained. "There's a perfectly good double bed in here," she continued, leading him towards one of the guestrooms.

"D'you know, I feel like some degenerate heroine out of a French novel. See the effect you're having on me!" At the back of her mind was the thought that under Robert's tutelage, she was rapidly morphing into a raging nymphomaniac!

"We're wasting time Fi," he protested, leading her right into the room and closing the door. Perhaps he was trying to lay a few ghosts of his own? Slowly, and very gently, he released her long auburn tresses from the pink head towel. As it dropped to the floor he began to run his fingers through her thick, dark mane. Then he reached down, pulling back the lemon duvet cover. Removing each other's clothes, they sank down onto the bed.

They took time to savour the delights of one another. Despite an underlying urgency, they controlled their needs masterfully for a while, their passion unfolding slowly – like a delicate flower. Only towards the end, when they were approaching ecstasy, their senses reeling, did they feel the need to increase the tempo. At that point, Robert behaved like a castaway on a desert island, who had been sex-starved for at least ten years. Fiona lay back, panting and exhausted, upon the bed.

"Christ, Rob," she protested, "it's a good job I'm younger than you are. Slow down. You'll wear me out!" Robert said nothing. He just collapsed beside her, with a contented smile. Reaching across, he grasped her hand tightly.

"This is so good for me, Fi. I could really get used to it," he sighed contentedly. "It's not just the physical side of our relationship... but our being together. It feels so right; as though it was always meant to be... somehow."

As Rob lay beside her she considered the mass of contradictions within him. On the one hand, he was intensely physical; on the other, he was an intellectual, of some standing. It was like having a relationship with Neanderthal Man and Albert Einstein, at one and the same time!

Over the next few days they made fresh discoveries about each other. They discussed their interests, their dreams and their respective achievements.

"Tell me about your earlier days in Oxford, during the seventies and eighties," she asked. "You've not said much about that period in your life."

"Barbara, Graham and I graduated together. All three of us were high-achievers in our field. Initially, we all gained First Class Honours degrees in Classical History, within the same year – a scenario straight out of Raphael's *Glittering Prizes*.

"Graham and I worked on the theses for our doctorates at the same time," he continued. "Mine was primarily concerned with Grecian History. He had already made the switch to Maritime History. The two of us eventually became the youngest Dons ever to be appointed: he to a London college – myself at Oxford."

He explained that Barbara was then hired as a junior research assistant, to a television producer of historical documentaries. "Roughly a year later," he elaborated, "without any prior knowledge on my part, she became his mistress. They spent a great deal of time together, you see, on location. I suppose it became too tempting – combined with the fact that I was completely absorbed in research for my doctoral thesis. Inevitably, we drifted apart. Once she'd become that bastard's mistress, there was no going back. I thought I'd never get over it. At one time we'd been absolutely inseparable, you see." This last sentence was said very wistfully. Fiona suddenly felt intensely sorry for him: not an emotion she was accustomed to feeling, where Robert was concerned. The tearful expression in his eyes went straight to her heart.

Kissing him tenderly on the forehead, she gave him a comforting hug. He simply melted into her arms. There was a more vulnerable side to him, after all; although he'd previously only allowed her brief glimpses of it.

Fiona showed him some of the synopses she had written for various novels, together with research folders, both for current projects and from her teaching days. She also revealed the usually jealously-guarded secrets of her poetry notebooks, including several abortive attempts.

Robert was interested in her bookshop work, and in particular, her relationship with Paul. Apparently, he had seen her stepping out of Paul's car on Tuesday evening. He had been consumed with jealousy, but had taken particular care not to show it, at the time. He wanted, at all costs, to avoid giving the impression that he was being overly possessive. After all, they had only known each other for a matter of weeks.

Fiona told him about her own Honours Degree, achieved by spending most of her leisure time studying, over a period of fours years, while engaged in full time teaching. She'd specialised in all aspects of English, particularly creative writing and literature. The course had also carried a maths component, together with research techniques and statistics.

CHAPTER NINE

She'd always maintained a strong interest in history, ever since her grammar school days. Most of her research in that field, she admitted ruefully, was concerned with local history studies. She showed him a range of files.

"It's nothing *like* the degree of specialisation that you're accustomed to," she said apologetically. "Don't undervalue your achievements darling," he chided her. "You're such a wonderfully creative person: your writing, your music, artistic skills, your love of nature. I'd say we're an ideal match."

Fiona told him that Patrick had mentioned the sunset painting in one of his letters. "How often does he write to you?" he retorted, more sharply than he'd intended. He was painfully aware of his acute feelings of jealousy, making a mental note to try to control them. No woman, not even Barbara, had provoked such a reaction in him. Usually, he feigned disinterest, but in Fiona's case, he didn't want any other man to touch her. As far as he was concerned she belonged to him!

"Did Patrick mention the other painting?" he asked.

"Which one would that be?"

"Well, we were having a drink in his apartment one night," Robert explained. "Patrick was showing me some of the work he'd completed, during the holiday. He showed me that seascape-cum-landscape that he'd helped you with. You know, the practice piece – for want of a better term."

She knew only too well. Although still a novice, she was very proud of her first efforts. In fact, she felt quite possessive about it. It was her creation – her baby!

"You didn't ask if that one was for sale?" she asked, in a belligerent, disbelieving tone of voice. "Well, actually, I did," he replied, sounding equally aggrieved. "He reacted quite passionately – told me it wasn't for sale!"

"I'm not surprised," she said quietly, almost to herself. Then, turning to him again she asked, "But why buy that one? It was only a beginner's piece you know; quite primitive and unsophisticated really."

"But that was part of its appeal," he explained. "Besides, there was another, far more important reason." "What was that?" "Do you *really* need to ask? Don't you know?" The expression in his eyes was darkly serious, almost tormented. "Because you created it… it's part of you," he added softly.

Fiona had several paintings and framed maps around the house. Most of the paintings were copies, although she had one original oil painting of Ullswater Lake, in the Lake District, by a local artist, bought from an exhibition in Ambleside. There was also a huge picture, entitled The *Landlords' Meeting* by Turner, in the dining room, on the wall behind the elegant mahogany dining table. It looked like an original oil painting but was, in fact, a clever copy.

Robert was particularly fascinated by one of the three gilt-framed pictures, which hung in the lounge – a copy of an original watercolour. "That's Warwick Castle, isn't it?" he asked, peering closely at the detail. The tree-fringed River Avon flowed through the centre of the painting. In the foreground were two figures in a boat. On the river bank to their right stood a solitary fisherman. His lady friend was kneeling on the bank, a short distance behind. Judging by their style of dress, it was a nineteenth century painting. In the distance was a small wooden bridge, beyond which lay the castle. The pinnacle of Saint Mary's Church rose majestically, to the far right. Fiona smiled, as he admired the picture.

"Ian and I bought it, on a visit to the castle, about ten years ago, I suppose. It was rather funny because the artist had a bizarre sense of humour. He'd painted another, almost identical version, but with a bear rowing the boat, instead of the two men: the Warwickshire bear, without his ragged staff, you see? We could have bought that one, but we 'chickened out' and bought the normal one instead!"

Robert suggested that they might have a day's outing to the castle, that weekend. The only local place that he had ever visited in the Solihull area was the Shakespeare Memorial Theatre in Stratford, a building which also stood on the banks of the Avon. His father Colin, an English Master, had taken himself and a party of schoolboys from his Torquay grammar school on a visit there, when he was fifteen years old. The play they had seen was *Macbeth*, one of their set books that year.

The three days that they had originally planned to spend together increased, as if by sub-conscious design, into the week-and-a-half, first suggested by Robert. They felt so happy, contented and fulfilled in one another's company that neither of them wanted such domestic bliss to end. It felt so right and natural to both of them... as though it had always been so.

On the days when Fiona was obliged to work, Robert just relaxed around the house, reading a selection of books from the hundreds which practically filled two or three rooms in the house. "You've got your own library here!" he said in amazement. "You should Dewey Reference it all." "Well I would – but it might take me a couple of years!" she retorted.

Many of them had belonged to Ian, but she also had a wide selection herself, including many children's books. "You teased me about my archives, on the boat – but look who's talking!" commented Robert.

He enjoyed shopping for the two of them, at the local supermarket and proved to be a capable cook – at least partly out of necessity, having reverted to bachelor status, several years ago.

CHAPTER NINE

They drove into Warwick that Saturday. Luckily the weather was ideal for viewing the castle and grounds. Approaching the castle entrance, they could hear the distinctive calls of peacocks, from the grounds beyond. "When I first visited here, as a child, and heard their calls," laughed Fiona, "I thought they were cats – in distress. My mother thought that was quite funny!"

Robert laughed with her, hugging her closely to him, as they walked. He felt so relaxed in her company. Everything seemed so right with the world, on such a fine summer's morning. It felt as if they had known each another for years.

Despite various sexual and quasi-romantic encounters, it had been many years since he had felt so much at ease, in the company of a member of the fair sex. Far too long, he acknowledged ruefully, to himself. Now he was going to move heaven and earth to make sure that Fiona didn't slip through his fingers. Just this one last voyage to Crete: hopefully a successful one. With most of his professional ambitions realised, it would be the ideal time to settle down.

According to their guidebook, the castle had remained the seat of the Earls of Warwick for nearly a thousand years. The Beauchamp family were responsible for most of the fortifications that Fiona and Robert saw, as they toured the site.

Gazing up at Caesar's Tower, Robert remarked, "You can just imagine, can't you, stones and boiling pitch being dropped from that parapet, on to the poor devils below!" They visited the dungeon, beneath the tower. Fiona cringed when she saw the grisly display of torture instruments. Carved inscriptions on the wall, made by beleaguered Royalist prisoners during the Civil War, put her imagination into overdrive. She could almost hear their moans and cries of anguish – abandoned to a grisly fate in that damp, dark place.

They visited the Madame Tussauds Exhibition, depicting one of Daisy Warwick's famous house parties, held at the castle in the earlier part of this century. There were several famous guests including a remarkably young, sandy-haired Winston Churchill.

Van Dyck's portrait of Charles the First, clad in armour and mounted on a white horse, hung in the panelled state dining room. It had attracted a whole crowd of tourists who stood around it in a kind of haphazard half-circle, admiring it. Fiona thought, cynically, that the portrait was rather idealised.

In the smallest room in the castle, the *Blue Boudoir*, they were surprised to find a silver-and-enamel clock, opposite the fireplace: it had once belonged to Marie Antoinette, before Madame Guillotine claimed her, in October 1793.

Linking arms, they walked out into the magnificent and extensive gardens. The bright sunlight was quite startling after some of the gloomier parts of the castle. They explored the topiaries and rose gardens. Fiona was delighted to find a peacock with its splendid tail actually *open;* strutting around in courtship mode.

"Let's find the church – the one in my picture!" enthused Fiona. "I think Richard Beauchamp's tomb might be in there." Leaving the castle, they hurried along the street of the same name, passing the Doll Museum, on the right. They didn't need a street map, but simply followed the distant peal of church bells. Walking on, past the Court House, then the Tourist Information Office, which was also on their right, they reached the busy main road junction with Jury Street. To their left lay the main High Street, crowded with shoppers. At this point the bells were much louder.

"I hope this is worth it!" yelled Robert – his voice almost drowned by the din. As they reached the library in Church Street, the bells, thankfully, ceased. Right at the top of the street stood Saint Mary's; its 174-foot high tower looming before them. So there it was, in all its Gothic glory; standing on arches that straddled the road – the actual church in her painting!

Beauchamp's effigy was indeed there; looking so peaceful, in its tranquil church setting, isolated from all the noise and traffic. His hands were raised towards the figure of Our Lady, in the vaulted roof. Robert whispered, "I wonder if he met a violent death. I mean, he looks so peaceful lying there. But he could have died on the battlefield; not necessarily in his own bed, poor chap."

The church pews provided a welcome resting place, for a while. All that walking had made the soles of Robert's feet very sore; his shoes weren't designed for long walks. Luckily, Fiona was wearing trainers.

They strolled back along the medieval streets, stopping for afternoon tea, in an old Tudor-style tearoom, adjacent to the Shire Hall.

As early evening approached, they headed back, tired but relaxed, to the car park just above Theatre Street. It was conveniently situated for the road back to Birmingham.

* * * *

The night before his departure they lay on the broad lounge sofa. He was stroking her hair, as he cradled her head in his arms. Robert explained that it was essential that he return to Greece. He planned to take his large, well-equipped motor boat, to Crete – for further investigation into the

CHAPTER NINE

location of the *Queen Isabella*: the Spanish galleon he had mentioned to her when they were on his boat.

"I've been meaning to ask you about the name you chose for your boat – *Silver's Arrow*. With your love of all things linked with the great Mr. Stevenson, it has to be the *Long John* connection – right?" "But of course," confirmed Robert, with a twinkle in his eye. "You see, for me Silver was always the quintessential anti-hero – the loveable rogue." "But how does the arrow come into it?" Fiona queried.

"Well, she's always been straight and true – served me well. I've had her for a few years now, since she was new. She's always taken me exactly where I needed to go; never once let me down."

One of the local sailors, Andreas, had offered to accompany him again, as on the previous voyage. Both he and Robert were experienced scuba divers. Armed with the latest, more accurate information from Graham Pilkington, they stood a much stronger chance of locating the wreck. "Graham's latest findings suggest that the cargo is likely to be worth far more than we'd originally anticipated; we could be talking about millions of pounds worth of gold bullion."

"Is that your chief motivation? Is the money so important to you?" she asked. Robert looked visibly hurt. "Well, of course not," he muttered. "It's mainly the satisfaction of locating a vessel of exceptional historical interest; for posterity, rather than for financial gain... at least, on my part. If we manage to raise her, we'll be *making* history. And the *Queen Isabella* will then be available to everyone – for all time."

He was clearly upset that she thought him avaricious, retaliating: "If we're discussing money, how about our mutual friend... Mr. Maitland? He's as rich as Croesus!" "What d'you mean?" she said, sitting suddenly bolt upright. "Well, he must have discussed it with you. He must at the very least, have *mentioned* it."

"We didn't discuss money at all!" Fiona was both puzzled and indignant.

"Well, that will be a first!" exclaimed Robert – equally surprised. "It's my understanding that in his past relationships with women, and believe me, there have been *quite* a few, the subject of money has always been high on the agenda. The man's a multi-millionaire, for heaven's sake!"

Fiona was totally speechless. "The subject never came up," she eventually repeated, trying to recover from the shock. Realising his mistake, Robert put his arm around her, saying, apologetically, "Well Fi... perhaps he shared your view... that it wasn't important..."

CHAPTER TEN

Lying in bed together that evening, Fiona felt a sudden, overpowering urge, to keep him with her. "Please Rob," she pleaded. "Stay with me – don't go back yet!" There had been precious little time to discuss his forthcoming voyage.

"What happens if you and Andreas actually find the galleon? What will the next step be?" "Inform the Greek authorities, I expect. There will probably be a substantial reward; there invariably is. Which reminds me," he continued briskly, "I have a business proposition to put to you."

"Really?" said Fiona, only half-believing him. "Do continue."

"I've been thinking about offering you a partnership," he said, watching carefully for her reaction. Her heart gave a violent leap and her pulse quickened. "What *sort* of partnership?"...she hardly dared ask. "Well," he replied teasingly, "I need a new research assistant. I had to sack the last one – far too incompetent. Would you be interested... maybe?" He raised a quizzical eyebrow. She looked at him – uncertain whether to laugh or cry.

"I hesitate to ask you," he continued. His facial expression and tone of voice gave nothing way. "It would involve re-location, plus months of travel. But you have such a beautiful home here – you probably wouldn't be interested." He stared directly ahead – the back of his head resting against the pillow.

"I, on the other hand, would be unable to leave Greece," he continued. "It's my natural home. Ever since I was a schoolboy in Torquay, delving into Homer's *Odyssey,* I've longed for a legendary kind of existence. I've always been fascinated by the sea and its islands. It's such an integral part of my psyche – I could never give it up...." He uttered the last sentence in a preoccupied, almost distant manner.

Continuing in a more light-hearted vein, he said: "As you know, my favourite book, as a youngster, was Stevenson's *Treasure Island.* Sheer fantasy! When I was younger still, it was his poetry – especially those that involved imaginative exploration. I've always found John Masefield's poetry rather appealing too."

Sitting up in bed, Robert's mood seemed to change. Taking her hand in his, he looked directly at her, with almost expressionless eyes, he asked:

CHAPTER TEN

"What arrangement did you make with Patrick?" Fiona remained silent, then answered guardedly, "What did he tell you?" "Like the true gentleman that he always is," replied Robert, "he told me absolutely nothing." Sensing that this particular approach wasn't working, he tried again: "During the final week... I happened to mention you... in passing. He didn't need much encouragement He was singing your praises to the hilt."

"You didn't tell him about *us?*" she asked, with some alarm. "No," he said adamantly. "I thought that best left to you – so that you could choose the right moment. Besides, I had no idea how to even *begin* to tell him. I just listened, trying to change the subject, as soon as there was an opportunity."

Fiona thought carefully. Normally, she would keep any arrangement between herself and Patrick completely private. After these past days spent with Robert she felt totally confused by this cryptic approach – offering her a working partnership on the one hand, but then making love to her in such a tender fashion and quizzing her about Patrick.

She found it impossible to get his earlier proposition out of her mind; it stirred up repressed feelings of anger: how *dare* he play 'hot-and-cold' with her emotions in such a cavalier fashion. This charade had to stop – right now. "I don't want to be *that* kind of partner!" she suddenly shouted at him. "What a crass remark! What sort of idiot d'you think I am? I'm in love with you – you bastard!"

As she shouted this last comment, she began pummelling his chest hard, with her fists. "Hey, wait! Just stop for a minute will you?" he protested, grabbing both of her wrists at once. "I love you too. I'm sorry that I teased you. I didn't mean it to go that far.... Only I wasn't completely sure. That's not the sort of partnership that I really want either. What I want... deep down... inside... is for you to marry me."

As he released her wrists, Fiona remained motionless. Then, looking him steadily in the eye, she said, "Would you please repeat that Mr. Osborne?" Placing his lips gently over hers, he kissed her with great tenderness. Then releasing her, he repeated, "Will you marry me Fiona?" "I love you Rob," she answered. "Right," he said, nodding his head in acknowledgement. Then, between gritted teeth, he snarled impatiently, "But will you please answer the *damned* question?!" "Yes," she said. Lying naked on the bed, they made love with passionate intensity.

* * * *

During breakfast the following morning, before Robert's departure for Heathrow, Fiona, summoning all of her courage, finally revealed that

Patrick had invited her to stay at his home in Victoria. Placing his half-finished slice of toast back on the plate, he said tersely,

"Then he can simply *un-invite* you, can't he?"

She explained that the original purpose of the visit was to get a more realistic picture of her relationship with Patrick, away from the romantic holiday setting. After further discussion, Rob reluctantly sanctioned the idea. Certainly, matters had to be resolved – once and for all. He had no wish to marry a woman who was secretly pining for another man. One divorce was *more* than enough, he reasoned. He also agreed for the sake of his friendship with Patrick – he owed him that much.

They agreed that, at an opportune moment, during her month's stay, Fiona would tell Patrick about Robert and herself; far kinder to do it in person than by letter, or over the telephone. Later, she and Robert would arrange a wedding date: once he had returned from Crete. They would probably settle on one of the Greek islands; the choice of island could be made later. For the time being they would leave it, rather appropriately, 'in the lap of the gods'.

Fiona agreed to keep Robert updated, by whatever means she could muster. As he was about to leave, he produced an exquisite ring. It had a broad band, and was made, from what appeared to be an antique, almost bronzed type of gold. He placed it on the third finger of her right hand. "This will have to do for now," he said. The ring had been willed to him, by his beloved grandfather, William, along with the treasure chest. According to William, the ring had once belonged to a Spanish noblewoman. "Please accept it as a token of my enduring love for you Fi," Robert said softly.

Their parting kisses were hot and passionate. As Robert began to reverse his hired Nissan out of the drive, she signalled for him to lower the automatic windows. He pressed the button. "What is darling?" he asked. "Where exactly did you put Patrick's sunset painting?" "On my bedroom wall – just above the bed," he replied.

"Why there?" she asked, laughingly. 'How typically Robert', she thought.

"Well, it's a salutary reminder for me darling," he explained. "That day, at Olympia Bay, was the only time we didn't make it – sexually speaking I mean. We were interrupted – if you remember."

"Am I ever likely to forget?" she joked. "It serves to remind me," he continued, "about how desperate I felt when I couldn't have you." Having positioned his vehicle for driving straight out, he switched off the engine, then jumped out of the car again.

CHAPTER TEN

"Come with me for a moment," he requested, as though something had suddenly occurred to him. Leading her back into the porch, he closed the door behind them.

He hesitated for a few seconds, uncertain about how to continue. Taking a deep breath, he said, "If anything should happen to me darling, for *whatever* reason, I want you to know that you are the only woman I have ever truly loved." "What could happen…" she began, but he interrupted her. "You mean more to me than my own life. I want you to promise me faithfully, that wherever you are in the world, at any time, you will always remember that. Never, ever, forget it."

"Oh Rob," she began to cry, "when we're married, we can put all of these worries behind us. I've waited half a lifetime to find you. We're soul mates – you *know* that. When you leave me now, you'll be taking my heart with you." As they embraced in a final kiss, Fiona was convinced that no one else would ever take his place. Two minutes later she was waving cheerfully to him, as his car drove out of sight.

But back in the house, the old feelings of depression returned, as she considered his parting words. It was just over two-and-a-half years, since she'd lost her beloved Ian. He was still a young man, in his mid-thirties, when he'd suffered the heart attack – probably stress-induced; he'd been working all hours that God sends. Before that fateful day, they'd had every reason to believe that they'd be spending the rest of their lives together. Her feelings of loss were still raw. There was *no* way that she could cope for a second time, should anything happen to Rob.

CHAPTER ELEVEN

The film on the miniaturised screen was a familiar one: the classic Jane Austen story, *Sense and Sensibility*. It had just reached the part where Colonel Brandon, played by Alan Rickman, had fallen in love with romantic Marianne Dashwood, but couldn't permit himself to show it, for fear of rejection.

In essence, it was the story of a young woman with two suitors. The first, in the shape of the dashing Mr. Willoughby, appeared to be eminently suitable. The denouement of the story, however, was that Willoughby's love proved fickle. Colonel Brandon's, by contrast, was of a much more genuine and enduring nature.

The film was far too 'close to home' for her liking. She removed the airline headphones and closed her eyes, hoping to banish that particular storyline from her mind. Most of her fellow passengers, oblivious to her private dilemma, continued to view the film quite happily, from their own mini-screens.

She tried to sleep: to dispel the disturbing scenarios that were tormenting her. After an hour or so she awoke. It was a strange sensation. One moment you imagine you're at home, in your familiar bedroom. Then, suddenly, wham! You're in the rarefied atmosphere of an aeroplane cabin; a faint hum of engines in the background, and the cabin staff moving about, like silent shadows: busy and efficient.

The pressurised atmosphere of the cabin with its muffled sounds, made her feel as though someone had cocooned her in cotton wool. Once she'd recovered her bearings, she felt quite cosy and cosseted.

Reaching into her large red shoulder bag, she reassured herself that the seaplane tickets were safe. Rather than make the tedious, often misty ferry crossing, from Vancouver to Victoria, Patrick had mailed her a return ticket for the seaplane: part of a package deal, which included transfer from Vancouver Airport to the harbour.

The flight from Heathrow to Vancouver seemed interminable. It took just over ten hours. Patrick had explained that the seaplane stage of her journey should be really enjoyable – the most spectacular part of the whole trip.

CHAPTER ELEVEN

As she boarded the seaplane in Vancouver Harbour, she had a magnificent view of Canada Place, from the water. To the right stood the impressive and relatively new Steamship Pier, hotel and convention centre. A cruise ship lay at anchor, close by, bound for Alaska. The roofs of nearby buildings were shaped like the peaked masts of ten white sailing ships: an ossified regatta! Their architectural style reminded her of the Sydney Opera House. A little way towards the hinterland, the magnificent space age Century Tower glinted and gleamed in the sunlight.

The plane skimmed the water at tremendous speed, soaring into the sky like an enormous buzzing dragonfly. She felt a great sense of elation, as though she were at the start of a truly momentous adventure!

As Patrick had predicted, the ocean views en route to Victoria were breathtaking. The pilot, Joe, was a Vancouver man. His friendly conversation added to her enjoyment of the flight. On arrival in Victoria, the seaplane deposited her at the landing stage, by the water's edge. Joe helped with her luggage. She tipped him generously and they exchanged a warm, farewell handshake.

The final stage of her journey now complete, she stood expectantly with her luggage, on the quayside. Miraculously, she had managed to catch *some* sleep on the initial flight from Heathrow. As she stood patiently waiting, however, she began to feel very drowsy; struggling to keep her eyes open.

She wasn't exactly sure who would be meeting her. Patrick hadn't been specific. She surveyed the area for some sign of assistance. Maybe it would be like a scene from a film – a stranger, dressed in a chauffeur's hat, might be holding a card – bearing her name. The pulse of the whole town seemed to centre on this harbour area. Whilst she waited, growing increasingly weary, seaplanes took off and landed close by, at regular intervals.

Then she saw him: leaning against a parked, dove-grey saloon car. He was dressed in a smart grey suit, white shirt and red silk tie; a red silk handkerchief carefully folded in his breast pocket. He looked very smart and debonair. His beard was much neater and less bohemian than on holiday. Obviously he'd paid a visit to the barber since then!

The moment he spotted her, he waved in recognition. Removing his hands from his trouser pockets, he began to walk cautiously towards her. Then his walk broke into a jog, and his jog into a run. The effect of seeing him so suddenly gave her renewed energy. She wanted to run to meet him too, but was marooned where she stood, because of her luggage.

He came to an abrupt halt, just in front of her. They stood there, looking at each other for a few seconds. Neither of them could quite comprehend that after all those weeks of separation, they were finally together again – albeit, in a totally different setting.

As they finally embraced, Fiona sighed deeply, in the sanctuary of his strong, loving arms. Patrick held her silently to him, for a while. Then, grasping the front handle of her suitcase, he wheeled it across to the car, while she carried her smaller, matching hand luggage.

As he drove, he explained that their destination was about half an hour's drive from the harbour, along the Nanaimo Road, on the northern shore of the island. In the course of writing to him, she had sent several photographs of the interior and exterior of her own house. Patrick, on the other hand, had made no recent reference to his home, in his letters, apart from mentioning that some parts of it were in the 'colonial' style. In view of Robert's revelations about Patrick being 'as rich as Croesus', she had strong misgivings about what lay ahead.

How could she hope to compete with his lifestyle, if that really *was* the case? 'Perhaps Robert was exaggerating?' she thought hopefully. She would feel much more at ease if he lived in an average type of apartment.

Twenty minutes or so into the journey, they appeared to be entering an exclusive residential area. Patrick swung the car off the main road, then produced a remote control gadget from the glove compartment, to open security gates – a large, black wrought iron gateway, leading to a sweeping, gravelled driveway.

It was then that Fiona began to realise the extent of her misconception. On either side of the driveway were areas of landscaped gardens, with exotic plants and beautifully laid out beds of fragrant roses. At the far end of the driveway was an amazing, gravelled courtyard. In the centre, a large elegant fountain played, surrounded by mischievous stone cherubs. It looked just as if it had been transported from Versailles and set down, in all its glory, right in front of the house!

His home was a spacious white mansion. The Greek columns adorning the main entrance were extremely grandiose. The facade of the house was rather like an extended Grecian temple. As the car swept into the courtyard, two grey-suited members of his staff, one male, one female, emerged. They promptly removed Fiona's luggage from the trunk of the car and into the house, before she could blink!

Patrick opened the passenger door, offering her his hand, as she stepped, completely stunned, out of the car. To the right-hand side of the entrance she noticed a green metal name plate trimmed with gold, bearing the legend *Tralee*. The spacious marble-floored entrance hall, with a sweeping, polished oak staircase, completely took her breath away!

CHAPTER ELEVEN

Turning a half circle, she gasped in amazement, at the sheer opulence of her surroundings.

Patrick had anticipated her reaction. Giving her a reassuring kiss, he linked his arm though hers, leading her into an even grander drawing room. It had two large picture windows, facing out onto a large gravelled patio, beyond which were extensive, well-manicured, lush green lawns.

Both members of staff had disappeared. Patrick invited her to join him on a large brown leather sofa. It had been placed at an angle to the windows, affording a generous view of the magnificent gardens. "Patrick," she began, "I didn't expect...." He placed two fingers, gently on her lips, then moving in closely beside her, gave her a gentle, lingering kiss. "Patrick, I wasn't prepared for this. Why didn't you *tell* me?" she demanded angrily. "Tell you what?" "About how wealthy you are."

"It didn't seem to matter," he replied. "But I feel so foolish," she protested. "Sending you photographs of my sorry little house, when you're living in a huge mansion. It's totally unfair of you!" She began to cry quietly to herself. Her tears provided a release. All those hours of travelling – and now this.

"You're tired darling. Besides, the photos of your house look grand. Just leave everything to me. Maggie, my housekeeper, has put a snack in your room. You must be hungry. Come on – you'll feel a deal better when you've had your sleep. It's probably the jet lag."

So saying, he led her back into the hall. He placed a strong arm around her shoulders, steadying her. Carefully, he helped her to ascend the grand, twisting staircase, and into one of the guest bedrooms. It was furnished in various shades of soft green. The large silk-sheeted bed looked wonderfully inviting. On a circular onyx table, over by a rather large picture window, she noticed a plate of cellophane-wrapped sandwiches and a cold drink.

Patrick eased her gently onto the bed, helping her to remove most of her clothing as far as her under-slip. Gently removing her elegant blue shoes, he eased her legs under the covers, pulling the cool green sheets over her. Silently he drew the heavy green brocade curtains, so that the sunlight would not disturb her. Then he squeezed her hand, kissed her forehead, and departed, as she sank rapidly into a deep sleep.

She slept soundly and awoke, feeling rested, but still rather disorientated. After resting on the side of the bed for a minute or two, she opened the brocade curtains a little, allowing some of the light to filter through. Her wristwatch had stopped; she'd had no time to replace the batteries, before leaving. However, according to the digital display on the bedside clock, she must have slept for at least twelve hours... unbelievable! It was now seven o'clock in the morning.

Trying to regain her equilibrium, she looked slowly around the room. It was both spacious and elegant. A partially-mirrored wardrobe, or closet – as she supposed she must now call it, ran the full length of the right-hand side of the room.

Fiona devoured the sandwiches hungrily. Struggling to remember the security code for her suitcase, she unlocked it, but unpacked only two or three items, feeling far too unsteady to deal with it all immediately. She laid a blue trouser suit out on the bed. As the room was en-suite, she decided to take a warm, rejuvenating shower. Feeling considerably refreshed; she put on the trouser suit. After adding silver jewellery and fixing her hair and make-up, she slipped on a pair of pale-blue casual shoes. They felt comfortably soft and welcoming – almost like slippers. Examining herself in the mirror, she felt quite satisfied with the result: ready to face the world again.

By this time at least another hour had passed. Opening the door quietly, in case people were still sleeping, she descended the huge, twisting staircase. Below her lay the elegant marble hall – so it definitely *hadn't* been a dream! She gingerly tried one of the doors on the left-hand side of the hall, unsure of what she might find. It opened into a large study furnished in black, white and green. The walls were lined with several bookcases, each containing a variety of books, many of them expensively-bound. Landscapes adorned some of the remaining wall space. She wondered if any of them were Patrick's.

Deciding to keep to a familiar route, still very much over-awed by her grandiose surroundings, she walked back through the hall, into the drawing room. She selected one of the single, brown leather armchairs. There was a comfortable-looking footrest to hand. Placing both feet upon it, she settled back in the armchair and closed her eyes.

On waking, she was surprised to find Patrick already sprawled across the sofa opposite, dressed in jeans, an open-necked, casual shirt and loafers. He was reading a copy of the local newspaper, *The Times Columnist*.

"Ah, the Sleeping Beauty awakes!" he observed, good-naturedly, folding up his newspaper. "Come on gorgeous – time for breakfast." He led her into a breakfast-dining room, which thankfully, was far less formal than the other rooms. A continental breakfast awaited them.

They sat adjacent to one another, at a circular, polished oak table. When they had eaten, Patrick suggested that, for the most part, they remain within the environs of the house and garden for the first day or two, until she had adjusted to her new surroundings. Fiona was happy to agree. That would be more than enough to handle, for the time being.

CHAPTER ELEVEN

Patrick gave her a grand tour of the house, followed by the gardens, which he drove her around, in a type of golf cart. The grounds of the estate were truly magnificent, covering several acres. They appeared to have been created, if not by Capability Brown, then at least by his Canadian counterpart! At the outer reaches of the estate, elegant lawns sloped gently down to the water's edge, providing an absolutely stunning view, across a wide bay area.

Patrick explained that, geographically speaking, this stretch of water, between themselves and the Vancouver mainland, was known as the *Strait of Georgia*. Not only did the strait provide a fantastic view, it was actually a neck of water connecting two seas. It was these same waters which flowed into their bay area.

A few yards away from the water's edge and at a considerable distance from the mansion stood a spectacular Victorian conservatory. Patrick took great pleasure in showing her around it. It consisted mostly of glass. Vast shafts of sunlight were streaming in. One half was furnished with ornamental furniture and a lavish array of plants; the other side, furthest away from the water, but still affording a partial view of the lake, had been converted by Patrick, into a studio. It contained an easel and painting equipment, plus several items of fairly worn furniture.

The two halves of this substantial glass building were divided by a large, but very attractive mobile screen of Japanese silk, split into four sections; each decorated with oriental bridges, trees and exotic flowers. The size, arrangement and location of the screen could be adjusted, according to the occasion.

They drove back towards an octagonal-shaped summerhouse, adjacent to the main building. Maggie, the housekeeper, whom Fiona had met on arrival, brought lunch out to the summerhouse for them. She wheeled it out on a glass trolley. Fiona rose quickly to help her, as she steered the heavily laden trolley up a short ramp and into the outbuilding. She had been obliged to wheel it out, through one of the mansion's side entrances, then a few yards across the lawn.

"Ah, don't fuss, me darlin'," she said. "Sure, the exercise will do me good!"

"She doesn't have to do this on a daily basis, you know," Patrick reassured her, once Maggie had left. "This *is* a very special occasion."

He explained that he had six staff working for him altogether. Maggie and his butler and manservant Charles, both lived on the premises. The remainder, who all lived locally, consisted of a chauffeur, gardener, housemaid and cook.

CHAPTER TWELVE

The third day of her visit fell on a Wednesday. Patrick had given her prior warning, that she was to have the dubious honour, as he put it, of being introduced to his two sisters. Patrick had seniority, as he was forty-two; Kathleen, at thirty-nine, was three years younger; Anna, the youngest of the three, was thirty-two: just a year younger than Fiona.

The sisters had lived with Patrick in the family home, until their respective marriages. Anna, the youngest, married a banker from an affluent local family. Kathleen's husband was a horticulturist, who ran his own, extensive family business. It had proved particularly lucrative in this wealthy *bay* area of Victoria; almost every home had its own variety of spectacular landscaped gardens, although relatively few were as extensive as the Maitland Estate.

The plan was that the four of them would begin with a grand tour of the centre of Victoria, aided and abetted by the chauffeur. Following lunch, the next 'port-of-call' would be the *Pacific Undersea Gardens,* which, by all accounts, were quite an experience!

Although normally reasonably self-confident, Fiona was rather apprehensive as she entered the drawing room. Anna and Kathleen were seated alongside each other, on the leather sofa. Her nervousness, she guessed, was because they were all family; having only known Patrick for a short while she still felt like an outsider.

The differences between the two sisters were apparent to Fiona, from the moment that Patrick introduced them. Anna was exuberant, direct and demonstrative. Kathleen, on the other hand, was more darkly reserved, with an acerbic tongue that might easily be construed as malicious. Anna had a similar, svelte figure to Fiona, but was an inch taller than Fiona's five foot seven inches. She was very attractive, with long, curly blonde hair and twinkling blue eyes. In contrast, Kathleen had a dark-haired, almost elfin beauty of her own, and was slightly smaller than Fiona. Her deep brown eyes bore a serious expression. Her hair was well groomed, in a short, cropped style. At that first meeting, she appeared to be more of an intellectual than Anna.

Whilst Patrick went to the kitchen, to arrange coffee, Anna quickly took Fiona by the arm, leading her to a corner of the room. "It's so good to meet

CHAPTER TWELVE

you at last," she said quietly, in a cultured Canadian accent. "Paddy simply *dotes* on you, did you know that? He's done nothing but talk about you since his return from the islands."

It took Fiona a second or two to realise that *Paddy* was Anna's nickname for Patrick. She hadn't thought of him as a Paddy, prior to that. "Where are your manners Anna!" admonished her more severe sister, coming over to join them. "Leave the poor girl alone! She doesn't want you pawing her and fawning over her, at your very first meeting." Fiona was about to remark that she didn't mind at all – in fact, she rather welcomed it, when she was stopped in her tracks, by the stony expression on Kathleen's face. Although she wasn't a scheming person by inclination, she realised that she would have to adopt a different approach, according to which sister she was with.

* * * *

The four of them sat drinking coffee. "Paddy tells us that you've taken up painting, under his *expert* tuition," said Anna enthusiastically; she was obviously very proud of her elder brother. They discussed the subject, for a while. Suddenly Kathleen said, "It must seem very *strange* to you, I guess, and perhaps a little disconcerting, coming to a house of this type, when you've been living in such a small place yourself." There was a painful silence. Fiona replied bravely.

"Well, my house isn't exactly *small*, you know." "Perhaps not, but you can hardly be described as *wealthy*, now can you. Also, what is it you do? Oh yes, let me see… you work in a bookshop, don't you?"

Fiona began to grow *very* hot under the collar. "I think, don't you," she answered, with all the sweetness she could muster, "that one's nature and the manner in which one relates to people, is of infinitely greater importance, than the amount of money one happens to possess."

For a split second Kathleen paused. Then, not prepared to be outdone, she continued in an exaggerated, sarcastic drawl: "Well, you know – the fact that we have servants here to do all the menial chores. It must be very galling not be able to afford one's own servants… not even a *maid*, for heaven's sake!"

Fiona rose to her feet, then headed straight out of the room, muttering about having "something in her eye." She ran straight through the breakfast room and out of a side door, into the garden. From there she headed for the summerhouse. "For Chrissake Kathleen! What the *hell's* gotten into you!" Patrick roared at her.

He slammed down his coffee cup. Having seen Fiona dash across the lawns, he took the short cut, throwing open the French windows, which led directly from the drawing room into the gardens. Patrick ran swiftly across the lawns, in hot pursuit.

She was sitting on the grass, in front of the summerhouse, crying with frustration. He helped her to her feet, hugging and kissing her so tightly, that she thought she might suffocate. "Don't cry darling – please don't cry," he implored. "For God's sake, *ignore* the sanctimonious bitch. She really isn't worth it!"

Fiona felt faint, so he helped her to sit down again on the bank, this time joining her. Speechless and upset, she felt like returning home immediately. Her hands were shaking. Patrick offered a large handkerchief – to dry her eyes.

"You said it didn't matter Patrick," she said, between sobs. "I couldn't care less about your bloody money. I didn't even know about it for God's sake!" "I know that honey," he reassured her. "Problem is Kathleen suspects the worst." They sat in silence for a while.

"I would never condone what she said to you," Patrick continued vehemently. "On the other hand, I can understand her *motive*. You see Fiona," he explained, placing an arm around her shoulder and guiding her head, so that it rested comfortably on his shoulder, "she thinks she has justification. In the past... and in the case of one woman in particular, before I met Julia, I was cruelly deceived. It's extremely difficult, when you're wealthy, to know if someone loves you purely for yourself, rather than for your money. I've been so badly hurt in the past – almost suicidal. I think Kathleen's probably afraid that history might repeat itself."

As he finished speaking, they were aware of soft footsteps, on the grass behind them. Turning around, they saw Anna. Her face was flushed – as though she had been arguing. Seating herself on the other side of Fiona, she placed an arm around her waist. "Please don't be upset Fiona," she pleaded. "Kathleen's bark is worse than her bite. You see, she believes that she's protecting Paddy. Do come back to the house."

As the three of them returned slowly back, across the lawns, Anna explained, "Kathleen's had some awful experiences herself, in that respect. One or two of her past suitors only wanted her for her money too. She became very embittered. She gave poor Pete a *really* hard time, before he married her. Thought he was a gold digger – until the poor guy pointed out that his folks could probably buy and sell us three times over – called him a common labourer, so she did. It hadn't registered that he was the owner of a multi-million dollar landscape business. Oh brother – was that a showdown!"

CHAPTER TWELVE

As they neared the house, Kathleen was standing outside the open French windows, waiting for them and watching closely; her arms folded across her chest. She seemed more contrite and subdued and had red patches on her cheeks – but she said nothing. Fifteen minutes later, they were preparing to leave, in the grey Bentley. Patrick was in the passenger seat alongside the chauffeur; Anna waited patiently in the back.

As Kathleen and Fiona were about to walk towards the car, Kathleen suddenly pulled her to one side, so that for a few seconds, they were both half concealed by one of the large Doric pillars. "Look Fiona," she said, still somewhat curtly, "I have to say that I owe you an apology. It's just that I couldn't stand to see Patrick hurt again. Since Julia died, he's not had any real happiness. Guess I've let my concern for him override my sense of your British *fair play*."

"I understand what you're saying," Fiona replied, "but could we please get one thing straight? I care a great deal about your brother, but I don't want his money and I don't *need* his money." "Okay… Fine… I'll take your word for it… friends?" Kathleen asked, offering her hand. "Yes, I think so," Fiona agreed, whilst shaking her hand. They began to approach the car once more, which was parked a little way out, along the drive. Suddenly, Fiona stopped short. Turning to Kathleen again she said: "There is just one matter though." "Oh, what's that?" "If you *ever* speak to me again, in that manner, I shall slap your sarcastic, sanctimonious face!" Fiona snarled at her. Then she added, sweetly, "Is that clear?"

"*Absolutely* clear," replied Kathleen, obviously well satisfied, and also much relieved. 'The girl's got spirit', she thought. 'I think I'm going to like her!' "Everything sorted ladies?" enquired Patrick, with a smile, and a twinkle in his eye, as they got into the car.

The remainder of the day went well. The chauffeur drove them into the centre of Victoria and then part of the way around. He eventually parked the car just around the corner from the enormous Parliament Buildings. It seemed to Fiona, as a newcomer, that such a grandiose structure was a little 'over-the-top' for a provincial town. The Canadian maple leaf lag flew majestically from the mast above.

They transferred to one of the horse-drawn charabancs, a popular but expensive tourist attraction. The charabancs had attractive red-and-white striped canopies, instead of roofs. The wheel hubs and seats were red; a pair of magnificent brown, red-plumed horses drew each carriage.

Normally, each vehicle carried six to eight passengers, but Patrick decided to reserve a whole charabanc entirely for themselves; for their own private tour. The name 'Tallyho' was emblazoned on the side of the carriage, each letter being centred within a large and separate, pastel-coloured card.

The coachman gave them a scenic tour of the city, pointing out all the significant buildings and landmarks. The entire trip took an hour and a half. It included some of Victoria's loveliest homes and gardens, together with points of historical interest. In addition, they were able to see more of the city centre, plus Chinatown and Antique Row.

Fiona would have liked more time to explore the fascinating inner harbour area. It held a special significance for her, as the place where she had disembarked. However, she consoled herself with the fact that they were to have lunch at a favourite seafood restaurant of Patrick's, close to the harbour. He assured her that there would be plenty of time during the remainder of the holiday, to explore other areas that appealed to her. He had already planned more private excursions, for just the two of them.

That afternoon the four of them visited the *Undersea Gardens*; situated, to her surprise, on a huge boat. The Gardens, at the south west entrance to the Inner Harbour area, were a giant floating museum of marine life. They descended into the bowels of the vessel, via a steep flight of steps. Each step was illuminated with rows of fairy lights – like strings of enchanted pearls.

Once inside, they viewed a series of large fresh water tanks, set out in a special sequence, following the outline of the vessel. There must have been at least thirty or forty such tanks, each containing its own fascinating display of marine life, ranging from crabs to octopuses.

The highlight of the visit was the most enormous underwater tank of all, actually located under the sea itself. A diver conducted the show from inside the tank, whilst a young blonde woman provided a running commentary about the sea creatures. As each creature was mentioned, the diver brought it to the window of the tank for the audience to view; like a compère, introducing a series of celebrities.

Patrick sat next to Fiona. He reached for her hand in the darkness. Anna and Kathleen were a short distance away, on the same long wooden bench. The tank was brightly illuminated – the water within being a vivid green. It was just like being at the cinema, except that the performers were live and there was no popcorn!

The diver was a great showman. He waved to the audience, and obviously had a great sense of humour. One of the creatures he displayed was an enormous, but hideous grey wolf eel, with bulbous eyes and sharp jagged teeth. Its looks, however, belied its disposition; it was very friendly and played games with the diver, delighting the audience with its antics.

CHAPTER TWELVE

As they sat in the semi-darkness, listening to the commentary, which lasted about half an hour, the woman's voice gradually, grew fainter and fainter. Fiona felt herself drifting off… into another dimension…

She was no longer in Victoria. Her memory drifted back to Thursday of the previous week. Robert had telephoned her; she had been amazed by this, as the cost of a long distance call from Greece, of about six minutes duration, would surely have been prohibitive.

He was suggesting that in the circumstances she should allow him to do most of the talking. Her latest letter had just reached him in Skiathos. Following his marriage proposal, she had felt compelled to ask him for an explanation about the early morning beach scene, between himself and Lydia.

He assured her that there had never been a sexual relationship between him and Lydia; she was far too young for that to ever be the case. She must learn to trust him implicitly; such trust was vital, he added, if their relationship was to flourish.

His principal reason for phoning was that it was the last opportunity for him to make contact, before his voyage to Crete. Robert had been giving a great deal of thought to Fiona's arrangement with Patrick: her forthcoming Canadian trip. Patrick, he said, although outwardly a gregarious person, was at heart, an intensely private man. The fact that he had actually invited her to stay at his private residence, for a whole month, must therefore be extremely significant.

"Let me put it like this," he explained. "I don't think that what he has in mind for you involves a scenic tour of the Rockies, or sampling the delights of the Maple Country Cookies!"

At this point, she recalled, there had been some interference on the line. He had been shouting for much of the duration of the call. When the line began to crackle and deteriorate his voice suddenly grew much fainter, but she was still just about able to distinguish his words: "Hold steadfast to our agreement Fi. Remember that my love for you will never diminish. I'll have to go…." At this point, they were rapidly losing the connection. She was just able to hear him say,

"Goodbye for now, darling… keep safe. I love you."

A peal of laughter shattered her daydream. Fiona was startled to find herself back watching the underwater show. She could hear the commentator announcing, "Ladies and gentlemen, here we have Armstrong, our *very* own Pacific Octopus."

Her eyes re-focused on the illuminated aquarium. The cause of the laughter, she guessed, was probably the witty choice of name, or maybe the way in which the diver was playing with the salmon pink octopus. It had a rash of large white suckers on the underside of each of its huge tentacles. Its colour made it stand out clearly against the vivid green water, as did the diver, who wore a bright red wet-suit. The audience found it quite incredible that he was actually *playing* with this exotic but potentially dangerous creature. Such a degree of sympathetic interaction was only possible, according to the commentator, because their divers had formed a bond of friendship and trust with many of the creatures. The diver further demonstrated a sense of humour, by means of his own solo performance; behaving as though he were an exhibit too, he waved to the audience, grinned, turned somersaults and blew bubbles at them!

The show completed, the four of them emerged, blinking, into the bright sunlight of Victoria. Anna linked arms with her affectionately, as they strolled along the downtown streets; exploring them and investigating an array of shops. Fiona noticed baskets overflowing with flowers, dangling from cinque-globed lampposts, situated at intervals along the streets.

The air was filled with the Canadian accents of pedestrians, intermingled with both their British and more cosmopolitan counterparts. Fiona noticed signs, pointing to the Maritime Museum: she could think of at least *one* individual who would have been particularly fascinated by such a place.

Kathleen explained, as they made their way back to the huge, domed Parliament Buildings, that at night the rooflines and green cupolas of the buildings were festooned with multi-coloured fairy lights. Even as a young child, she observed, it had seemed incongruous to her that such dainty lights should be used to decorate such massive buildings – like fleas on an elephant!

The chauffeur finally collected them at just after five o'clock in the evening. Anna lived within a few miles of Victoria. She and Kathleen were dropped off at the gateways to their respective, homes. In Kathleen's case, this involved taking a considerable detour, before returning to *Tralee*. On parting, both sisters kissed Fiona, each suggesting further meetings, in the near future. Anna gave her an affectionate hug. By the time they returned to *Tralee*, Fiona was exhausted. It had been a long day. Patrick helped her out of the car, leaving the chauffeur to drive it round to the garages, at the rear of the house.

Later still that evening, after a sumptuous meal, specially prepared by cook, the two of them ascended the staircase. This time, however, instead of Fiona retiring to the green room, Patrick suggested that she should join

CHAPTER TWELVE

him in his own, even grander apartment. "I'm hoping that you've had enough time for settling in, darling," he observed.

Fiona lay beside him in a huge, unfamiliar, four-poster bed. Patrick wore only pyjama trousers. She was wearing a beautiful green satin nightdress; each strap decorated with a daisy-shaped silk flower. It clung to her shapely, nubile body, accentuating all of her contours and curves. Such close proximity to Patrick, during the past few days, after a dearth of intimacy, had already succeeded in inflaming her desire. Patrick moved the bedclothes away from her. Lying on his side, he allowed his eyes to rake her body, with obvious pleasure.

"Oh God!" he moaned. She put her hands around his tanned, muscular shoulders, then moved slowly down, examining his hairy chest. They slipped off his trousers and her nightdress, so that they were both totally naked. "It's been a *long* time, honey," he whispered hoarsely. "Come on darling," he urged, as they began to make love. Patrick grabbed her right hand, and held it tightly.

A short while later, he said, very seriously, "You have to stop taking the pill – right away. Remember… we talked about it on Skiathos. I just can't stand the thought of you taking it any longer."

"I'd no way of knowing how it was going to be between us, at least, not for certain," she explained. Secretly, she was thinking, 'How on earth can I stop? What about Robert – he'd never forgive me!' She continued, "I thought it better to wait and see; to give ourselves time. What if you decided you'd made a mistake? I don't want to bring an innocent child into the world on that basis. It just wouldn't be right."

Patrick paused momentarily, then asked, "Do you recall my telling you on Skiathos that Julia died in childbirth? I mean, she was only twenty-six years old – you know?" His voice began to break. "I've been so traumatised… for such a long time. Having a child with any other woman has remained totally out of the question – it would have seemed like betrayal… somehow." He regarded her intently. "I lost Julia nine years ago. Since then, my life has been one long saga of change and bereavement. I've had nothing of real… value… or permanence – that is – until now.

"I want to make you pregnant," he continued. "I want us to… extend the Maitland family line. I honestly never thought Fi, that I'd *ever* hear myself say that again – you have to believe me!" He was close to tears. Fiona pulled him to her, kissing him ardently. With each passing day, her need for him had been intensifying. Dramatically. Now, it was almost impossible for her to bear. What could she to do? There seemed to be absolutely no escape from such a dilemma. She couldn't possibly abandon him, under such circumstances. It would be totally heartless.

Words from the ballad, which she'd heard that evening on Skiathos, came flooding back to her:

Thinking of two lovers
Loving them the same
Loving's for eternity – it isn't just a game.

CHAPTER THIRTEEN

The following day was a Thursday. This was traditionally the servants' day off, giving Patrick and Fiona the opportunity to be alone together. Fiona discovered yet again, that Patrick had risen early – and prepared a light breakfast for the two of them. Seated at the table, she demanded, "Why are you always up ahead of me?"

"We – ell," he drawled, "It's to do with... the light." As she looked decidedly puzzled, he clarified the matter. "Ya see, since way back, when I was a student of Fine Arts, at the university, in Victoria, maybe even before that, light has always played a crucial part in my work. For example," he continued, "the quality of light, as you know, varies according to the time of day, seasons, and so forth. If I wanted a certain effect for one of my paintings, I'd have to be up at the crack of dawn – to capture it. Guess over the years, the habit has remained."

They were still in their dressing gowns, having decided to take full advantage of the servants' absence. After the previous night's lovemaking, Fiona felt much more relaxed in Patrick's company. Breakfast completed, she linked her arm through his, kissing him tenderly on the lips. He responded at once with a more lingering version. As they rose to their feet he kissed her ferociously, his tongue moving deep inside her mouth: playing havoc with her senses. Finally he released her. They were both breathless.

"Come on," he said, "before we're totally fazed. There's something I want to show you." He led her up the winding staircase, then up two additional flights of stairs, until they had reached the top storey of the house – a part of the building that she hadn't yet seen.

They walked along the top corridor, then turned right, through a set of white, colonial style double doors. She found herself in an enormous, high-ceilinged, corniced library. Huge bookcases filled with all manner of books, lined the major part of the room.

In the centre of the library was a long, highly polished mahogany table, in Sheraton style: dating from the Georgian period. Fiona immediately recognised the design, as she had a reproduction version, at home in England – although judging by the Maitland family fortune, this was probably the genuine article! The accessories suggested that the table served a dual function: for important meetings and elegant dinner parties. Fiona could imagine such parties; she marvelled at the sheer style and opulence of the setting. Two large library windows overlooked the grounds, at the front of the house. The fountained courtyard below appeared even more impressive, from this vantage point.

Taking her hand, Patrick led her towards a recess in the wall, to the right-hand side of the double doors. He switched on a brass spot-lamp, which illuminated the whole area. To her astonishment, an entire family tree was displayed there, in photographic form. His maternal grandmother, Rosaleen Kirkpatrick, originally began the wall. Her photograph was at the base or trunk of the tree, alongside that of her husband, James Maitland, 1906–1972. Her photograph bore her name and the dates, 1905–1970.

His paternal grandfather's family had been bankers, spanning at least two centuries. "Émigrés from the Home Counties originally," Patrick explained, with a twinkle in his eye. "Grandmother, on the other hand, came from rough Irish peasant stock. Her family were originally from Tralee, in Southern Ireland – hence the name of the house. They were a bunch of *grafters* though – or so I've been told. The guys in the earlier generation of the family worked as navvies on the railways, when they first came over here.

"My great grandparents were both from that part of Ireland, you know? Not far from Killarney, near Bantry Bay," he continued. "Sure, it's a grand part of the world, all right. We still have folks living there. Being a musical family, we've flown over for the Celtic Music Festival in Tralee, several times; stayed with descendants of the original family – had a grand old time. Grandpa and his brothers pulled themselves up by their bootstraps; made a whole pile of money over here. Guess it was the heyday of the railways, back then."

"Did they settle in Victoria originally?" asked Fiona; his family history seemed such an intriguing one. "No, my grandparents settled initially in Quebec, then worked their way across Canada, by degrees. By the time Rosaleen was ten years old, they'd begun to move up the social scale. That's the reason they moved out to Victoria."

"But why settle in Quebec?" wondered Fiona. "They were Catholics. Sure, Quebec was a Catholic province – made things a whole lot easier for them – in the early days," explained Patrick. "Anyways, as you can see, Grandma married James Maitland," he continued, indicating the photograph. "They married when she was just twenty years of age – a mere slip of a girl. By that time she was an heiress."

CHAPTER THIRTEEN

"It was certainly a good match… financially at least," observed Fiona.

"'Twas a great deal more than *that* my girl," he corrected her. "It was also a grand love match if ever there was one. They named me after the Kirkpatricks, you know!"

Following the branches of the tree upwards, she was startled to discover a photograph of Patrick, with Julia alongside him. She was an attractive, blue-eyed blonde… her face was serene and smiling.

Noting her reaction, Patrick admitted, "I hesitated to show you this room until now; especially after that fiasco with Kathleen, the other day."

"That's okay darling," she said, linking her arm through his. "I think my ego can stand it. Besides," she added, "she looks such a caring sort of person… was she?" "Oh yes… indeed she was," he sighed, his eyes suddenly moist at the thought of her. "And now me girl," he said, switching to mock Irish brogue, "'I'm after taking you below… for a trip in me boat!"

As they left the room, Patrick closed the double doors behind them. Placing one hand on her shoulder, whilst turning her towards him, he whispered, conspiratorially: "I'm thinking of adding another branch to Grandma's tree… quite soon."

"Are you now?" Fiona half joked with him, but her legs felt as though they might buckle beneath her, at any moment. Descending to the second floor, they went to their respective bedrooms to change into more suitable clothing. Having changed, she seated herself at the dressing table and took out her jewellery case – she needed some immediate reassurance. Contemplating her reflection closely in the mirror, she could feel her resolve about keeping her relationship with Patrick strictly on a light-hearted basis, continuing to ebb away, at an alarming rate.

Regarding the jewellery case, with some trepidation, she unzipped a small section inside it, removing a tiny tissue-wrapped package. Nestling right in the centre of the paper was the precious antique gold ring, which Robert had given her. Placing it in the palm of her left hand, she began to examine the engravings.

So engrossed was she, in examining the fine details of the ring, that she was oblivious to anything else. Robert had intended his gift to serve as a talisman: a constant reminder of the unshakable bond that had been forged between them; a charm to keep her safe, until he could return safely to her.

"That's a helluva ring, I must say!" Fiona nearly jumped out of her skin. When she turned around she was painfully aware that she was blushing. "I'm sorry if I startled you darling," said Patrick, "but the last time I saw anything resembling that, was in an Art History book."

Fiona muttered something about it being a family heirloom and quickly replaced it in the case, making a mental note to find a more secret hiding place, at the first opportunity.

* * * *

A few minutes later, all thoughts of the ring apparently forgotten, Fiona found herself at the passenger end of a rowing boat, heading out into the bay. Patrick was rowing smartly towards a small island, located a half mile or so from the water's edge. Five minutes later, with assistance from him, she stepped out onto a jetty and from there onto a mossy green bank.

He had brought a wicker picnic hamper, carefully prepared by cook, to his instructions, the previous evening. They carried the basket between them, to a small clearing in the centre of the islet; placing it alongside a rough wooden bench, which had been built by James Maitland, many years before. Spreading a red-and-white checked tablecloth, they ate lunch at once, as it was about noon.

As they lay sprawled out on the grass, enjoying their meal, Fiona remarked, "I know this sounds totally crazy, but this is rather like that episode from *The Wind in the Willows*, by Kenneth Grahame. D'you know it? The part where Ratty rows Mole across the water for a picnic, and they have a wicker hamper with them. I've read it hundreds of times, to pupils; it's one of my favourites."

"Yes, it's a classic: I know it well," replied Patrick, much to her surprise.

"Ya know, I can't help wondering if my father, God-rest-his-soul, only bought me that damn book, because of Grahame's financial connections. Guess he'd been a kind of role model for him, as a boy, you see – almost a folk hero! As he was fond of telling me, Grahame was not only a first-rate storyteller, he was also a Scot, who at the age of thirty-nine was the youngest ever Secretary of the Bank of England."

"Surely that wasn't the only reason?" replied Fiona. "I mean, the story's enjoyable for its own sake." "Ah, but you didn't know my father me darlin': obsessed with all things financial, he was!" replied Patrick. "He was *so* determined to make a banker of me. Poor guy... didn't stand a snowball's chance in hell!"

Having re-packed the basket with the remains of the picnic, they stowed it under the bench. "We'll leave it there for a while. Follow me," he commanded. He led her to a secluded spot, just a short distance from the clearing, surrounded on three sides by overhanging trees and plants. A

CHAPTER THIRTEEN

fourth side led down to the water's edge. There was a gap in the undergrowth, through which the water could be seen.

"This was a favourite spot, for Anna and myself," he explained, "since she was old enough to hold a sketchpad and pencil. The two of us used to row across here – we'd sketch for hours. It's an artists' paradise, with the wild life and all – our own secret place. My sister's very talented you know. She had her own full-time freelance business, before she married and had kids. Ah, but didn't we have a grand time of it out here!"

"What did she do exactly?" asked Fiona. "Not *did* but *does*," corrected Patrick. "She still runs the business on a part-time basis – illustrating children's books; designing greetings cards, stationery and so forth. All the designs are taken straight from nature.

I call her my Canadian Beatrix Potter – and I love her dearly," he added. "I know – I can tell," said Fiona. "The feeling's obviously mutual."

The hot afternoon sun was beating down upon the little islet, making their secluded haven all the more welcoming. Slowly, they removed their clothing, lying naked in each other's arms. "Did you take your pill this morning?" asked Patrick. "No. I'm not sure why," she replied. "Perhaps it was last night that persuaded me?"

"That's just fine by me," beamed Patrick, his hands stroking her breasts very gently. "Make me a promise, Fi," he said softly. Unlike Robert, Patrick very rarely used the abbreviated form of her name. She found that she liked it – more than she could have imagined. "Promise me," he continued, "that when we get back to the house, you'll trash your entire supply of pills." "What – all two month's supply?" "That's the deal." With that, he lowered himself on top of her and they began to make love, to a steady rhythm. Apart from their sighs, and lovemaking, all that could be heard was the gentle lapping of the water around them.

Suddenly, a strange sensation came over Fiona, making the hairs on the back of her neck stand on end. Looking up, she couldn't believe the surreal nature of what she was experiencing. Instead of Patrick's face looking down on her, it was *Robert's*! She froze… in panic… and immediately stopped moving.

Two seconds later, Patrick was looking down at her again – with obvious distress: "What is it Fi? Are you okay? You look as if you've seen a ghost!"

"I'm … I'm sorry Pat," she stammered. " It's nothing… nothing at all."

They resumed their lovemaking. Fiona was gradually becoming more and more aroused; Patrick's manoeuvrings were becoming more erotic, with each passing second.

But then she felt the same sensation again. Only this time it was even more pronounced. Something was happening which was totally beyond her comprehension. Once again, Robert's dark, swarthy face was moving above her. But this time, even the body above her had changed. It was that of a taller, heavier man, much closer to Robert's physique than Patrick's!

A split second later, it was as though Robert was actually there – taking her to great heights of ecstasy. "No, no, stop!" she cried out. But whoever, or *whatever* it was, *couldn't* stop, as great ripples of release shot through her. Then she rolled over and lay very still… exhausted, and unable to move: in a trance-like state.

Regaining her senses, she opened her eyes. Someone was calling her, from a distance: "Fi, Fi!" Her eyes focused: Patrick was leaning over her; his naked body against hers; stroking her forehead. "Fiona honey, what happened? What the *hell's* the matter?" He was yelling at her, in obvious bewilderment. As she recovered her senses, Patrick realised that she was in a state of shock.

"What happened darling? One moment you were with me, the next I thought you'd passed out! I'd better get you home." She was shivering with cold. While they dressed quickly, he tried to make light of it: "Don't you go catching anything at this stage, young lady. I can't have you ill for the rest of the month!" Secretly, he was really worried about her: she looked as white as a sheet. She sat down by the boat, far too exhausted to do anything else, while Patrick collected the now much lighter picnic basket.

By the time they'd returned to the house she'd begun to recover. Patrick felt guilty. Perhaps he'd been overdoing it, he thought ruefully; they *had* been rather going at it. Although with a woman like Fiona, he reasoned, a guy can't exactly blame himself!

CHAPTER FOURTEEN

After resting on the drawing room sofa for an hour or so, she felt much better. However, she still had no rational explanation for what had happened, over on the island. Nothing that appeared to make any kind of sense, that is.

Perhaps she was losing her sanity? Maybe the cumulative strain was to blame? After all, in the space of just three months, her whole world had been turned completely, and irrevocably, upside-down.

That evening she and Patrick enjoyed a quiet meal together. As it was cook's day off, Fiona produced a simple spaghetti bolognaise, washed down with a bottle of Chianti, which Patrick had selected from the cellar. They ate in the much grander dining room: across the hall, from the smaller and more intimate breakfast room.

Patrick arranged the table especially for the occasion, using the best silver and cut glass goblets. Fiona had laughingly protested that it was only a simple meal: totally unworthy of such grandeur. Patrick was much relieved to see her restored to her normal good-natured self; however he insisted that she should humour him in this respect. He seemed to regard it as a kind of game. To heighten the sense of occasion still further, he suggested that they dress for dinner.

He wore the same smart outfit that he had worn on that memorable evening at *Taverna Persephone*. Fiona chose a long black skirt, combined with a shimmering Italian-design evening top, decorated with gold sequins.

The serviettes, or *napkins* as Patrick called them, were of dark burgundy linen, rolled between silver serviette rings. Initially, Fiona had found it quite difficult to accustom herself to the vagaries of the Canadian language. Gradually, however, it was becoming more familiar. The boot of the car was the *trunk*, the bonnet was the *hood;* a dressing gown was a *bathrobe* and a hall was referred to as a *vestibule* or *lobby*, in some cases. Serviettes were *napkins*; napkins were *diapers* and so on.

After dinner Patrick presented her with two gift-wrapped packages. Kathleen had dropped off the larger of the two at the house the previous morning. The gift tag read, '*A peace offering – looking forward to seeing you again*'.

She opened it. It was a large box of *Rogers' Chocolates*, presented in a red rectangular box, trimmed with golden edges. In the centre of the lid was a picture of the Parliament Buildings – of all places! Patrick explained that *Rogers* were an old established firm, famous throughout Canada for their confectionery. Their local premises were close to the Art Gallery in the centre of Victoria; they had passed them on the charabanc ride. He suggested a closer inspection, some time.

The second, much smaller package, was from Patrick. It was a Fabian Dawson CD. While they were in Greece, Fiona had mentioned that he was her favourite male singer. Patrick played the CD for her, after they adjourned to the drawing room, for coffee. At a certain point he stopped the music. Taking her by the hand, he said very quietly, "I bought it for you for a special reason Fi. I have an identical copy myself. During those weeks when we were separated, before I could see you again, I was haunted by feelings of desperation: like some kind of premonition. They kept returning... couldn't get them out of my head. Ya see, I kept imagining you in someone else's arms – making love to another man. Can you believe it?!"

The expression in Fiona's eyes, as he made this confession, slowly changed to one of bewilderment. She said absolutely nothing. What could she say? "I'm sorry Patrick, but your instincts were absolutely right?" There was no way that she could hurt him that deeply.

"There are some lines in one particular number," he continued, "which say it all." He found it on the disc. "This is the song: it's called *I'm Oh So Blue*. This is the part," he said, as he listened apprehensively.

> *Think about you day and night*
> *But something's happening that's just not right.*
> *Got a feeling, oh so strong*
> *Come back to me, where you belong.*

The song continued as they drank their coffee in silence. The CD played on, while they slid down onto the sofa and made passionate love. This time however, the music had a profound effect upon Fiona. She suddenly realised, in a single, lucid moment, the true depth of Patrick's love for her. The realisation released such passion in her, that she made love to him, free from all inhibition.

As she lay in Patrick's large double bed that evening, staring up at the fringed canopy, the memory of that revelation returned. Any deception on her part had only been possible while she thought that Patrick's love for

CHAPTER FOURTEEN

her might change. Up until this point, she had managed to convince herself that such a strategy was purely for her own protection.

Now however, she lay tossing and turning with indecision. Owing to the sheer size of the four-poster bed, Patrick slept peacefully beside her – unaware of her restlessness.

Why, oh why, did I ever take that Greek holiday? She knew that she had done so for the most sensible of motives: the need to escape from her worries; to shake herself out of a depression and give her a clearer perspective on life.

However, the nagging voices inside her persisted – like a two-way argument. *Ah yes, but if you'd stayed at home, life would be far less complicated.* In the event, Fate had transformed her, from a caring, level-headed widow, into little more than a two-timing conniving bitch!

She had been attempting the impossible: to remain faithful to two lovers at one and the same time. It *couldn't* be done. How could she have ever thought it possible? Her conscience was torturing her – almost beyond endurance. Maybe she should just catch the next plane back to England: simply try to forget Patrick and wait... until Robert contacted her? Then perhaps this nightmare would finally be over.

After attempting to sleep for a couple more hours, she gave up, slipping quietly out of bed and into her slippers. With her silk dressing gown draped over her shoulders, she carefully opened the large, frosted-glass doors, on the right-hand side of the bedroom. They led directly onto a balcony, with a distant view of the bay.

Softly, she closed the doors behind her, anxious not to disturb Patrick, and to be alone with her thoughts. She gazed out uneasily, towards the moonlit bay; as if something out there might provide the solution that she so desperately needed. As the water was a fair distance away, she took a pair of binoculars, from a special holder, close to the balcony rail. They provided the magnificent, yet soothing sight that she was seeking. The light from the full moon was reflected in the ripples of water. Silhouetted against the sky, were the dark trees of the island. Adjusting the focus on the binoculars brought everything into stark relief.

There was a panoramic expanse of water, as far as the eye could see. It seemed so vast and eternal. As she gazed reflectively across the bay, her thoughts returned once more to Robert. She knew that he was somewhere out there... but thousands of miles away. He and Andreas, sailing in *Silver's Arrow*, on the Ionian Seas.

She wondered where he was, at that precise moment. What was he doing? Had they found the shipwreck? Having found it, would he finally be able to settle down, his ambitions realised – and be at peace with himself? She prayed for some kind of guidance or insight.

As these thoughts ran through her mind she felt a pair of strong hands on her shoulders. It was Patrick. He had woken and seeing only an empty space beside him had come to find her – to make sure that she was safe.

"It's beautiful, isn't it darling?" he murmured. "Mother used to love it… said it reminded her of County Kerry, back in the Old Country; all the lakes… and the green of it all." They both stood, gazing out at the view, for a little while longer. As they returned to their warm bed, Patrick said: "Fiona love. Something happened tonight, now didn't it?" "Yes Pat," she agreed, smiling at him and squeezing his hand. "I don't understand exactly what it was," he continued. "All I do know is that you truly gave yourself to me. I know that you've been holding back from me, from the moment you arrived. Sure, it's been like a chasm between us. Suddenly, that feeling's gone." Fiona made no further comment, but snuggled her head into the protective cradle of his body, and fell into a contented, untroubled sleep.

* * * *

The following week seemed to fly by. Patrick had booked a table for afternoon tea, at the *Empress Hotel*, in the centre of Victoria. It was one of Anna's favourite places; she described it as "an unforgettable experience."

The walls and front entrance of the *Empress*, including both pillars, were almost entirely enveloped in a gigantic waistcoat of ivy. Patrick had reserved a table for exactly three that afternoon. The flight of white stone steps leading up to the entrance was swamped by a host of visitors, ascending and descending from its hallowed portals – like Jacob's Ladder – minus the angels!

Two white Victorian lamps, each crowned by a single globe, stood either side of the entrance, resting on columns of white stone slabs. Red salvias paraded in neat rows just outside the building, at pavement level. A huge feathery conifer stood sentinel, to the right of the entrance. The decoration above the doorway was in Palladian style, embellished with a green and white crest above the portal. Multi-coloured flowers, cascading from hanging baskets, enhanced the sheer elegance of the place.

The old colonial image of the *Empress* was reinforced, as they entered the lounge area. There was the usual cosmopolitan mix of expensively-attired tourists, found in many sophisticated international hotels. Added to this however, were a large number of elderly ladies, dressed in cardigans, sensible shoes and tweed suits – like a Miss Marples Convention! It was

CHAPTER FOURTEEN

difficult to distinguish between those who were bona fide British Columbians of British descent, and others, possibly from the Home Counties or English seaside towns – looking as though they had reached retirement and were taking a fortnight's celebratory holiday.

To the left of the restaurant entrance was a superb, highly-polished grand piano. Seated at it was an equally highly-polished, smartly-attired lady pianist, in Victorian costume. She was playing a medley of songs, from the Victorian and Edwardian eras, as they approached. The frosted glass sign above the entrance was engraved with the legend, *Palm Court*, the name of the restaurant, which was also printed in gold lettering, on the two elegant reservation cards which Patrick presented.

They were escorted to a table for two, on the right-hand side of the restaurant. The floor of the enormous room was decorated, like a black-and-white chequer board: an opulently-splendid version of a traditional Victorian tearoom. Each circular table had its own pristine white tablecloth, decorated with silver table accessories. In the centre stood a three-tiered bone china cake stand; the lower plate contained delicate triangular sandwiches, made with a selection of wholemeal or white bread, to cater for all tastes. There was a choice of fillings: salmon and cucumber, shredded boiled egg and ham.

The remaining two tiers contained cakes and scones of all sizes and descriptions, together with sachets of butter and jam – what a treat! Tea was served from a silver tea service. The cups were exquisitely delicate and of the finest porcelain. A plate of vol-au-vents had been placed to one side of the display.

The pianist's repertoire changed to a light classical style. The whole atmosphere of the tea-rooms was one of sartorial elegance and charm. It was like stepping back into a bygone age. All of the guests were dressed in grand style especially for the occasion. Patrick and Fiona were no exception.

Each table had been assigned a highly-skilled, attentive waiter. Despite his Victorian garb, their waiter was an articulate and charming Irishman. During the course of conversation he happened to mention that his family were from Limerick. "Well, there's a coincidence," said Fiona enthusiastically. "My great grandparents, on my mother's side, were originally from Croom: a rural village, just outside Limerick."

When the waiter had departed, Patrick leant over to her, saying, "You kept that quiet Fi. Why didn't you tell me that you have Irish blood in you?"

"I didn't think it was important; after all, I'm only one eighth Irish. I mean, I've hardly kissed the Blarney Stone, now have I? Anyway, my father's side of the family are pure Anglo-Saxon."

"Ah, but the Irish side of you would explain a great deal," he insisted. "I wonder which particular eighth of you is Irish. D'you suppose we could have fun finding out?"

Afternoon tea was a very traditional affair: everything was done 'just-so'. When it was almost complete Patrick said, "Fi, I have a suggestion to make." He was about to elaborate when the waiter returned, asking if they required souvenirs. They ordered four gift baskets, containing sachets of *Murchie's* tea – 'famous since 1894'.

The tea was an exclusive blend, especially produced for the *Empress*. The baskets were to be presents for Anna, Kathleen, Fiona's mother and one of her three sisters. For herself, Fiona ordered a similar collection of tea sachets, together with an Irish linen tea towel, with a recipe for maple cookies printed on it. She intended these to be souvenirs, which she could take back home to Solihull. Patrick thanked the waiter, but added, "We'd like ten minutes to ourselves, if you don't mind."

"Certainly sir," he replied with the utmost courtesy.

When they were alone again, Patrick returned to his previous subject. "I have a suggestion to make... but I'm not quite sure how you'll react to it. I mean, you've referred to your journey back to England several times already."

She was about to protest, but he interjected quickly.

"Okay. So maybe it was just a passing reference, but I'm getting the distinct impression that you regard it as some kind of lifeline."

Fiona didn't answer. She was acutely aware that there were frequent moments of telepathy between Patrick and herself: his assessment of her state-of-mind was uncannily accurate. "Here's how I figure it." He hesitated, then continued quickly, "Oh to hell with it Fiona! How'd it be if you stayed for at least another month? I can't stand the thought of you going back." He put his right hand on her knee. "Say you'll stay!" he pleaded. "For God's sake, forget about the damn tickets!" Fiona paused, deep in thought, for a few seconds. Then putting her hand on top of his, she said, "Patrick, I don't want to be parted from you either. Of course I'll stay longer."

It was only while they were descending the hotel steps, a few minutes later, that the implications of her change-of-plan suddenly dawned on her. What would happen if Robert tried to contact her in England, after he returned from Crete? How would he react, when he realised that she was still with Patrick... in Victoria?

As yet, she had caught only fleeting glimpses of Robert's 'short-fuse': his impatience and his quickness to anger. But maybe it was simply a matter of time? In such an ambitious and passionate man, she knew that it was there – simmering – just below the surface.

CHAPTER FIFTEEN

The remaining fortnight of Fiona's first month in Canada passed very quickly. She wrote to her niece Samantha, who was living rent-free in her park-side house, while she was away. Samantha was a first-year music student at Warwick University: a level-headed girl who could be trusted to treat her home with care. A fellow student, whom Fiona had previously met, was sharing with her. Samantha readily agreed to an extension of their arrangement. She wrote back saying, 'You can make it a year if you like!'

Patrick and Fiona were invited to a dinner party, which also included a few close friends, at the home of Anna and her husband David, near the centre of Victoria. Patrick had placed the investment side of the Maitland family business in David's capable hands. He was an expert financier and business consultant, with a proven track record. The family held six-monthly board meetings, chaired by David, in the library at *Tralee*, to ensure that everything was running smoothly.

A few days later, Kathleen and Peter invited them to spend a day at Butchart Gardens: reputedly, the most splendid of all the gardens in British Columbia. Peter, being a horticultural expert, had volunteered to give them a guided tour.

Meanwhile, Patrick had an even greater surprise in store for her. At the end of August there was to be a performance of Fiona's favourite ballet, *Swan Lake,* at the Concert Hall. She discovered that, ironically, they had their very own Swan Lake, a relatively short distance away from the bay area, at the southern end of the Saanich Peninsula. Patrick pointed it out to her on a local map, adding,

"I'll take you there some time."

Their visit to Butchart Gardens was arranged for the following weekend. The gardens were situated approximately half way between Victoria and Swartz Bay. Peter and Kathleen lived in a house overlooking the bay. Fiona had caught a brief glimpse of it, from a distance, on the day they returned Kathleen there, following their tour of Victoria.

According to Patrick, the grounds of Kathleen and Pete's home were indescribably beautiful, as one might expect from a man of his talents.

They included a collection of rare and exotic plants; the most delicate of which were nurtured in extensive greenhouses, near the back of the estate.

They had arranged to meet outside the main entrance to Butchart Gardens. On arrival, they found them standing in front of the wooden entrance sign, which had a circular window of flowers in its centre. Fiona had her camera with her this time. Not only was she a keen gardener, she also enjoyed photography.

Kathleen introduced Fiona to her husband. "Just call me Pete," he said exuberantly, shaking her firmly by the hand. He had keen intelligent eyes and a slightly aquiline nose. She soon discovered that he had a well-developed, almost brash, sense of humour; 'he'd need it with Kathleen', she thought wryly. Pete explained that the Gardens spanned about fifty acres in total. "It's going to take at least two hours to do them justice," he advised.

They paid the entrance fee. Fiona was becoming accustomed to converting English pounds into Canadian dollars – and vice versa. It was relatively easy: there were roughly two Canadian dollars to every English pound. This time she insisted on paying the entrance fee for the four of them; the family had already paid for so much on her behalf.

A clearly-signposted pathway directed them round to the right, then in an anti-clockwise direction. The pathway sloped upwards to a higher level, bringing them to a position where they could look down, onto the remaining acres of garden, lying over to their left. Eventually the pathways, which meandered in and out of each of the gardens, would lead them in an almost complete circle, back towards the exit.

Everywhere was a magnificent riot of colour. Pete explained that the permanently lush effect was maintained by a highly sophisticated watering system, which had been installed throughout the complex. Each section of the grounds had its own theme. After a quick flick through the brochure, the most promising of these, from Fiona's point of view, were the Rose, Japanese and Italian Gardens, together with the most intriguing of all – the Sunken Garden.

According to Pete, the entire site had once been, amazingly, a barren limestone quarry. As they made their tour, he discussed the various species of plants with her in some detail. He was very amiable, and particularly pleased to be in the company of a fellow enthusiast. They also discussed the differences between gardening in England, compared with this part of Canada.

Patrick photographed her, standing on a red lacquered bridge, in the Japanese Gardens, surrounded by exquisite rhododendrons and azaleas, in

CHAPTER FIFTEEN

various shades of pink and white. Each garden had its own unique vista. Fiona envied the standards achieved there – if only she could grow specimens of that calibre in her own garden! There were so many species of flowers and shrubs throughout the whole development. She found it an overwhelming experience.

Kathleen and Pete had already decided that her brother and his young lady would need some privacy, especially in such a romantic setting. Having provided Fiona with a wealth of information, they took their leave, arranging to meet in an hour's time, at the Gift Shop.

Fiona was amazed at the sheer size and quality of the blooms on show. Some of the species were familiar to her, being of the English Country Garden variety; others were much rarer and more exotic.

The collective fragrance, emanating from the Rose Garden, was heavenly. Roses, of every variety imaginable, were intermingled with gigantic blue delphiniums, standing erect like blue sentinels. Black Victorian lamp posts towered, at intervals, above the multi-coloured rose beds, their lamps of yellow glass reflecting back the warm sunshine; with their tall, black pointed 'hats' they resembled groups of stately, but static mandarins! Patrick explained that the ultimate experience was the illuminated evening tour of the gardens. It was then that the lamp-lit pathways, throughout the length and breadth of the gardens, were at their most spectacular.

There was a trellised arbour on the left-hand side of the Rose Garden. They strolled arm-in-arm along the path leading up to it, sitting on a bench directly underneath the arbour, at the end of the pathway. The entire structure was covered in fragrant roses. From there they had a glorious view of the many other rose borders – and also a little more privacy. In the background they could hear the distant voices of other visitors, wandering along the pathways.

Patrick put his arm around her and kissed her. "Happy darling?" he asked. "Absolutely," she replied, with a heart-warming smile. After a while she ventured, "Patrick, you haven't mentioned either of your parents, apart from the morning we were looking at your family tree. Forgive me for asking, but why is that?"

He paused... and sighed deeply. Fiona recalled Robert's comment about Patrick being essentially a rather private, sensitive person. There was further silence, and then he began, rather hesitantly, his eyes fixed firmly on the ground.

"My father, Roger, died four years ago... from a heart attack. He was still fairly young, relatively speaking: just sixty-four years old. They said it was stress-induced. He'd been following a punishing schedule at the time, with various financial deals and so forth. Two years later, my darling mother Mary followed him. The doctors attributed it to a combination of factors, resulting in kidney failure... but I'm pretty certain that she died of a broken heart – you know?"

He turned tearfully towards her, taking her hand between his. "They were so close Fi. He used to call her his *Rose of Tralee*, like the song... Mary, you see." "I'm really sorry Pat', she said, linking her arm through his. "I didn't realise."

"No reason why you should," he replied defensively. "I've had no wish to speak of it. It's far too painful... with Mary going so soon after Da, as she did. You'd have loved her darling; she was a fine woman. I know you'd have been *great* together," he added wistfully.

They rested in the secluded arbour, in sombre, contemplative mood, for a few minutes more; such sad memories contrasting sharply, with the beauty and tranquillity of their surroundings. All the while, Fiona stroked his hands, trying to comfort him. Eventually, to lighten the atmosphere, she said cheerfully, "Tell me about your exhibition Pat. We've had so little time to talk about it." Patrick described the exhibition's success in some detail. He had sold seascapes, landscapes, and a few abstract paintings. Fiona felt tremendously proud of him. His spirits revived as he described his work in passionate detail, as though his paintings were his children.

After a while he said: "Come on honey, I almost forgot. You've yet to see the most outstanding of all the gardens. I'm hoping to secure a commission to paint this one – at some stage."

Standing at Patrick's side, a short while later, they admired the breathtaking view he was referring to... the lake in the Sunken Garden. Fiona took a rather artistic photograph of Patrick, against the backdrop of the lake; its deep, spring-fed waters reflected the leaves and exquisite blossoms. "Can you imagine painting this?" asked Patrick. "The intricacies of the detail alone would have given Monet a few sleepless nights!"

While he took an investigative stroll around its shores, with his sketchbook, Fiona descended a little lower onto the bank itself, close to an overhanging willow tree. Its delicate leaves were reflected in the water. She knelt down on the bank, seeing her own reflection smiling back at her. Being a tranquil summer's day, the surface of the lake was quite still – like a mirror.

At that precise moment, a slight breeze caused a rippling of the millpond surface. Fiona's eyes were drawn into its emerald-green depths.

CHAPTER FIFTEEN

She could see something else now; what appeared to be a rocky reflection, with something white leaning against it. With mounting curiosity, she peered ever more closely. Then, she stared in disbelief.

The white object appeared to be some kind of boat, but it was leaning to one side, as though it had capsized. Another gust of wind caused further rippling.

In an instant, the rocks and the boat had disappeared, without a trace. It was amazing – the tricks one's eyes could play!

Searching for Patrick, she eventually found him sketching, on the far side of the lake. Having checked their watches they decided to find Pete and Kathleen. They were already in the Gift Shop, close to the exit. Adjacent to that was a restaurant.

"We thought you might like a quick look around," suggested Pete, "then maybe a bite to eat afterwards?" He and Kathleen were already familiar with the shop, having visited it on several occasions. To Fiona however, it was an Aladdin's Cave – even the simplest of items proved fascinating! In a round wicker basket she discovered large pale-blue packets of seed labelled *The Perennial Collection*. Each envelope contained five smaller packets of seed, culled from the gardens: gypsophila, hollyhocks, Shasta Daisies, Sweet William and Icelandic Poppies. She was about to purchase them when Patrick stopped her.

"Why are you buying these?" he snapped. Fiona was puzzled. This was so unlike him. "When I eventually return home, I can plant them in my garden. There's plenty of space at the front of the borders," she explained patiently. "But you won't be needing them!" he replied tersely.

"What are you talking about?" She was becoming quite annoyed by this time. What *was* the matter with him? They were about to continue the argument, when the manageress came hurriedly over to him. "Mr. Maitland," she said, somewhat uneasily. "Yes Maria?" "We've been trying to locate you," she explained. "I've just sent two of the guys off, on a search around the gardens." "Why, what's going down? What's the problem?" he asked, frowning.

"We've just had a phone call, from your manservant Charles. He's in quite a state; 'think he might blow a fuse! Seems they've just received an urgent telegram. He said that he'd got a bad feeling about it… asked if you could get back there – right away!"

By this time, Pete and Kathleen had come over to investigate. It was decided that they should return at once. Pete and Kathleen offered to accompany them, but Patrick insisted that they return to their own home, promising to update them later. He drove back to *Tralee* as quickly as possible, although it still seemed like an eternity. They turned back into the drive with a screech of brakes, slamming the doors behind them.

Hurrying into the house, they found both Maggie and Charles waiting. Maggie was pacing the floor in an agitated state, clutching the telegram in her hand. They all moved quickly into the drawing room. Patrick and Fiona seated themselves, while Charles and Maggie hovered in the background. Patrick examined the envelope, turning it over and over in his hands. He was gripped by a sense of foreboding. Glancing anxiously at Fiona, he slowly opened it. The message read as follows:

Skiathos Greece 14 – 08 – 97 10. 00 hrs
Please telephone. Emergency. Silver's Arrow wrecked off Gulf of Charnia.
Robert and Andreas believed missing.
Miklos.

Patrick stared at the telegram in total disbelief. Slowly, without raising his head, he passed it across to Fiona, who was sitting in the adjacent seat. She read it, then saying absolutely nothing, rested her head on one hand.

The note dropped to the floor. Maggie retrieved it. Both she and Charles read it together. Having done so, they quickly left the room. Fiona joined Patrick on the sofa, trying to comfort him. He was speechless with shock.

There were no words to describe how Fiona felt, although she was trying to be brave – for both of their sakes. Maggie returned with two cups of hot sweet tea. Patrick took a quick gulp, then headed immediately for his study, found the phone number for *Club Skiathos*, and rang long distance, from the telephone in the hall. As Fiona was seated some distance away from the vast hall, she could just make out an occasional word in Patrick's conversation.

Returning to the drawing room, Patrick looked ready to collapse. Fiona helped him to his seat. "Tell me. Tell me!" she insisted, trying desperately not to sound too hysterical. "What did he say?" she persisted.

Maggie quietly intervened: "Excuse me madam, but he'll be needing a moment – don't you think?" After a little while longer, and a few more gulps of tea, Patrick was able to explain. According to Miklos, Robert's boat had been found, partially wrecked, but totally abandoned, off the Northwest coast of Crete. There was no sign of Andreas, his co-navigator, but there were *definite* signs of a struggle.

CHAPTER FIFTEEN

Patrick hesitated. Then looking into Fiona's eyes, with an expression of complete anguish, he whispered, almost inaudibly, "They found one of Robert's shirts. It was heavily stained... with blood!"

At that moment, everything went black for Fiona. She remembered nothing further until she came round, hours later. Opening her eyes and trying to focus, she realised that she was lying in bed, in the green room. Someone had removed her clothing. She was wearing a nightdress. There was a terrible throbbing in her temples, and at the back of her head. All of a sudden, it came back to her: the telegram; Patrick's reaction; the telephone call.... everything.

She began to shake from head to foot and then she was crying. She cried as if her heart would break. At the same time, she tossed and turned from side to side. Turning over, she hit the pillows, again and again, with her fists. She remained in this hysterical state for at least five minutes, until her energy began to wane. Then her beautiful, tear-stained face gradually sank back into exhausted oblivion.

Some time later Maggie came into the room, with a tray of tea things. As Fiona sat up slowly, looking mournfully at her, Maggie placed an affectionate arm around her, then hugged her. "Now then miss," she said, as she consoled her.

"Fiona – it's Fiona," she answered haltingly, still in a daze.

"Right you are Fiona," said Maggie, gently placing an extra pillow behind her for support. "You just relax my love. You've had a terrible shock – you both have."

"Patrick. Where's Patrick?" she asked, in the same laconic voice. "I have to see him." "Sure, he's in almost as bad a state as yourself," Maggie commented. "Have your tea first my dear. I think he's in the garden."

Fiona managed to eat and drink a little. Then she stood up, on very shaky legs, putting on slacks and a woollen top, with some casual shoes. Although it was the height of summer, she was shivering with cold. Maggie returned and, fearing that Fiona might fall, assisted her down the staircase and out into the garden.

Patrick was seated alone at the patio table, outside the French windows. His head was in his hands. As he looked up she could see that he had been crying. It suddenly occurred to her that this was the same patio area, the same setting that he had previously described; where he had spent those last few precious moments with Julia, before driving her to the maternity hospital for the last time. An empty tea tray lay on the table beside him.

He rose to his feet quickly, as she approached. They both threw their arms around each other. "I love him Fi," he sobbed, holding her tightly to him. "He's like a brother to me. If anything were to happen to him…" They clung together, trying to comfort one another.

* * * *

The ornate wooden bench was situated at the water's edge. Two days had elapsed since the telegram arrived. Patrick and Fiona sat facing the lake, discussing events in a calmer, more rational manner. "I'm sorry I over-reacted Pat," she was saying. "I suppose it was the shock of seeing you in such a state." "There's no need for explanation," replied Patrick. "We're just going to have to deal with the situation, as best we can."

An hour or so later, Miklos arrived, post haste from Greece. Patrick had arranged that he should stay with them, although their friend was uncertain about how long that was likely to be. He arrived in an agitated state, explaining that it had taken a day or so, to make all of his arrangements.

Once he had settled in, he was able, over dinner, to give them a more detailed account. Even under normal circumstances, Miklos was inclined to be emotional. It was immediately apparent that Robert's disappearance had had a devastating effect upon him. He seemed to have aged by at least ten years, since the last time they met; his face was pale and drawn and there were heavy bags under his bloodshot eyes.

"I cannot believe that he is no longer with us," he was saying sorrowfully. "If only I had realised the gravity of the situation I could have prevented him from taking such a trip."

"I guess we all feel the same way Miklos," replied Patrick, reaching out to put a comforting hand on his arm. "He is my very dear friend," Miklos continued, "like a younger brother. I cannot bear the thought that I may never see him again."

"We don't know that for sure Miklos; they may still find him you know," ventured Fiona, desperately trying to reassure herself as much as anyone. Making a supreme effort to remain calm, Miklos continued, "The police, you see, well, at first they thought it was an accident – that maybe some freak storm had thrown them off their course. After making enquiries, however, they found that no such storm had occurred that day. Also, there is the matter of Andreas. No one can find him. I simply do not understand why," he said, shrugging his shoulders. "How can two people suddenly disappear like that?

"The blood-stained shirt," he continued, "and the state of the cabin, have persuaded the authorities that it could be a case of – how do you say? – 'foul play'."

CHAPTER FIFTEEN

"What about this place where *Silver's Arrow* was found?" queried Patrick.

"Ah yes. The Gulf of Charnia, as the tourist brochures call it. For the Cretans, you know, it is sacred, the spiritual capital of their island. We Greeks know it simply as *Harnia*." Miklos was particularly puzzled, because it was an area of coastline which Robert knew extremely well; in previous years he had visited several archaeological sites in the same area.

"Normally, it is such a beautiful, harmonious place," Miklos continued. "Harnia, she was originally a peaceful fishing village, nothing much ever happened there. Nowadays, she is more like a 'Little Venice': so full of life, so how d'you say – vibrant. The White Mountains, they stand so proud and tall behind her. The boats in the harbour, they are just like gondolas."

"How exactly did they find *Silver's Arrow*?" enquired Fiona. "I mean, who actually discovered the wreck?"

"Some local fishermen," replied Miklos. "They came back from the night's fishing. It was dawn. They found his boat lying broken, on the rocks; no one inside. It was a great *mystery* to them."

"What about his shirt?" asked Patrick. "Ah… well, that they did not discover until later, when they searched the cabin more thoroughly," replied Miklos. "The police, they have checked the blood group. I regret to say it is the same as Robert's."

It was decided that they would all have an early night, as they were so emotionally exhausted. Patrick went to the kitchen to find Maggie and make arrangements for the following day. While he was gone, Miklos came swiftly over to where she was sitting. He spoke hurriedly, but in hushed tones. "Fiona," he whispered, "may I call you that?" "But of course. You did on Skiathos. Why change now?"

"Fiona, I have to see you urgently – by yourself – without Patrick." "But surely…" she began. He hushed her. "No, I am sorry," he insisted. "Please do not argue – we have very little time! It is most important that I speak to you *alone*. I must depart at twelve noon tomorrow. Perhaps we can find some way of arranging a private meeting?"

Just at that moment Patrick returned. They bid each other goodnight. Miklos was assigned a room in the west wing. Once in bed, Patrick pulled her gently towards him. Lying together in the darkness, they clung closely to each other, for comfort. Later, Patrick disrobed her, and removed his pyjamas. The heat of their naked flesh aroused a great hunger.

Slowly, Patrick began to caress her. After a while, he sighed and said, "You know Fi. The most creative act, for a man and woman, is the making of a new life. Now that you've quit taking the pill, every time that we make love, we have the chance. Think of it that way baby. It may be that I've lost the precious life of someone dear to me, but we can always create a new life, to replace it." Patrick placed his moist lips on hers and she responded, willingly.

They slept peacefully until the morning, her head cradled against his strong, virile body. She felt so safe and secure... in his arms.

CHAPTER SIXTEEN

Charles was carrying a breakfast tray across the hall, in the direction of the patio. It was a fine, bright morning. "Oh there you are," she said, stopping him in his tracks. As he turned to face her, still balancing the tray, she enquired, "Do you know where Mr. Maitland, is Charles?" "I believe he left earlier this morning madam," he replied. Fiona smiled to herself – such impeccable manners, this English manservant. He added, "Something to do with the gallery, I understand."

Thanking him, she followed him towards the patio. Miklos was already seated at the table. Charles arranged the breakfast things on a side table. He passed half a grapefruit with a cherry in its centre, served in an elegant glass dish, to Miklos. "Would you care for breakfast Madam?" Charles enquired.

"Certainly!" she replied, with deliberate affectation. She liked playing butlers and aristocrats with Charles. He was still a fairly young man in his mid-thirties, and wasn't above a joke. He returned her smile, then departed.

"Thank goodness we have not had to resort to the subterfuge," Miklos said, with a sigh of relief, once they were alone. "I'll second that," agreed Fiona.

"Even now, I am appalled at my own duplicity Fiona," he continued. "I find myself in what I believe you English call a *cleft stick*. Mr. Maitland, he is such an honourable man. I truly have no wish to deceive him."

"Of course not," Fiona said, with a reassuring smile, reaching across the table to press her hand upon his. She had a soft spot for Miklos. Despite being a shrewd businessman, he had always been considerate and avuncular towards her; for some reason, ever conscious of her welfare.

Charles returned with a cooked breakfast. After the exertions of the previous night, she felt ravenous. When the butler had left them for the second time, Miklos, facing her directly across the table, leant across in conspiratorial fashion. "We have to talk," he reminded her.

Once breakfast was finished, Fiona suggested a walk through the cottage garden, behind the summerhouse; it would provide sufficient cover and they were unlikely to be observed. "Wait... Just one moment," cautioned

Miklos. Going into the hall, he grabbed his jacket from the Victorian coat stand. "It's a warm day Miklos," she remarked. "Surely you won't be needing that!" Miklos placed a conspiratorial finger on one side of his nose, like a character from a classic, 'who-dunnit' movie. He clutched his jacket even more tightly, as they strolled across the lush-green, manicured lawns. Once by the summerhouse, she led him through an archway, into the cottage garden at the rear.

He looked around carefully, satisfying himself that they were completely alone. Then reaching into the deep pocket of his smart navy blue jacket, he pulled out a plain white, unaddressed envelope. Indicating a two-seater bench, beneath some trees, the two of them sat down. All was quiet, except for the sound of birdsong.

Miklos gave a short, somewhat nervous cough, beginning cautiously: "I have been asked to give this envelope to you. It was a very special request of Robert's. My instructions were to hand over the envelope, only in the event of his death."

Trying to ignore the look of alarm on her face, he continued: "You see, he had begun to suspect that there could be an element of danger in this latest enterprise of his. Like a fool, I accused him of having an over-active imagination. Can you believe it?" As he handed the envelope to her, his hands were shaking. "Please put it away – out of sight – immediately!"

Fortunately, Fiona was wearing a tunic with a pocket on either side. Without a word, she quickly slid the envelope into the left-hand pocket. "I believe that it contains a letter," Miklos continued. "It comes with strict instructions. Firstly, read it only when you are *completely* alone. Secondly, you must not mention its existence, nor show it to *any* other living soul. I myself have had to refrain from doing so: Robert was *most* particular about that point."

"Do the Greek police have any idea what has happened to him?" asked Fiona. Miklos' expression as he regarded Fiona, was one of deep sadness… such a tragic thing to happen to such a lovely young lady. Fate could be so cruel. Her eyes were brimming over with tears, as she questioned him.

"The police suspect some sort of underhand dealing," Miklos elaborated. "Some subterfuge – involving treasure trove; probably involving huge sums of money. They paid me a visit, shortly before my departure for the airport."

"Did Robert actually *find* the *Queen Isabella*? I know that he made fresh discoveries about its location." It was Miklos' turn to look surprised. "I'm not sure how much he told you," he commented warily, scrutinising her face.

CHAPTER SIXTEEN

"Well, I know a few of the details. With hindsight, and judging from his last, rather cryptic letter, I'd say that he was trying to protect me from something."

Reluctantly, she described the incident on the beach, involving Miklos' niece, Lydia. When she had finished, he seemed rather crestfallen. Pausing to consider, he elaborated: "There is, I fear, a rather complicated explanation for all of this. And, regrettably, there's a strong possibility that my niece Lydia is in some way involved."

According to Miklos, Lydia had been having a clandestine affair with the young student, Jean Pierre Lefevre. They had originally met the previous year, during his first visit to *Club Skiathos*.

"Did you see anyone else on the beach, apart from Robert and Lydia?" he asked. "No, although there was a motor boat, at some distance behind them – heading for what appeared to be a large ocean liner. I saw the back of a man's head in the boat, but there could have been other passengers. Lydia had been swimming – I think."

"Ah, now it begins to make sense," Miklos observed. "It is quite possible that the man you saw at the helm of the motor boat, was Jean Pierre and that Lydia had been, perhaps, talking with him... maybe even passing something to him. Also, it is possible that the ocean liner was...." Here, he paused, adding, "Ah, but who knows? This is all conjecture. The only thing I know for certain is that Jean Pierre duped poor Lydia into falling in love with him, for what now appears to be his own selfish gain. Then he tried to elicit certain information from her. He is certainly a user, that one."

"But he seemed such a charming young man," said Fiona, wistfully.

"But of course. It is often the way!" replied Miklos, rising to his feet. "My dear Fiona," he said, taking her by the hand, "I am most anxious that you hide the letter somewhere else, where no one will find it – without further delay. Remember my advice, in that direction. Please go now, before Patrick returns."

As they walked back to the house, Miklos spoke of the Greek sense of honour, or *philotime*, as he called it. He was very distressed that his niece's part in the whole affair had not only endangered Robert's life, but was likely to bring disgrace upon their family.

On reaching the house, Fiona ran quickly upstairs, along the corridor and into the green bedroom. Then, opening her suitcase, she carefully sandwiched Robert's envelope between two layers of clothing, near the bottom of her case.

Patrick returned from the Halcyon Art Gallery in Victoria Street, in the centre of Victoria, about an hour before Miklos was due to depart. The two men remained in the drawing room, in animated conversation, for most of the remaining time. The French windows were slightly open. Fiona could hear the rise and fall of their voices, from the garden bench where she was seated. She was attempting to read a novel, thinking it preferable to avoid further contact with Miklos, following their conversation that morning. It might be easier for both of them, under the circumstances, she decided.

In the event, Miklos said his final goodbyes in her absence. Patrick came out into the garden afterwards, to find her. "Poor guy; seemed to be in a tremendous hurry to leave us," he commented. "Guess he's had more than enough of grief sharing. Probably wants to get back to familiar territory."

"Did he say much before he left?" Fiona enquired innocently. "Well, the Athens police paid him a visit, just prior to his departure," explained Patrick. "They're working in liaison with the Crete police and Interpol, who've been pushing a few buttons. Seems that far from being a simple case of nautical misadventure Robert may have gotten himself caught up in a complicated web of financial intrigue and double-dealing."

"Miklos mentioned something earlier, about a French financier, named Lefevre," interjected Fiona. "Yes. Reckon he's the guy who put up the initial capital for the Cretan project. I seem to recall Robert mentioning it, about two years ago, when the *Queen Isabella* project was first put to him. Trouble was they always conducted transactions with Robert through a third party – an Italian, I believe. So he never actually got to meet the top man. I remember commenting at the time – such a weird way of doing business! But Robert seemed reasonably happy with the arrangement; he always *was* a little unconventional! Besides, nothing came of it. I assumed the deal had fallen through. He hadn't mentioned it since – at least, not to me."

Later that afternoon, Patrick received a further phone call from the gallery. Sales of his paintings over the last few years had been so profitable that he had become a major shareholder and partner, in the gallery. His co-partner, Arabella, wanted him to visit one of their more temperamental young artists, at his home.

It was at least an hour's drive from *Tralee*. Arabella was having problems with some of the finer details in the artist's contract. Patrick's diplomatic skills were required, to smooth things over. "I'm sorry about this sweetheart. I've left instructions that I'm only dealing with urgent gallery business right now, whilst you're here. Unfortunately, this looks like another problem that can't wait."

Fiona suggested that he should go ahead; it would also give her some time to herself. "I might even row over to the island," she ventured. "It's

CHAPTER SIXTEEN

only a short distance." "Well, it's your funeral," he said. Then, realising the irony of his comment, added, "That is… What I meant was… Ah, you know what I mean," he said, gesturing with his hands. "If you're using the boat, just be careful honey." With that, he grabbed his briefcase and was off.

Following Patrick's hasty departure, and with a little tricky manoeuvring, Fiona drove one of the golf carts to the lakeside. Despite feeling rather apprehensive, she managed to row across the bay, to the island. Adopting the same strategy as Patrick, on their previous visit, she used the painter to secure the boat safely to its customary post.

Making for the hideaway that they had shared on that memorable occasion, she lay down in the shelter of the trees, hidden completely from view. At *last* she could read Robert's letter, without fear of interruption.

Opening the unlabelled envelope, she began to read the contents with some trepidation – desperate to learn its secrets. Perhaps it would throw a significant light upon Robert's disappearance; maybe even help with his rescue?

But the more she read, the more thankful she became that she had chosen such a private location. It was written in his usual, copperplate handwriting, on four sheets of notepaper.

My Darling Fiona,
As I write this letter, my eyes are filled with tears and my heart is aching. For I know that you will only be reading it in the event of my death. It is my fervent wish that you will never have to do so and that Miklos will be able to return it to me unopened, as a secret souvenir, once I arrive safely back in Skiathos. Maybe it will end its days as a faded piece of writing, which I can surprise you with, in years to come – which we can laugh about when we are old and grey and out of harm's way? I most fervently hope so.

A series of threatening letters and anonymous phone calls have prompted me to take this precaution. Already, it may be too late to save the situation.

It is a source of great sadness to me that a cause so essentially noble and well motivated: the historical exploration of a Greek island, and the subsequent recovery of a shipwreck, may have an altogether crueller and more degenerate aspect to it. It now seems that purely malice and greed may have, after all, motivated individuals whom I previously trusted – that there may be a more sinister, covert and dangerous side to Paradise.

At this stage, I still have no conclusive proof about the identity of these unseen enemies. You once likened me to Odysseus, sailing the 'wine-dark seas'. In a way, my love, my whole life has been an Odyssey. But a futile and empty one, until the day I met you. The sea god, Poseidon may be our only hope now.

ADRIFT IN PARADISE

Since our first meeting, on Skiathos, I knew instinctively that we were meant for each other. As you yourself realised, we are like two lost halves of the same soul, searching for one another, throughout eternity.

I weep when I think of the life we could have had together. Our children; our island home. I want you to know that I have never loved any woman, as deeply or as passionately, as I love you. Above all, I beg you not to allow my tragedy to destroy your hope of future happiness. I could not bear that to happen.

Patrick is a close and very dear friend of mine. Should things have developed between the two of you, in the way that I suspect they might, seize your opportunity for happiness my darling, with both hands.

He is the only man I know who would have the capacity to love you with the intensity that I do. Please cherish our ring. It is a talisman by which I shall recognise you in future times. Wear it often and think of me. It would have been your wedding ring, my love.

Miklos will confirm that I have already visited the priest, to arrange a marriage for us, at the hillside chapel of Saint Nikolas, on Skiathos. It was to have been my surprise for you, and was due to take place this October.

This time, tragically, fate has intervened and snatched away our happiness. But know this, beyond any doubt that I shall be waiting for you again in the next life. Some day, my love – some day. Take care and have courage.

Please forgive the simplicity of the following poem. There was not time to compose a more erudite one. Hopefully, all of this is just a false alarm, and I'll be able to write you a whole book of poetry, on my return. I hope with all of my heart that you have not had to read this.

> *My lonely ship sails out to sea*
> *Where it is bound I cannot see.*
> *We two shall meet, take my advice,*
> *Though we're adrift in Paradise.*

No matter what the outcome remember Fiona, that my heart and soul are forever yours.

Yours for all eternity,
Robert.

She had been lying on the grass, as she read the letter. Owing to its complicated and rather cryptic nature, she re-read it several times, until she had grasped its full significance.

Her second course of action, an irrational one in view of the fact that the island was completely deserted, was to protect it from the gaze of any

CHAPTER SIXTEEN

other human being. She replaced it in its envelope and then concealed it quickly in her pocket, bitterly disappointed that it contained no further clues, to aid his rescue.

She could no longer hold back her anguish. Lying prostrate on the ground, she cried as if her heart would break – long, anguished sobs, whimpering and groaning like a wounded animal. The tears were heavy and prolonged. Her whole body was racked in an agony of remorse.

Why hadn't he warned her about the danger? Why had he tried to protect her? She would willingly have died protecting him, a thousand times over. She could have gone with him; together they might have stood a better chance of overcoming his enemies. He was worth far more to her than her own life; it was meaningless without him. Fiona felt fairly certain that whoever had done this must have taken him by surprise. But what had he meant about Poseidon?

Recalling his words about their future marriage on Skiathos, she became almost delirious with grief; beating the ground with her hands, tearing up huge handfuls of grass and throwing them about her; throwing anything she could lay her hands on.

For several minutes she remained in this frenzied state. Caring nothing about anything or anyone but Robert. If she couldn't have him, she might as well join him where he must surely be by now... at the bottom of the ocean.

Eventually, little by little, she began to calm down again. Her sobs became more subdued. Slowly, she internalised her agony, pushing it resolutely inwards. No one must suspect *anything*.

Raising herself on one elbow, she dabbed her puffy eyelids with a handkerchief and blew her nose. With slow, faltering steps, she managed to seat herself on the bench behind her. She remained there for several minutes, in a complete daze, staring between the gaps in the weeds, at the water flowing beneath them. It seemed strangely cool and inviting... it would be so easy to step into it... it would be over in seconds – and all the pain would be gone – forever.

As she stared and grieved, she contemplated an uncertain future: unsure as to whether she even had one. Finally, after spending over an hour on the island, she rowed wearily back across the bay. Around the half-way stage, she suddenly remembered the surreal nature of her previous visit; the way she had suddenly felt that it was Robert making love to her, not Patrick. What had that been all about? She was suddenly seized by an irrational fear – that something even more sinister was about to happen to her – before she could reach the jetty. Whatever it was that had destroyed Robert might now be hunting her! She began to row desperately back to shore.

With trembling hands, Fiona secured the boat on the other side, alongside the boathouse, still haunted by the same thoughts. With hindsight, could it have been some kind of telepathy: Robert trying to communicate with her – perhaps in his *precise* moment of mortal danger? Hadn't she had read somewhere that paranormal phenomena such as this could be triggered by extremely intense emotion?

The golf cart was still parked where she had left it: adjacent to Patrick's studio, close to the lakeside. She drove it back to the house. As she trudged dejectedly, through the main hallway, she mentally checked herself for entertaining such morbid thoughts: 'I must be stark, staring mad!' When Patrick returned that evening, he found her slumped out across the four-poster bed, sound asleep.

CHAPTER SEVENTEEN

Over the next few days, her relationship with Patrick appeared to undergo a sea change. It began when he reminded her that, as it was again the servants' day off, they could make use of the main, more elegant dining room on the ground floor, which they had used once before. It would make an ideal setting for a really sumptuous evening together.

They laid out place settings with the best silver, cut glass goblets, even candelabra, on this occasion. They cheated a little, ordering gourmet food; delivered around six thirty, that evening, from the *Lobster Pot*, a local restaurant. They had both dressed elegantly, if a little unconventionally, for dinner. Patrick sported a particularly smart light brown worsted suit and waistcoat, over a cream silk shirt, with shamrock green tie, but no jacket; Fiona wore a long green silk gown, with a slit up one side and a low-cut bodice. The built-in bra raised her breasts into a highly seductive décolletage.

The whole evening was designed to relieve the depression that had engulfed them. Both had descended into their own personal Sloughs of Despond, since the news of Robert's disappearance. A spot of play-acting might be fun; hopefully it would distract them from the grim reality of their present situation.

Fiona wore Robert's antique gold ring. Once the property of a Spanish noblewoman, it complemented her style of dress well. Besides, she mused, it had been Robert's express wish that she should wear it. After what had befallen him, wearing what should have been her wedding ring was the least she could do; no one would be any the wiser. It was her secret alone. Patrick had no inkling of its history. As far as she was aware, Robert and herself were the only two people who were aware of its true significance.

Dressed as the lord and lady of the manor, they sat down to dine. Patrick gave her a conspiratorial glance, as they took their places at either end of the elegant, polished mahogany table; a slightly smaller version of the one in the upstairs library. The meal lasted some considerable time, during the course of which they consumed two bottles of extremely potent, full-bodied red wine. They became progressively merrier and less inhibited, as the evening wore on.

From time to time, Fiona would study the ring on her right index finger and toy with it a little. Patrick observed this, but made no comment. He merely gave her an enquiring look, raising his eyebrows slightly. The music of Mozart and Chopin played elegantly in the background. Normally, when they finished a meal, they would retire to the drawing room for coffee and perhaps a brandy. But something strange was happening to them... imperceptibly... and by degrees.

They began to feel rather light-headed: 'probably the wine', thought Fiona. Then, without warning, Patrick, still seated, suddenly called out to her, in a mock-Elizabethan style of speech, slapping his thighs as he spoke: "Come hither wench!" "Why certainly my liege!" she responded.

Entering into the spirit of things, and, as always, with a keen sense of the dramatic, she walked seductively down to him, from the far end of the table, placed both hands on his shoulders and began to massage them. Patrick made a sudden grab for her, but she ran across, to the other side of the table, laughing.

The main lights had all been dimmed. He pushed back his carver chair.

"Sit here," he continued, motioning to his lap. Sitting astride him, she looked straight into his sexy brown eyes.

By the time she crawled into the four-poster bed that night, she'd discovered a new, more primitive side of Patrick, which she had only caught brief glimpses of before. He lay slumped out by her side, on top of the bedclothes.

Throughout the whole of the following day they remained locked in an almost manic state; as though some hidden force held them in its power. Fiona continued to wear her antique ring. It felt so perfectly in place, on her right index finger – as though it had always been there. The two lovers made every effort to be alone. Patrick took her up to the dusty attic, right at the uppermost part of the house. It was so high; it was almost like being in heaven. Yet what she experienced there was more like being in the other place!

The room was full of cobwebs. It was mostly a storeroom, for old forgotten paintings and furniture. They found a clear corner. Patrick picked her up bodily. The most remarkable thing about the whole episode was that she was actually enjoying it!

That afternoon, they rowed across to the island, to their secret hideaway. Later that night when they were finally in bed, it seemed as if they were trying to purge their souls of all the accumulated pain that they had endured, not just over the last few days, but over many years.

Robert's apparent death seemed to have triggered a kind of desperation in both of them, which demanded to be assuaged... like some form of

CHAPTER SEVENTEEN

exorcism. Throughout that period, Robert's ring, his talisman, remained securely on her right index finger.

Much later, lying in a sort of twilight state – half asleep, half wake, she realised that Patrick's present brand of lovemaking reminded her of someone else; someone who had stolen not only her body, but her very soul. She twisted his ring upon her finger and settled down … contentedly.

* * * *

A shaft of sunlight attempted to force its way through a gap, in the heavy blue curtains. Patrick and Fiona lay in a deep stupor. It was already midday. Maggie was becoming quite concerned: both of them were normally such early risers. Finally, in desperation, she buzzed the intercom machine, which was connected to the master bedroom.

Bleary-eyed, and still in a daze, Patrick rolled over and pressing the button down, answered it. Several minutes later, although they'd struggled out of bed, they decided to have brunch in the breakfast room, still clad in bathrobes. Understandably, they both looked rather pale and haggard. Maggie darted them a look of disapproval, but said nothing. Moving across to the drawing room, they read newspapers and magazines at a leisurely pace.

But there was something different about them. Glancing across at Patrick, who was engrossed in the local journal, Fiona realised that they both seemed calm and more relaxed. Thank the Lord for that! She breathed a sigh of relief. The pace had become too much for her.

Later, as they dressed in the bedroom, Patrick said suddenly, "I almost forgot. Today is a very special one, my love." Fiona was extremely relieved that he seemed to have returned to his familiar self again. Neither of them mentioned the events of the last two days; it remained like a secret, but unspoken bond between them.

Opening a draw in the bedside table, below the lamp, he announced: "Do you remember my mentioning *Swan Lake*? Here are the tickets. The performance is this evening." Fiona was overjoyed. Throwing her arms around his neck, she kissed him exuberantly. She was actually going to see her favourite ballet – at last.

"Before that, I have an additional surprise for you," he continued. With obvious pride, he led her to the uppermost floor of the house. They walked past the library-cum-boardroom. Then following the corridor, they turned sharp left. This was a wing she hadn't seen before. In such a large mansion, it was difficult to keep one's bearings; they seemed to be somewhere on the far left-hand side of the building. Perhaps this was the west wing, where Miklos had slept?

With great ceremony, he flung open two white colonial style doors, similar to those that led into the library, to reveal... a Music Room. There was a large grand piano, so highly polished that Fiona could see her face in it. Around the room, which smelt slightly musty, were a variety of musical instruments: mainly woodwind, brass and percussion. An even wider selection of musical books, some quite worn, lined the shelves. They ranged from musical scores and instruction manuals, to books on ballet and opera.

The floor was almost entirely covered with a huge, exquisite Indian carpet. Looking out of a casement window she could see a large area of distant woodland, plus a tiny part of the bay. Running one finger lovingly along an edge of the piano, Patrick said softly, "Mother used to play the piano for us. She had a beautiful, mezzo-soprano voice." Slowly, he seated himself on the piano stool, carefully lifting the piano lid, then staring at the keys.

"Play something for me Pat." He hesitated. "Something that Mary used to sing," she encouraged him, recalling their conversation in Butchart Gardens. Again, he hesitated. Then, slowly, he began to play and sing, in a rich, deeply resonant, baritone voice.

> *The pale moon was rising above the green mountain;*
> *the sun was declining beneath the blue sea*
> *when I strayed with my love to the pure crystal fountain*
> *that stands in the beautiful vale of Tralee.*
> *She was lovely and fair as the rose of the summer*
> *yet 'twas not her beauty alone that won me*
> *Oh no! 'twas the truth in her eye ever dawning*
> *that made me love Mary, the Rose of Tralee.*

As he played and sang the even more poetic words of the second verse, his baritone voice echoed through the room; breathing life once again into it. His performance was so awe-inspiring, that it rendered Fiona utterly speechless. The second verse, with its image of the moon, shedding her pale ray through the valley, was even more evocative.

Only when he had completely finished, and was looking up into her astonished, blue-green eyes, did she recover her voice. "Patrick my darling," she whispered. "That was *incredible!*" "I'm glad you liked it sweetheart." He stood up, closed the piano lid, then kissed her gently on the cheek. "I hadn't

CHAPTER SEVENTEEN

realised you could sing and play like that," Fiona continued. "You sound so professional."

"Well, at one time I actually did have a singing tutor, but that was as a boy. All three of us play an instrument: that's how I first met Julia. Kathleen plays the clarinet and Anna the flute. They still practise here, from time to time. We used to have our own family ensemble… once," he added wistfully. Fiona imagined Patrick and Julia playing piano duets together – long before Patrick even knew of *her* existence, thousands of miles away, across a great ocean.

Two young people, living in a cosy unsuspecting paradise, here by the shimmering lake – totally unaware of the cruel blow which fate was about to inflict upon them – and any future family that they might have. At least she and Ian had spent a few years together. Patrick and Julia's marital bliss, by comparison, had been a mere drop in the ocean.

Lying to one side, propped up against a wall, was an acoustic guitar, made from pine-varnished wood. It looked as if it had seen better days. Fiona picked it up and, seating herself, began to tune it, by ear. Once tuned, she strummed a few chords, and sang a couple of songs: the *Ballad of the House Carpenter* and the *Beatles* song, *Yesterday*: the latter, in the circumstances, seemed particularly apt.

When she had finished, Patrick applauded enthusiastically. "Well done Fi," he said. "It's been many a year since someone actually played that instrument. I believe it was my father's, originally."

Seated in the garden later, she became quite cross with him: "Fancy hiding your talent from me like that!" she complained. "You can be so secretive sometimes Pat – allowing me to ramble on about my choirs and guitar – and my music teaching. Yet in reality, I'm nowhere near as accomplished as you are!"

"Relax," he said, putting an arm around her shoulder. "Besides," he added, "it wasn't deliberate. I haven't played or sung like that since Mary died, two years ago. I hadn't the heart to do it. The whole experience traumatised me… far too much; especially after losing Julia and Da.

"With you by my side," he continued, "I have the power to put all of that behind me. You've given me the most precious gift of all Fi," he murmured, touching her cheek gently. "You've restored my faith and my purpose in life."

* * * *

The Bentley drew up outside the concert hall. An immaculately-dressed couple emerged: she in a sequinned black evening dress, he in elegant evening attire. Entering the hallowed portals of the concert hall, and up two flights of stairs, they presented their tickets. A small side door in the theatre was opened. Ascending by a narrow staircase, they entered a private box, from the rear. It was surrounded on three sides by dark red velvet curtains.

As they settled themselves, the lady removed her long black evening gloves, one finger at a time. The gentleman laid his white leather pair, across the top of the opera glass holder in front of him. There was a subdued, fan-shaped light, in the centre panel of each balconied box, with floral decorations on either side. Hushed whispers emanated from the auditorium, far below. The high ceiling dripped with chandeliers. The orchestra tuned their instruments. The conductor tapped his baton. Slowly, by degrees, the lights dimmed.

An expectant hush fell across the whole audience. Someone coughed. Tchaikovsky's music gradually permeated their senses, as the orchestra began to play. It had a magical quality of fantasy about it. It mesmerised its audience.

The opening act of *Swan Lake* thus began. Fiona felt as though she were in a dream, a dream from which she might never awake. There, seated beside her, was her own handsome prince. He squeezed her hand tightly as he turned smilingly towards her. Patrick was so proud to be with her. His eyes filled with tears. 'This is the happiest moment of my life', he thought. 'I've finally found a woman whom I truly love... without reservation'.

The music of this particular ballet had always had a profound effect upon Fiona, from the moment she first heard it, as a young child. There was such a haunting, magical quality about it: one moment so noble and majestic, the next so poignant and full of despair. It touched her heart strings and completely seduced her senses.

As the ballet opened, celebrations were under way for Prince Siegfried's twenty-first birthday. A flock of swans was gathered around the lakeside, led by Odette, the Swan-Queen. They had all been transformed into swans, by Rotbart, an evil magician, but resumed their human form in the moonlight. The spell could only be broken, when a man swore faithful love to one of them – and kept his vow.

Fiona was terribly saddened by this part of the ballet, as she remembered the vow she had made to Robert, symbolised by his ring; a vow that would now be impossible to keep. Tears filled her eyes as she squeezed Patrick's hand ever more tightly.

Memories of her school teaching days came flooding back. Thousands of miles away, in Solihull and Birmingham schools, she related the story of this, and other ballets, to the children, her pupils; playing extracts from the

CHAPTER SEVENTEEN

music, in the hope of awakening their youthful senses – just as her own, exceptionally-gifted music teacher had done for her, years before, at grammar school.

Now here she was, under such different circumstances, seated in a theatre box in the capitol of British Columbia, watching the very same ballet, live, accompanied by a man whom she loved with all her heart. Fiona smiled at Patrick. He kissed her lightly on the cheek, revelling in her obvious enjoyment. His beard tickled her.

She recalled that *Swan Lake* could be interpreted on a more intellectual level: as a psychological allegory. Odette represented the soft, elusive, romantic image of a woman. Odile, the black swan, symbolised the scheming, aggressive side – the two sides of womanhood.

Fiona was transfixed by the whole performance. As the last act opened, Odette was heartbroken by what she mistakenly considered to be the prince's betrayal, with Odile. The prince, meanwhile, was searching desperately for her. Odette forgave him. They made a suicide pact.

As Odette began to slowly drown in the lake, something inside Fiona snapped. Her mind transported her back, by degrees, to Patrick's island – a few days earlier – when the water had suddenly seemed so inviting.

This final part of the ballet struck a chord, too painfully close to the feelings she had been trying to repress: something to do with the presence of water... and drowning. As Odette drowned, the prince closely followed her. Instead of the prince, however, Fiona suddenly imagined the handsome, virile body of her own beloved Robert.

He was drowning. He couldn't breathe. He had fallen overboard. Everything seemed to be playing in slow motion. Water was gradually closing in around him, filling his lungs. He was struggling – unable to escape!

Suddenly, she *herself* couldn't breathe. She hadn't been there for him; not in the way that Odette was for her prince. She hadn't known about the danger.

She was overwhelmed by feelings of guilt and helplessness; he had been condemned to die alone, in a watery grave, with no one to comfort or save him. She should have been there, with him.

Fiona began to sob gently to herself, as the beautiful, haunting violin strains of the *Dying Swan* filled the theatre. It was all too much. She could still see him under the water – her beloved Robert... alone, and dying. In the cold, deep waters of the Mediterranean. The image just wouldn't go away.

Initially, Patrick had supposed that Fiona, being of a sensitive nature, was merely reacting to the emotional intensity of the ballet. But when he saw the anguish in her eyes, as the tears began to fall, and looked once again, at the scene being enacted below them, realisation slowly began to dawn on him.

She buried her face in his shoulder, stifling her sobs; painfully aware that no matter what, she mustn't spoil the enjoyment of the surrounding audience, or embarrass Patrick. Gradually, the music changed. She took out a handkerchief and dabbed her eyes, resting her head on Patrick's shoulder again, trying to calm herself.

Fiona stared, with mounting incredulity, while the final apotheosis of the ballet unfolded. The prince's proof of their true love had destroyed Rotbart's power.

The final act ended as Odette and the prince sailed away, reunited in a better world. The scene so dramatically matched the words of Robert's poem, in his last love letter to her. They suddenly returned to her, with blinding clarity: his faithful promise that *they* would be reunited again, in the next world. The parallel between her real-life tragedy and that of *Swan Lake* became suddenly only too clear.

And, in that precise moment, she also realised her own destiny: regardless of her own safety, she must try to discover the truth, about what had happened to Robert. She knew that she would have no peace until, at the very least, she attempted to find him. Had the situation been reversed, there was no doubt that he would have been out there... looking for her.

* * * *

The cool evening air provided welcome relief, as the couple emerged from the theatre. Both of them, for different reasons, maintained a stunned silence. Luckily the chauffeur was already parked and waiting for them, directly outside the side exit. The prospect of having to wait for transport, possibly for minutes, after such an experience, was unthinkable.

Soon they were speeding homewards in the car. Patrick cradled Fiona in his arms. She was still in a state of shock. Solemnly, he pressed a button and an automatic smoked glass screen came swiftly up, between themselves and the driver. The screen was soundproof, providing them with much-needed privacy. Patrick hugged her to him, ever more tightly and protectively.

If only he had *known*, he thought savagely. But, fool that he was, he hadn't suspected a thing. He had never made the connection. Why should he? It was too fantastic for words. He could hardly believe it – even now!

Fiona rested her tear-stained face in the arc of his shoulder, moaned gently and began to sleep. He eased her head into his lap, placing his

CHAPTER SEVENTEEN

folded jacket underneath, for a pillow. He began to stroke her forehead. Her previously troubled expression gradually relaxed, into a more peaceful one.

As he comforted her, he tried to think the situation through, to the extent that his shattered nerves would permit him. It had all been there, he realised, if *only* he'd had the wit to see it. Everything suddenly began to fall into place. He had quite naturally assumed that Fiona's emotional reaction to Robert's death had been because it followed so closely upon that of her husband, Ian.

Now, as he remembered Robert's acquisition of the sunset painting, combined with his additional, even more puzzling request for her first efforts at painting, everything seemed so much clearer: like finding the missing pieces of a jig-saw.

Glancing down at the antique ring, which Fiona still wore on her right index finger, he began to question its origins. This line of thought was soon abandoned, however, proving too painful to even contemplate.

As the car sped swiftly along the Nanaimo Road, he recalled that last week in Robert's apartment, on Skiathos. He had been extolling Fiona's virtues to the hilt, in such a proud fashion – with Robert himself of all people! He marvelled at his friend's forbearance and self-control under such circumstances. How could he have been so blind? *Surely* he should have read the signs earlier?

With Fiona safely sleeping in the green bedroom, he collapsed wearily onto his four-poster bed and spent a sleepless night alone; dreaming of drowning bodies shipwrecks, swans, and phantoms... bloodstained boats drifting slowly out to sea.

Above all else, the question that most tormented him centred upon Fiona's reasons for visiting him in Canada. How could she have been so cruel? Just at the point when she'd restored him back to life again. If she had been so hopelessly in love with Robert, why had she even bothered to come to Victoria? Why not simply cancel the arrangements?

Why, in *God's* name, was she tormenting him like this?

CHAPTER EIGHTEEN

On waking that morning, the events of the previous evening had come flooding back – all too quickly. In desperation, she immediately removed Robert's ring and placed it in its original pocket, in her jewellery case. She was resolved to leave it there. Since the moment she'd slipped it on her finger, events seemed to have escalated out of all control.

Taking a quick sip of fruit juice, she hurried from the table, to find Patrick. Just at that moment however, the doorbell rang. A package had arrived by registered mail, addressed to both of them. She signed for it, but took it to Patrick's study, depositing it in the top draw of his desk. It would have to wait until later. She had far more urgent matters on her mind.

Having tried several of the downstairs rooms, to no avail, she was obliged to ask Maggie if she knew of Patrick's whereabouts. "I believe he's in the studio. He's been there since six this morning. Is everything all right madam?" she added, with obvious concern.

"I hope so," replied Fiona anxiously. Full of trepidation, she raced across the lawns, to find a golf cart – all dignity forgotten. How would Patrick react? What if he refused to see her? The prospect of returning to England, under such a terrible cloud, filled her with despair.

She put the golf cart into gear and drove along the winding pathways, towards the lake. Luckily there were two such vehicles on the estate. Patrick had parked the other one, outside the conservatory. Entering by the studio door, she found him, apparently engrossed in his work. He wore a pair of faded blue jeans. A paint-splattered shirt hung loosely about his hips. His hair was a mess. He looked worn, tired, and suddenly, much older. As she entered, he gave her a sidelong glance, then immediately resumed his work.

Normally, he painted with a quiet concentration, but now he was almost slapping the paint on; taking vicious stabs at the canvas with a thick brush. Still he said nothing, but kept his back to her. "Patrick," she began, after two or three minutes waiting. The only reply she got was a surly "Yes?"

Unable to take his indifference, she put her arms around his waist, kissing him from behind. "Damn it woman! You'll get paint all over you! Wait a minute can't you?" With this last comment, he slammed the palette

CHAPTER EIGHTEEN

and brush down on the rough wooden worktable, wiping his hands on an old turpentine-soaked rag.

"Please Patrick," she whimpered, sitting resignedly on one of the older, wooden, studio chairs. "I just want to *explain*."

"What is there to explain?" growled Patrick. "My best friend and the woman I love were having an affair, but neither of them bothered to mention it. But – hey... *it's no big deal*!" By this time he was roaring at her. He slammed his fist down hard upon the table, his back half turned away.

As he turned to face her, he kicked the table leg savagely. His face was contorted and crimson with rage; a vein on his forehead stood out, thick and swollen.

* * * *

Resting a hand on his workbench, to steady himself, he slowly sat down. After a few moments' silence he said, in a broken voice, "My God, Fiona. This isn't a game! What the *hell* have you been playing at? Don't you *realise* what you've done to me?"

"I didn't plan it this way Patrick. Truly. It just *happened*. Neither of us wanted to hurt you. We both *love* you... please believe me!"

"Then you've got a *damned* peculiar way of showing it!"

Unable to take any more, Fiona collapsed into tears, her head in her hands, crying bitterly. She ran towards the door – anything to get out of there. Patrick's anger quickly turned to concern. "Oh, come here darling, come here!" he remonstrated, heading for the door, to prevent her leaving. He led her to a two-seater bench close to the wall. Gradually, by degrees, her sobbing subsided. Patrick cupped her chin with his hand and began to kiss her tear-stained face. Then passing her a large but rather grubby handkerchief, stained with flecks of paint, she attempted to dry her face.

"What I *can't* understand," he said, at last, "is if you were *so* committed to Robert, why didn't you just come clean? I mean, why come to Victoria at all?"

"I had to be certain about my feelings for you. I was *totally* confused. If I hadn't come, I would never have known for sure."

"But Godammit Fiona! What if Robert hadn't disappeared? What then?"

Even as he asked the question, he was dreading the answer. She began to stroke his hair and kissed him tenderly on the lips. Reaching tentatively for his hand, her beautiful eyes still moist with tears, she spoke softly.

"Please believe me Patrick. Long before Miklos' telegram arrived, I realised that I'm still *desperately* in love with you." Gazing earnestly and sincerely into his eyes, she said, "There is no other man on this *earth*, whom I love more than you."

"Then show me Fi, Godammit," he whispered… "show me," his eyes brimming over with tears. He strode purposefully to the windows, pulling down each shutter in turn; blocking the light completely. Then he switched on a small green table lamp. He spread a thick grey blanket onto the studio floor, rolling up an old jumper to use as a pillow. Half an hour later, not a *trace* of doubt remained.

Some time later as they sipped martinis on the patio, Fiona suddenly remembered the package, which had arrived earlier that morning. Patrick went into his study, to retrieve it from his desk. It was addressed to Mr. Patrick Maitland and Mrs. Fiona Eastley. He returned to the patio, so that they could both read it. The thought of opening it held no appeal at all; they were both developing an aversion to this kind of correspondence. The letter was from Miklos. It began:

My dear friends,
  I hope that you are already coming to terms with our terrible loss and that you are therefore in a more suitable frame of mind to receive this latest information.

Although Miklos had spent the major part of his life on Skiathos, he was a well-educated Greek, who had attended Business College in Athens. His studies there, combined with half a lifetime of various business enterprises, of which the tourist industry was but one, had furnished him with a more than acceptable standard of English – certainly a lot better than their Greek!

The main part of his letter was concerned with up-dating them about police enquiries concerning Robert. Before leaving, he had promised Patrick that he would keep him posted. Subsequent investigation had placed Claude and Jean Pierre Lefevre high on the list of suspects. It now appeared that Andreas, the missing fisherman, had been employed by Claude Lefevre, unbeknown to Robert, right from the outset; when they made their initial, exploratory voyage to locate the *Queen Isabella*, two years before.

As a result of evidence obtained from his fellow fishermen, the Greek police had built up a dossier on Andreas, which included a personality profile. The picture that had emerged was of a very determined, physically strong, and at times, rather devious individual. Although Robert had apparently trusted him, it now transpired that, over a period of years, Andreas had been involved in petty theft and several brawling incidents with

CHAPTER EIGHTEEN

other fishermen, some of whom were in no doubt about his predilection for violence – they had the scars to prove it! In short, Andreas' profile was hardly that of a victim.

Miklos, who had also known him for several years, was of the opinion that if Andreas and Robert had come to blows, the former would have proved a formidable opponent, despite Robert's undoubted physical prowess.

Owing to both the prestigious and the political nature of Robert's research, plus the vast sums of money involved, a fourth organisation, *Europol,* had also been assigned to the case. *Europol* had informed the Greek police that both Lefevres had disappeared since the incident, to parts as yet unknown, thus implicating themselves still further.

An additional matter of concern was that the police had failed to find two documents belonging to Robert, which might provide crucial evidence. Firstly, a daily journal, which, Miklos assured the police, had been kept by Robert meticulously, with daily entries, ever since he had known him. The second missing document was the logbook, usually kept in a certain draw of his cabin; a more thorough search of the boat revealed that it was definitely missing.

According to Miklos, a substantial part of the wreck had been brought back to shore. Classified as 'Police Evidence', it was currently being stored in a local boatyard, under lock and key. Although still concerned about his family's *philotime,* Miklos had conclusive evidence that Lydia had indeed passed certain information about Robert's project, to Jean Pierre. Although reluctant to tell the police, she admitted, to her uncle, that, in all innocence, she had told her lover about the likely increase in value, of the treasure trove and had also made copies of maps.

Having no reason to doubt her integrity, Robert had, unfortunately, confided in her. The fact that the stakes had become substantially higher provided the Lefevres with an even stronger motive for murder, or at the very least, abduction. It was possible, explained Miklos, that Andreas had deliberately sabotaged the vessel himself, causing it to capsize. Perhaps Robert had tried to stop him?

At this stage, however, much of this was speculation. There was as yet, no firm evidence either way. The thought that Robert might be held in some remote hideaway, possibly in an injured state, or, in the worst-case scenario, been murdered, was extremely distressful for both Fiona and Patrick.

However, the most surprising part of Miklos' letter had been saved for its conclusion. He referred them to a photocopied document, several pages long, which was enclosed. It was from a Mr. Nikolias Theodepolous, whose offices were located in the main business centre of Athens. He was, explained Miklos, not only Robert's lawyer, but also an old and valued mutual friend, whom he himself had originally introduced to Robert.

Turning their attention to the lawyer's letter, Fiona and Patrick were astonished by its contents. The lawyer explained that as it was necessary to apply the laws of *habeas corpus*, and as no body had yet been discovered, it would be essential to allow a reasonable length of time to pass, before settling Mr. Osborne's affairs. The date for a preliminary enquiry, to be held in Athens, had already been set for the following month.

Once a reasonable period of time had elapsed and given that Robert did not suddenly reappear, Mr. Theodepolous would then be at liberty to reveal the full contents of the will. However, without going into any great detail, he felt it only fair to reveal at this stage, that Robert's closest living relatives, namely his parents and his sister Naomi, were likely to inherit royalties from his books, together with a substantial additional amount, from other business interests.

Patrick put the letter face down, on the wrought-iron coffee table in front of them: "His financial affairs can be of no interest to us. What the hell is the point of all of this?" He put his head in his hands, visibly shaken by any inference that his friend's death, if indeed he was dead, could possibly be of financial benefit to anyone. He rose to his feet, saying, "Dammit Fiona. I need a drink!" Fiona had never seen Patrick drink liquor during the day; it was a pleasure he usually reserved for the evenings, and then only in moderation.

Returning shortly with a double whisky for himself and a small brandy for her, he passed it to her solicitously: "There you go darling. This will steady your nerves." As Fiona put the glass to her lips, she realised that her hands were shaking. The letter had had more of an effect than she had realised.

Patrick remained unwilling to read any further. Fiona, however, was concerned that the last few pages might contain vital information. As she began reading the closing section her eyes widened in astonishment. Then she suddenly burst into tears, passing it back to Patrick. "I can't," she gasped. "That's unbelievable!" Reluctantly, Patrick read its conclusion, with mounting disbelief.

Robert's lawyer was at great pains to stress that the information that he was providing could only be given, at such an early stage, in the strictest of confidence. It seemed, however, that both of them were likely beneficiaries of Robert's will.

Apparently, within the space of the last few months, Robert had added two further codicils. Patrick stood to inherit a half share in *Club Skiathos*,

CHAPTER EIGHTEEN

together with Robert's apartment. In an explanatory note, he had written that he realised how much Patrick loved the islands and that he would prove an ideal guardian for such a legacy. He would be in joint partnership with Miklos. He further hoped that the legacy would serve as a token of the abiding respect and affection between himself and Patrick – a reminder of the good times they had spent together.

The reason for Fiona's reaction suddenly became crystal clear. In the penultimate paragraph, Mr. Theodepolous spoke of a very special legacy for her, which was to be of a two-fold nature.

Firstly, a *dwelling place*, up in the hills of Skiathos, known simply as *The Den*, together with all its contents. Special mention had been made of the second bequest; his grandfather's old sea chest and its contents. It appeared that Robert, having had a strong premonition of danger, had removed the chest from *Silver's Arrow*, shortly before sailing.

Patrick could only guess at Robert's reasons for making such a bequest. His previous feelings of jealousy and rage began to resurface. This time however, he clenched his fists, making a Herculean effort to contain his anger. He was acutely aware of Fiona's present state of mind and didn't want to add to her distress.

* * * *

Seated on one of the more respectable studio chairs, the top half of Fiona's body was naked, save for a green chiffon scarf draped strategically across her shoulders. Her deep auburn hair cascaded over her elegant shoulders, to a point half way down her back. Beautiful blue-green eyes gazed lovingly towards Patrick, as he began sketching her portrait, onto a fresh canvas. There was silence for a minute or two.

"How long do I have to remain in this position Paddy?" she asked. "My neck's getting stiff already." Patrick stopped momentarily. It was the first time she had ever used that particular term of endearment, normally used only by his sister Anna. Fiona's use of the name created an even greater and delicious feeling of intimacy between them, which was irresistibly seductive. She grinned back at him mischievously. "You don't *mind* me calling you Paddy, do you?" she asked, coquettishly. "It suits you – you great brute of an Irishman!"

"No, I don't mind at all," he replied softly. Putting down his sketching pencil, he came over to her, kissing her tenderly on her luscious lips. He adjusted the scarf, which had moved slightly. Resuming his work, he continued to sketch her head and shoulders.

Fiona's thoughts strayed to Robert. Would she ever see him again, or was he lying at the bottom of the ocean? It was a mystery that might *never* be resolved, unless she took some form of action. Patrick eventually broke the silence, after a further twenty minutes or so: "I hope you realise what an honour this is me darlin'," he quipped. "I only do portraits for close family members, you know."

"How close is close?" she said, from between clenched teeth, still trying to maintain a posing position. She could only see him out of the corner of one eye. Reverting to his usual deep-voiced Canadian drawl, he replied,

"That rather depends upon you, my love." Turning full faced to him, in surprise, she noticed the twinkle in his eye. This time he put the pencil in his pocket. Instinctively, she pulled the lightweight jumper back over her head. He led her slowly by the hand, moving the Japanese silk screen just sufficiently to allow them passage through, to the other section of the conservatory.

They seated themselves in this more elegant part of the building. There was a moment's pause. Then Patrick spoke very incisively: "This affair Fi – between yourself and Robert. We have to get this *absolutely* clear between us. I've had enough pain, of late, to last me a lifetime, and there is no way on God's good earth, that I can be expected to compete with a ghost – even if he was a good friend of mine!" He added this last sentence with a wry grin.

"I *am* trying to come to terms with it Paddy," she explained, "to get it into some kind of perspective. But it has to be said, there are certain things that have happened to me, since Robert's disappearance, which have no rational explanation."

Patrick was too preoccupied with his own train of thought, for her last comment to register. "I can understand you falling for the guy Fi," he continued. "I mean, that fella could charm the birds off the *trees* if he'd a mind to. You know, over the last few years, until you showed up on Skiathos, I'd noticed a gradual waning of his enthusiasm, in that particular area. He seemed to have become disillusioned with the type of women he'd been meeting. That may account for his renewed interest in the Cretan project."

Fiona considered returning to her previous point, by telling Patrick about the surreal incidents on the island, and in the lake at Butchart Gardens. Then she thought better of it – 'He'll think I'm losing my senses!'

She was still wondering whether she *ought* to tell him or not, when Patrick spoke again, although this time he'd become rather tongue-tied. "Well now," he stammered. "That is... I.... Oh, to *hell* with it. I'm going to do this thing properly!"

CHAPTER EIGHTEEN

So saying, he produced a small black box out of his right hand trouser pocket and knelt down on one knee, directly facing her, looking up into her gorgeous eyes. Fiona looked on in amazement: unable to comprehend what was happening. "My darling Fiona," he said earnestly, taking her right hand in his. "The love of my life… will you marry me?" Producing an exquisite diamond solitaire engagement ring, from the black box, he held it out to her. She was so overcome with emotion that she couldn't speak. She began to cry with happiness.

"For God's sake *say* something," he pleaded. "Me knee's seizing up!"

She laughed with joy. Holding his handsome head between her two hands, she kissed him passionately. Patrick placed the ring on her left index finger. "I've waited *so* long for this. Tis all yours, Mrs. Maitland," he said softly.

They kissed in a passionate embrace, lasting so long, that in the end they both had to come up for air. A wave of euphoria enveloped her, as she closed her eyes. In that moment she knew, at last, despite matters that still had to be resolved, that she really *had* come home.

CHAPTER NINETEEN

Fiona and Patrick were married just before Christmas 1997, in a local chapel, close to *Tralee*, where Maitland family ceremonies had taken place for generations.

Fiona's parents and two sisters flew over for the wedding. Most of the Kirkpatrick and Maitland clans attended, some making the trip across from Southern Ireland. Pat's mentor, his Uncle Daniel, a relatively youthful sixty-five year old, was still a practising artist. He was much-relieved to find his nephew restored to his former, more positive self, after years of heartache.

Shortly after the wedding, Patrick's new portrait of Fiona was given pride-of-place, to the right of the library window, which overlooked *Tralee's* sweeping gravelled driveway.

A few months later, Robert Osborne Maitland, their first-born son, was christened, on the November 10th 1998. Within the space of the following four years, two more children were born: a daughter Mary and a second son, Patrick Junior. In due course their photographs were added to Grandmother Rosaleen's family tree in the library – on the wall opposite their mother's portrait.

Thus, at the dawn of a new millennium, the Maitland dynasty continued to expand and thrive.

* * * *

In July 1998, four months before the birth of their first-born, the mystery of his namesake's disappearance remained unresolved. The Greek police subsequently declared Marine Historian Robert Osborne 'missing, believed dead'. A subsequent coroner's enquiry confirmed the verdict.

Nevertheless, both *Europol* and *Interpol* continued their investigations and insisted on keeping their files open. Their enquiries had uncovered a substantial network of international crime, demanding further investigation. Robert's two missing documents had yet to be found.

His will was then read and his property divided, in the way that his lawyer had previously outlined. When the time came for Fiona to visit

CHAPTER NINETEEN

Robert's *den*, a property which was now legally hers, she drove alone, high into the olive-clad hills of Skiathos. Patrick was reluctant to accompany her, due to his unease about the personal significance of the place and the memories that it still held, for his new wife.

Fiona's heart was heavy as she opened the heavy oak lid of her former lover's old sea chest; discovering half a lifetime of memories below its red padded top. There were albums, some quite old, some more recent, of Robert and family members; also snapshots taken with friends; examination certificates; research notes – neatly filed; a copy of each of his published books and articles. All kinds of memorabilia: all laid out in neat compartments and methodically ordered.

She wept as she examined each item, thinking all the time of her lost love. She could almost imagine his handsome face, smiling at her and feel his muscular body, enfolding her. With no one there to witness her grief, she gave full vent to her feelings. Wiping away the tears, she made a reviving mug of tea, just as Robert had done for her, on that unforgettable day. Having rested on the bed for a while, she resumed her search.

Right at the bottom of his grandfather's chest, beneath a pile of old school reports and bundles of letters from friends, she found two hardback books, which were beginning to fade and turn yellow with age. Labels on the inside covers revealed that they had been awarded as school prizes for English, at his Torquay grammar school. The first was *Treasure Island*, by Robert Louis Stevenson, who had inspired him so much; the second was a collection of sea poems by John Masefield. There was a photograph of the poet on the second page.

* * * *

As the months passed and still no body had been found, Patrick and Fiona decided to host a private memorial service, for close friends and family, as it was impossible to have a conventional funeral.

In August 1998, they made arrangements for Robert's parents, sister and friends to stay at *Club Skiathos* for a few days. It was almost exactly a year since Robert's disappearance. Fiona was seven months pregnant, but she refused to let this dissuade her. Besides, if the child inside her proved to be a boy, he would bear Robert's name, so the occasion seemed particularly apt. She was uncertain about how much Robert had told his family, about their relationship.

However, she and Patrick felt that Robert's memory should be honoured in some way. At a more subliminal level, Fiona was eager to discover exactly what it was about Robert's family that had produced such a unique individual, with such a compelling personality. Had it not been for the twist of fate that took Robert from her, she would have become an Osborne too.

Over two hundred guests attended, both from his earlier, academic years and those whom he had made more recently on the islands. It proved to be a very cosmopolitan collection of people. Several had made arduous journeys to be there.

Miklos, as his closest friend, played a key part in the ceremony. Professor Graham Pilkington, who had flown in from London, remained extremely morose throughout. He was particularly upset by the whole proceedings; feeling, albeit misguidedly, that if he hadn't assisted Robert in his latest quest for the *Queen Isabella*, his friend might still be alive.

Although at times he had been capable of great stubbornness, even irascibility, Robert had a gift for arousing strong passions in people. Ironically, Fiona realised, this tendency to provoke and 'stick to his guns', may have played a major part in his downfall. A very contrite Lydia also attended, having been released by the police, pending further enquiries.

This international company of people, from all walks of life, gathered together, one hot summer's evening, on the private shingle beach below *Club Skiathos*. As the sun was setting, a large wooden fishing boat was pushed out to sea. It contained a myriad of personal mementoes, placed there by the mourners; each of them having placed within the boat a special keepsake, which they associated with Robert. On top of these were piled a cornucopia of wreaths.

In view of Robert's abiding love of the sea and of ancient history, the ceremony was conducted in Viking style. As the boat was pushed out to sea, Miklos said a prayer for him: a translation of a Greek sailor's prayer. He spoke the words with great emotion, unable to hold back the tears, which streamed down his anguished face, almost choking him.

Then Fiona stepped forward, lighting a beacon of twigs placed at the ship's bow to light its way. As it began to burn, five of his strongest friends, including Patrick, waded out into the sea, pushing the ship firmly on its way.

The tide carried it forwards, inexorably onwards – out to sea. Each person said his or her own silent prayer. As the boat gradually began to disappear into the distance, Fiona read aloud the particular verse from Rupert Brooke's poem, which she and Robert had so loved. It was a great effort to project her voice sufficiently… it was so choked with emotion.

CHAPTER NINETEEN

Where lies your waiting boat, by wreaths of the sea's making
Mist-garlanded, with all grey weeds of the water crowned,
There you'll be laid, past fear of sleep or hope of waking;
And over the unmoving sea, without a sound,
Faint hands will row you outward, out beyond our sight,
Us with stretched arms and empty eyes on the far-gleaming
And marble sand...
Beyond the shifting cold twilight,
Further than laughter goes, or tears,
Further than dreaming.

Early the following morning, two women took a stroll along the Skiathos beach. Shiny wet pebbles crunched beneath their feet. Frothy white waves ebbed and flowed onto the shingle; missing their feet by inches. One of the women was tall and prepossessing, with Robert's dark good looks and piercing blue eyes. Her hair was somewhat greyer now, partly with age, but more recently with grief. The other was a younger and beautiful, auburn-haired female.

Both women were anxious to speak to one another privately. Sarah explained to Fiona that her family had received a letter from Robert, just before he sailed for Crete.

"I thought it best not to mention it in front of the others, and particularly for Patrick's sake. We all know how close he and Robert were, so we've agreed not to dredge up old memories."

"I've wanted to meet Robert's family for some time," Fiona explained tentatively. "I thought about writing to you, but I was unsure of your reaction."

"Well, we'd hoped to meet you last October – under *completely* different and much happier circumstances," replied Sarah, reflectively. She hesitated for a moment, then, as if to change the subject, she continued: "We owe Patrick and yourself a tremendous debt of gratitude, for arranging all of this."

Again, she paused. The conversation was proving difficult, for both women. When she began again, Sarah was close to tears: "Robert told us about the arrangements... you see... for your wedding at Saint Nikolas... here on the island. He absolutely *worshipped* you, Fiona. You had only to read his letter, to realise that. When his father and I spoke to him on the telephone, he sounded so much happier than he'd been... for a long time."

The strain was becoming too much. As the two women looked at each another, they began to cry. Sarah held her tightly for a while. Neither of them spoke.

They continued along the beach, so preoccupied that they covered quite a distance. As Sarah dried her tears, she began to explain that Robert had been most like William, his volatile and passionate grandfather. Fiona tried to imagine the old seafarer. She pictured him with leathery, weather-beaten skin and flowing white locks: like a picture of *The Old Man of the Sea* that she had once seen, back in her childhood. She wondered how accurate her imagination really was. Fiona described the contents of the old sea chest, which Robert had bequeathed to her.

"William took it with him, on every voyage," Sarah explained. "Robert used to tease us about it – said there was a concealed panel in it – for hiding secrets. It became a kind of family joke – but we never really gave it much credence!"

As they continued their walk, his mother explained that her husband, Colin, now a retired head teacher of the same Torquay grammar school which Robert had once attended, was by comparison, a much milder-mannered, conventional man. She had reached the conclusion long ago, that it was probably a reaction against having a less stable, rather unpredictable home environment, whilst his father was off on his various voyages of discovery.

"Robert loved his grandfather; they were so close," Sarah said wistfully. She and Fiona seated themselves on an outcrop of rocks, at the end of the stretch of beach; both rather tired now – emotionally and physically.

"They were kindred spirits," she reflected. "You had only to see the two of them together to realise that," she added, with a faint smile. "Ever since Robert was a boy, they'd spend *hours* together on William's boat, discussing voyages, pouring over old maps or charts. He often moored his boat, *The Falcon*, in the Kingsbridge Estuary. Robert was fascinated by it all. I suppose the sense of adventure simply skipped a generation."

Being able to share such a profound grief, since the loss of her son, by talking to the woman he had loved, was particularly cathartic for Sarah. Being in such close proximity to Fiona helped her to feel somehow closer to Robert.

Looking into Sarah's eyes, it was abundantly clear where Robert's passionate nature came from. Sarah reached out momentarily, grasping Fiona's hand tightly. Then she released it.

"Colin is the intellectual in our marriage," she observed. "I expect Robert explained that to you." "Not in any great detail," replied Fiona. This time it was her turn to reach out and clasp the older woman's hand, for comfort. She added tearfully,

"You see, Sarah, what really hurts is that we had so *little* time together."

CHAPTER NINETEEN

She spent most of the two remaining days with Robert's parents and his sister, Naomi. His father Colin, was certainly a more reserved and formal person than his wife, but he thanked her for choosing the Rupert Brooke poem. "I thought it a particularly apposite choice my dear," he commented. "After all, Brooke died in the Aegean, you know, in his twenty-sixth year. He's buried on the island of Skyros." Fiona nodded. That had been one of the reasons for her choice.

Four days later, most of their guests had departed from the 'shaded isle', to their various destinations. Just before their departure, Robert's sister, Naomi, a thirty-year-old advertising executive, took her to one side. She said stoically, wiping away a tear, "I don't believe for one moment that he's *really* dead Fiona. Please don't give up hope. I certainly shan't. Believe me, I know my brother! Although there was quite a difference between us, age-wise, we've always been pretty close. We had a sort of telepathy – almost like twins. If he's survived, somehow, I know he'll move heaven and *earth*, to be with you. You'll see. He'll suddenly walk in... out of nowhere... take us all by surprise! He was forever doing things like that."

Long after they had taken their leave, Naomi's words still rang in her ears. If *only* she could be certain that they were true. There was also something else... something niggling away at the back of her mind. In her present, highly emotional state, she couldn't quite pinpoint what it was. But, if Robert were to return, how would he handle the present situation? Even if such a miracle occurred he would have *far* greater reason to simply disappear from her life forever, in view of the present circumstances.

When he realised that she had married Patrick, and was soon to bear his first child, he would have even more cause to assume the Sydney Carton role, to Patrick's Charles Darnay.

Having spent time with Robert's family, she was seized by an urgent impulse – to visit the *Den* once more. As she was so heavily pregnant, Miklos offered to drive her up there the following day, taking the opportunity to visit a local hill-farmer friend, whilst Fiona spent further time there... remembering.

Recalling Robert's words, when they were on *Silver's Arrow*, she felt a sudden compulsion to reach for a leather-bound volume of Dickens' *A Tale of Two Cities*, from one of Robert's bookshelves. Seating herself on the bed, she turned to Sydney Carton's closing speech, on the last page of the celebrated classic. She read with mounting incredulity. Certain sentences and passages seemed to stand out from the rest.

I see Her with a child upon her bosom who bears my name.

She realised with a start, how incredibly apt that might turn out to be. Reading further, her eyes alighted upon the following:

I see that child who lay upon her bosom and who bore my name, a man winning his way up in that path of life which once was mine.

Fiona's heart began to beat faster. Would it really be that way for their child? Was it possible that her unborn child would grow up to be some kind of historian, or, at the very least, a student of ancient history? Perhaps even an explorer?

Sydney Carton had imagined Lucy Darnay's child as a prominent judge, in adulthood; in the same legal profession as himself, but rising to even greater heights. But surely that sort of thing only happened in romantic novels – not in normal, everyday life? However, recent events in her own life had led her to realise that *nothing* was impossible.

As she was so heavily pregnant, her movements were slow and cumbersome. Kneeling down in front of Robert's old sea chest, she carefully opened the heavy lid, rearranging some of the contents, so that their order was more to her liking.

From the carved wooden side panel of the chest, the sea gods gazed up at her. There was Poseidon, once again, in the centre of them all, with his enigmatic smile. What *was* it that Robert had said about him? Something… about… hidden secrets. He could be so mysterious and cryptic when he wanted to be. She still thought of Robert in the present tense – refusing to acknowledge, even at this stage, that he might actually be dead.

The figures were thickly carved, standing out in sharp relief. Fiona's delicate fingers reached down, tracing the outline of Poseidon's smile. Feeling the contours of his lower lip, she was startled by a sudden click. Looking more closely, she realised that something in the side panel, the upper part of Poseidon's face, had twisted around, very slightly.

Investigating further, she was shocked to discover that the two halves of the sea god's face had suddenly opened up, like a miniature door. Her legs were shaking as she staggered to her feet. Carefully, she carried one of the smaller chairs over to the chest, seating herself in front of it. For a few seconds she rested, trying to take stock of what had happened.

With shaking hands, she eased the two halves of the miniature door even further apart. Behind them was a tiny lever. As she pulled it, she heard the cranking noise of some ancient mechanism, as the side of the chest parted in the middle, revealing a hidden compartment. There was just sufficient space to reach in carefully and move her hand around. She offered a silent prayer that there was nothing lethal hidden in it – but there was definitely *something* in there.

CHAPTER NINETEEN

Her hands were trembling, as she pulled out a package, wrapped in two layers of polythene covering; unwrapping it, she could hardly *believe* the contents: a smart red leather journal, with Robert's name, inscribed in his copperplate handwriting, on the inside cover!

Although her immediate inclination was to hide it, she hastily scanned the pages, discovering dates, map references, detailed notes about the missing galleon – even part of an old map! This could be precisely the information that Robert's enemies had been searching for, otherwise, why would Robert have concealed it? Assuming that it *was* Robert...

The most sensible course of action must surely be to get rid of it – to hand it over to the proper authorities, as a matter of urgency, as soon as she and Patrick returned to Canada. There was no *way* that she was going to place their lives, or the lives of any future family, in jeopardy. There had probably already been one murder committed, as a result of all of this. She had no wish to add to the list.

CHAPTER TWENTY

Father Darius, the bearded young priest at the Skiathos chapel of Saint Nikolas, executed his duties meticulously each day, preparing for the various services.

From time to time, while engaged in these duties, he caught a fleeting glimpse of a solitary figure. A simple shawl of fine black lace invariably covered her beautiful head. Twice a year, and for some reason always in the months of June and October, she appeared from nowhere, repeating the same ritual. The pattern never changed.

The early morning sunlight streamed through the chapel windows as she entered. She began by kneeling in front of one of the pews, on the soft green cushion provided. Usually, she would remain somewhere towards the back of the chapel, bowing her head in silent prayer for several minutes.

Then raising her head, she would stare fixedly in the direction of the altar; as though imagining a scene being enacted there… one which no one else could see. Approaching the altar via the central aisle, she crossed herself, lit a single candle and knelt before it, with sorrowful, world-weary eyes. Finally, without a word, or so much as a sideways glance, she would slip silently out of the chapel. Moments later, it was as though she had never been there.

On this particular occasion, Father Darius was able to catch a closer glimpse of her from the back of the chapel. He had no wish to disturb such a lonely soul, as she seemed totally absorbed in her private world. But he noticed a rather unusual gold ring – on the index finger of her right hand.

* * * *

Despite Patrick's reluctance to visit, the children would often accompany Fiona on her drive up into the Skiathos hills – to Robert's den – during their bi-annual trips to the Greek islands.

Young Robert Maitland was fascinated by the unusual collection of books. He enjoyed the wildness of the ancient hills and olive groves surrounding them. He listened, wide-eyed, to his mother's suitably

CHAPTER TWENTY

abridged stories about his namesake – his Uncle Robert. As she related them to her young son, she was again reminded of the final thoughts of Sydney Carton, recalling them almost exactly as Dickens had written them, but substituting the pronoun 'him', as it was in the book, for her own pronoun, 'her'.

I hear her tell the child my story, with a tender and faltering voice.
If only he *could* hear her.

* * * *

Patrick and Fiona continued to share a deeply loving relationship. Their passion for one another increased with the passage of time. Although they took frequent holidays abroad, the majority of their life was spent back home in Victoria, with the family, in the sanctuary of their beautiful home, *Tralee*.

It was a safety that Fiona was determined to maintain. She had kept Robert's journal well hidden, until a few months after the birth of her first son, having decided not to hand it over to the police after all. Who knows? There could be corruption within the police service itself, which might explain why no further headway had been made. In any event, she was unwilling to take the risk.

With her health fully restored, on a day when Patrick had business at the Art Gallery, she rowed out alone to their secluded island. After placing the journal in a large metal box, she buried it in a secret place, where no one would *ever* find it. Years later, she promised herself, she would return to the spot, when all danger had passed... and perhaps read it more closely.

* * * *

Despite Fiona's resolve, to free herself from Robert's ghost, it proved far more difficult than she had anticipated. His influence over her was of no earthly order and could not be explained by the normally accepted laws of nature. The bond between them seemed to derive from a source of tremendous power and intensity; transcending all normal boundaries of human experience.

His spirit consumed her with a fierce all-pervading intensity: an unseen, but spiritually protean presence, capable of assuming many forms. It would suddenly take hold of her, without prior warning. At such times she was convinced that his sister, Naomi was right. That Robert wasn't *really* dead after all, but desperately trying to communicate with her, from some unknown place, by the only means available to him – asking for her help.

During such moments she would feel his physical presence beside her, holding her, kissing and arousing her to the same supremely sensual heights, which she knew, instinctively, she could experience with no one else – not even Patrick. Sometimes, in the half-light of dusk, or early dawn, she would be transfixed by the sight of a solitary boat, drifting across the bay... perhaps bathed in moonlight or at other times, sailing into a magnificent sunset.

She might be on the second floor balcony, or watching from the Victorian Conservatory, down by the water's edge... in the twilight. In these magical, otherworldly settings, she found herself yearning for him; repeating, in a mere whisper, the lines of the simple, yet poignant poem contained in his final letter.

My lonely ship drifts out to sea,
Where it is bound I cannot see.
We two shall meet – take my advice,
Though we're adrift in Paradise.

Despite the happiness which marriage to Patrick and their three lovely children gave her, there was another, intensely private part of Fiona, which kept a lonely vigil. In these sad moments, the final words from his letter would drift into her consciousness. Softly but timelessly, his voice would call to her, across the ether:

"Some day, my love
Some day..."

CHAPTER TWENTY-ONE

Seven long years had passed since she'd lost him; slowly, the memory of him began to fade. Supported by the love of a husband who adored her and three beautiful children, her grief seemed to be gradually subsiding; replaced by a calmer more resigned realisation, that fate had not meant them to be together – at least, not in *this* lifetime.

The children were a source of constant joy. Ironically, Robert's namesake, although already tall for his age, was otherwise totally unlike him from a physical point of view. He was much more like his father. As a young baby, he had been very content: always chuckling. As he grew, he retained his sunny disposition. She pictured the fringe of golden, wavy hair, hanging over his brow; two handsome brown but intense eyes, staring from beneath.

Mary, on the other hand, was a bit of a tomboy; so determined about everything. She loved to climb trees and join in with the rough games of her older brother and cousins... apparently without fear. All situations, no matter how difficult, were a challenge to her. Already, at the tender age of four, she had begun piano lessons.

Patrick's time was divided between painting and running the art gallery, leaving precious little time for extra-curricula activities, apart from family holidays. Surprisingly, Kathleen volunteered to give Mary piano lessons, despite the fact that the clarinet was her first love. Fiona was amazed by her sister-in-law's uncharacteristic patience, as she guided Mary's stubby little fingers to the correct keys.

Kathleen and Pete had been unable to have children of their own, despite a whole range of expensive, gynaecological treatment, from a top specialist. Finally, the couple resigned themselves to the situation, becoming like surrogate parents to Fiona's three.

As Fate would have it, Patrick Junior, despite the absence of any genetic connection, was destined to become most like Robert. He was a rather stout little two-year-old with a shock of thick, dark-auburn hair and a serious, sometimes stubborn side to his nature. Even at this early stage he was showing signs of exceptional intelligence and perception.

One of the back rooms on the ground floor at *Tralee* had been converted into a spacious playroom for the children. Several antique Maitland toys had been rescued from the attic. With the cobwebs dusted off, and, in some cases, a fresh coat of paint, they had proved quite a novelty. Particular favourites were a rocking horse, two old teddies, one with an ear missing, and an Edwardian doll's house. Its miniature furniture had been stored carefully away, years before; someone had gone to a lot of trouble to see that it was well preserved.

But for the time being, the enormous mansion of a house was empty of everyone, apart from Maggie, Charles and herself.

* * * *

Fiona's daydreaming about her family came to an abrupt halt, as a pile of haphazardly stacked folders collapsed in a landslide, landing with a resounding thud on the elegantly tiled floor of the conservatory. Alongside them were additional piles of assorted notes, folders and books.

She had been trying to sort them into some kind of order. The more successful results of her labours were stacked on tables and chairs. But now she was growing weary. A lock of hair fell across her eyes, obscuring her vision. She pushed it back impatiently, sighing with exasperation.

For the past four years she had been collecting all available material concerning the Maitland family and its numerous branches. Being an influential family in Victoria, their fortunes and escapades were well documented in local archives and old newspaper cuttings. Some of them were yellowing with age, in family scrapbooks. But Fiona intended to investigate far beyond that.

Endless hours had therefore been spent in the reference library, sifting through information. Each folder had a different colour, one for each member of the family. She had built up at least thirty of these – hence the landslide. Such work, unfortunately, could only be done when her role as a wife and mother permitted it.

From the moment that she met Patrick, she had known instinctively that anything or anyone associated with him would make fascinating material for a novel. Her trip to Victoria, all those years ago, had more than confirmed this.

That first, unexpected sight of Rosaleen's family tree had caused her to consider that perhaps the non-fiction genre would be more suitable, after all. The sweat and toil of the Kirkpatrick branch of the family; their sheer determination and untiring energy, became her principal inspiration for the project.

A photographer friend of Patrick's took some excellent shots of the pictorial tree, with its photographs and labels, some of which had to be re-

CHAPTER TWENTY-ONE

written more clearly; these he scaled down to size, enabling them to fit more easily into Fiona's burgeoning manuscript. They would have prominence on the opening pages. How proud Rosaleen would have been!

Fiona sank back into the regency striped chaise longue, a wedding gift from David and Anna. Adjusting the cushions behind her, she swung her legs up, stretching them out lazily in front of her.

Facing the window, she had an excellent view of the natural lake, within the bay. The dappled afternoon sunlight played upon the water, reflecting back in ripples onto the conservatory walls. Insects and birds skimmed its surface.

The island, although just out of view, was forever in her thoughts: for its solitude – and what lay hidden there – concealed from everyone.

Still staring towards the lake, she suddenly imagined that she heard a noise: rather like music… but not quite. It was a distant but somehow insistent sound, which begged to be heard, rising and falling upon the ether.

Moving slowly towards the window, she was startled to find that it seemed to be coming from the direction of the island. Closer and closer. It had almost reached her now.

A cold, clammy sensation began to creep across her body. She shivered, then returned to the chaise longue, feeling rather unsteady on her feet. Sinking back once more, she relaxed into a peaceful sleep.

When she awoke, the conservatory was in almost total darkness, save for a glow cast by the lamps, which encircled the lake. Something was moving in the water, perhaps a vole or some kind of amphibian; there were hundreds of toads and frogs around the banks. Whatever it was, dived into the lake, then, in an instant, was gone.

Fiona switched on two green table lamps on either side of the room, then hastily tidied her files and papers as best she could. It was time for bed. At least when she resumed her task in the morning, there would be some semblance of order.

Patrick had taken the children on a three-week holiday to England. They had agreed to do this on alternate years. She had felt unable to abandon her park side home in Solihull, when they married. A compromise had been reached. Her young niece, Samantha, continued to live there. Jonathan, her bachelor brother, had moved in to keep her company and help with living expenses. This seemed a mutually supportive arrangement, at least for the foreseeable future. In return for such luxurious accommodation they took care of her house and garden.

The visits became almost like a pilgrimage, to Fiona's home country; staying in the house which had once been the centre of her universe, with all of her possessions around them, to explore and wonder at. Right now, it was spring and her back garden would be blooming with the masses of spring bulbs she had planted over several years. She could almost smell their fragrance.

Unfortunately, Fiona had been unable to visit two years ago, as Patrick Junior was just a tiny baby and Mary had been too young to travel without her. Patrick and young Robert had therefore made the trip together.

They hired a Nanny for this second trip, so that all three children would be able to accompany their father. She was particularly needed to keep an eye on boisterous Mary! The two younger children were very excited about seeing mummy's house.

Fiona was determined to make as much progress as possible with her book, in the family's absence; to work most effectively she needed to be totally free from distraction. She promised herself faithfully that once this project was complete, she and Patrick would fly over to England – just the two of them. Then at last she would be able to see her precious house once again. For now, it remained a distant memory.

Maggie had left supper on a tray in the bedroom. As soon as this was finished, Fiona settled down for a good night's rest. The large four-poster felt so strange and empty without Patrick. She was overcome with fatigue. Once she began any project, she found it extremely difficult to give any thought to even the most basic things, like food and relaxation.

* * * *

It was almost dark when she awoke again. A shaft of moonlight had insinuated its way through a gap in the curtains. Suddenly, she sat bolt upright. Something was wrong. She slipped into her bathrobe, then opened the frosted glass doors, which led out onto the balcony. Of all the magnificent vistas afforded by this grand old house, this was the most evocative of all: a moonlit view of their bay. It never failed to soothe and reassure her, especially when she was troubled.

Her family would be well settled into the Solihull house by now. Patrick, considerate as ever, had promised to maintain telephone silence for the first few days, unless there was an emergency. She knew, therefore, that all must be well with them. So why this unease? She had expected to sleep like a log.

A new moon hung over the island, which was silhouetted in the distance. Memories stirred... old memories. She shivered, wrapping the bathrobe more closely around her. An inexplicable compulsion stirred, deep within her: an overwhelming sensation. In an instant, everything became crystal clear... she *knew* what must be done.

CHAPTER TWENTY-TWO

Dawn was breaking, as Fiona rowed across to the island. An onlooker might have thought her totally mesmerised. She headed for the spot, known only to her, where she had hidden Robert's documents.

She had no idea *why* she was returning there, only that it must be done... and as quickly as possible. The metal box was buried several feet deep: she'd had no intention of recovering it, until many years had passed. Throwing the spade to one side, she lay down on one side, then reached into the hole, struggling to retrieve the contents.

Seated on James Maitland's wooden bench, she began to examine the red leather journal. Six years ago, she had buried it with great trepidation; the implicit danger, including Robert's murder, or at the very least his disappearance, had been uppermost in her mind. This time, she could examine the contents in a more leisurely manner; safe in the knowledge that there was no one to see, or grasp the significance of what she was doing.

Everything in the journal was just as she remembered it. As she sifted through, paying particularly close attention to the map of Crete and its surrounding islands, she chewed her lower lip in frustration. *Something* was missing. It was designed to span the years 1995–2000. The 1997 section was packed with entries, almost one for every day. But it ceased abruptly – in mid-August.

Leafing through the remaining pages she found them all empty – all that is except one. Her eyes filled with tears as she read the entry for October 10th 1997, made in advance. The date had been circled. There was one sentence, in blue ink:

Fiona and I, united... forever.

She had thought that she was over it; that the intervening years had healed the pain. How wrong she had been. She began to sob. With shaking hands, she closed the page quickly, to avoid obliterating his final message, with her tears.

Later that day, she re-examined the diary in the sanctity of Patrick's study. Remembering that Robert's birthday was on Midsummer's Day, she turned to June 23rd, curious to know how he'd celebrated it, as she'd already returned to England by that time.

Four sentences, which appeared to be complete nonsense, were written there. They were written in pencil, which was most unusual for Robert, and in neat, capital letters. She must have turned two pages together during her initial search. Copying the sentences onto a separate sheet of paper, she studied them more closely, by the light of Patrick's angle-poise desk lamp.

Since boyhood, Robert had been fascinated by anything involving secret codes or messages. Whilst in England, he had regaled her with stories of schoolboy pranks and passing messages to his friends, which only they could decipher.

For the next twenty-four hours she puzzled over the lines. In exasperation, she drew biro squares around each letter, to make them stand out more clearly. That evening, she left the paper lying on the dining room table. She would have to enlist expert help, she decided. It really was beyond her.

* * * *

Breakfasting the following morning, she waited, while Charles poured coffee. Then she noticed her sheet of paper, lying face downwards on the table, in rather a crumpled state. She almost spilt her coffee! Someone had crossed out most of the squares, in red biro, so that only a few remained, forming an anagram. These had then been re-arranged into three words, at the foot of the page:

SUNSET TWO FIVE

As Charles returned with breakfast, he enquired,
"Have I cracked the code d'you think? That was quite an easy one. I hadn't realised that you're a fellow enthusiast."

Fiona stammered her thanks, joking that she would have to make it more difficult next time. Closer examination revealed that it was the deleted squares that formed a pattern. It was what you crossed out that counted!

She must act quickly. A telephone call to Miklos was her first priority. At first, she was unable to reach him. According to his secretary, he was travelling around Athens, on business. Miklos took care of Patrick's business interest in *Club Skiathos*, as he had precious little time to do so himself. Just over two hours later, Miklos returned her call, from his estate manager's office in Athens. She explained what had happened, as briefly as she could.

Miklos admonished her for concealing the existence of the box, for so long, but sympathised when she explained about her fears for her family's

CHAPTER TWENTY-TWO

safety. He agreed to return immediately to Skiathos and to telephone her from there.

She was woken by the call, in the early hours of the morning. Miklos had, at her request, removed Patrick's *sunset* painting, the first word in the coded message, from the bedroom wall of the penthouse suite. "There was no need to damage it," he explained. "You were absolutely right. I have now in my possession, a key that was taped to the back of the picture. Alas, I could find no further instructions with it."

They agreed that she would take the next plane out to Skiathos. He would meet her at the airport. "Just like old times my dear," he commented. Together, they would surely stand more chance of resolving the mystery. "Whatever happens – not a word of this to Lydia – I still don't trust her," she cautioned him.

Fiona left strict instructions with Maggie and Charles that when Patrick telephoned they should tell him that she was visiting Skiathos for a few days. The break would do her good; improve her creativity and thereby her work on the forthcoming book.

At this stage, the fewer people who knew precisely what was happening, the better. Besides, she didn't want to worry Patrick: he had the children to think about. Also, the trail might fizzle out and she would feel extremely foolish.

* * * *

The sea view, from the balcony of Miklos' apartment was breathtakingly beautiful. A gentle sea breeze was blowing, as they sipped cocktails, reviewing the events of the last two days. Between them, on the table, lay a tarnished silver key, together with the increasingly crumpled sheet of paper.

Miklos picked up the key, examining it more closely as he turned it around, between his thumb and forefinger. "Having seen your decoded message, I am pretty certain that this could be the key to some kind of luggage locker, or maybe even a cupboard," he said softly.

"Number twenty-five maybe?" interrupted Fiona, glancing at the paper. "But where do we start?"

"If I'm right, it seems so obvious," commented Miklos. "That's undoubtedly why he had to use a code. The only place, outside of the Club, to which Robert had quick access and used frequently, would be the airport. At the very least, it's worth a try."

* * * *

Two hours later, Miklos was attempting to fit the key into locker twenty-five at Skiathos Airport. Fiona was irritated by the chatter of passengers, constantly moving to and fro' behind them; she would have preferred more privacy. She shut her eyes tightly, hardly daring to look. What if the key didn't fit?

The key was very stiff; the locker obviously hadn't been used for a considerable time. Feeling a tap upon her shoulder, she opened her eyes very cautiously. Miklos stood facing her directly. He placed a package in her hand.

"This is all there was," he remarked simply. Moving to a private corner, she tore open the parcel. There in front of them, at last, was the missing logbook!

A few hours later, having dined together, they examined the entries in the book. The opening section was devoted to Robert's initial quest for the *Queen Isabella*, and their subsequent conclusion that they must have the wrong location. In his usual methodical way he had included lists of provisions and equipment, together with a proposed itinerary. The entries revealed that he and Andreas had searched for almost six weeks. The terse nature of Robert's later entries echoed his frustration. In the back section were two rather dog-eared maps, plus a series of nautical references.

Miklos and Fiona continued to examine the contents of the log book late into the night, anxious to discover any possible clues concerning Robert's fate. Just at a point when they were both beginning to doze off, Fiona noticed a Good Luck card from Graham Pilkington, sandwiched between two other documents.

Inside the card, on a separate, folded sheet of paper, was a small sketch map of an un-named island. Despite its distinctive shape, Fiona couldn't quite place it. A section of the island's southern coastline, which jutted out into the sea, was marked with a black felt tip cross; other than that, no additional details were shown.

When she showed the map to Miklos, he immediately recognised it as the island of Rhodes. "The cross is just about where Lindos would be. The airport is to the north-east – Trianda. This is Rhodes Town, and look here, you see – that must be Faliraki!" he pointed out, excitedly. "But I don't see the connection," observed Fiona. "I mean, the cross obviously means something, but it hardly helps us. Why would he leave the map in his logbook? The card looks years old."

Miklos offered her the use of the penthouse for the evening; it now belonged to Patrick after all. She declined however – too many ghosts.

The following morning she phoned Graham Pilkington, in Greenwich, London. One of the joys of being a millionaire's wife was that she no longer had to worry about telephone bills! Graham was rather surprised to hear

CHAPTER TWENTY-TWO

from her, as they hadn't spoken since Robert's memorial service. When she asked about the Good Luck card and the sketch map inside it, there was a few moments' silence.

"Last time I saw that card was a couple of months before he died." He seemed to be choosing his words carefully. "What on earth are you doing with it? Robert brought his logbook with him to London, so that we could compare notes. He was using my card as a bookmark." Then he repeated: "What on *earth* are you doing with it? I understood that the police were unable to trace the logbook."

Fiona tried to side step the question – saying that she had found the card in Robert's sea chest, which was, in a way, true. "Do you know if he ever visited Rhodes?" She asked the question with all the casualness she could muster. Graham replied that twelve years ago the two of them had spent a working holiday on Rhodes, exploring the ruins of Kamiros.

They were both short of cash in those days, but had rented a simple wooden shack from one of the hill farmers. He couldn't remember exactly where – just that it had been quite conveniently located just a few kilometres out of Rhodes Town. "Why all the questions?" he asked. "Just a hunch," she replied, "nothing definite. I'll let you know if anything turns up. Thanks for your help."

Her head was buzzing with ideas as she replaced the receiver. Rhodes was such a distance from Crete; any connection would surely only be a tenuous one. But why leave the sketch map inside a card that wished him luck on his voyage? Maybe it was pure coincidence?

Sadly, it was the only clue they had. She would fly to Rhodes for a couple of days; just to satisfy herself that there was no possible connection, then return to Canada to resume her research for the Maitland book. If nothing else, the trip should be an interesting one. Miklos offered to accompany her, but she preferred not to waste his valuable time on a fool's errand. "I'll contact you if I need help," she promised.

* * * *

The plane touched down on the runway, in the middle of the afternoon. She booked a single room in a likely looking hotel near the harbour. The taxi driver chatted to her in Pidgin English as they drove from the airport to the centre of the town. When she mentioned Lindos, he remarked, "You must have the strong knees, yes? For the hills. But the views, they are very very good."

The following morning, she rose very early. Since marrying Patrick, they had spent several holidays exploring Mediterranean towns and cities, yet the town of Rhodes, sheltering within medieval walls, seemed more fascinating than any she had yet encountered. Perhaps it was the early morning light or the mysterious nature of her quest – who could say? She only knew that everything felt surreal, as though something extraordinary might happen, in a place such as this.

She lunched at the hotel. The manager, Kostas, made her very welcome. They chatted together for a while, in the restaurant. He was curious: a wealthy European with a trace of a Canadian accent. Added to which she was attractive, although surprisingly, alone.

Fiona met Kostas again, an hour or so later, in the bar. Continuing their conversation, and, as time was of the essence, she asked whether there had been any male strangers around town; possibly someone who had been there for several years, but of whom little was known.

Simple explanations were the best, she reasoned, so she told him that she was searching for someone who had been missing for seven years, although it was purely a long shot. "As you may imagine," explained Kostas, "an island like this has many such people. *Lotus-eaters*, I call them. There is for example, a whole community of writers and artists – all searching for inspiration. Inevitably, there are also those who are trying to escape their past."

They spoke for a while longer. He recommended that she try the *Kontiki Bar*, a popular venue for the smart set, situated a little further around the harbour. It was about a five-minute walk away. "Ask for Dmitri, behind the bar. He knows everything there is to know about the locals – and more besides."

Dmitri turned out to be a large, rather handsome bartender, with curly black hair and a moustache to match. At first, he was a little wary of her; suspicious of her motives. He'd met all kinds of neurotics, eccentrics and assorted weirdoes in his line of work. By the time she was on her second glass of wine, she was beginning to doubt her own sanity. Maybe she should simply hire a private investigator? It might be a lot easier. Her instincts, however, told her otherwise.

Dmitri eventually came over to her table. Having observed her for a while he decided to join her. During the course of their conversation, she discovered that he actually owned the bar. She described Robert in more detail; also Andreas and the Lefevres. After all, she had no idea, which of them, if any, might provide the most likely lead.

"Your friend, I think, would be in quite a state if he had survived. Also, this character... Andreas. You would be better asking my friend Christos. He is a fisherman and knows all there is to know about these waters." Fiona offered

CHAPTER TWENTY-TWO

Dmitri money but he declined. "You come back to my bar again – yes?" They shook hands. In the early evening she searched for Christos, down by Mandatui harbour. He was seated on an up-turned lobster pot, mending nets.

"Many such people are drowned... no-one ever hears of them again," the gravel-voiced old fisherman told her. "A legend tells us that our island itself once lay below the ocean. Then it rose out of the sea – a gift to the sun-god Helios. Ah well! There is beauty and at the same time – there is also death." Disappointed, she turned to go. Right now, she could do without that morbid kind of philosophy. Then a sudden thought occurred to him. He called her back.

"There *was* one such character, some years ago. But he was very rough: more like this... Andreas you talk about. I pulled him out of the sea myself. He was very close to death." Christos explained that he had taken the man to his sister, a retired nurse, who lived in a village a few kilometres out of town. She had nursed him for a while, but that was all that he could tell her.

Fiona thanked him profusely, giving him a generous amount of money for his help. This was the first real lead she'd had. Even if it turned out to be a completely false trail, at least she'd tried.

Armed with this information, the following day, she took an afternoon bus to Lindos, where Christos' sister Sofia lived. She found also an apartment set into the hillside. It had its own swimming pool, although she wasn't planning to swim: there wouldn't be time. Lindian accommodation, she soon discovered, tended to be of a basic, unsophisticated nature. The evening sun hung low on the horizon, adding a comforting glow to her room, as she settled down for the night.

Everyone in Lindos, it seemed, knew Sofia. She lived near the centre of the village. It was a fifteen-minute walk downhill, along narrow lanes. Donkeys were the main form of transport. Making her way down, she passed numerous tavernas and courtyards. On several occasions she paused, to allow donkeys and their owners or riders to pass. Once a donkey was set on course it was wise to give it right of way! There was no arguing with their stubbornness.

Christos had already telephoned his sister about Fiona's intended visit. On reaching the attractive, brilliant-white villa, she was greeted warmly by the ageing Sofia. She had received a better education than her brother, enabling her to maintain a responsible position as a nursing sister at the local hospital, for many years.

"The man you speak of, and the one I nursed back to health cannot be the same person. This Robert of yours – he was an attractive, educated man you say?" "But he may well have changed," interjected Fiona.

"No, I don't think so," Sofia said sadly, handing Fiona a cup of tea. "The creature I nursed back to health was much more primitive – like an animal – a wounded, frightened animal." She described how, for eight weeks, she had nursed him in her own home, with the help of some of the locals. At first, he was unable to speak and could only make animal noises: grunts, groans and whimpers. No payment had been received for her trouble. But time lay heavily on her hands since retirement, so she had been glad to help.

"Sometimes I was frightened, you know? He could be quite gentle – and *such* a smile. But he had mood swings. At times he could even be violent."

"What happened to him?" Fiona asked, steeling herself for the answer.

"I knew I would have to get rid of him, eventually," she explained. "It was a very difficult situation. He was so dirty – could not even wash himself. In the end Christos came down and helped him to bathe."

Sofia described how one particular day she had visited the market. On returning, she discovered that the stranger had just vanished – disappeared into thin air. Nothing further was heard of him. Then a few months later, he was seen buying goods in one of the village stores. He obviously had money, though no one knew from where. There were various rumours about how he might have obtained it.

One shopkeeper, in particular, eventually refused to serve him. Unable to speak, he would point to items and the owner would take the required money from a wad of notes, which the man offered. The trouble arose when he couldn't make himself understood: he became aggressive. On one occasion, he swept a whole row of goods off a shelf. Some of the locals thought that he must be living up in the hills; but Sofia feared that he might be dead.

"No-one could survive up there by themselves," she said, "at least not without food." Fiona decided that she should make some attempt to find the man, and if possible, view him from a distance. Her only chance would be if it were Andreas. She felt sure that he would be identifiable: Miklos had provided her with an old photograph of him, in company with a group of friends. It had been taken several years ago, but he had a wedge-shaped scar just below his right eye. Although hardly visible in the photograph, it was apparently unmistakable. If the man turned out to be a total stranger, she would return to Skiathos. It was at least worth a try.

"I have to warn you," said Sophia, clasping Fiona's hand between hers and squeezing it. "It will be a shock when you see him. You see, this man does not only have one scar. The sea and rocks can be very cruel. Most of the right-hand side of his face has been damaged."

CHAPTER TWENTY-TWO

Returning to her apartment that evening, Fiona felt very depressed. Sofia's warning about the possible danger weighed heavily upon her; she had three small children and a husband to consider.

She re-examined Robert's sketch map of Rhodes and the area close to Lindos – marked with a cross. If the map was accurate, the area he had marked was likely to be somewhere up in the hills, possibly an hour or two's walk from her present position. Fine for two young men, like Graham and Robert, but for a woman on her own...

At least she could find out what the mark represented. Then she would be on her way again... back to civilisation.

CHAPTER TWENTY-THREE

Wearing trainers and a tracksuit, Fiona headed into the hills. Thankfully, after Patrick's birth, she'd attended aerobics classes and was consequently in good shape; she'd need to be!

She carried a large rucksack containing food, drink, one change of clothes, including a week's underwear; also, a compass and a folded sun hat. Andreas' photograph was stowed in a smaller section, together with a first-aid kit. Following the main, but narrow pathway up into the hills, she made an early start – determined to find that crucial landmark, marked with a cross, by midday at the latest. All around her was the steady hum of insects. It was a beautifully fresh morning. A donkey would have been very handy, at this point.

An hour or so, and three insect bites later, she reached a fork in the pathway, either side of thick undergrowth. From this point she had an absolutely stunning view of the Acropolis. Looking back at the village below, then following the distant coastline, towards Rhodes harbour, the full scenic splendour of the island was suddenly revealed to her. But being so intent upon her purpose, such breathtaking beauty seemed relatively insignificant.

Half an hour later, she began to feel as though she had been going round in circles. She had made regular compass checks, but the vegetation and scenery, under the hot sun, seemed to merge into one. She could have sworn she'd passed that same clump of trees ten minutes ago – seen the same view below.

Glancing at her watch she realised that it was eleven thirty. There was not a soul in sight or a single dwelling place, for miles. In panic, she feared she might be lost

There was a shady spot a few yards away, in the shelter of some bushes. She was in tremendous need of a rest. Having settled there, she applied cortisone ointment to ease the irritation from insect bites, then returned the tube to the First-aid kit in her rucksack. After a hasty snack she rose to her feet. It was then that she heard the distant sound of a donkey braying. Civilisation couldn't be too far away, after all. She laughed with sheer relief. There it was again!

A much narrower pathway to the left was barely visible. Although someone had attempted to clear a way through, it was still very overgrown.

CHAPTER TWENTY-THREE

The braying seemed to be coming from that direction and was becoming more insistent.

She had to bend almost double in places, to follow the pathway; it was treacherous underfoot and branches scratched her face and limbs. Eventually she reached a clearing. Smoke was drifting upwards from somewhere, just beyond a clump of trees. Following the smoke drifts and the almost choking smell of wood smoke, she could just make out what seemed to be a derelict wooden shed. The smoke was curling from its ramshackle chimney.

A donkey was tethered to a nearby tree. No wonder it was complaining; the poor thing looked so malnourished! Insects were buzzing around its nose. She approached the shed cautiously, listening at the door. There was no sound. Hinges creaked as she pushed the door open. It was deserted; no sign of life save for the embers of a fire, slowly dying in the grate.

The furniture was ancient; one of the wooden chairs had an entire back missing. A foul stench of rotting food and neglect filled her nostrils. She stepped back in disgust. A sudden gust of wind caused the branches of a tree, growing just outside the one dingy window, to bang up against it.

Slowly, the seriousness of her predicament began to dawn on her. Until that point, although a little afraid, she had felt able to cope with any eventuality, fired by sheer determination and a singleness of purpose.

But whoever lived here might return at any moment. She was alone and defenceless... miles from anywhere. *Anything* could happen. Her mouth went dry with the realisation and the hairs on the back of her neck stood on end.

Turning to go she tried, with clammy hands, to close the door from the outside, so that no one would be any the wiser. To her dismay she realised that the door's hinges had dropped with age; she hadn't the time or energy to lift it back into place. Then she heard the cracking of twigs: someone was coming! She headed in desperation, for a gap in the bushes, crouching down in terror. Her heart was beating wildly, as though it would burst. She was trembling. She *must* try to remain calm.

A tall but hunched figure with unkempt grey hair, shuffled into view. Hurling a couple of dead animals straight through the open doorway, it began to stomp in after them. The creature paused at the door, growled angrily and looked around. Then heaving it up from the inside with the weight of one shoulder slammed it shut.

Fiona crept out cautiously and began to hare back along the rough track that she had entered by. She must get as far away from this spot, while she could... and quickly. After running and tunnelling through the undergrowth for at least a minute, until her face and arms were torn and bleeding, she suddenly stopped. What *was* she doing?

This was the closest she had ever been – or was ever likely to be – to solving the mystery about a man she had once professed to love – more than her own life. Was she going to abandon the chance – when she was so close? She lay panting on the ground for a minute or two, trying to collect her thoughts.

If she could only get sufficiently close to see his face. She could creep back, taking care not to be heard. Then she'd only to peer through that filthy window. Anything was possible. She *might* be able to see him. All was not lost.

She carried out her plan. Stealthily, by degrees, she crept back towards the shack. It's now or never, she realised. It was fortunate that he couldn't hear her heart beating! Cautiously, she slipped under the bough of the tree and peered through the window. Thank heavens she was tall!

He was putting logs on the fire, so his face wasn't visible, just his revolting mangy hair, which hung down his back in rat's tails. Fiona crouched low for a few seconds, then decided to take a second look. The leaves underfoot crunched as she raised herself once more. It was very difficult to see anything. There seemed to be no form of lighting.

With a startled cry, she turned round: the savage was upon her. She was face to face with her quarry! Grabbing her by the shoulders, he dragged her, kicking and screaming into the shack. With full force, he flung her down onto one of the beds, tying her arms to the posts on either side.

Fiona screamed and shouted in blind terror. He forced an evil-smelling rag between her lips, gagging her. She continued to struggle as best she could, but to no avail. Finally, unable to take any more, she fainted.

* * * *

The evil, foul-smelling stench filled her nostrils once more, as she regained consciousness. Suddenly, the full terrifying realisation of what had happened hit her. She felt certain that he was going to kill her!

Images of her children… and Patrick flooded through her mind as tears streamed down her face. Please God. Don't let it end like this. Perhaps any moment now she would wake up… and it would all be just a terrifying nightmare.

Gradually, she calmed herself, breathing in deeply through her nose, as her mouth remained gagged. By degrees, she tried to relax. On the opposite side of the room her captor was sleeping for the time being, snoring gently. At least she had some respite… time to formulate a plan.

Slowly her eyelids closed once more. When she awoke, to the sound of creaking, it was light. The creature was seated in an old wooden rocking

CHAPTER TWENTY-THREE

chair adjacent to the fireplace, rocking backwards forwards, backwards, forwards. The effect was quite soporific. He seemed to go on for hours.

He was staring straight ahead, as though in a trance, ostensibly, oblivious to her presence. The rhythm of the chair seemed to comfort him. The faintest of smiles was discernible upon his lips. Bit by bit the rocking slowed down, then finally ceased. Turning his head, his eyes met hers for the first time; but there was nothing behind them – just a vacant stare.

Easing himself from the chair, he moved wordlessly towards her, flexing and un-flexing his fingers. Then he produced an evil-looking knife. She closed her eyes, offering up a silent prayer: please God, don't let it all end – here and now – in this squalid little shack. Perhaps this is what happens in life, she thought. Once you've experienced ecstasy and real happiness the Piper must be paid; sooner or later life will call you to task.

Her eyes remained tightly closed. If she was going to die, she didn't want to see the face of her killer. Daylight streamed through the window. She was aware of movement, close to one of her hands. Suddenly, she felt the knots loosen on one side and then the other. Reluctantly, she lifted her eyelids – and wished she hadn't!

In normal circumstances daylight could be cruel; but this was positively *grotesque*. The entire right-hand side of the creature's face was twisted and contorted, by one massive scar, running from just below his half-closed right eye, where Andreas' original scar should have been, to a spot just above his jaw. The whole area must have been slashed open at some point, then healed badly, through neglect.

Fiona gasped, then looked away, swinging her legs over, to the other side of the bed, so that she was sitting up. Dismayed by her reaction, the recluse returned grim-faced to the chair, concealed the knife, and began once more, to rock himself.

She moved instinctively away, to a far corner of the room, into the shadows. From there she watched him warily – waiting for his next move. She had no idea what to expect. She massaged her wrists to restore the circulation.

The next two days were spent in a cat-and-mouse type of situation: each watching the other, trying to weigh up the odds; neither one trusting the other. There was total silence – brought about by habit in the one party and fear in the other. He provided food and drink, mostly in the form of meat and berries, so maybe he intended her no immediate harm? Following her initial reaction, he studiously avoided any further eye contact.

There was a broken mirror propped up on the mantle-piece, so he must be aware of his appearance, she reasoned. But he had probably received the same reaction hundreds of times, from others around him. No *wonder* he'd become a recluse!

Having conquered her fear to some extent, during the hours that followed, Fiona decided that she must do something to show that she meant him no harm. Besides, the inactivity was driving her mad! By degrees, she made an effort to tidy the interior of the shack. It looked as though it hadn't seen a broom or duster for many a year. Despite her efforts, at times the stranger seemed totally indifferent to her activities – almost as though she was invisible.

He allowed her outside, briefly at first, to answer the calls of nature; bushes being the only available solution to this; there was no toilet. A nearby stream provided water and washing facilities. It was a profound relief to discover that he was prepared to give her privacy, at least for short periods of time. Should she stay outside the hut for more than ten minutes at a time however, he came looking for her.

She had the feeling that he was constantly watching her. If she made one wrong move – tried to escape – she feared the consequences; he might produce that knife again. This time he might not hesitate to use it!

Cooking was done outside in a pot suspended over an open fire, or on a makeshift spit that he had concocted. He seemed to have retained sufficient intelligence to carry out basic chores, but otherwise appeared to be in permanent shock.

By the third day of her captivity, having made the place reasonably habitable, as opposed to a cesspit, she summoned up all of her courage. Reluctant to reveal her true identity, on the remote chance that this *was* Andreas whom she was dealing with, she coughed nervously, then began:

"My name is Mary," she offered cautiously, her daughter's name springing readily to mind. Pointing to him she asked, "What is yours?"

He seemed not to understand the question, turning his head away. She repeated the two sentences again, but to no avail. Refusing to be beaten, she decided to talk frequently as she busied herself, both inside and outside the shack. Years before, she had worked with children who had learning difficulties. Now she put this experience and the techniques she had learned, to good use. Surely he would eventually sense that he could trust her?

* * * *

It was her fourth night as a captive. They had the glow of the firelight and one candle that she had managed to find, to see by. A gruff voice broke the silence.

CHAPTER TWENTY-THREE

"Israel." Just one word. He was sitting on the edge of his bed, staring towards the firelight. "Israel!" he repeated, more vehemently this time, to no one in particular.

Summoning all of her courage she moved slowly towards him, kneeling down in front of him. Clasping one of his rough, callused hands between hers, she looked directly at him. She repeated "Israel," several times over, smiling at him. He laughed – then did the same. Sensing that she wasn't afraid, he allowed himself to trace the features of her face, slowly, one by one, with his hand. He seemed fascinated by her beauty: a face without a single blemish!

Over the course of the next few days, sensing that she meant him only good, and that she provided him with companionship, he began to open up much more, even allowing her to feed his donkey. He must have been lonely for so long, thought Fiona, beginning to feel sorry for him.

Gradually, he made an effort to communicate, albeit in disjointed sentences, combined with a kind of sign language, about the simplest of things: objects about the place, things he brought in from the area around the shack, chores they were doing. Often the sounds that he uttered were incoherent – occasionally they made sense.

Each time, she reacted as though she fully understood, trying to build up some contact with him; hopeful that in a few days time she would gain her freedom. To her amazement, the following day, he took her by the hand, leading her down to the village, accompanied by his faithful donkey.

They shopped together in a relatively civilised manner. Fiona did all the talking for him. The shopkeepers were so amazed by this new companion of his, that they made no objection. She could so easily have made her escape, at that point, but she was determined to persevere.

That afternoon, having made the steep climb back up from the village, he sat in his rocking chair, trying to keep still. He had bathed in the stream and now he was allowing her to cut his hair. All that she had for the purpose were the small, but sharp pair of scissors from her first-aid kit; but at least they were better than nothing.

Fiona's rucksack lay where she had concealed it – under the bed. She needed to keep it hidden, for inside were photographs and other items which revealed her true identity. There was one photograph that she desperately wanted to show him: the one that Miklos had given her of Andreas and his fellow fishermen. Luckily, Robert was absent from the picture.

Whilst he was putting out the remains of the fire over which, for the first time they'd cooked an afternoon meal together, she quickly removed the photograph from its small section within the sack and slipped the scissors back in. Then she hurriedly pulled out her change of clothes. She tucked the photograph into the back pocket of her clean jeans: out of sight.

Earlier that day, whilst shopping she had hastily bought a packet of disposable razors and some shaving foam; her companion's attention having been focused elsewhere. With some trepidation she now showed the shaving implements to him. At first he was very reluctant, but when he felt the gentle touch of her hands on his face and neck and smelt the fragrance of the creamy foam, he allowed her to shave off the moustache and other areas of facial hair, which he had neglected himself. She had to cut some of the more bushy parts off with the scissors first. Judging by the state of his partial beard and facial cuts, he must have previously tried to use a knife for the purpose. She winced at the thought of it – especially on the injured side. Particular care was needed as she negotiated that part.

Stepping back to admire her handiwork, her eyes suddenly met his. This time he held her gaze for several seconds. An incredibly primal urge welled up from deep within her. Hurriedly, she looked away, blushing with discomfort. This couldn't happen; he might be a mass murderer – for all she knew!

Just before going to sleep that night she summoned her courage and showed him the photograph. She had bought a powerful torch at the shop, with its own adjustable stand, enabling them to see much more clearly. It illuminated an entire section of the room, casting a large disc of light onto the wall.

For a few seconds he stared at the photograph – in complete silence. Then he became extremely agitated. He began to thump the table several times shouting "Israel Israel Israel!" Alarmed, she quickly put the photograph back in her pocket. She stroked his hair, gently calming him down by degrees.

Lying on her bed that night in the stygian darkness, she tried to analyse his reaction. Something in the photograph had obviously touched a raw nerve. Perhaps he had recognised his erstwhile handsome features and was lamenting his altered state.

She was thankful that the evening before leaving her apartment for her trip into the hills, she had telephoned the manager at her Rhodes hotel to explain what was happening, providing him with Miklos' telephone number – just in case. In confident mood, she had explained that she would be perfectly safe. However, it was agreed that, should she not return to the hotel within seven days, he would contact Miklos.

Anxious to keep track of time, she made notches on the wooden bedpost: one for each day that passed. By her calculations, only two days

CHAPTER TWENTY-THREE

remained, before the deadline. If she were to make any further progress, it would have to be the following day.

Late that night, a shadow fell across her bed. Looking up, she saw him standing over her, holding a lighted candle fixed onto a saucer with melted wax. She wondered why he hadn't used the torch. He placed the candle on the nearby table so that it shed a weak light across her. She opened her mouth to speak, but he placed two fingers across her lips: to silence her. The upper half of his body was totally naked and was particularly hairy and muscular. He was breathing heavily and seemed quite agitated. Since she had shaved him, and with the left-hand side of his face turned towards her, he appeared quite handsome, at least, by candlelight. The light danced across his eyes and she could just make out the blueness of them.

Gently, and quite reverentially, he stroked her dark-auburn tresses then slowly removed the old shirt that he had given her as a makeshift nightdress. She began to struggle but his lips came down firmly upon hers, silencing her protest.

'This can't be happening', she was thinking. 'Why now? I can't cope with this. I don't even know who he is!' Her thoughts flew to Patrick. What should she do?

She recalled Sofia's warning, about the stranger's mood swings. If she pushed him away, who knows what his reaction might be? By this time he had undressed almost completely, except for a pair of worn shorts. Fiona was totally naked.

The heat of his body was alarming, as he wrapped himself closely around her. How she wished that the bed had been larger. She clenched her teeth and closed her eyes, dreading his next move. She was aware of his male hardness, pressing against her inner thigh.

Straining to prevent herself from arousal, she kept telling herself that this man, or a man very like him, was probably responsible for Robert's death. Then, by degrees, she began to realise that he intended nothing further. Her fears were unfounded. He just wanted to huddle close to her for physical warmth and comfort. That was all. He was lonely. It seemed likely that, at least for that evening, he would make no further demands upon her.

He gave a deep sigh. She, in turn, allowed her muscles to relax. They remained in that position all night; their arms locked around each other, breathing gently.

CHAPTER TWENTY-FOUR

She was woken by birdsong. Leaving her companion, who was still sleeping, she went out for an early morning dip in the stream.

Stepping out of the water, she blushed. He was standing, absolutely naked, staring at her through the trees, which lay between the stream and the shack. She had no idea how long he had been standing there.

As she approached him, he stepped out of the shadows. He placed his hands on her shoulders, then gradually worked his way downward to caress her breasts. His tongue sought her nipples. He began to suckle each one in turn.

Playfully, she pushed him away, anxious not to arouse his anger. She ran back to the shack as quickly as she could. He pursued her. By the time he entered, she was lying on the bed, pretending to be asleep.

Instead of pursuing her further, he backed away outside. She could hear him shouting and throwing things about. The poor donkey began to bray loudly, stamping the ground with its hooves. Then everything went quiet.

She crept out, cautiously, and was just in time to see him bring an axe down on a tree stump. He had begun to chop wood. He continued for at least an hour, until he had an enormous pile of logs. She dared not go near him – not with an axe in his hand! All of a sudden, he dropped the axe, then ran towards the stream and jumped into it. Fiona felt inexplicably guilty, as though she had abandoned him. She made a fire and began to cook breakfast.

A few minutes later he joined her, dripping with water. He dressed himself in a pair of old corduroy trousers and an open-necked shirt. They sat in preoccupied silence, side by side. As she prepared breakfast, she puzzled over his obsession with the word *Israel*.

He didn't appear to be Jewish, but maybe he was a terrorist – in hiding from the authorities. Something was trying to register at the back of her mind. Was it the country he was referring to – or maybe, even... a name?

Yes, that was it. Her heart leapt within her! Now it was beginning to make sense. It *was* a name... surely? A picture flickered into her consciousness: a sailing ship with an old sea dog high up in the mast. Israel... Israel Hands!

CHAPTER TWENTY-FOUR

Her brain made an immediate connection. It had been in an old Treasury book of children's stories. Then the recollection was gone, as fast as it had appeared.

Fiona passed a plate of porridge to him and a mug of tea. Placing them on the ground to one side, he drew her closely towards him in a passionate embrace, his lips desperately seeking hers.

"Come," he said. Taking her by the hand, he led her back towards the shack: towards his bed. Just as they were about to enter, he froze in his tracks. There was a movement beyond the bushes. A man's voice was calling:

"Fiona. It's Miklos. Where are you?"

"Don't be afraid," she told him quickly, her hopes raised, but anxious that he shouldn't overreact when she was so close to freedom. "It's okay – really – he won't harm you."

At that moment Miklos emerged from behind the trees, accompanied by a doctor friend, Alexandra, whom Fiona immediately recognised from her visits to Skiathos. He was carrying a small medical bag. Unwilling to take any further risk, the hotel manager had telephoned Miklos two days earlier than planned.

Fiona took her companion gently by the hand and led him towards Miklos. He followed in silence. As the two men faced each other, for just a fleeting second, a flicker of recognition passed between them. "Ah Fiona," said Miklos lightly, "aren't you going to introduce me to your friend?"

The doctor, meanwhile, was circling around, behind the stranger. Out of the corner of one eye, she saw him place his case quietly on the ground behind him, having taken a syringe from it. Too late, the stranger turned around in alarm to confront him. But he had already stuck a hypodermic needle firmly, into the stranger's upper arm.

CHAPTER TWENTY-FIVE

"Imagine if you can," said the doctor, leaning back in his chair and placing the tips of his fingers together, triangular-fashion, "that you are on a long and arduous sea voyage. You have been searching for something, which is of tremendous importance to you." He paused for a moment to consider. "With you on that voyage is a companion of several years standing, whom you trust with your life... someone who has *never* let you down."

Rising from his seat, Yannis Stavros, a specialist in his field, moved to the window, gazing down into the street below. Then he turned back to face them.

"You are on the brink of making the discovery of a lifetime. All your plans, your dreams, are finally coming together. Then – without warning – your supposed friend, the man you have trusted for years, turns on you... *drags* you to the floor. He has a knife and he is going to kill you.

"A desperate fight ensues. You suddenly realise that it is your life or his. The choice must be made instantly. Blood is oozing through your shirt. He drags you out on deck. It is almost *certain* that you are going to die, but once on deck, you manage to grab some kind of blunt instrument. He holds you over the side; the spray is soaking your face. You can taste the salt.

"Luckily, you manage to turn the tables on your assailant – your close friend – right at the last moment. It is he, not you, who is now hanging over the side. You take a split-second decision: with your last ounce of strength you bring the weapon down on his skull, several times, smashing it to pieces. Then you toss his body over the side."

The couple seated at his desk made no reply. Then the woman began to cry. Removing a handkerchief from his breast pocket, her husband passed it to her. "Jesus Christ!" he exclaimed, as the full horror of the situation hit both of them.

Fiona had collapsed with nervous exhaustion on her return from Rhodes, falling into a deep sleep lasting almost two days. For several weeks, since their return, Yannis had been trying to unravel the mystery of this man, whom Fiona, Miklos and his doctor friend had brought back to

CHAPTER TWENTY-FIVE

Skiathos. Miklos had immediately telephoned Patrick in England, who arranged an immediate flight for himself to Skiathos. Their ever-reliable Nanny returned to British Columbia, with the children, the following day.

Patrick and Fiona decided to remain on Skiathos while the psychologist pursued his investigations. Patrick was as anxious as she, to discover whether the recluse could throw any light upon Robert's disappearance. Initially, he had been rather angry with her, for risking life and limb, on something that might simply have proved an illogical hunch. However, when he realised how exhausted she was, the strength of her determination, and the positive outcome, his anger dissolved into concern – followed by admiration – for her bravery.

Later that afternoon, the couple returned to *Club Skiathos*. Seated in the penthouse lounge, they discussed the psychologist's latest findings. Under hypnosis, it emerged that the Lindos recluse had become deranged, as a direct result of having killed his friend: the quintessential 'laughing fellow rover' of Masefield's poem, who had transmuted so horrifically, into Blackbeard.

A type of hysterical amnesia had swiftly followed the tragedy. But the stranger was by no means out of danger. For, only moments after this terrible event, the dead man's accomplices, anxious to secure their plans, had pulled up alongside the boat, in a much larger cabin cruiser.

Realising that their original plans had gone badly astray, they nevertheless bundled the injured man onto their own boat, after hiding his bloodstained shirt in the cabin below. They still needed vital information from their captive, so dragged him onto their ship, intending to grill him about the location of the missing wreck.

What they hadn't realised was that their victim was in total shock – incapable of uttering a single word. Heading at top speed for the Turkish coast, the murderous conspirators therefore tossed him overboard, onto the rocks; convinced that the impact alone would kill him. Instead, it ripped the side of his face open.

"By all the laws of nature," Yannis observed, "this man *should* be dead. But luckily, he has a remarkably strong instinct for survival. Also, by some strange quirk of fate, the passing fisherman, who rescued him, lived on an island with which our hapless victim was already familiar."

"What amazes me is that despite most of his memory being shot to pieces, he could still remember certain details," mused Patrick. "I guess his brain must have switched on to some kind of automatic pilot." "Like the location of a shack he'd once rented," added Fiona.

"God help us if you'd known each other's true identity," said Patrick with a grimace. "I wouldn't have been too happy about it – that's for sure.

I hate to think what might have happened between the two of you, under those circumstances!" Fiona thought it best not to mention that, had Miklos arrived just ten minutes later, she probably *would* have discovered the man's identity – albeit in a rather unorthodox fashion!

The following day she returned to the hospital. This time she was alone. The doctor had advised that, for the time being, she should be his only visitor. She felt very optimistic about the future – it was the year 2004 after all. In the last few years rapid advances had been made in the field of plastic surgery. She felt sure that, given time and patience, his poor face could be restored to something resembling its former glory. Canadian plastic surgeons were reputed to be amongst the best in the field. Once he had returned with them to British Columbia, arrangements could be made. They would also hire the best psychiatric help that money could buy; to continue the good work that Yannis had begun.

As a result of this new information, Europol had renewed their search for the Lefevres. Their new enquiries now spanned the whole of Turkey, from the Bosporus to the southern borders. This time there would surely be no escape.

Fiona and Mr. Stavros spent well over half an hour discussing the prognosis for his patient's recovery. "I hope that you are a good actress, Mrs. Maitland," began Yannis. "You will certainly need to be, to execute the scenario I am about to propose."

He explained that treatment had progressed to a point where the patient could now recognise her. For her part, she must pretend that it was still 1997. The second Cretan voyage, once again unsuccessful, had just ended. "You must agree that you are about to marry Robert," he instructed. "Your husband is visiting me later today. It is fortunate indeed that he and Robert were such good friends. He has already assured me that, like you, he is willing to do whatever it takes."

Yannis likened the situation to suspending a delicate tightrope across a vast gorge. "If we can maintain this pretence over the next few weeks, we could be well on our way to resolving the problem, once and for all. You must give no indication whatsoever that time has moved on and that you are married to Patrick – that would be completely disastrous! Make no reference to your husband, or the children. Do you think that you can do it?" Fiona assured him once again that she would do anything she could to resolve the situation. By prior arrangement with the doctor, she clutched a photograph of Andreas, in her hand.

"You should be perfectly safe," Yannis reassured her, as he escorted her down the labyrinth of corridors, towards the stranger's room. "He is sufficiently sedated to prevent him from giving you any serious problems."

CHAPTER TWENTY-FIVE

They paused, just a few yards away from his room. Yannis noticed, just in time, that she was still wearing her wedding and engagement rings. Lowering his voice, he advised her to remove them immediately. She felt rather foolish for having overlooked such an important detail; as far as the patient on the other side of the door was concerned, she was most definitely single!

"Remember my advice Fiona," Yannis cautioned, placing a paternalistic hand on her shoulder. "Be very gentle with him," he said, almost in a whisper... "No sudden shocks. At the moment he's lost seven years, he's trapped in 1997 – expecting things to be exactly as they were before he set sail. In heaven's name, do not disillusion him!

"It's a good thing that you found him when you did," he added. "A few more months of living on the edge and I think we'd have lost him for good." When she considered how close she had come to abandoning the whole search, her blood ran cold. What she Miklos and the doctors had achieved between them was nothing short of a miracle!

The man waiting for her, as she entered the private room, was scarcely recognisable as the savage whom she had encountered on Rhodes. He was well-groomed and smartly dressed. The injured side of his face was hidden by a large surgical dressing.

Seating herself beside him on the sofa, she spoke gently to him for a minute or two, then showed him the same photograph that she had shown him on Rhodes.

"I finally remembered. Israel Hands – in Stevenson's *Treasure Island*. If I'd known it was you, I'd have made the connection earlier," she explained. "He tried to kill the cabin boy, Jim Hawkins, didn't he?"

"It was a life or death situation – I realise that now," replied the stranger. "There was no choice." There was a substantial pause, then he jumped to his feet: "We have to hurry Fiona!" he said, grabbing her by the hand. His own hands were shaking. "Father Darius is expecting us. Come – there's no time to lose!"

"But we have all the time in the world," she assured him. "We'll make you better – now that I've found you at last." Thanks to the sedative, she was able to coax him back into his chair, without too much difficulty. She added: "We'll make you well again – I promise!"

If she could only tell him about her visits to Saint Nikolas, the church where they were to have been married and the lonely vigils she'd kept there, since his disappearance. But she must keep such thoughts locked away inside her. A relapse at this stage would be unthinkable. Maybe some day, when he was fully recovered, she could help him to understand what she'd been through? But how could she speak to him about the past seven years, when for him the new millennium hadn't even begun?

She hoped that after transferring him to a Victoria clinic, the doctors would be able to ease him towards the present day; across the threshold into the 21st Century. Slowly, his emotional and physical scars would heal, in the nurturing environs of *Tralee* – her family's Canadian paradise. Until that time, they would all need infinite patience.

She kissed him gently, on the cheek, half wishing that the two of them actually *could* be suspended in time; transported back to their hideaway – to live out the rest of their days amongst the fragrant pines and olive-clad hills of Skiathos.

* * * *

Gazing across the lake at *Tralee*, the fading light of a Canadian summer's evening slowly drew a veil across all of her memories. She watched as their intrepid explorer friend steered the motor boat safely back, towards the jetty, after a day spent on the island. Patrick and their three children were seated safely on deck.

For just a few fleeting seconds, her thoughts returned to the Skiathos clinic, three years ago. He'd responded passionately, pulling her closely to him. The kiss lasted for several heart-stopping, but impossible moments. Then, with a long, deep sigh she'd said:

"Welcome home Robert."

* * * *

Once the news of his survival spread, those who had inherited his property were only too delighted to return it to him. After several more months, in Mr. Stavros' clinic, although increasingly prepared to face the outside world, he returned to England for a year or so, to stay with his family.

This present holiday was the third short vacation that he had spent with the Maitlands at *Tralee*. A week every year, under the same roof as Fiona, was as much as he could bear, in the circumstances. There were still days when depression set in; specialists predicted that it could be several years before he was free of these mood swings. The Maitland children proved ideal therapy at such times. Robert delighted in telling them tales of the high seas and hidden treasure; making up adventure stories for them.

CHAPTER TWENTY-FIVE

He now planned to have another boat ready, in a few months' time; very similar to the one that had been wrecked. It would keep the same name, *Silver's Arrow*, despite the unhappy associations.

Robert described the new *Silver's Arrow* to the children, showing them detailed plans of the interior and the exterior, equipped with all the latest 21st Century technology.

He invented even more action-packed tales about the adventures they would share together, on board the new ship, with Robert Junior as the admiral and himself as captain. Mary, he suggested, could be First Mate; Patrick Junior would be Cabin Boy.

"But what about mummy?" asked Mary. "Oh, she can be ship's cook," he replied, winking at Fiona.

As the week ended, Robert flew to Athens, where work was to begin on the new craft.

In her dreams, Fiona began to imagine even more fanciful scenarios, on board the new ship. For it seemed to her that Life itself is like a brightly-glowing fire. The events that happen in people's lives are like sparks that shoot out, intermittently, from the fire. Some will burn themselves out, as they hit the ground, but others will ignite, beginning new fires of their own.

One thing that she had learned, since that fateful holiday on Skiathos, was not to be afraid of the sparks that life might throw at her. Robert's proposed voyage, on the new *Silver's Arrow*, began to kindle her imagination. Who could say where such an exciting enterprise might lead?

* * * *

During the six months that followed, however, the Maitland family heard nothing further from Robert. Just as they were fearing that he might have had a relapse, a letter arrived, together with a gold-embossed invitation card. In the covering letter, Robert explained that the brand-new 'high tech' version of *Silver's Arrow* was now ready for her maiden voyage. The card was an invitation to the Launch Ceremony, in Athens. Fifty or so other close friends were invited to the celebrations.

Patrick suggested that they should combine this with a week's holiday in Athens, giving them a few extra days with their old friend.

A couple of days after the Maitlands received their invitation Robert telephoned to explain that the Athens press had, somehow, got hold of the story about his miraculous 'Return from the Dead'. Consequently, the Launch was to receive television and radio coverage too. He could hardly contain his excitement – what a reversal of fortune!

The Launch was a huge success. Television producer Helena Nikolaos decided to do a follow-up documentary about the unsolved attempt on Robert's life. Who exactly had tried to murder him? And why were the murderers still at large?

Helena, an attractive blonde, spent several days interviewing Robert and gathering a wealth of background information. During the weeks that followed, a relationship began to grow between Robert and Helena. They began dating.

The initial documentary was so successful and the viewing figures so high that her television bosses immediately proposed a further series of programmes, but this time about *Silver's* maiden voyage. There would be a television crew of three: Helena – the reporter; a cameraman and a sound technician. All three would be on board with Robert, as he departed for the Azores. He was resolved to give Crete a 'wide berth' – despite Helena's suggestion that they should re-visit the Gulf of Harnia – the scene of the crime. Robert explained to her that he couldn't foresee a day when his psyche would be sufficiently recovered from such a trauma, to pay a return visit. Secretly, he feared a relapse, should he attempt to do so.

Before his voyage to the Azores, Robert had undergone a series of plastic surgery operations. Although the injured side of his face would always be scarred, the surgery was, by degrees, making his appearance more tolerable.

Robert and the television crew were away for several months. Patrick and Fiona received an e-mail from him, every two or three weeks, updating them about the trip, their 'ports-of-call' and various incidents that occurred en route. He mentioned Helena frequently and with tremendous affection. Fiona gradually began to accept that her own relationship with Robert had become a thing of the past. She was simply thankful, she told herself, that she had been able to rescue him, before it was too late.

Meanwhile, she completed her book: *An Illustrated History of the Maitland Family*, which was successfully published. Patrick's career as an artist went from strength to strength, as he acquired an international reputation, presenting a range of exhibitions at home and abroad, accompanied, in some cases, by Fiona.

The three children were doing well at school. Apart from her husband's career, the family now occupied most of Fiona's time, together with the day-to-day running of *Tralee* and a broad range of social occasions. Life *seemed* to be entering a more harmonious and settled phase for Patrick, Fiona and Robert, compared to the turmoil of previous years. At last, there was time for them to relax – and begin to get some real satisfaction out of life.

CHAPTER TWENTY-SIX

Since the late 1980s, visitors to Palm Beach, Florida, have aspired to stay 'down by the breakers'. As Helena and Robert set sail for the Azores, on a balmy day in May, security cameras posted around *The Breakers* complex, picked up a cream-coloured Daimler, its windows glinting in the sunlight, as it swept into the courtyard of Henry Flagler's opulent establishment.

Henry, the son of a Presbyterian minister, was born in Hopewell, New York, on January 2nd 1830. He had accumulated a vast fortune, through innate business acumen, boundless energy and sweeping vision... a man after Josh's own heart! Flagler made a vast fortune in Cleveland and New York, as a partner of John D. Rockefeller, in the Standard Oil Company. From there he turned his attention to becoming a resort developer and railroad king.

There was valet parking at *The Breakers*, so Josh could forget about the Daimler, until Saturday evening. He was greeted in the porte-cochère by the doorman: "Good afternoon sir. Welcome to *The Breakers*."

Josh Martinez had just one medium-sized suitcase. He only planned to stay a couple of days, then he'd be off on his travels again. Having loaded the case onto the bellman's cart the porter ushered Josh through the front door. He checked in at the marble reception desk, in the lobby.

The Breakers was a miniature metropolis, with five hundred and sixty rooms, including fifty-seven suites. Several hundred guests checked in and out of this ocean-front city every day. Its eight restaurants catered for several thousand people.

On entering his suite Josh headed immediately for the window. He remained spellbound, for a while... gazing out at the Atlantic Ocean. Although he had stayed at the hotel on four previous occasions, he never failed to be impressed by the sheer luxury of the place and its spectacular setting.

He took a few minutes' nap on the comfortable bed, settling back on to the feather-down pillows. Noticing the CD alarm clock to his left, he made a mental note to rise early, the following morning. As it was only 2pm he planned to play a round of golf later, on one of the hotel's two courses, followed by dinner at 7pm in the *Italian Restaurant*.

The evening meal fulfilled all his expectations. It began with a soft-shell crab appetizer and an entrée of rack of lamb. Meanwhile turndown attendants had begun the evening service. Between 6 and 10pm each one of them would enter about forty empty guest rooms, turning down the bed, tidying up the bathroom; leaving fresh towels and chocolates.

Returning to his room, later that evening, Josh found that the attendant had put a compact disc in the CD player, welcoming him back with the sleep-inducing sound of the ocean. What a place! The bathroom, which had resembled a bombsite when he left it, was once more neat and tidy. He smiled to himself... such are the trappings of wealth – and by God, he'd earned them!

* * * *

"Good morning Mr. Martinez. This is your wake-up call. It is 7am. The forecast is for fine Florida weather today, in the high eighties. Have a wonderful day!"

Today was Friday – the end of an extremely busy week. Dragging his naked body out of bed he reached for a white terrycloth bathrobe.

The living area had an oversized armoire with a colour television. There was also a dual telephone line, with voice mail, and a data port in each phone; high-speed Internet access, play station, video games and in-room movies – a 'high-tech' aficionado's paradise!

After a relaxing bath, he plugged in his laptop, to confirm that the breakfast-brunch meeting, hurriedly arranged the previous morning, had not been cancelled. But all was well. Still dressed in his white bathrobe, he worked at his laptop, collecting information for his new clients.

At 10.30am he selected his second-best suit, exiting his room just before 11am – heading for the *Oceanside Seafood Bar*, where he'd reserved a table for three. As he waited for his guests, he sipped a club soda, with ice and lemon, at the bar. He intended to keep a clear head; this might prove a tricky situation – although nothing that he couldn't handle.

Ordering a second club soda, Josh reflected on the colourful history of the hotel's founder, Henry Flagler, a partner of John D. Rockefeller. Despite several tragedies in his life, including two fires at the hotel and the tragic deaths of close family members, Flagler's spirit persisted. In 1926 he produced this Italian Renaissance-style landmark, where Josh was staying. There's determination for you... what a character he must have been!

His guests arrived at 11.30. The three businessmen were then escorted to their table. To their immediate left, as they looked out of the windows,

CHAPTER TWENTY-SIX

was a walkway, bordered by a wall; beyond which lay a breathtaking view of the ocean. The three men regarded each other rather nervously, as the waiter took their order.

The younger of Josh's two guests seemed preoccupied with watching the breakers roll in. The older man appeared to be the main spokesman. Martinez knew precious little about his new clients – except that they were foreigners, with some kind of merchandise to sell.

The older man introduced himself as Monsieur Gautier; the younger man was an Associate of his. They were in the Import-Export business. Josh came highly recommended, by a former, highly satisfied client. He took a file out of his black leather briefcase, referring periodically to the documents that it contained.

As the conversation progressed, Monsieur Gautier made it clear that if the three of them were to do business, he would require the utmost discretion from Josh. He understood, from this mutual acquaintance that he'd mentioned, that Mr. Martinez could be relied upon to keep all business dealings strictly confidential.

Over the years, Martinez had acquired a wealth of business associates and contacts, catering for a wide range of special services. Monsieur Gautier's informant was confident that Josh would undoubtedly be able to help. They had certain highly valuable merchandise to dispose of, which would require his particular expertise. The commission should therefore be considerable – several thousands of dollars.

Once their terms of business had been established, over a lunch of beef tenderloin, profiteroles and an excellent cabernet sauvignon, Josh invited the two Frenchmen to join him in a round of golf. The younger man, who had remained silent until that point, quickly explained that, regrettably they were unable to stay, as they had other pressing matters to attend to.

Two hours after their arrival the two strangers departed for a large cabin cruiser, moored within reasonable walking distance of the hotel. As the Frenchmen made their exit, three ground-keepers were mowing the grass, edging and weeding. A fourth gardener was planting flowers alongside one of the pathways.

Josh returned to his room for a short siesta, and to mull over the notes that he had made, during their lunchtime meeting.

There was something about these new clients that he found a little disturbing. He hadn't remained a successful entrepreneur for all of these years without developing an instinct for such things. The older man, for example, had been rather vague about the origins and precise nature of the merchandise... never a good sign. His younger colleague had been edgy throughout the meeting, glancing nervously at fellow diners, on adjacent tables, from time to time.

The two men were renting a beach house on South Beach, Miami. Josh had agreed to a second meeting there, in a few days' time.

After making a number of telephone calls, to 'sound out' some of his contacts, including the ever-reliable Kurt Lobowitz, a hard-bitten private investigator, Josh settled down for a siesta, making a mental note to take a trusted colleague with him, to the South Beach meeting. Brad Carnegie had been in this game far longer than he had. If there was something suspicious about these clients, he could be relied upon to suss it out.

Josh left *Breakers* around noon, the following day, calling in at the Signature Shop before his departure, to buy some Guerlain cosmetics for one of his lady friends. He was not a monogamous guy – never had been. Why settle for one woman? As a successful businessman he could afford to pick-and-choose, changing partners whenever he pleased.

CHAPTER TWENTY-SEVEN

Miami, otherwise known as 'the magic city', remains a crossroads of cultures – an eclectic mix of neighbourhoods, which are still evolving.

Having visited South Beach a few times, during the last decade, Josh was in no doubt that although Miami had matured, transforming itself into a global hotspot for design, arts, stellar restaurants and clubs, its roots as a tropical wild child were still there... somewhere just below the surface. The irony of such a meeting place, with these particular clients, was not lost on him, as he and Brad Carnegie motored down, from West Palm Beach.

South Beach's fabled waterfront strip, representing the Miami that the world had come to know, through the *Miami Vice* television series and other media, had undergone a metamorphosis of its own. Nowadays it was becoming known as America's Riviera, with many upmarket restaurants and clubs.

Brad, dressed in chauffeur's uniform, was driving the silver Rolls Royce, with Josh playing the role of his employer, on the back seat. It was a ploy which the two friends had used several times before, not only to protect their backs, but because it appealed to Josh's wicked sense of humour.

The strategy had worked like a charm, whenever clientele seemed less than reliable, enabling Brad to remain close at hand, for any eventuality. So far, no one had suspected that anything was amiss. Not only was Brad a shrewd businessman, and a consummate actor, but he also had a Black Belt in Judo. Thankfully, he'd never had to demonstrate his skills – but there was always a first time!

The Rolls was one of a collection of five magnificent cars, which Josh kept under lock and key in his spacious, bungalow-sized garage, back in West Palm Beach. The collection also included the Daimler, which he'd driven to *Breakers*, a Jaguar, an Aston Martin and a Porsche.

En route to Miami, Brad and Josh discussed possible strategies. Brad had suggested a series of subtle questions, designed to extract further information from the two Frenchman, regarding the merchandise that they proposed to sell. The only certainty, apart from the considerable value of their booty, was that a significant quantity of gold was involved. In all likelihood, the items couldn't be 'fenced' in their present form. Where possible they would have to be melted down into ingots, and shipped elsewhere.

Josh was anxious to ensure that this wasn't a police 'Sting' by Europol, Interpol, or some other organisation. Some of his colleagues, whose greed had made them a little careless, were currently serving prison sentences, as a result of undercover operations. He had no plans to join them!

South Beach comprises twenty-three southernmost sections of an island, separating Biscayne Bay and the Atlantic Ocean. Originally purchased in the 1870s, surprisingly, for coconut farming, it was the first section of Miami Beach to be developed, in the early 20th Century.

There had been numerous changes, man-made and natural, over the years. These included a booming regional economy, increased tourism and the 1926 hurricane, which destroyed much of the area. It had risen from the ashes to become a 21st Century major entertainment destination, with hundreds of boutique hotels, nightclubs and restaurants; popular with American and international tourists alike.

Following the attack on Pearl Harbour, in 1941, the Army Air Corps took command of Miami Beach. In 1966 it became even more famous when the *Jackie Gleason Show* was filmed there. By the late 1970s and throughout the 1980s, South Beach had become, for the most part, a retirement community. Most of its ocean-front hotels and apartment building were filled with the elderly, living on small fixed incomes.

Josh recalled being taken there, by his father, to visit his Uncle Bernie, an elderly, ex-Marine who had fallen on hard times. If anything was guaranteed to convince a young Josh of the power of the almighty dollar, that was it – it was never going to happen to him... he shuddered whenever he thought about it!

As they grew closer to their destination, Josh described his uncle's misfortune to Brad: Bernie had had some really tough breaks, not least of which were the sleazy neighbours, who gradually took over the area.

"There were the drug dealers to deal with too – and the junkies," commented Brad. "Do you remember *Scarface* – Al Pacino and the rest of those guys? The film came out around 1983, I guess – all those 'cocaine cowboys' using the area as a base. Your uncle must have thought he'd died and gone to hell... poor guy!"

"They didn't have to look far, location-wise, when they made *Miami Vice*. It was a gift!" Josh replied. "They had their pick of derelict buildings on South Beach for the thugs and drug addicts – no need to build special sets – must have saved them tens of thousands of dollars in overheads!"

"My cousin Sondra, you know – the one who's a top fashion designer? She got started in South Beach, way back in '89," continued Brad. "The fashion industry had a kindov Renaissance in the area, back then. That's where she got her first big break. She's worth millions now – lucky bitch!"

CHAPTER TWENTY-SEVEN

From Interstate 95 they took a left onto the 395, after Wynwood, crossing Biscayne Bay Beach to South Beach, which separates the Bay from the Atlantic Ocean. The numerical streets criss-crossing the neighbourhood, ran from east to west, starting with First Street and Lincoln Road: largely pedestrianised – between 16th and 17th. Josh had plenty of time to study the map. He'd counted thirteen main roads, running from north to south – one helluva network!

From the Biscayne Bay side, he noted, there was Bay Road, West Avenue, Alton Road, Lenox, Michigan; then Jefferson, Meridian, Euclid and Pennsylvania Avenues; Drexel Avenue, Washington Avenue, Collins Avenue (Route A1A) and finally Ocean Drive.

Josh and Brad headed for one of South Beach's most 'up-and-coming' neighbourhood's, Collins Park: an area enclosed within 17th Street to the south; 23rd Street to the north; to the east was the Atlantic Ocean, to the west, Washington Avenue and Pinetree Drive.

Jules Gautier's beach house lay to the east. Like *Breakers* it enjoyed spectacular views of the ocean. Monsieur Gautier had provided plentiful supplies of beer and sandwiches. His younger colleague, Marc Chagrin, was away on other business. The three men discussed the proposed deal, in generalities, over lunch. Then Brad retired to the adjacent lounge, where he picked up a journal, pretending to read it.

Rather reluctantly, Jules gave out snippets of information to Josh – one piece at a time; like a fisherman, slowly extending his net – a rather apt metaphor, considering they were in Gautier's lanai, with the distant sound of breakers crashing onto the shore.

The Frenchman oozed charm, explaining quite plausibly to Josh, that the reason for his caution was because the articles, which happened to have come into his possession, fell into the Treasure Trove category. Due to various legalities, which he felt sure that a man of his experience would understand, he had to be completely sure about who he was dealing with. It would be so easy for the authorities to have someone 'planted' on the inside, filtering all of the information back to them.

Josh used all of his diplomatic skills to glean as much extra information as he could. Two or three beers later, however, the one thing that Jules had neglected to mention was where the merchandise was stashed; it was probably in an extra large Dade County bank vault… like looking for the proverbial needle in a haystack!

Josh couldn't help concluding, from some of the phrases that the French entrepreneur was using, that he had probably worked for a financial establishment, at some point.

Jules also handed him a partial list of the items: at least fifty per cent were various kinds of antique jewellery – some with precious stone settings. Josh reassured his French client that he would get back in touch, once he'd been able to run the list past certain specialists in the field of antiques. Over thirty items were of solid gold. By these means, explained Josh, he would then be in a position to offer Monsieur Gautier a fair price for the merchandise – allowing, of course, for expenses incurred.

Gautier seemed totally unconcerned about the historical significance of the treasure and more than happy to have some of the items melted down and transformed into ingots. He simply wanted to get them off his hands, with all possible speed. At this point he revealed that he was merely a 'Go-Between' – acting on behalf of a wealthy lady friend of his, who also lived in Collins Park. She needed to liquidate some of her assets – as quickly as possible.

The neighbourhood, he elaborated, was currently undergoing considerable gentrification: many of the old apartments from the 1980s, some of which still had bars on the windows, were being purchased by major real estate developers, who planned to convert them into condominiums. His lady friend, Thelma, wanted a piece of the action.

Despite adopting Brad Carnegie's tactful style of questioning, which he'd had years to perfect, Jules steadfastly refused to give Josh further details regarding his lady friend's identity, explaining that she was a former paramour of his – so Josh must surely see that he couldn't *possibly* betray her trust. Meanwhile, Brad sat quietly in the lounge, the other side of the lanai's slightly open doors, maintaining the role of dutiful chauffeur, but listening… intently.

* * * *

Motoring back that evening, Josh and Brad discussed their options. Top of the list was running a check on the merchandise. As Gautier wouldn't reveal his sources then police contacts would have to be employed, to see if any of the items were on the Hot List of stolen goods. Meanwhile, the ever-reliable Lobowitz would be assigned the task of tracking down Gautier's former mistress.

A safe distance away from the beach house, Brad pulled over, tossed his chauffeur's jacket and cap onto the back seat of the Rolls, then jumped into the front passenger seat alongside Josh, who had slipped in, behind the wheel. Brad was relieved to ditch the jacket: the temperature had shot up several degrees. He loosened his collar and tie, as Josh inserted a James Brown CD, to ease them through the heavy Rush Hour traffic.

CHAPTER TWENTY-SEVEN

* * * *

He and Josh rendezvoused for coffee the following morning, in Josh's office, to plan their investigation in more detail and to make several phone calls. They had collaborated on a range of projects over the years – this one should be a piece of cake. Smooth as clockwork, they planned each of the stages that would be needed to see the deal through.

Brad left just before lunchtime, bound for a meeting with a certain police inspector, with canny Gautier's only half-completed list of merchandise in his inside pocket. They would need to access Europol data, to crack this one!

Josh had given his secretary the day off. He sat with notepad in hand, gazing at his waterfront view. E-mails and faxes were not an option in this case: too easy to copy or hack into. It would be strictly handwritten notes and the indispensable shredder!

He jotted down a list of everything that they'd covered to date, on the Gautier project. Enquiries via the local force would be insufficient this time. In addition to *Europol* he and Brad had decided to enlist the combined help of a Fine Arts expert and an Art Historian. They'd employed them, as a partnership, on a previous project, seven years before, with excellent results. Hopefully, they hadn't retired. Even if they had, he would make it well worth their while to rejoin his payroll.

CHAPTER TWENTY-EIGHT

Kurt Lobowitz's office was hardly of the Mickey Spillane variety – a burgeoning list of wealthy clients had seen to that! He had a roomful of state-of-the-art technology, to speed up his data processing, turning out reports to satisfied clients at record speed.

Such was his success that the word had spread like wildfire, over the past five years. Now they were practically queuing at the door.

Nevertheless, Kurt could always spare time to see Mr. Martinez, even at short notice. He owed Josh a great deal, including the initial financial backing he'd needed, after retiring eight years ago from the Force, to set up on his own as a Private Investigator.

Josh had loaned him thousands of dollars, without interest. Kurt subsequently worked off the debt, via various cases that his benefactor put his way. After three years, he was in the clear – the debt was paid. What could be better? The relationship between the two men, as Kurt was a few years younger than Josh, was like that of a younger and older brother.

As he entered Kurt's office that morning, Martinez was in an uncharacteristically sombre mood. There was something about the Gautier proposal that didn't quite scan. The details that he was able to give Kurt, to open an investigation into the mysterious 'Thelma', were sketchy, to say the least! Somehow, the treasure trove had come into her possession, but how unlikely was that? And who was she anyway? She could be operating under a totally false name. Perhaps if Kurt, or one of his staff, were to 'tail' Gautier for a few days, they might come up with something.

Following his meeting with Kurt, Josh departed to a local wine bar for a well-earned lunch, still feeling uneasy.

Lobowitz, on the other hand, couldn't wait to get started. This was a job that demanded his personal touch, rather than assigning it to one of his associates.

During the two weeks that followed, he trailed Monsieur Gautier, practically around the clock. But the Frenchman was nobody's fool. If the mysterious 'Thelma' was still his mistress, he was taking great care to have no contact whatsoever with her.

CHAPTER TWENTY-EIGHT

A change of approach was called for. Kurt perused his copy of the partially-completed merchandise list, which Gautier had given to Josh, then phoned his client to see whether their police contact had succeeded in linking any of the items, with stolen goods. The antique jewellery seemed the most likely way of finding a breakthrough.

Josh, however, informed him that, despite hours of searching police computer records, no information about the origin of any of the items had yet been found.

At this stage, another, even more urgent case required Kurt's attention, so he assigned the Gautier case to one of his associates, Karen Brady. Armed with the list, she spent two days in the Museum of Fine Arts, delving into history books and computer records, to find a connection.

Early in the morning of the third day, when she was beginning to weary of the whole business, she suddenly made a breakthrough, by cross-referring two of the rings on the list of treasure trove. Two Search Engines later, she discovered references to a Spanish galleon – the *Queen Isabella*. Returning to the office, for more privacy, she 'Googled' the name of the galleon into the home page of her laptop.

Near the top of the list of references that this produced were three entries about a television documentary, concerning the near-death experience of Dr. Robert Osborne. Immediately below these were a couple of headings: *Silver's Maiden Voyage*.

Karen made a long distance phone call to the television company in Athens, which had produced the *Return from the Dead* documentary. Within two days, a CD of the documentary arrived in Kurt's Office, by Special Delivery.

* * * *

Kurt and Josh sat in Josh's office later that evening, watching the documentary, over several beers. The programme emphasised the point that the criminals responsible for the whole, sordid affair, had still not been found; despite the concerted efforts of Europol and Interpol, they continued to give police 'the slip'.

Josh almost choked on his beer when he realised the brutality and callousness involved. What had started out as a lucrative business proposition was now changing into something far more sinister. "We'll have to turn these guys over to the cops," insisted Kurt.

But Josh had other ideas: "The loot could be stashed away somewhere, maybe in that fancy beach house of theirs. If we search the place ourselves, we could make some money out of this, on the side. What say we take a trip down there – and find out for ourselves? We could have a fifty-fifty split."

"But even if we find some of the treasure, we've still got the problem of getting rid of it and turning it into hard cash," protested Kurt.

"You can leave that to me Lobowitz," retorted Josh. "It's never been a problem before!"

* * * *

But Josh and Kurt weren't the only people to happen upon the story. During a return business trip from California, Gautier's younger business associate, Marc Chagrin, had been casually leafing through the pages of an in-flight magazine.

Suddenly, he flicked over to an article about the up-and-coming TV Journalist, Helen Nikolaos; he was only half reading it – normally he found such publications quite tedious: there wasn't much that he hadn't already done or experienced before, so what could a magazine like that teach him?

But suddenly he sat bolt upright! Helen's rise-to-fame, according to the article, had arisen from her documentary work about a certain Dr. Osborne, whose boat had been shipwrecked off the Gulf of Harnia. Chagrin read the article with mounting incredulity. His face turned bright crimson. Where was that stewardess? He needed a drink!

* * * *

Gambling on the fact that both Frenchmen would be away for the evening, Lobowitz and Josh motored down from West Palm Beach to Miami. If the Frenchmen were at home then they'd simply stay a day or two longer. However, their luck was in – the beach house was deserted.

The sun was setting over South Beach, as the two men completed their search of Jules Gautier's premises, but to no avail: they searched every inch, but found nothing.

Josh decided to find a hotel and departed, to book two rooms for the night. Kurt, meanwhile, determined not to be beaten, took out a torch and began to search the wooden structure below the house: maybe there were hidden, waterproof packages underneath there somewhere? Perhaps they'd been looking in the wrong place? After all, these were cunning men they were dealing with.

Half an hour later, he'd still found nothing. He slumped, exhausted, on the beach, a few yards away from the house, waiting for Josh to return.

CHAPTER TWENTY-EIGHT

Minutes later, there was still no sign of his colleague. The evening air was growing chilly. Kurt pulled his coat collar up, to keep him warm.

Growing ever more impatient, he shuffled out across the sand, towards the waves. As he walked further away from the beach house, the beach became darker. There was only a half moon. Standing by the water's edge, Kurt watched the distant lights from passing ships.

One of the ships sounded its horn. It was the very last sound that he heard. As a rock smashed the back of his skull, his face was pushed below the reddening ocean.

His lungs began to fill with water...

CHAPTER TWENTY-NINE

Sleep came very slowly that night, as he lay at anchor. He'd been at sea for several days and nights, with no definite plans in mind.

The trip to the Azores had been highly successful and had been broadcast in sixteen different countries. Magazine articles about him had followed, plus radio and television appearances, by himself and Helena. They had made quite a name for themselves.

But now they had parted company. Helena had been headhunted by a top American television network and was spending a great deal of her time in the States. He had visited her for a fortnight or so, in California, just three months ago, but the fields in which each of them was now engaged, seemed worlds apart.

Robert was determined to return to maritime exploration, once he'd taken a few more months of recreational cruising. He needed time out, to consider his future plans, particularly with regard to his relationships with women – which seemed to be going nowhere!

Helena, on the other hand, seemed hell-bent on pursuing a career as a top producer of documentaries. The sexual chemistry that had existed between them was rapidly dissipating as they pursued their individual goals.

The nightmares that had plagued him, ever since significant parts of his memory began to return, were thankfully becoming less frequent. The most horrific of these was, unfortunately, the last to leave him: the memory of Andreas' blood-soaked skull, staring eyes and the sheer weight of his body, as he hauled him over the side – to a watery grave.

During the more rational daylight hours, Robert reassured himself, over and over again, that he'd had no choice – it was kill or be killed. But those startled eyes continued to haunt him.

He was also tormented by a notion, which kept niggling away at the back of his mind and refused to go away – that he and Andreas had actually *discovered* the wreck of the *Queen Isabella* – making two dives, to bring pieces back for authentication.

But he'd made so many dives in the past. How could he be sure that these weren't simply older memories returning, out of context?

CHAPTER TWENTY-NINE

He discussed this dilemma with the neurologist who was treating his memory loss. But, as the only person who could collaborate the success or otherwise of their mission lay somewhere at the bottom of the ocean, it was a mystery that would probably remain unsolved. Certainly, no sign of treasure was ever found on *Silver's Arrow*.

However, it seemed of little consequence now. What was really important was that he was alive and well, having been saved by the Love of his Life. He thought about her constantly. Even though he now knew that he could never possess her, no power on earth could erase her from his mind. Love of that magnitude couldn't just be switched on and off, like a tap. She was the first person he thought about on waking, every single morning and many times, throughout each day; at night she was there, in his dreams.

Absent-mindedly leafing through the pages of his Log Book, which the police had returned to him in due course, he turned back once more to the opening page, which bore the inscription:

Twenty Years from now, you will be more disappointed by the things you didn't do,
than by the ones you did.
So throw off the bowlines, sail away from the safe harbour.
Catch the Trade winds in your sails.
Explore. Dream. Discover.

Those words had been so inspirational for him as a young man, setting off on his earlier voyages of exploration. Although the author was unknown to him at that time he copied it into his Log Book, it sounded like the kind of observation that someone like Mark Twain might come up with!

Immediately below the quotation, in his customary, meticulous way, he'd made a note, that if you actually did as the author suggested and set sail following the trade winds, you would end up at the equator. He'd added a postscript to this, observing that Trade Winds, in both the northern and southern hemispheres, sweep easterly, because of the earth's rotation towards the equator.

* * * *

In her lakeside mansion at *Tralee*, Fiona was finalising her travel arrangements for a trip to Ireland. Patrick and the children had already departed for Bantry Bay, three days before, for the start of his Irish tour, which he'd been planning with great enthusiasm, for some time.

Over the next four weeks, he would be making a series of personal appearances, giving lectures – and working on two commissions for the O'Hanlon brothers, who were both wealthy landowners. Declan, the younger of the two, whose house was in Galway, had requested a family portrait. His older brother, Sean, had asked Patrick to paint the family mansion, set amidst the rolling countryside of County Clare.

Seated at a Drawing Room desk, she busied herself with her itinerary for the next two days, before her departure.

Tralee was such a huge responsibility. Thankfully, the staff salaries were paid by direct debit, so that was one less problem to think about. When the telephone rang, Fiona was so engrossed in her task that she decided to ignore it – the Answer-phone could pick up any messages. Their butler, Charles, was in Victoria, on business, otherwise he would have taken it for her.

It wasn't until Maggie brought in a lunch tray that Fiona took a break to check who the caller was. Most of the phone messages were routine matters and could be easily dealt with. As she came to the last message, there was a long pause. Fiona was about to press the Exit button and replace the receiver, when a tearful woman's voice, interspersed with heavy sobbing, left two numbers: a mobile and a landline – asking her to return the call urgently. The voice seemed vaguely familiar, but still quite difficult to identify, as the speaker was so upset.

Dialling the long-distance landline number, Fiona waited anxiously for someone to pick up the receiver. After just three rings, the phone was snatched up, at the other end. "Fiona, is that really you?" "Yes of course. Who is this?" she asked, in exasperation.

"I *had* to phone you!" the voice continued. "I'm probably the last person you want to hear from, but this is Lydia," the caller persisted. Fiona calmed her down and reassured her that what had happened between them was now in the past. Secretly, she could never forgive Miklos' niece, for her part in Robert's ordeal, but there had to be something terribly wrong for her to have phoned – and to be in such a state.

Fiona had been standing when she made the call, but as Lydia continued the conversation, Fiona sank into a nearby chair. Her legs felt as though they would buckle underneath her, as Lydia's story unfolded.

Despite her past history with Jean Pierre Lefevre, and the cruel way in which he had used her, she had remained secretly in love for him. But as the years passed and he and his father continued to evade the police, she reconciled herself to the fact that she would never see him again.

Then suddenly, just a week ago, she had received a letter in the post, written in capital letters, asking her to meet the sender in Room 30 of the

CHAPTER TWENTY-NINE

Hotel Athena, in the business quarter of Athens. If she did so, the writer promised her, she would learn something to her advantage. Enclosed with the letter was a banknote for a thousand Euros, to cover all expenses and make it worth her while.

The writer turned out to be none other than Jean Pierre, although he was registered in the hotel, under a different name. Under normal circumstances nothing would have induced her to keep such a rendezvous. Lydia had endeavoured to put her disastrous youth behind her and was now a successful businesswoman. But the style in which the letter was written must have triggered something in her subconscious.

In no time at all, despite her best intentions, Jean Pierre seduced her; once again they became lovers. Despite his greying hair, she still found him irresistible. However, Lydia reassured herself that this time she would remain in control. This would only be a fling, for a few days. Jean Pierre would depart and she would return to her sensible lifestyle.

But after one of their lovemaking sessions in Room 30, his mood suddenly changed. He began to describe being on a beach. One of his 'enemies', as he described him, had been about to hand him over to the police. "There was only one way to stop him," he told her, "he *had* to be destroyed! He'd found out about the treasure, you see?"

Terrified, but unable to escape from him, Lydia pretended to be sympathetic.

The following morning, he's shown her the copy of the in-flight magazine, which he'd slipped into his briefcase, on the plane. The article, about Robert's rescue, described Fiona Maitland's search and dramatic rescue of her former fiancé. Jean Pierre's eyes were full of malice as her cursed her: "If it hadn't been for the meddling of that interfering bitch, no one would ever have discovered what really happened. The trail would have gone cold by now and my father and I could have begun a new life."

Lydia suggested tentatively, "But if you simply disappear again now, you may still be able to escape the police," – but to no avail.

She began to sob again: "Fiona, you're in terrible danger. He means to kill you – and Robert. He's calling himself Marc now – and he's totally obsessed. He's convinced that if he eliminates the two of you, all of his troubles will be over."

"You must find Robert and warn him," she continued. "Uncle Miklos knows people who can help me lie low for a month or two. I managed to escape from the hotel at two o'clock this morning, so Jean Pierre will be hunting for me too, in case I warn you."

"Where are you now," Fiona asked, fearfully. "I'm with Miklos. He's waiting for me in the car, to take me up to the hills. I was meant to go two hours ago, but I had to wait for your call, so that I could warn you. I have to go now. Please Fiona, hurry! Get away from *Tralee* as soon as possible. He knows where you live!"

Lydia hastily replaced the receiver, leaving Fiona totally stunned. Seconds later, she raced to her laptop, to see if Robert had left any e-mails for her. They normally kept in touch by this means, at least three times a week. Thankfully, there *was* an e-mail from him, sent the day before, which she hadn't yet opened.

The e-mail explained that he'd logged on to the Maitland Family Website and discovered that Patrick was making a month's tour of Ireland.

He suggested that he should sail over to the Bantry Bay area and find a place to moor his boat. He could be there in twenty-four hours. It would be a great opportunity for them all to meet up again.

With trembling fingers, Fiona e-mailed him, on 'High Priority', summarising Lydia's warning. He must avoid Bantry Bay at all costs, as Patrick and the children were staying there, at least for the first fortnight of the tour, possibly longer. 'We must draw Jean Pierre away from the area', she wrote. 'If you can moor somewhere a few miles away, I'll meet you there. We can use our mobiles to keep in touch. There's not a moment to be lost'.

Luckily, Robert sent confirmation within a minute or two, that he'd received her message. Fiona instinctively deleted all of their e-mails, quickly packed a travelling bag, then grabbed her keys, money and travel documents. Handing a hastily-written note to an astonished Maggie, asking her to contact Patrick about her early departure, she drove into Victoria, then boarded a seaplane for Seattle.

As their family website was easily accessible, Jean Pierre would have no trouble in tracking down the family's itinerary for the next month or so. At all costs, she and Robert must draw his attention away from her family. At this very moment, the murderous Frenchman might be en route for the West of Ireland too! She had to find a way of letting him know that she'd changed her plans about joining her family at the Bantry Bay hotel – that she was heading for a new destination.

As soon as she landed at Dublin Airport, she must phone her contacts in Europol. Over the last decade, as a result of Robert's case, there were at least five police officials of varying ranks whom she could consult. The most vital call would be to arrange immediate protection for Patrick and the children. As mobile phones couldn't be used on the plane, she couldn't even send a text until they'd landed.

CHAPTER TWENTY-NINE

The moment she'd cleared Customs at Dublin, she made a couple of calls on her mobile, at which point the Irish Gardai were immediately alerted. There was a text from Patrick on her mobile, confirming that Maggie had phoned him, long distance, alerting him to the danger. He insisted that she should come to their Bantry Bay hotel immediately, so that he could protect her.

She sent a brief reply, saying that the local Garda should be at his hotel shortly, but she avoided confirming that she was on her way there too. As she had previously demonstrated, Fiona could be very determined, to the point of stubbornness, when the lives of her loved ones were at stake.

Just hours later, she rendezvoused with Robert, having chartered a small aircraft to fly her from Dublin, to a private airfield on Bantry Bay. He was waiting for her in his four-by-four. They headed back with all speed, to *Silver's Arrow*.

The plan was to spend the next day or two, aboard the boat, formulating a plan to ensnare Jean Pierre once and for all, with the help of various European Police Forces. Two of the men assigned to the case, on behalf of Interpol, were already waiting for them, when they arrived back at the boat. Robert had moored his boat in Dunmanus Bay, the next bay south of Bantry Bay, below the headland of Sheep's Head; a location sufficiently removed from Patrick and the family, but still within travelling distance of their hotel.

Robert's immaculate cabin cruiser was moored just out of sight, below one side of the concrete pier at Durrus, a short distance from the local church. As Fiona descended from Robert's vehicle, the church steeple was still visible.

Robert unloaded the vehicle, assisted by the officers, while Fiona explored their location, anxious to see what cover might be available in an emergency. On the bank to their far right lay the ruins of an ivy-clad, derelict stone building, its many gaping windows open to the elements.

On the front left-hand side of the pier, immediately in front of her, a small blue-and-white boat was beached, bearing the legend, the 'S310'. In a small field just beyond that, six caramel-coloured cows grazed nonchalantly. Three warning signs were displayed nearby. The first showed a black car on a yellow background – about to tip over into the water; the second, on the back of a post, was a cautionary Customs Duty notice, about Drugs; a third, on the wall right at the back of the pier, close to an abandoned, rusty old trailer, had been issued by the Food Safety Authority of Ireland. It warned against the dangers of eating Irish shellfish, due to a potentially toxic plankton. But right now, they had a lot more to worry about than dodgy shellfish!

Once they were all aboard *Silver's* Arrow, the two officers informed them that, to the best of their knowledge, since a recent murder, Jean Pierre, alias Marc Chagrin, was acting independently of his father Claude, aka Jules Gautier.

An undercover agent, they elaborated, working on their behalf and posing as a businessman, had made contact with Jean Pierre three days ago, in the Maitland's home state of British Columbia. The combined effect of Lydia's terrifying phone call, a hectic flight schedule – and now this additional news... that her enemy was already trying to hunt her down, back on Vancouver Island, left Fiona feeling completely dismayed and exhausted. She fell fast asleep, as soon as her head hit the pillow, on the bunk bed that Robert had prepared for her. The Interpol officers were to remain on full alert, throughout the night – protecting them.

Shortly afterwards, Robert popped in, to switch off Fiona's bedside lamp. He stood there, framed in the semi-darkness of the doorway. A light from the outside deck shone through the cabin window, illuminating one side of her beautiful face. Robert remained motionless, as he watched her sleeping... peacefully at last.

That monster Lefevre had a lot to answer for. Had it not been for his wicked intervention, he and Fiona would be married, his face wouldn't be so disfigured and they'd be raising a family by now. Given *half* a chance, he was going to make that evil bastard pay!

CHAPTER THIRTY

Bantry House, the ancestral home of the Earls of Bantry, had been carefully selected by Patrick, as a base for his month's tour of Ireland. He discovered that although the title lapsed in 1891, the house was still owned and occupied by Egerton Shelswell-White, the direct descendant of the Ist Earl of Bantry, and his family.

The House and Garden had been open to the public on a daily basis since 1946, between Mid March and the end of October. It was a particularly suitable venue for Patrick's exhibition as it housed its own collection of art treasures, the majority of which the 2nd Earl had collected on his grand tour.

Patrick and the three children strolled through the Italianate Gardens most evenings, after driving down to Bantry Square for the 'Early Bird' menu, at *O'Connor's Fish Restaurant*, which was served from 18.00h. The business of the day being over, they could take time out to relax together, save for the odd occasion when Patrick's lectures or painting assignments took him too far afield to return the same day. The children were looking forward to their mother's imminent arrival. Once she was there, she'd be able to take the family out on all sorts of excursions. Seated on a bench by the fountain, one of their favourite spots, they would discuss the events of the day with their father, before turning in for the night.

The food at O'Connor's was renowned for its quality. Patrick was delighted to learn that in 2009, the restaurant had won the *Seafood of the Year* award for the whole of Ireland. Anne O'Brien, one of the owners explained to Patrick that Georgina Campbell was the actual critic who selected restaurants for the award, sponsored by the local Fisheries Board. Anne and her husband, Peter, had also received other accolades, including the *Good Food of Ireland* seal of approval.

The restaurant had an intriguing history: in 1914, Margaret O'Donovan opened a fully-licensed Bar & Grill, which was subsequently purchased by the O'Connor family in the late 1960s. In early 2003, Anne O'Brien, the great grand daughter of Margaret O'Donovan, and Peter, relocated to Bantry, to take over the restaurant – so it was back in the family again!

As Patrick's daily schedules were rather hectic, Robert, being the oldest son, was assigned the daily task of looking after his two younger siblings, nine-year-old Mary and Patrick Junior, who was seven. Whenever possible, the family took breakfast together at Bantry House, in the rose coloured Breakfast Room, before their father departed in a hired Mercedes, on his next assignment.

The Breakfast Room was exquisitely decorated; framed pictures of a variety of roses adorned the walls. The pendulum of an antique clock on the left-hand wall ticked comfortably in the background, as the Maitlands, in lively conversation, ate from the best china. No one would have guessed that this charming room was formerly a coal cellar!

The children lunched together in the West Wing Café Bistro, Patrick Junior having been instructed by his father to be on his best behaviour. They also enjoyed the various exhibitions, theatre productions and other entertainments, which the House provided.

* * * *

As a police officer-turned-art-dealer, Kyle Danzig, Jean Pierre's informant, was well aware of Patrick's glowing reputation as an international landscape and portrait artist. Logging on to the Maitland Family Website, he printed off two copies of Patrick's Irish itinerary, for the month of July. "It's a piece of cake," he informed Jean Pierre. "We know exactly where this guy's going to be, throughout the whole month – you can't go wrong!"

Unbeknown to Lefevre, however, Kyle's main assignment, on behalf of Interpol, was to lure his so-called friend to Robert Osborne's boat, moored in Dunmanus Bay, to the south of where Patrick and the children were staying.

After all, Fiona and Robert were the Frenchman's primary targets; he'd made it clear that he was hell-bent on destroying them. Although Kyle already knew the location of *Silver's Arrow*, he spent a few hours, pretending to search for them, contacting a couple of supposedly 'bent' police officers, who, for a fee, would provide him with the information that he needed and 'surfing the net' for additional details regarding Fiona's travel arrangements. "Thank the Lord that the old days of sleuthing are behind us my friend," he remarked to Jean Pierre. "We don't even have to leave the office. We can track people down using mobiles and other high-tech gadgets. No worries!"

Back on *Silver's Arrow*, Rob and Fiona watched and waited. A Police Launch was moored, just out of sight, on another side of the pier: its

CHAPTER THIRTY

occupants ready to pounce at a moment's notice. On the bank, a fisherman, and four other 'tourists' waited patiently, at various points in the vicinity, checking in with the Launch, by mobile, every few minutes. The scene was set. By the end of the day, their troubles would be at an end; they could relax... and resume their normal lives once more.

By the end of the second day, however, it became clear that their quarry was not going to show. A decision was made to escort Fiona and Robert to Bantry House. They travelled in a convoy of three vehicles, to the new destination, situated on the outskirts of Bantry, about fifty-five miles from the city of Cork.

As Robert drove back, sandwiched between two unmarked police vehicles, along the winding R591, Fiona was totally preoccupied: had Lefevre decided to give up the chase, or did he have more sinister plans for them?

She glanced nervously a they passed two cream-coloured bungalows, lying down in a dip, on the right-hand side of the road – there were relatively few houses along this route. Every hedge seemed to threaten an assassin with a machine gun – the sooner they reached their destination the better!

Eventually, the convoy turned left onto the main Bantry Road – the N71. Just before the town's main square, they turned sharp right, through a narrow stone tunnel, signposted 'Bantry House – Accommodation'.

They negotiated this access road very slowly, as there were several speed-bumps along this alternative route to the House. All three vehicles entered through a large iron gateway, then drew up, alongside the East Wing.

Patrick was there to meet them. He unlocked a small white door, affording them private access to their accommodation. Passing the Reception Desk, the whole party ascended the twisting staircase.

Patrick had rented two rooms on the first floor of this East Wing: rooms 21 and 22 were side by side, off the same corridor. The boys had been sharing Room 21; Room 22, at the end of the passageway, overlooked the gardens to the south and the sea to the north. As it was a spacious double room, Mary had been sharing it with her father, in Fiona's absence. Robert was assigned Room 21. The fact that both rooms were side by side simplified the security arrangements.

The children, meanwhile, had been dispatched to another hotel, several miles away from the Bay, under the careful supervision of two women police officers from the Garda, plus a detective constable.

Gazing out over the Italianate Gardens, the Fountain and the famous Hundred Steps, Fiona felt secure again, for the first time in days. Placing his hands on her shoulders, Patrick turned her around gently and kissed her, passionately. "You're not to leave my side now, honey, until this awful business is resolved," he cautioned her.

Although Patrick doubted whether their arch-enemy would have the nerve to show his face again, officers were nevertheless appointed to guard all access points to the apartments; regular staff, employed by the House, were also placed on High Alert. Jean Pierre had already proved himself a master of disguise, so this would be no easy task, should he decide to pay them a visit. One of the police guards, posing as a tourist, pretended to browse nearby, in the grandiose library, examining its unique collection of books and other exhibits. The Maitland rooms were just a few yards away and up the staircase, from the connecting door to the library.

Back in Paris, Claude Lefevre had been placed under House Arrest. Tired of wandering the globe for so many years, he had returned to his former apartment, on the banks of the Seine, a broken man. As the old man no longer presented a threat, confining him to his apartment seemed, to the Sûretè, the best solution, for the time being. Once they had captured Jean Pierre, father and son could then be tried jointly, although the son would face far more serious charges, including the brutal murder of Kurt Lobowitz.

Claude had plenty of time to reflect on his inglorious past. All that he wanted to do now was to make up for lost time with his grandchildren, Evette and Thomas. Their father, Giles, was Claude's oldest son. He was a studious man, a Professor of Foreign Languages at a university just outside Paris. Claude reflected, with much chagrin, how as a youngster he had often chided Giles for not being sufficiently adventurous, describing him to friends as "rather dull." Now those words returned daily, to haunt him.

His younger son, Jean Pierre had always been ambitious. Even from infancy, Claude had encouraged him to take risks in everything that he did. To come out on top, to win, was the most important thing in life, he advised him, time and time again. If he did not always come top in class, or in other projects that he undertook, his father would chastise him, making him feel worthless. In retrospect Lefevre Senior could see the disastrous error of his ways – he had created a monster!

Claude's wife, Giselle, had left him for another man, years ago, once she realised that her husband and youngest son had become permanent fugitives from the law.

Evette and Thomas were young adults now. The Sûrétè permitted them to visit their grandfather once a fortnight, together with Giles and his wife. Claude wanted to make his peace with them now – they were all the

CHAPTER THIRTY

family that he had left in the world. He had no expectations of ever seeing his younger son again, other than through prison bars!

Back at Bantry House, time passed slowly. Patrick was obliged to cancel his engagements for the next few days, until the situation had been resolved. But as the days passed uneventfully, a decision was made to downsize the number of bodyguards, leaving a skeleton team of just three men. Patrick resumed some of his engagements, safe in the knowledge that Robert and the three police officers were on hand, to protect his wife.

On the penultimate Saturday before the close of Patrick's tour, Robert and Fiona decided to take the self guided tour of three floors of the house, which included Drawing Rooms, tapestries from Versailles, the Dining Room and the Library. In 1820 Richard, the 2nd Earl of Bantry, had enlarged the house, by adding two of these Drawing Rooms. They collected laminated information sheets, linked together in book form, from Egerton's daughter Julie, in Reception, to assist them with the tour.

After an early lunch, in the West Wing Bistro, they took a stroll through the Gardens.

There were eight terraces altogether, the house itself being situated on the third. Four other terraces rose at the south side of the house, connecting the formality of the house with the wilderness of the woodland.

Every aspect of the house had its own character. To the east lay an imposing statue of the goddess Diana, holding a young deer captive, within a circular bed. Her statue was close to the private door leading to their rooms. The western aspect of the gardens overlooked a lush, sunken garden, while to the south they discovered her family's favourite spot for a pre-bedtime chat – the fountain, in the centre of the parterre. The ancient circle of wisteria, at its best two months before, had now faded.

After a tremendous effort, Fiona and Robert managed to reach the top of the Hundred Steps, where they were rewarded with one of the best views that they had seen, anywhere on their travels. The entire estate was surrounded by fields, woodland, walkways and a little stream leading up to the walled garden. On such a beautiful day it seemed like Paradise on Earth, reminiscent of the paradise that the two of them had shared all those years ago, in Robert's hillside hideaway on Skiathos, before Fate has cast them adrift... parting them for so many years.

Eventually, they made their way, hand-in-hand, down the northern side of the house: past sweeping lawns and fourteen circular beds, leading towards the sea. It was a glorious summer's afternoon. 'Had this been another time and another place this woman would have been mine', reflected Robert, sadly.

As the evening wore on they decided to explore an overgrown pathway, leading to an area know as 'The Pond' – a saltwater inlet of tidal water, flowing in from the Bay. According to one of the gardeners, many years before, a road had been built, separating Bantry House from the Bay. The Pond was therefore the only remaining area of water that could be directly accessed from the House.

Robert and Fiona inched their way, single-file, along the winding, muddy pathway, which then opened out into a large, shady copse of four massive beech trees. From there, the pathway narrowed again, until they eventually reached a metal-barred gate, which was padlocked. They clambered through a small gap, where two bars were missing, then out onto a large area of marshy grassland. A gravel pathway, encircling this area of sodden grass, enabled them to walk around to the Pond – a large area of marshland and water, with a sizeable island to the left, reinforced with rocks around the base, to prevent further erosion. A variety of bushes were growing on the island.

On the far right of the Pond was a Lodge. To the extreme right and close to the metal gate through which they had squeezed was a boatyard. Although no workmen were actually visible, someone was working late in the yard, as they could hear the sound of hammer on steel.

The couple continued further along the path, towards the island on the far left. Beyond the Pond, the N71 was busy with traffic. Fiona could just make out the green Bantry road sign. In the distance, beyond the road and over to the left loomed a substantial graveyard, its gothic tombstones pointing towards the sky, like an army of evil invaders! Fiona shivered. With dusk approaching, Robert put an arm around her shoulder, as they both stood there, surveying the scene.

Suddenly their reverie was interrupted by Fiona's mobile phone. "It's Patrick," she explained. "He expects to be back any time now, so I've asked him to meet us down here, by the Pond. He could do with some relaxation – he sounds quite stressed out. Apparently he's been down here before with the children, so he knows the way."

Being one of the busiest weeks of the year, Bantry House and the Gardens had been crowded all day with visitors; as closing time was fast approaching, their numbers began to dwindle. But standing in this tranquil spot, away from everyone else, they once again contemplated the tranquil waters of the Bay, lost in thought.

This time it was the turn of Robert's mobile, with Mozart chimes, to suddenly break the moment. "Damnation!" he exclaimed, "the joys of the modern world!" It was his father, ringing him from Torquay, on important

CHAPTER THIRTY

business. Unfortunately, Robert had forgotten to charge his phone batteries the night before, so he had to dash back to the house, to use one of the landlines there, as transmission was very weak.

"I won't be long," he assured her. "That's okay. Patrick will be here soon," she replied. As Robert headed for the gate, Fiona turned back towards the lake, fascinated by a swan, gliding on the water. As she watched the elegant bird preening its snow-white feathers, memories came flooding back, of the very traumatic evening, years ago in Victoria, when Patrick took her to see the ballet, *Swan Lake*.

This was the moment he had been anticipating. For two whole days he'd been pretending to make a tour of the Gardens... waiting for his chance. He'd followed them, from a safe distance, down towards this isolated spot. Kyle Danzig must be mad if he thought he could trick him into laying siege to Osborne's boat. It was an obvious trap! As for Lydia, yet again she was a mere pawn in his End Game. He knew very well that she'd warn Fiona. Then he could lull her into a false sense of security, striking when she least suspected anything. He would *always* triumph; his superior intellect would always come out on top. They were such fools. He was *far* cleverer than the rest of them... always one step ahead!

As Robert progressed back along the muddy path, towards the house, Jean Pierre jumped out from behind thick foliage, where two alder trees, a large Yucca and a bronze Berberis were growing together. A gun was too cumbersome to carry as a tourist, but a knife would do the job just as efficiently.

He ran towards her, with a manic expression on his face, preparing to plunge the knife into her heart. She had been his enemy for far too long, meddling in his affairs. He would send her to a place where she could never harm him again. He would have his revenge!

As Fiona turned and screamed, she was aware of another man, running swiftly from behind her, as if from nowhere, screaming "No!!" In seconds, this other man had thrown himself, with tremendous force, at Jean Pierre, at the same time grasping the hand holding the knife.

The two men fell into the water, with a tremendous splash. The knife flew out of Jean Pierre's hand, as they disappeared into the murky depths, for what seemed an age. When they eventually resurfaced, gasping and spluttering, both men filled their lungs with air, preparing for the inevitable second dive. Fiona watched, in horror, as they both disappeared again, the one man forcing the other's head into the marshy water, trying to drown him. She screamed as loud as she could: "Somebody, please... help!!"

Within seconds, her three bodyguards appeared from nowhere, having been maintaining a discreet distance. They jumped into the water – in quick succession. Meanwhile, one of the two assailants had hit his head on a rock, as he went under for the second time. The water was turning bright red. But grabbing his opponent around the neck, her protector held on… choking the life out of the Frenchman – refusing to let go.

By degrees, Jean Pierre's lifeless body sank slowly down, to the bottom of the inlet. Fiona's bodyguards emerged from the marshy water, carrying the body of her rescuer between them, to the side of the bank, where they administered the 'kiss of life'. Blood was oozing, from the back of his head. Everything went black, as Fiona fainted.

* * * *

When Fiona came round, she began to sob, as she realised the full implications of her plight and how close she had come to death. As the memory of her rescuer's skull, staining the grassy bank red, returned to her, she became hysterical. A doctor was called, to administer a sedative. Lying in what had become Robert's bedroom, she went in and out of consciousness.

Suddenly, she was back at *Taverna Persephone*, amidst the wooded hillsides of Skiathos, laughing and joking with Jean Pierre; dancing with him – sharing a joke! How could that carefree, highly intelligent young Frenchman, with the world at his feet, have turned into such a paranoid sociopath? His face suddenly morphed into that of a murderous madman, as she slipped back into unconsciousness.

Minutes later, she revived again. It was spring. She was on a Greek island with Robert – their children were laughing and playing around them. But that was impossible. She must learn to control such fantasies.

Gaining consciousness for a third time, she recalled her realisation, all those years ago, that if one lived in Paradise, sooner or later, one would be called to task. Because there was always a darker, more sinister side to an idyllic lifestyle, which eventually, insisted on revealing itself. Once more the Fates were playing with her; laughing at her for believing that such happiness could be sustained.

Although the sedative was beginning to wear off, Fiona made a concerted effort to sleep again – to banish such morbid thoughts from her mind.

But somewhere, at the back of her troubled mind, lay the image of a man whom she had loved for so many years… but would never see again.

* * * *

CHAPTER THIRTY

He sat by his friend's bedside, clasping his right hand tightly in his. The paramedics had decided, having stretchered him back through the side door in the East Wing, to Room 22, that there was no point in trying to move their patient again. A large, blood-soaked pad lay against the back of his head, which was propped up against three pillows.

The two friends had, at their own request, been left to spend the last few minutes together privately. Suddenly, the injured man's eyes opened again, as he attempted to sit bolt upright. "Where's Fiona?" he demanded. "Is she safe?"

"She's in Room 21, next door, but she can't move, because the doctor's given her a sedative. But she's perfectly safe. If you haven't arrived when you did, she'd have been dead… You saved her life… mine too probably. The Frenchman's where he belongs – at the bottom of the marsh. He can do no further harm to any of us now."

"Thank God! That's alright then… that's all I needed to know," responded the injured man, his face, momentarily, lighting up with relief.

As the minutes ticked by, the eyes of Fiona's rescuer gradually began to glaze over. His hand slipped from his friend's grasp. Seconds later, as his eyes opened again, he motioned to him, to rise from his bedside chair… and come closer… with one of a pair of hands that had helped to create such beautiful images of nature, for people across the globe to enjoy. Representing all that was good and positive in the world, it was, nevertheless, one of its evils that had destroyed him.

Drawing his tear-stained face closer to this brave and selfless man, who had been his best friend for so many years, his companion was barely able to discern his parting request, delivered in the faintest of whispers:

"Look after my family. Take care of Fiona. Love her for me… Robert."

BY THE SAME AUTHOR

King of Clubs, Brewin Books, 2007
Auf Wiedersehen Pat, Brewin Books, 2006
Finally Meeting Princess Maud, Brewin Books, 2006
Pat Roach's Birmingham, Brewin Books, 2004
The Original Alton Douglas, Brewin Books, 2003
If - The Pat Roach Story, Brewin Books, 2002
There's More Out Than In, Brewin Books, 1999